COLORS INSULTING TO NATURE

ALSO BY CINTRA WILSON

*A Massive Swelling: Celebrity Re-Examined
as a Grotesque Crippling Disease
and Other Cultural Revelations*

COLORS INSULTING TO NATURE

A NOVEL

CINTRA WILSON

4th Fourth Estate
An Imprint of HarperCollins*Publishers*

HarperCollins books may be purchased for educational, business, or sales promotional use. For information, please write: Special Markets Department, HarperCollins Publishers Inc., 10 East 53rd Street, New York, NY 10022.

FIRST EDITION

Printed on acid-free paper

Library of Congress Cataloging-in-Publication Data

Wilson, Cintra.
    Colors insulting to nature: a novel/Cintra Wilson.
      p.   cm.
    ISBN 0-00-715460-7
    1. Teenage girls—Fiction.   I. Title.

  PS3573.I45685C65   2004
  813'.6—dc21   2003054955

04 05 06 07 08 WBC/BVG 10 9 8 7 6 5 4 3 2 1

For Kent, who is like Abe Lincoln.

And for all the child-stars in my family:
Meghan, Grant, and Adam Dickerson, Abigail and
Roscoe Bernard, and Ava and Una Ankrum.

Especially Adam, a great actor and a righteous American.

Just don't read this until you're 17, unless accompanied by an adult.

. . . he had to admit that the paintings of the Dutch School exhibited in the Louvre had led him astray. They had in fact served as a spring-board from which he had soared into a dream world of false trails and impossible ambitions, for nowhere in this world had he found the fairyland of which he had dreamt; nowhere had he seen rustic youths and maidens dancing on a village green littered with wine casks, weeping with sheer happiness, jumping for joy, and laughing so uproariously that they wet their petticoats and breeches.

—J.-K. Huysmans, *À Rebours* (Against Nature)

COLORS INSULTING TO NATURE

ARE YOU THERE, GOD? IT'S ME, LIZA

(A Heartwarming, Young-Adult, Coming-of-Age Tale)

July 23, 1981, Novato, CA

HE FACES OF THE JUDGES revealed, although they were trying to hide it, deep distaste for the fact that the thirteen-year-old girl in front of them had plucked eyebrows and false eyelashes. Something about her well-worn miniature stiletto heels and her backless black evening dress—side slit up to the fishnet hip, with rhinestone spaghetti straps—was unsavory to them. The girl looked way too *comfortable*. Equally unsettling was her performance.

". . . and now, I'd like to perform a little something by someone who has been a huge influence on my work. This lady has the most incredible pipes in the business. I'm speaking, of course, of Ms. Barbra Streisand. Vincent?" she asked, addressing the horrified pianist, who was busying himself with the mosaic of colorful buttons on his Yamaha DX-7 that promised such sounds as "oboe" and "tympani."

"Could you give me 'Clear Day' in F, sugar? You're too good to me."

The child took the microphone and Cher-ishly flipped back a long strand of zigzag crimped hair with fuchsia fingernails as the pianist rolled into the opening bars. Her vibrato, though untrained (learned, most likely, by imitating ecstatic car commercials) was as tight, small, and regular as the teeth on pinking shears.

"On a Cleee-yah Daaaaaaaaaaayy
T'Wheel Asssssh-TOUND Yewww . . . thank you," she spoke, as if the judges had just broken into spontaneous applause.

The mother, visible mouthing the lyrics from the wings in an exaggerated fashion, was clearly responsible for this travesty, this premature piano-bar veteran of a youngster.

"Yew can sheeeee Fah-REVAH,
ond EVAH."

The moderately talented girl was emoting with her hands, seemingly tweezing the adult male heart out of its sexual prison with her kitten claws, all too professionally. The judges squirmed in their seats, intensely disliking the thought of their own daughters or nieces belting out a song in this seamy, overwrought fashion—parroting the stage acts of overripe chanteuses, moist with the rot of numerous alcoholic disappointments in both Love and Life. The mother would probably be devastated if her child didn't land the gig . . . she might, in fact, lock herself in an all-peach-colored bedroom and wash down handfuls of muscle relaxants with cheap Polish vodka from a plastic handle–jug; her unfortunate daughter would be left for days without milk and forced to eat lipstick. It was this thought that brought large grimaces of feigned appreciation to the faces of the judges as the girl collapsed into the bow as if she'd just wrung every drop of hot life out of herself and was now utterly spent. She blew a few kisses toward the judges and urged them to "give themselves a hand."

The mother, whose diaphanous, mango-colored pantsuit was trumped in visual loudness only by the Louis IV–style stack of conical curls on her strawberry-blonde wig, came forward and shook the girl playfully.

"Say goodbye to the nice judges, Liza," she mewed.

"Goodbye to the nice judges, Liza," the girl cracked, with a wink.

"Go outside and amuse yourself while Mommy talks grown-up-talk."

Liza pouted theatrically, then waved bye-bye to the group of middle-aged men as she wobbled on her heels out of the conference room. Seconds later Liza was visible through the one-way windows on the lawn of the industrial park, trying to swing on one of the large, nautically themed boat chains that roped off the parking lot. As she yanked one of the nagging rhinestone straps back up onto her porcelain doll-shoulder, the judges were petrified with worry that the miniature disco Lolita would be spotted from the freeway by a predator on a quest for this particular banquet of perversion, who would swoop down the on-ramp and yank the spangled child into a dirty van. The girl seemed blithely unaware of such dangers and, as evidenced by the trembling of her lower lip, was apparently singing again at top volume as she jerked back and forth on the heavy chain.

Peppy Normal took a spread-eagled stand in front of the judge's fold-out table with her hands on her hips. Her mouth unfolded into a glossed, yellow alligator-smile.

"She nailed it, didn't she. You know she nailed it."

"We have a lot of kids to see before we decide anything, Mrs. Normal."

"Boys, for Chrissake, it's a TV commercial, not a goddamn Nobel Prize. Just cut to the chase and tell me: did she nail it, or what?"

The colorless klatch of balding men looked at each other helplessly and squirmed in their orange plastic seats. The bravest among them spoke candidly.

"The spokes-child that the OtterWorld Fun Park is looking for . . . how can I say this . . . we were maybe thinking of a kid who is a little less sophisticated."

"You wanted Shirley Temple schtick? I thought you were looking for *talent*."

Liza had given up trying to swing on the sunbaked chain and was now pressing her nose and forehead against the tinted window. Peering in, she could make out her mother violently gesticulating at the cringing group of men. Two of the judges glanced miserably out the window at her; her Nude Beige pancake makeup had made a small figure-8-shaped smear on the smoked glass. Liza saw her mother grab her oversize, gold-buckled handbag and storm out of the room. Knowing her cue, Liza smiled and waved goodbye through the window again and tottered through the grass toward the car.

Peppy drove angrily, her long brown cigarette pointing out of a crack in the window.

"You were great. They were shoe salesmen. They didn't get it."

"I ate a plate of dicks again, Mom."

"No you didn't. And don't say that, say you 'ate the midget.' You're too young to use nightclub slang, it makes people uncomfortable."

"*You* make people uncomfortable."

"They were uncomfortable in their own asses. They exploit otters, for Chrissake."

Liza's brother was already visible at the bus stop in front of the shopping center, because his silver ersatz car-racing jacket (selected by Peppy because of the word LANCIA written down one sleeve) made his chunky, fourteen-year-old upper torso look like a Mylar balloon. Ned stood alone with his heavy bag from the hardware store, outcast from the summer cliques of wealthy, mall-wandering Marin County teens, who dazzled the eye in erotically tight designer jeans, sun-bed-tans, gold anklets, frosted hair, and top-dollar orthodontics . . . all the procreative bounty of sustained wealth-eugenics; the attractive rich exclusively breeding with the attractive rich for at least five generations.

"Where are your sunglasses?" Peppy screeched as the guano-battered Honda Civic jerked to a stop against the curb. Ned, releasing a sigh of infinite pathos, produced the mirrorized aviator frames and wrapped them slowly onto his wide, flat face. It was sadly amusing to Ned that his mother would want him to wear the glasses in order to disguise the fact that he had a lazy eye, but she felt no compunction about picking him up in a birdshit-encrusted economy hatchback while the glamorous kids were slinking into the leathery backseats of gleaming BMWs and Mercedes-Benzes.

"You nail it?" Ned asked Liza.

Liza shook her head.

"You eat a plate of dicks?"

Liza nodded. It wasn't painful anymore, she was used to rejection. In the last three months, Liza had botched commercial auditions for Tender Vittles, Silly Sand, and The Colorforms Barbie Sun n' Fun Gazebo and failed to impress the casting agent for a horror movie entitled *Suffer the Children*, yet another in the long line of *Omen* and *Rosemary's Baby* knockoffs wherein innocent youngsters parented by the Dark Lord telekinetically cause the head-exploding death of nannies, bus drivers, and priests. It barely occurred to Liza, at this point, that she was auditioning *for* anything; the evening gown, fishnets, and sky blue eyeshadow had become her uniform, inasmuch as any soccer girl donned shin guards and cleated shoes.

"What's in the bag?" Liza asked her brother.

"Science," Ned whispered cryptically, squeezing the bag more firmly shut.

(A note to the Reader:

In the beginning was the word, and the word was written according to certain unimpeachable rules and formats.

Flashbacks are to be avoided if it is at all possible. Exposition is painful enough all by itself; but to then be enshrouded in the horrible spectacle of the same actors playing heavily filtered, pressed-powdered, and pigtailed versions of themselves is just too disturbing—it threatens the suspension of disbelief. Nonetheless, you are being asked to plummet uncomfortably backward in time. Prepare yourself for the ugly g-force as we slam on the retro-jets.)

BACKSTORY:

Penelope "Peppy" Normal, née Pinkney, had been married to Ned and Liza's father, Hal Normal. Hal had been dazzled by Peppy's topless juggling act ("Best Juggles in the Business"—*Reno Nitewatcher*) at the Lady Luck casino in Reno, NV, in May 1965. It was a low point in the life of Peppy, who at twenty-two had been living with her mother following a daring period of LSD experimentation, which culminated with her boyfriend, Chet Borden (who had Seen the Light and changed his name to Blessed Ram Baku), fatally swan-diving off the roof of their Oakland apartment building in a rapturous hallucinogenic brain-rage. A month later Peppy found herself grieving and half-naked before the Reno multitudes. Her act culminated in juggling four pins with tasseled pasties to "Do You Believe in Magic" by the Lovin' Spoonful. She was a "good-looking chick," five foot two, freckled and curvy, who was partial to wigs, because she had suffered the charring effects of a bad perm after cutting off her waist-long, ironed hippie locks. Even though her hair (light brown, a noncolor) had grown back, the wigs were easier to put on for work, and they made her feel as if she was in costume or disguise; eventually she wore them all the time.

The "Dentist from Duluth," as Hal Normal signed the cards on the single red roses he sent backstage ("cheap," she thought, "romantic," he thought), seemed to Peppy as good an escape route from her mother as any. He was a good height, anyway, and had most of his hair, and she had always wanted capped teeth. Sharon, a topless, redheaded magician's assistant whom Peppy had befriended at work, said he looked like a younger version of Karl Malden. After dinner dates at various Denny's-esque restaurants every night of his National Dental Workers conference, Hal proposed, and Peppy, figuring she must either escape her current situation or risk murdering her mother with a serrated steak knife in a Southern Comfort–induced tussle, agreed to marry him the next day in the "Little House of Love" twenty-four-hour chapel, a tiny, shingled building built to look like a gingerbread house, replete with footstool-size concrete "gumdrops" studding the Astroturf lawn. It was all over in fifteen minutes. Sharon, who had only known Peppy for four months, had the dual job of being the wedding's only witness and covering Peppy's mother's Ford Country Squire station wagon with shaving cream and novelty condoms. Peppy regretted the marriage with a stomach-dropping certainty immediately afterward, especially during dinner at her mother's house later that evening, when Hal pontificated at length about the nauseating new developments in hydraulic flossing.

Peppy had insisted that Hal move from Duluth to Reno; he realized the wisdom of this decision, knowing that his Minnesota Methodist crowd would not warm to a new female who looked like the cartoon lady in the champagne glass from *Playboy*. They moved into a new, three-bedroom tract home in southwest Reno with a chimney pressed together out of concrete and large flat rocks.

The stressful demands of baby rearing while trying to establish a newlywed life were enough to keep the poorly matched couple distracted from the fact that they loathed each other until late 1972.

Edward Norbert Normal had been born on February 17 in 1966 and Elizabeth Lynn on October 25 in 1967 (*Scorpios have hot pants*, said Grandma Noreen, Peppy's mother). The photos from the hospital bed of Peppy, smiling her modeling-school smile and holding a pruny red newborn-wad in a light blue or light pink blanket, suggest that she had been in full Cleopatra cat-eye makeup during her entire labor and delivery process, and that her tall dome of red (or ash-blonde) hair also remained unmussed by the primitive bringing forth of life. Other photos showed the new mother (brunette) smiling bustily at the photographer whilst her long brown cigarette hung perilously close to baby's eye.

By the time Ned was six and Liza almost five, Hal had been permanently barred from the nuptial bed with the white headboard, on which two carved swans kissed in a heart-shaped symbol of lifelong monogamy. Peppy had a new, Osmond-size set of blue-white upper teeth and an impressive aptitude for painkiller consumption. Hal had a string of dental assistants named Kim, Wendy, and Lois, each of whom was persuaded to inhale balloons full of nitrous oxide after office hours and let him have sex with them in the reclining dentistry chair, in exchange for his looking the other way on their moderate embezzlements.

It all came to a head when Peppy was roused from her pill slur at the sight of one of Lois's hickeys on Hal's abdomen when he stepped out of the shower. It was the moment Peppy had been waiting for: a True Crime on which to hang the demise of the loveless marriage, which, due to the presence of toddlers, she would have felt too guilty to leave otherwise. Hal lied with loud indignation about the mouth bruise, but it was all over, and both were relieved.

After a hi-speed divorce (forty-eight hours to Nevada residents with children and property, 192 times the length of the marriage ceremony), Peppy was legally free, Hal having expressed virtually no interest in custody of the children, and having agreed with surprising ease to sign over the new family car and the equity on the house in exchange for Peppy releasing all future claims to alimony or child support. The divorce cost $270. Hal paid; Lois was waiting for him in the parking lot with a bottle of pink champagne. "Woo woo, lucky you," Peppy cracked at Lois, packing the children into the conservative new 1973 Oldsmobile Toronado. Afterward, the children only saw Hal for their annual checkups. They dreaded his guilty nervousness far more than the tooth cleaning, but he always gave them $50 each to compensate for the birthdays and Christmases that he routinely ignored.

The three-bedroom Reno house was rented out; after paying the mortgage, this provided Peppy with a moderate monthly income. Peppy and the kids moved back in with her mother. Grandma Noreen babysat while Peppy played the field, the field being Bil's Red Turkey Tavern, where Beer Nuts were sold, beneath a mirror covered with Bil's favorite bumper stickers:

Free Mustache Rides

No Laugh-a, My Car, Eh?
You're Goin' To Hurt Its Feelings

HEY PAL,
Watch My Tail. . . . Not HERS!

Peppy was often the only woman in the bar, which made her virtually irresistible to the pockmarked clientele.

Noreen couldn't understand where the daughter had gotten "the Look-At-Me bug," as she called it. Peppy eventually called it "artistic flair" and claimed it came from the father she'd never known. Noreen had known WWII veteran Clemont Pinkney less than a month when they were married in 1946, and wasn't prepared to say whether he was inclined toward fits of exhibitionistic dancing and loud show-tune medleys or not, since he was found dead a mere five days into their honeymoon, wearing her store-bought wedding dress and hanging by the neck from a coat hook by a pair of ruined nylons she'd thrown away earlier that day.

Naturally uncomplicated, hardworking, and less vain than her female counterparts of the time, Noreen went back to wearing her wartime combat boots during her pregnancy. She would never wear dresses or girdles or marry again, choosing instead to live modestly off of Clem's navy pension, and repress the unwanted remains of her sexual energy through vigorous, tight-mouthed housecleaning.

From the moment she could voice her wants, Peppy had always craved tap-shoes, ballet classes, tutus, mirrors, cosmetics, and pink tinselly things. She lit up at the prospect of being photographed and went into swooning deliriums at the movies, moving her lips to the dialogue with her eyes locked on the lead actress, genuflecting weirdly in the dark. Strangers pointed at her, laughing. She didn't notice. She was a girl who would buy anything advertised with a kiss, and who never questioned the benevolence of Hollywood Magic. The movies were the home of her heart, where she relaxed, opened like a flower, and let any suggestion float into her unchecked. (In short, she was doomed to lifelong consumer slavery.)

In 1955, after weeks of hysterical pleading, Noreen reluctantly allowed her daughter to enroll in Miss Marquette's School of Photographic Modeling and Acrobatic Dancing for Young Ladies, where Peppy learned the elements of tumbling, baton twirling, and how to smile with her lips slightly parted, her eyes open wide, and her upper teeth freshly glossed with saliva. Noreen had imagined that Peppy would learn how to be charismatically adorable, like Shirley Temple, or perhaps adorably wisecracking, like Jackie Coogan. What emerged instead was a pocket-size version of Gypsy Rose Lee. Like many fatherless young girls, Peppy was man-crazy and through osmosis somehow picked up her mother's abandoned sex drive from its cold storage locker and sashayed around in that sublimated man-fever like a lynx G-string. Her mother found Peppy's dance numbers disturbingly burlesque. "Throw a man in the room, any man," Noreen lamented, "and that child will put on a bathing suit and do exotic backbends." Confused insurance agents or dishwasher repairmen shuffled nervously as the preening child wantonly grabbed their attention by doing the splits on the area rug; they often gave her a dollar to go away, creating in Peppy a Pavlovian template for her future employment.

Grandma Noreen's stoic road through single motherhood made her largely unsympathetic to Peppy's freewheeling, drunk style of child rearing, but she took Peppy's evening absences at the Red Turkey as an opportunity to carve Proper Moral Understandings and A Respectable Work Ethic into the little kids, who, she secretly vowed, would never want for respectable, nontopless employment. She taught Ned to stuff and lick envelopes, she taught little Liza how to bag groceries, beer cans first, bananas last. The children slept in Noreen's small sewing room beneath a framed copy of a silent film poster, the 1917 melodrama *Babes in the Woods*; Noreen had picked it up at a rummage sale to spruce up the bare wall. It was a rather chilling illustration of a pudgy boy and girl, pinkly angelic and barely past the toddler stage, clutching each other at the foot of a large, threatening black tree. The boy is trying to be brave as his little sister weeps tears of terror; the tangled and sinister woods behind them seem to be conspiring to eat the innocent tots like succulent capons. The poster gave Liza nightmares. She did not want to be abandoned in the woods with Ned, who would think it futile to intervene and probably just watch with scientific curiosity as badgers dragged her by the hair into a dark, wet hole.

In 1976, during this period of Noreen's regular babysitting, the Montreal Olympic Games were on television; the children, now eleven and nine, were mad for them. They tried to reenact various gymnastic events on Noreen's living room settee; knees were pressed through the cheap pink cloth of nightgowns; rug burns bearded little chins. Liza was especially affected, particularly in her vivid mental moments before sleep, during which she had a rich and ego-gratifying fantasy life. Liza, at an age when every glory in life seemed possible, would beat out Nadia Comaneci, in slow motion, for a gold medal in the floor routine, to the haunting strains of *Nadia's Theme (Theme from The Young and the Restless)* every night. The fantasy expanded during the Winter Olympics in Innsbruck, with Liza taking to the ice and beating Dorothy Hamill for more gold medals in figure skating. Everyone would be watching— Peppy, Noreen, Ned, her kindergarten classmates, her teachers, the president. Everyone would clap and cry as she swirled beautifully, her legs in the splits over her head in any direction, her arms swanning upward. As adoring fans wrapped her in an American flag, she would drift into a giddy, love-filled, and triumphant slumber. *That is what it will be like, when I am fourteen.*

Liza's waking hours, however, were not spent backflipping over gym mats, or gyrating in empty skating rinks. After school, Liza and Ned watched six to nine hours of television each day; a practical hobby in that they could do it almost anywhere.

Peppy would often hook up with men vacationing in Reno, and the children would be taken on long car trips through the desert and into the Sierras, then deposited on atrocious carpets in faceless towns for periods not less than three days (school holidays) but no more than six weeks (summer vacation). There was a multitoned green shag carpet full of pennies and dog hair in Concord, CA, that belonged to Ray Tilper, who ran a drapery cleaning service. There was a coffee and oil-stained pink carpet with large blue roses that sat in the middle of the linoleum floor of the home of Dennis Van Kittelstrom, who ran a certified Bultaco dirt bike repair shop in Williams, CA. There was blood-red carpeting that aggressively complemented the golden couch legs in the TV room of Luigi Fontanesca, who had recently taken over his grandfather's veal sausage factory in Elko, NV. This rash of brief and unserious unions finally came to an end in 1978 when Peppy fell in actual love, with (and there should be a drum roll):

THE AMAZING JOHNNY BUDRONE
(cymbal *Clash!*)

Johnny Budrone had been a promising rodeo bull rider in his youth until a particularly nasty throw crushed one of his vertebrae and tossed the muscles around it into a splintery mélange he called "crabmeat." Peppy first saw him performing at the Lucky Seven club with his air gun act; with one in each hand, sporting a pair of yellow-tinted aviator-frame glasses, he would shoot a flurry of pellets into large, formless heaps of white balloons, loudly sculpting them into a kind of pneumatic topiary: rabbit heads, hearts, clubs, spades. The rest of the time he drank alone, a lot, to offset his constant back pain. Being another regular at Bil's Red Turkey, the solitary woman at the other end of the bar, who sometimes had jet-black hair, sometimes auburn, became a compelling enigma. One night Johnny was drunk enough to approach Peppy, who was wearing her Natural Honey Blonde wig, and drawl, "So what's your hair down there like, anyhow"—gesturing at her crotch with his Marlboro—"Neapolitan?"

It was not the best pickup line Peppy had ever heard, nor was it the worst. The worst was: "You wanna come in the john with me and put Bactine on my stump?" (Dan "Claw" Haverman, June 1974.) Johnny's line, at least, suggested a sexually viable man with an active, if tasteless, sense of humor.

Apart from the exploded veins, bowlegs, psoriasis, and gangrenous-looking assortment of blurring tattoos, Johnny was a handsome man, and Peppy felt a warm twinkling in herself that had almost nothing to do with the four or seven Fuzzy Navels she had consumed. The subsequent affair with Johnny Budrone was actually the closest she'd ever come to the kind of ovary-squeezing, sublimely unbearable, ice-cream headache-y love she had imagined as a hormonally exhilarated teen.

"That Johnny knew how to treat a lady," Peppy would sigh, later.

He would pick Peppy up at her mother's house in a clean gingham cowboy shirt and his newest Wranglers. She would run giggling to the screen door in hanging earrings and a pair of beige high heels. He would smell of Mitchum deodorant and Wintergreen Skoal "chaw," she of Jean Naté body spray and talc, with a hint of Wicked Wahine Eau de Toilette around the pulse points; a gambler's whisper of hope for the jackpot honeymoon in beautiful Hawaii.

At around 5 a.m. his Falcon Ranchero would growl mufflerlessly up the street again and they would park carnally in the quiet, the sleeping residential block unaware of their hot bourbon tongues and denim-searing concupiscence.

Forty-five minutes later the car would start again, and the white-steamed windshield swabbed from the inside. Peppy would step out onto the lawn, kiss her fingers and wave, her wig askew, her shoes unstrapped, sighing deep pink sighs.

"That Johnny was a real man," Peppy would say, later.

Johnny was a man of few words, but he made each child one sincere overture of friendship. Ned was twelve and already starting to display what would be a lifelong proclivity toward introverted lumpiness. Johnny bought him a Daisy air rifle and took him out in the desert to shoot cantaloupes; Ned fainted from the heat and wet himself while unconscious. Ned was profoundly embarrassed, but Johnny was understanding and friendly about it. He bought Ned a new pair of pants, a bag of pretzels, and a Gatorade, and never told Peppy about the mishap, but Ned had a shameful association with the gun afterward and stuck it in the back of his closet.

Johnny took Liza out for bubble-gum ice cream and was not angry when she picked all the gumballs out with her fingers and lined them up, mouth-sticky and bleeding primary colors, on the dashboard of the Ranchero, where the sun baked them into semipermanence; they could not be removed from the aged vinyl surface without ripping it down to the foam. After that, Johnny pretty much figured they were a family.

The children mostly loved Johnny for his gallery of smeared tattoos.

Johnny would lie on the brown and orange-striped couch with a burlap throw pillow embroidered with a yarn owl under his mangled middle-back, and the children would pry his sleeves up and gaze insatiably at the fading wonders: a horse head framed by a large horseshoe, with the name ZIPPO under it. A crudely wrought parrot with a long curlicued tail. A cowgirl in a skimpy fringe dress, with a gun and spurs. Yosemite Sam standing incongruously on a bed of roses. On special days in the summertime the children could see the bull that ended Johnny's rodeo career—a large blue-black, bucking monster with the unlikely name FEELIN' GROOVY written on a sash between Johnny's shoulderblades, over his six-inch operation scar.

"You gotta give credit to the things that crush you," Johnny explained when asked why he decorated his body with the bull that made him wince through the better part of every day. Ned and Liza were impressed by this philosophy.

The year 1978 was also when Ned and Liza took the bus to see a Saturday matinee and witnessed the cinema phenomenon *Ice Castles*. ("When Tragedy Struck, Love Came to the Rescue," promised the movie poster.) This film would lodge itself firmly in Liza's psyche; it was the pole around which the sprouting bean-plant of her mind would twist for years to come.

Ice Castles is a proto-Coming-of-Age movie featuring doe-eyed and growly-voiced Robby Benson (whose sexual appeal to the seven-to ten-year-old girl crowd invoked national epidemics of pillow kissing), paired up with Lynn-Holly Johnson who plays pretty, blonde figure skater Lexie, a simple country girl bursting with natural ice-talent.

Ice audiences adore Lexie, even though she lacks formal training; the audience is so moved by her rural pluck, they erupt into a standing ovations and hurl red carnations at her whilst Robby Benson swoons in a delirium of love and pride.

(Liza was already *being* Lexie, soul-crushingly in love with Robby Benson and feeling every double axel on-screen in the muscles of her own pelvis.)

Lexie's curmudgeonly dad, after a few tearful door-slams, hard truths, and violin music, reluctantly agrees to let a top ice-coach transform diamond-in-the-rough Lexie into a polished Olympic contender in six months (introducing the Ticking Clock, Hollywood Formula Obstacle #1).

"You've got all the raw talent," says the coldhearted new coach, "but you're virtually untrained. I'm not sure we'll be able to pull it off. . . . How much do you really want to win?"

(*I want to win so bad I am wetting my pants because I do not want to miss one minute of this film*, thought Liza.)

Right as Lexie wins the Big Preliminary Competition, Robby Benson busts her kissing a Fancy New Guy, and runs away from her; she is crushed. (Obstacle #2, plus Ironic Reversal: her Greatest Triumph comes at the same moment as her Greatest Loss—producers love that shit.)

Overnight, Lexie trades her blonde pigtails for a Sophisticated Hairstyle (Hollywood symbol of losing innocence and/or Coming-of-Age) and marvels at her own budding breasts in the mirror, touching her new chest tenderly (with blouse still on, natch, but this is very *serious* Girl-Becoming-Woman fodder, although no teen girl has ever done that, ever; it has only ever happened in the porn-infected male screenwriter mind).

Frustrated by the shallowness of the big-league skating world, Lexie slips out of a fancy party at the rink, puts on her skates, and attempts the forbidden triple axel. The *Ice Castles* theme song is played in a mordant, minor key (Warning!).

Lexie jumps, she crashes into a bunch of patio furniture, she goes blind. (The Grandaddy of all Obstacles #3.)

Smash-cut to the CAT scan—Lexie has a blood clot in her brain that may or may not go away, but certainly not in time for her to compete (Ticking Clock redux).

Lexie goes tragically home to Iowa and becomes depressed, self-pitying, and feral, with matted hair. (Probable Producer comment: "She should be having a Helen Keller moment, here." Screenwriter: "Agreed.")

Enter Colleen Dewhurst in her trademarked characterization of the crusty New Englander Who Is Gruff and Difficult but Whose Heart Is Golden.

"You wanted to find a way *out* when you took that jump," barks Crustbucket, baring her teeth. "Nobody's going to blame an *invalid* for giving up," she sneers.

(The classic "What are you, a Quitter?" speech. The Hollywood Formula pinball machine lights up! *Ding ding ding!* Extra balls!)

Sightless Lexie tries to punch and kick Colleen Dewhurst, who subdues her in a brutal rasslin' hold. Both end up in tears à la *Miracle Worker.*

("You're *crying*," whispered Ned, amused.

"I am not!" sniffed Liza, embarrassed, wiping her tear-slick cheeks on her sleeve.)

Act III Turning Point:

Nobody can persuade Lexie to get back on the ice, until . . . Robby Benson returns! Slighted boyfriend to the rescue! With just enough Love and Hate mixed together to berate and abuse blind Lexie back into championship condition, pitilessly barking out stadium dimensions so she can mentally calculate how many feet she has before she smacks the wall.

In just one week of hard work, Robby Benson's fierce love saves the day. Nobody at the competition even knows Lexie is blind as she takes her final bow until she trips over the carnations that audiences can't resist hurling at her, and can't figure out how to stand back up. As she gropes around the ice on her knees, the entire screaming stadium falls into an abrupt, pin-dropping, cricket-chirping silence.

Robby walks out on to the ice and takes her groping hand.

He guides blind Lexie to the middle of the stadium, where the crowd goes wild again for the two of them, holding hands.

"Stay with me?" begs Lexie.

"You bet," Robby Benson assures.

Roll credits to the sounds of "Through the Eyes of Love," as sung by Melissa Manchester!

Liza, age ten, was devastated by the film's beauty and power.

She wanted more than anything to go blind and have Robby Benson restore her, through Tough Love, to athletic championship, in both skating and gymnastics. She began singing the theme song, imitating the large, throaty warble and power-enunciations of Melissa Manchester around the house.

"That's a hell of a voice you got there," Johnny would say, and Liza would blush, then imagine herself with long, wavy hair, wearing an all-white fringe ensemble and holding a white tiger cub on her album cover, her slick lips parted, her eyes emanating prismic rays. Her album would be called, simply, *Castles.*

Johnny and Peppy bought stylish rings and moved with the kids into a condominium complex called The Snooty Fox in Sparks, NV. "Reno is so close to hell you can see Sparks," went the classic joke. The children had to enter a new school district. Ned had fewer problems in new schools because he'd always been a freak, who eagerly sought out the company of kids with handicaps, harelips, or expansive facial birthmarks. Ned liked finding these people with whom striking up a new friendship was relatively easy.

Liza had more difficulty, socially. The provocative clothing Peppy routinely bought for her perplexed everyone but the black and Mexican fifth-grade girls, who embraced her immediately. The white girls decided that Liza was "a scrounge" and made it their business to exclude her. So Liza "went minority" for a couple of years, much to Peppy's panic. She sang Michael Jackson songs from the *Off the Wall* LP with all the wet gasps and carnal hoots, and learned rhythmically advanced, contrapuntal, and pelvic jump rope jingles:

> *Ain't yo mama pretty*
> *She got meatballs for her titty*
> *Scrambled eggs*
> *Between her legs*
> *Ain't yo mama pretty*

Liza also wrote hieroglyphic notes to girls named "Lil' Pants," and "LaFlamme" in an advanced lowrider graffito-font, which was illegible to authority figures, but if you had a Rosetta stone–like alphabet guide sheet, could be translated into several themes:

1. "Keshawn is so fine" (*response: Jerell finer but he a dog*)

2. "Diane think she so bad" (*all flaring that booty in them stanky white jeans*)

3. "What do you do if Michael Jackson came in your house?" (*!!!!die????*)

For the Normals, 1980 was a big year. Shortly before the June date that Peppy had arranged for them to go to the frontier-themed "Chapel-

Chaparral" and get married, Johnny Budrone left. It was unannounced and unprovoked, according to Peppy, but it probably had something to do with the fact that he snooped into her bottom drawer and read her turquoise, pink, and lavender diaries and, thus informed, held her entire sex life previous to meeting him against her.

> *Dear Peppy*
> *Sorry about everything not working out but theres many things a man*
> *shoud handel by himself and one thing is his "wife". Also the back pain*
> *is to unbarable and I geuss I am just a Solitary Man by nature. No hard*
> *feelings & I hope the kids understand but I just can't go threw with it.*
> *I'm truly sorry and I hope happiness comes your way for you do diserve it.*
> *JB*

The spittoon was devoid of black juice. Faded cowboy shirts hung like Mitchum-scented corpses in the closet. He took the burlap pillow with the owl on it, the Ranchero, Ned's unused air gun, Peppy's blondest wig. He left $1,600, in twenties, on the table with the note. Peppy was devastated. She made a lot of hysterical phone calls; sea lion *orks* of guttural despair came out from under the bedroom door.

She was unable to reconcile herself to life without the man with whom sex had been revelatory—a breakthrough connection with The Mysterious, on par with discussing God in sign language with a baboon. Possessing no internal emotional governor or reasonable boundaries, Peppy spun into an unchecked cyclone of outrage, prompting Sharon (the topless magician's assistant and only witness to her first wedding) to pick up Ned and Liza and take them to Noreen's house with a stack of Hungry-Man TV dinners. Peppy splintered glass ashtrays against the wall and railed against Johnny's "chickenshit" emotional cowardice until her fellow tenants at the Snooty Fox had the police knock on her door. Fortunately, Sharon returned from Noreen's at the right moment and was able to convince the cops she had "everything under control" by having them watch Peppy down two phenobarbitals with a large glass of water. Peppy's caterwauling rage finally sank beneath a toxic slumber, on the striped couch where there was still a concave imprint of Johnny.

The next day, awaking to the raw brain-wounds of the pill and grief hangover, Peppy took her Oldsmobile and drove for three and a half hours, deep into the Central Valley of California, near Chico, where she knew of a cliff in a town called Paradise where people went when they wanted to End Things. It was a beautiful valley; a miniature version of the Grand Canyon, writ green and Mediterranean. The whole surrounding area was flat and agricultural; a rich, honey-scented fiesta of almond orchards, rice paddies, and fast, cool tributaries of the Sacramento River, with small farms laid out in green patchwork under high small clouds. The valley came like a surprise: the ground ahead sank down abruptly, a mile-wide crack dipping deeply into the earth, where the trees looked sea blue and compact as broccoli. The place was now an infamous gawking landmark that the local government took no pains to put a guardrail around—the guardrail, they felt, would imply that they were somehow responsible for the ever-growing pile of mangled cars at the bottom of the gorge. Peppy knew about this popular suicide locale from her ex-boyfriend, the dirt-bike mechanic in nearby Williams. Most of the adults in the surrounding areas—Chico, Forest Hills—had considered this route, more than once in their lives. It was akin to the comfort of a handgun in the closet, or a bottle of Seconal in the medicine cabinet—you didn't need to use it to be glad it was there.

Peppy spent a terrible, drunken half hour staring at the unsympathetically pretty landscape and considering the failures of her life. The children, she reasoned, would go to Hal and Lois or Hal and whatever dental assistant he was currently schtupping, or remain with Noreen, and would be better off. After that thought, she dispensed with thinking of her children and focused on her own woes, in the typically selfish way of the suicide. She opened, with some difficulty, the prescription bottle containing the last of Johnny's muscle relaxants, and reverently dry-swallowed all five.

Life had not turned out the way Peppy had anticipated. All she had wanted was a little show in a nice hotel lobby somewhere like Lake Tahoe, where she could wear a beaded champagne dress, hold a microphone, and ask people Where They Were From before singing "Alone Again (Naturally)" with a sadly ironic smile; then she would break into a little redemptive tap solo while the small horn-section played tight three-part harmonies, and shirtless, smitten dancing boys in cummerbunds and harem pants would lead her around the stage by the hand. She had wanted men to compete against each other for her backstage attentions, offering her turquoise jewelry and trips to Acapulco and leather trench coats, which she would or would not graciously refuse.

Nobody had ever given her the type of attention, or the amount of it, she believed she deserved. For Johnny Budrone to leave was the final insult heaped upon an unscalable shitload of insults, for despite the fact that she loved him with all of the depth, craziness, and thrilling impurity a dysfunctional, narcissistic, codependent, sex, alcohol, and pill-addicted woman could love, she secretly believed he was beneath her, and that he should have been grateful until his dying day that she had nobly condescended to love him.

Johnny's pills took hold with a woozy surge of blankness, and with a final blast of "Nights in White Satin" on the eight-track, Peppy revved up the sizable engine, floored the gas pedal, and drove in a blast of shameful glory off the cliff, plummeting into the deep green forever of Paradise, CA.

The 1973 Oldsmobile Toronado was the first car on the market equipped with a driver's-side air bag, an automotive phenomenon Peppy knew nothing about. After taking the nauseating plunge over the side and falling thirty-plus feet down with a sickening crunch onto the pile of other cars, Peppy assumed, as the pillowy plastic embraced her, that her guardian angels had manufactured the illusion of a painless death, and it was in deep and final relief that she nodded into a shock and barbiturate slumber, which was only disturbed forty-three minutes later when the paramedics interrupted her soft and deathful dreams by chainsawing her door open.

Peppy was taken to the hospital. Her stomach was pumped, and she was held for observation, but she was unscratched; her suicide had resulted in nothing more than a broken Lee Press-On nail. The air bag had cushioned her fall, the wig had absorbed the flying glass, the muscle relaxants had made her as pliable as an ink spot during impact. In short, while it had the best intentions of a real suicide and was clearly not a bid for attention, it was, in Peppy's words, "an ass-out failure." A legal hassle awaited her when she got out of the hospital; charges having to do with her willful destruction of the car and the potential endangerment of others ("Endangering who?" Peppy shrieked. "All the happy people picnicking in the mashed cars under my car? Shrub elves? Who?!"). After a weepy trip to the courthouse these charges were converted into a $500 fine, pending proof that Peppy was undergoing counseling.

The brush with eternity shook Peppy. For a few weeks she was a gibbering half-person who stared into middle distance and sprang into tears unprovoked. Her children worried about her. They were especially kind, and this was interpreted by Peppy as a confirmation that she was quite mentally ill. The inexpensive counselor Noreen had found in the Reno phone book was an Earth-shoe-and-gauzy-blouse-wearing Jungian-in-training named Gerald, who was sympathetic to Peppy's weeping tirades but basically ineffectual, and offered her few tools with which to reassemble her psyche.

During the evenings, Noreen, sweet mother that she was, remembering Peppy's childhood affection for the magical distractions of the big screen, would drive Peppy and the kids to movies, where the kids treated Peppy like a brain-damaged person, holding her hand and shielding her eyes from the violent parts. As a result of this concern, the children, who normally would have opted for nudity or gore when accompanied by an adult, increasingly stood in line for gentler, PG-rated films. *Fame* seemed appropriate, given Peppy's emotional fragility.

The children sat on either side of their mother and enjoyed the movie, but were terrified by the fact that Peppy sobbed through the whole thing.

(Most people seem to have nothing but a subconscious idea that movies are as deep a primordial template for living as the original myths were to the Greeks when Zeus was Sky God. Bad movies full of recognizable clichés are particularly influential. They suggest intrinsic, universal laws and patterns of cause and effect; equations that seem mathematically true:

1. **Goodness = Reward [both earthly and personal]**
2. **Believing in Yourself = Reward [both earthly and personal]**
3. **True Love = Possible for Everyone [via perseverance]**
4. **Proof of True Love = Personal Sacrifice**
5. **Want-Something-Badly-Enough = You Can Get It [via perseverance]**
6. **Rich People = Bad [until they learn the Valuable Lesson; see #9]**
7. **Poor People = Noble [unless tempted to become rich; see #9]**

8. **Hard Work = Golden Ticket to Fame and Reward [see #1, #2]**
9. **Money = Not Everything**
10. **Good-looking = Good**
11. **Too Good-looking = Bad**
12. **Too Good-looking + Rich = Outright Evil**
13. **Quitters = The Worst**

Can we say this logic has not affected our lives? Can any of us say we have not been brainwashed to believe that if we adequately perform the prescribed mambo steps laid out on the Hollywood life-template floor mat, we will earn our heavenly reward on earth?)

Though Peppy could not articulate it, *Fame* (a Coming-of-Age film, but also the Ur-text of several 1980s "Victory Through Uninhibited Dance and/or Music" gems of the screen) represented a world in which talent obliterated every other worldly inconvenience: genetics, poverty, race, even New York traffic. If you were a dancer, why, you *tour jeté'ed* out the door and pirouetted down the street to the mailbox, and traffic halted to admire you. Musicians spontaneously played the violin while eating chili in the lunch room. Drama kids expressed unctuously tender Personal Truths without fear of ridicule, singing the Body Electric with gusto and pride. Talent was its own planet, free of barriers, free of shame, where there was no color, no language, only oversexed teenagers in thin body stockings, frayed leg warmers, and shredded toe-shoes, dry-humping to joyous disco music on the roofs of taxicabs: the molten core of *life*. The truth of it bashed Peppy like a gong: each talented child held a thunderbolt which (s)he could hurl at the world and make it *fucking pay attention*.

As the movie ended, Ned and Liza stared at their tear-drenched mother.

"Mom?" Ned asked cautiously, touching her knee. "Mom? Are you OK?"

Peppy didn't seem to hear him; she was fixated on the rolling credits, trembling.

"Mom?" asked Liza, trying to look into Peppy's eyes. "Is something wrong?"

"Nope," Peppy said, snapping out of her trance. "Nothing's wrong. I'm just happy, because I know what I have to do now."

Ned and Liza shot each other looks of dread. Peppy gave them a desperately hopeful smile.

"You kids are going to go to the High School of Performing Arts in New York City," Peppy sobbed happily, her eyes as loose, intense, and toxically shiny as balls of mercury.

This mania did not abate as the children thought it would in the days that followed, when a film usually loses its grip on the viewer. Noreen assumed it was merely an improper pill combination or a hormonal power surge that set Peppy reeling about *Fame,* but it didn't go away. Gerald the psychologist regarded the movie as a breakthrough for Peppy; he told her that in her lost, unhappy, and bewildered state of mind, *Fame* acted as a mythological Golden Stag that would lead her out of the forest of doubt and misery.

"Golden *what?*" snarled Peppy, lighting another long brown cigarette.

"Stag. Like a buck. A male deer. The Golden Stag appears to the lost hunter and guides him to safety. It appears in quite a few European and Asiatic mythologies; it's a symbol of regeneration and virility, knowledge, life beginning anew. Its antlers grow back when they're broken." Gerald smiled his smug hippie smile. "Maybe your antlers are growing back."

The only buck Peppy noticed in the film was Leroy, the hot black dancer guy, who certainly was an inspiration but not of the beacon-in-the-dark-night-of-the-soul variety, per se. Still, *Fame* definitely suggested a new path, toward art and freedom. Peppy went around for weeks announcing to people, "*Fame* is my Golden Stag." But nobody had any idea what she was talking about.

(Curious Reader: The Romanian version of the Golden Stag fable bears an uncanny resemblance to *Hansel and Gretel*: small children are purposefully abandoned in the woods by weak and selfish parents. The young boy transmogrifies into a Golden Stag and carries his sister to safety.

Coincidentally, *Babes in the Woods*—the poster in Noreen's sewing room—was also a retelling of *Hansel and Gretel*. There is something pan-continentally compelling about the image of

little children, abandoned by their parents to the hostile elements in the dark woods. Who hasn't, at some point in the forced march of life, felt as helpless, and deserving of unqualified sympathy?)

First Peppy put the Reno house on the market, where it quickly sold. With the proceeds, she purchased a yellow Honda Civic station wagon and a commemorative tattoo—her personal "Feelin' Groovy" homage to the thing that crushed her. Rejecting Yosemite Sam and the bucking bull ("not ladylike,") she opted for a horseshoe over her left breast, signifying three important life-things:

1. How Johnny stomped on her heart.
2. How she will nonetheless remain emotionally available "to whoever the shoe fits."
3. How her botched suicide proved to herself she was both lucky and indestructible as pig iron.

During their final session, Gerald the Therapist told Peppy he liked the tattoo a whole lot. Peppy blushed with pride.

Peppy embarked on several car trips along the coast of California, intending to move the kids closer to Hollywood, as a baby step toward New York. She got as far as Fairfax, a town on the outskirts of Marin County, near San Francisco, for it was there that she took a pit stop at the Lady Tamalpais Café/Bar and befriended a gay couple in their late thirties, Mike LoBato and Ike Nixon.

Mike had been a pot-smoking Santa Cruz surfer until the *Ziggy Stardust* album came out and he was cupid-struck by a love of Glam Rock. When he paddled out into the lineup at Steamer Lane early one morning with high orange hair, silver eyeshadow, and a lightning bolt stenciled on his wetsuit, Mike got the shit beat out of him, which prompted him to hitchhike to San Francisco, where he enjoyed all the wild high life of the gay San Francisco 1970s, eventually working backstage for rock-show impresario Bill Graham.

Soft-spoken, compassionate Ike, who had grown up in a farming community in Sebastopol, had been on the fast track to Franciscan priesthood when he met Mike at the Mill Valley lumberyard. Mike was instantly attracted to Ike's kind, subtle demeanor and gravitas, while

Mike's black-Irish coloring, swimmer's body, and leather pants put a halt to Ike's religious ambitions altogether. Ike left the seminary to help Mike carry speakers for the last leg of Alice Cooper's *Billion Dollar Babies* Tour, and the two were inseparable thereafter.

Finally exhausted by the all-night, rock 'n' roll party lifestyle, Mike and Ike were now freelance handymen, comfortably settled down into a quiet, happy suburban degeneracy.

The funky charm of Mike and Ike, in conjunction with the sleepy wealth and cultural intelligence Peppy perceived in Marin County, was all she needed, along with a few Harvey Wallbangers, to put in a bid on one of the town's dilapidated landmarks: the old Fairfax fire station, a quaint, large, two-story clapboard structure that had been abandoned and had fallen into disrepair after the fire department was given a larger, new, windowless, popcorn-stucco building that looked like an oversize Pizza Hut.

Her love for the building's "vibrations" made her rash and impulsive. The firehouse had been subjected to the whims of unchecked entropy—extensive water damage made the ceiling of the top floor sag and peel down in the corners like moldy paper, termites had eaten sections of the joists and the main support girder until it was as spongy as coral, cockroaches and earwigs were firmly entrenched in the marrow of the wall studs. The minimal kitchen was embalmed in dusty grease; the bathroom contained a wall of urinals.

"I dunno," said Ike, blowing a rich, piney vapour of pot smoke down the hole in the second-story floor where the fire pole went through. "Considering what they want for this crate, you'd think they'd at least throw in a couple of firemen. *Black* firemen." He smirked, hugging the pole to his plaid chest and squeaking down out of sight.

"They should have torched this dump. Who'd accuse the fire department of arson? Nobody," countered Mike, following Ike down the pole.

Peppy didn't care. Her brain was romping on its wheel. Nobody could tell her this firehouse wasn't the repository of her future good fortune; the promised sunny clearing after suffering through the dark and predatory woods: the castle of the Golden Stag.

To rehabilitate the firehouse Peppy was going to need more money; she eventually bullied Noreen into selling her Reno house to come live with her in Fairfax. Noreen abhorred the idea of giving up the modest security she had so patiently assembled, but her fear of what would happen to Ned and Liza if Peppy raised them alone outweighed her worry about her own future. With great reluctance, Noreen allowed red-jacketed realtors into her home. "A gem," they proclaimed it. "I know," Noreen responded, knowing full well how much elbow grease she had frenziedly rubbed in over the years, keeping it free of rust, grime, and decay, and hopefully, *sin*. When Noreen saw the chewed-up firehouse for the first time, she was shocked by its decrepitude and cried a little. But she liked Fairfax, a little valley tucked inside round, dark green hills that gave the feeling of a soft catcher's mitt lying open, cool and snug. The air was piney and quenching. Noreen had forgotten about the appeal of green areas, her yard in Reno having contained only a tendrilled century plant, some small cacti in pots, and a ceramic lawn-burro loitering in a semicircle of decorative pink rocks. "The kind of garden you'd have on Mars," as Ned called it.

"The kind of garden you'd have on Mars if all Martian landscapers were blind," as Peppy called it.

"And Mexican," added Liza.

Peppy rejected three pricey contractor bids and hired Mike and Ike to perform the renovation, boldly tearing up her city work permit and opting to do the construction on the cheap and sly. Mike was a reasonably competent plumber and builder; Ike was a talented finish carpenter and master electrician. Dressed identically in plaid lumberjack shirts, red suspenders, and skin-tight jeans, they filled Dumpsters with sooty lath, plaster, and urinals, sistered a few joists, and hammered up fresh drywall. They left the fire pole and installed, where the fire engine once resided, a stage with a proscenium arch, a respectable theatrical "black box," replete with a backstage area and rest rooms (retaining an original urinal on the downstairs level, after deeming it "quaint and nostalgic"). In the area before the stage, where future audiences would sit, Mike installed a wall of mirrors and ballet barres. The firehouse was painted bright red. Peppy had a brass plaque made, thereby christening the former firehouse:

THE NORMAL FAMILY DINNER THEATRE
EST. 1981

Noreen, Peppy, Mike, Ike, Ned, and Liza posed for a photograph next to the sign. It was May; Fairfax was in bloom with furry yellow acacia. They squinted into the bright, cool day, giving the camera a thumbs-up.

The family lived on the top floor. Ned and Liza slept in the room with the fire pole. Noreen had the other little bedroom in the front, separated from the kids' room by the staircase.

Peppy claimed the master bedroom in the back, where she hung a dramatic array of hats, masks, and feather boas, arranged all of her wig heads on a long shelf, and installed a waterbed ("You sure you need a waterbed?" asked Ike, jumping up and down. "The floor is a little springy."

"You bet your ass I want a waterbed, honey, and don't you dare try and stop me. A girl's got to get some pleasure between the sheets.")

Once moved in, Peppy set her sights on hiring instructors. It was her intention to start "The Juilliard of the West."

Mike and Ike became a part of the Normal Family routine; they loved the whole idea of the theatre, and Peppy's amusing vulgarity promised that it would be something more rambunctious than the average community stage. Ike recruited Ned's help, sensing that the boy was lonely and underused, and the two of them purchased and hung all the stage lighting: long fly bars on the ceiling, draped with an array of PAR can-lights and a follow spot.

Ike knew theatrical lighting well; he had been the lighting designer and engineer for a San Francisco cabaret/bar called The Brig, where the drag comedy *I Hate You, Hannah Kingdom!* had played for a nine-month run.

Ike enjoyed his nerdy, informational friendship with Ned, who had a bright, fifteen-year-old geek's love for intelligent-sounding trivia.

"Hey, Mom, did you know that 'PAR' is an acronym for Parabolic Aluminized Reflector? Those are 1,000-watt Fresnels, see, that one is frosted, and that one is stippled, for a wide beam, and did you know that follow spots used to be actual limelights? They were like these burning jets of oxygen and hydrogen pointed at, like, this cylinder made of lime, that rotated."

"I don't want anything burning in here, the fire marshal will be on my ass like last year's ski pants."

"They don't use limelights anymore!"

"That's good. Don't use them."

.   .   .

Peppy had bigger things on her mind. Her plan was to start a school for teens, then cull the better talent from the classes and cast them in a full production that would run for the month of August. She put an ad in the *Marin Gazette*:

FAMOUS?
Spread some of your stardust
Teaching kids 11–18
Actors, Singers, Dancers Needed
For New Performing Arts School
Full Musical Production Impending
Submit photo, letter, résumé

Peppy received around fifty application letters, many with headshots; black-and-white 8 × 10 glossies featuring an idealized full-face portrait of the Actor or Actress. The more expensive versions featured a photo-collage, on the opposite side, of the actor in various "roles," to show the actor's "versatility." The headshots seemed to call out for talk-balloons:

"Ladies, I may wear a leather jacket with no shirt underneath for motorcycle riding, but I can also don horn-rimmed glasses and trans-form into that English professor you wanted to have sex with, or throw on jeans and get a laugh out of washing my Old English sheepdog with several neighborhood four-year-olds. Am I not the Original Man?"

Or:

"Choosy Mom in curlers, executive businesslady (with eyeglass-stem thoughtfully in mouth), oversexed newscaster or just plain Pretty Lady, why, I am Every Woman to all people, especially you, handsome casting agent."

Peppy had imagined that there were scores of semiretired Broadway, TV, and film stars studding the hills of Marin County who would leap at the opportunity to nobly pass their glitter batons. What she found were careers that had never made it past the embryo stage: (*Bob Lo-quasto, Professional Air Guitarist; Popo the Children's Clown—Birthdays, Gatherings, Corporate Events*). Many chalked up their failures to bad luck, or a lack of "connections," or had a story of how they'd been "ripped off" by a celebrity who had stolen and was living their rightful lives, e.g., a jittery, chain-smoking comedian who insisted his "entire schtick" had been stolen by the comic Gallagher: "I was the first guy ever to kill a watermelon with a croquet mallet, at the Holy City Zoo in '73, when that asshole was just a busboy."

Some of the people Peppy met were genuinely gifted but too odd-looking, bizarre-acting, or otherwise unfit for mainstream entertainment.

Among these people, there seemed to be a pervasive sense of denial: none of them could admit that the unrolled blueprint of their lives was the green felt of a craps table. None could believe that if they worked hard, nurtured their talent, and persevered heroically despite crushing opposition, their careers in showbiz might go nowhere anyway. This is an unfairness that many artists can't swallow, having been raised on the "Real Talent Will Win Out in the End" myth.

According to Peppy's schedule (and the dictates of her draining bank account), the theatre camp would run for five summer weeks. Rehearsals would begin mid-July for the yet-to-be-named Musical—the more talented kids in the classes would be drafted for the production. The show would run for three weeks until the beginning of the school year. During this time, Peppy reasoned, Ned and Liza would be whipped into triple-threat musical theatre prodigies at breakneck speed by trained professionals (Ticking clock, dramatic Obstacle #1). She would zip them off to New York City, and they would audition for the High School of Performing Arts, slay the judges, and go on to live the heightened, Technicolor life of *Fame*. If anything happened to obstruct Peppy's plans, these were bridges she would bulldoze when she came to them.

Peppy hired three instructors out of her twenty-some applicants:

Neville Vanderlee, an acquaintance of Mike and Ike's—a morosely thin whippet of a man with oversize vintage 1950s suits, a platinum swoop-wedge hair-helmet wrought in mousse, and pointy yellow shoes. He would be the camp drama teacher and direct the upcoming musical. Neville had earned local praise as the director, coauthor, and star of *I Hate You, Hannah Kingdom!*, the production that Ike had done lights for. Neville had thought the success of that production would bring him more legitimate offers, but they never materialized.

Barbette Champlain, aging former ballerina—a regal, imperious, chain-smoking spider of a woman with long, emaciated limbs who

Peppy hired to teach jazz dance, tap, and ballet; she would also be "movement coach" and choreographer for the musical. Barbette was vain and miserable, having found herself needing a job after her husband, an investment banker, traded up to a younger model of her as soon as she hit thirty-five. She was a capital-D Dancer, down to her snap-happy, osteoporosis crayon-bones, a victim of all of the steep trade-offs dancers make early on in life for the privilege of being physically superhuman while young. Her personality was whiny and condescending from getting too much slavering attention as an icy young beauty, her mind was weak and spoiled from underuse, her angry black liquid eyeliner and watertight, face-lifting hair-bun were bitterly nostalgic throwbacks to her *Swan Lake* days. The aging process was the first betrayal by what had been her faultlessly obedient body; her prime had been devoured like a wedding cake, and she loathed all the possible outcomes of her darkening future. But Peppy was impressed by Barbette's legitimate résumé (all *sylphide* and cygnet roles that ceased abruptly in 1972) and by the enclosed black-and-white picture of her, a lithesome feral bird, walleyed and starving, arabesque-ing in better days.

Lalo Buarque was a hangdog-looking Brazilian pianist and guitarist, whose sole function, it seemed, was to keep all women within a fifty-mile radius lactating with a romantic need to save him from himself. He was swaybacked, built with long, slender muscles buttered with just the merest quarter inch of subcutaneous fat. His body was the sun-kissed color and softness of blonde calfskin, matching the dirty gold of his oily bed-head. He was preternaturally relaxed to the point of abject laziness. In his musky, faded T-shirts, handlebar mustache, sunglasses, and bleach-frayed, cock-hugging jeans, his entire visage gave the impression that undersea Venus on the half shell finally got sick of him as a lover and rolled him onto a hot beach for the next woman to frustrate herself over. Lalo sang, drank, cried, and smoked unfiltered Camels with a languid sensuality; grown women who could smell his unwashed armpits bit their knuckles and considered abandoning their families for a chance to lick the salt off his neck.

His letter:

This letter is someting I don't write good, for to tell you my singing is good is no good, you must hear the singing also piano and mime. You can say good that the starlite on osean is beautiful, but with not see the stars or osean, its is not same thing? It is someting, ART, coming from my soul as a man with love and emotianal joy and sad and phisical not with paper and pensil. See me and I will show you someting, this is like big gift to me, I give it to you and to the childrens also.

Peppy would have thrown Lalo's letter away had there not been a Po-laroid photo enclosed of him in whiteface, shirtless, wearing shrunken cutoffs, smiling rapturously in the sun, juggling four grapefruits. *Yep, topless juggling can be a wise career move*, thought Peppy, moving the letter to the IN pile, deciding that Lalo could be "musical director" and pos-sibly much, much more.

Each instructor was hired with an explicit addendum to their job description: in addition to teaching the regular students, they would also have to help Ned and Liza prepare their auditions for the High School of Performing Arts—one song, one dance, one monologue. "When I say dance, I don't mean disco ass-wagging," Peppy told her new employees, solemnly shaking her cigarette at them. "I want them to think the kids have some *class*." Neville, Lalo, and Barbette dreaded this aspect of the job, but none of them were in any position to turn down regular employment.

Young people (girls, mostly) and their mothers arrived at the Nor-mal Family Dinner Theatre by the tens, intrigued by the ad:

THEATRE DAY CAMP
FOR TEENS 12-18
Singing, Acting, and Dancing
Work with Professional Performers
Fairfax Today, Broadway Tomorrow!

These were the miserable children of Marin County parents, mostly the daughters of orthodontists and real-estate agents, at their most hor-rible stages of adolescence: hateful and lazy creatures with noses jutting out like doorknobs, mouths dark with metal, skin and breasts erupting into sore red boils. Peppy accepted forty new students out of the forty-two that applied—she turned down a precocious five-year-old Suzuki-method violinist, and a very cheerful nineteen-year-old girl in a wheelchair who wanted to be a "sit-down comic." Most of the boys dropped out in the first three days when they realized how outnumbered they were. What remained was a surly mass of jailbait: thirty-one pouting, slouching, eye-rolling mounds of baby fat and lip gloss between the ages of twelve to sixteen, wearing their ill-fitting bodies like detested school uniforms.

This was Liza's first encounter with the local teens. She was thirteen, but even the older girls were threatened by her tube top, satin hot pants, flesh-colored nylons, and high, corrugated-plastic-soled platforms that made her look like the child-hooker from *Taxi Driver*.

There were no other disabled or malformed kids around to deflect scorn from Ned—he was presciently terrified, knowing that it was only a matter of time before the monstrously judgmental girls made his life unlivable.

But both Ned and Liza were floating down Peppy's plans for them like paper bags on whitewater. The mania of it gave them a strange, hopeful tickle of otherness, which separated and protected them from the rest of their peers (*perhaps*, thought the bags, *we are seaworthy!*). Resistance to Peppy's Master Plan was futile; if their mother believed they could become talented enough to go to the High School of Performing Arts in one summer, well, maybe they could.

Liza, secretly, had already taken the fantasy to its extreme.

Not only would she be admitted into the *Fame* school, but they would be leveled by her genius. The *Fame* instructors would be the Redeeming Eyes, her Ideal Audience; they alone would have the proper amount of knowledge and training to recognize the unbelievable talent she knew (as all thirteen-year-old girls know) that she alone possessed. A hush would fall as instructors in other rooms of the building came, like kings to the starlit manger, to witness her song.

Some would be jealous of her, some would weep. Agents would be telegrammed. She would radiate warmly in a bright halo of homecoming.

"I don't know how to thank you all," Liza would say in the mirror next to the downstairs firehouse urinal, when she didn't think anyone was around. "I've worked so hard and waited so long for this moment. . . ."

And then she would sing "Superstar" by the Carpenters, a song too sad and personal to sing for anyone but the long-lost family of people who were capable of appreciating her. She would stand in the light of a simple pinspot, wearing a strapless, white leather minidress, white high-heeled cowboy boots, and multiple concha belts slung about her hips.

Yeewur guita-a-a-ar, it sounds so sweet and clear
But yew're not really here, it's just the radio-o

Don't chu remember you told me you loved me bab-y
Bap-BADDA DAH DAH (Liza would also sing the horn
section part)
Ya said you'd be comin' back this way again, bab-y
Bap-BADDA DAH DAH
Baby, Baby, Baby, Baby, . . . (she would drop to a whisper)
Oh Baby,

A crystalline tear would roll down one cheek.

I lo-o-o-ove you . . . I ruhlly do . . .

At 5:20 every evening, on the camp days, cars pulled up and lined the street in front of the theatre, waiting to get their teen talent back. The moms looked expectantly at their daughters, hoping to see them transformed into longer, stronger, thinking people who could enunciate in the king's English, sing in medieval choral style, and move without looking like they'd been assembled out of water balloons. Day to day, they looked for a change and could see none.

At the beginning of the day, Barbette would lead the class through ballet barre and jazz-inspired floor exercises. She would sit on a tall stool, wearing ginger-colored tights, tan jazz pumps, and a brown, wrap-around leotard cut high over her knobby hip bones and low down her fleshless sternum, revealing an abdomen loosening into a gelatinous vodka bulb. Barbette would bang a broomstick on the floor to the beat and berate the resentful girls, disgusted by their clunkiness.

Ned, the only boy, seemed to draw all of Barbette's dislike of males in general.
"Ned, was that a *grande battement* or were you trying to shake blood into your foot before it died?"
The girls snickered derisively.

"For God's sake, Ned, pull your bottom in, you look like you're trying to dry it over a campfire."

The girls *tssssed* and eye-rolled cruelly.

"Ned, pull in your gut, we aren't doing 'Dance of the Maytag Repairman.'"

Ned went crimson with shame every time but pretended not to care, and obediently danced on through the rest of the forty minutes even though a crying jag was sitting in his throat like a lump of lye. Since Barbette, an Authority Figure, was mean to Ned, it was perceived by the worthless girls as tacit license to be fiendish to the limit of their abilities. They decided Ned smelled of urine and wouldn't stand near him. Within days, to be looked at by Ned in class was tantamount to courting disease.

"Eeeu! Ned, your gross eye is looking at me! Stop it!"

(Girls congratulating the insulter sotto voce: "Oh my God! That was *so tight*." "That was so *fully harsh*." Giggles.)

Even Liza was helpless to put a stop to their unchecked viciousness; she was on the ropes already, with the crueler girls. They tortured her in the dressing room. Despite Liza's provocative dress-style (which she was unaware was provocative), being the child of a woman who was essentially a nudist made Liza neurotically modest. She always wore thick underwear under her leotard and tights. ("What are you wearing under there, a diaper?" hissed Barbette.) She hated puberty, hated what her chest was doing, couldn't abide pubic hair. She used the extent of her flexibility to contort in and out of her leotard in a way that would conceal her nudity from the other girls. The other girls were hip to this, and since they were already outraged by Liza's clothing, they began to taunt her by belligerently frolicking naked in front of her.

"This is the *NBC Nightly Nude* with Dan Rather," one would scream, and the others would enact squealing, raunchy ballets, kicking over Liza's head and singing in falsetto while Liza hid her eyes. Sometimes girls would put her platforms on and pretend to hitchhike, as Liza, naked and gyrating.

"Are you going to wear that tube top to school when you go to Miwok Butt?" Desiree Baumgarten once asked Liza with a sneer in her nose, referring to Miwok *Butte*, the local public high school.

Liza was ashamed and furious.

"I'm not going to Miwok. I'm going to the High School of Performing Arts in New York," Liza snapped, exiting the dressing room to a chorus of "*Eeeeeeuuuuu!* I'm *Liza!* I'm going to the High School of *Performing Arts!* In my *wildest!* And I'm wearing a tube top *every single day!* Because I'm *special and unique!*"

You will all see me and cry, thought Liza.

Barbette saw that Liza was going to be a hard case: she knew that Peppy had a vision of Liza as a willowy little ballerina, waddling backstage at great concert halls with turned-out feet fetishistically clad in pink toe-shoes. The fact of the matter was that Liza, while she had a slim, proportional body, had no organic dance talent whatsoever. She was uncoordinated and abnormally bad at memorizing step combinations, being unable to determine "right foot" and "left foot" with any reliability. Her limbs turned inward, her hips were inflexible, and she had no sense whatsoever about what to do with her arms, which hung in a palsied fashion like the wings on a baked chicken despite Barbette's constant abuse. But Barbette knew that Peppy would fire her if any mention were made of Liza's lack of ability; also, it being Marin County, there had recently begun to be mention of lawsuits threatened by the parents of children who had been told such things by dance instructors. "What do you *mean* Mindy isn't prima ballerina material?! How dare you *limit* my child by *discriminating* against her body-type!"

The word *discrimination,* Barbette mused, once meant the educated ability to determine and appreciate subtleties of taste and value—now, she sighed, it meant she was a Nazi. "It's the French revolution," Barbette groaned, when discussing American culture in general. "Anyone with enough refinement not to shit in their own armchairs is getting their head cut off."

Liza, in the meantime, was only aware that she was not as good as some of the girls, but not as bad as Ned.

The teen girls were confused by Lalo; they didn't understand the complicated flavor of his crimson adult sexuality (being Children of the Television, they only consciously responded to boys who dressed in the fashions prescribed to their demographic), but their bodies knew something was afoot with the pheromone-blizzard surrounding Lalo, and they acted squirmy around him as they sat in folding chairs around the rinky-dink upright piano.

Lalo led the girls through warm-up scales, which they mumbled through tunelessly ("Scales are *so gay*"). Once those were completed, Lalo boinked out remedial accompaniments of his favorite songs, all of which were invariably about sex or God (Lalo's two big topics), e.g., "Day by Day" from *Godspell*, Dylan's "Lay Lady Lay," and "My Sweet Lord" by George Harrison; songs that sounded weird and unwholesome when sung by a chorus of nasal little girls.

The last section of the class was arranged so that a few girls, if they wanted to, could sing a solo. For the first week there were no volunteers. In lieu of any takers, Lalo would sing them one of his own compositions: swirling, watery songs of tormented passion, in Portuguese, that involved a lot of mushy pedal work. The girls would watch Lalo pour out his carnal grief with confused doll-eyes, fidgeting and discomfited by any form of emotional exuberance. Ned liked it. He could tell that Lalo was a hypersensitive person (like him) transformed into a Real Man—he was cool, and he was kind to Ned. Whenever Lalo smiled at him, Ned's bashful blood rushed hotly into his cheeks.

"Why do none of you want to seeng?" Lalo grumbled, the second week. "You, Liza, you do this. I know you like to seeng, I hear you seeng in the battroom sometime."

Unbeknownst to Lalo, Liza had been lying in wait for this moment—she was dying to sing, but her tenuous social position made it impossible for her to volunteer. Liza sprang to her feet and thumbed through Lalo's *Easy Rock Hits of the 70's* music book and found Melissa Manchester's "Don't Cry Out Loud," splayed it open on the piano, then turned to face her rude and lumpen audience.

Lalo plunked away at the opening bars, and Liza, with no hesitation, opened her throat and hollered the song at top Melissa Manchester concert-volume, wailing into the first vibratos . . .

*"Baby cried the da-a-ay the circus came to towwwn
'cause she dii-dn't want thah parade to go pahs-ssing
By Her . . ."*

The girls were shocked. None of them could believe Liza's cringe-inducing brazenness, being too repressed, swinish, and conservative themselves to ever do anything that five or more of them couldn't do simultaneously, to avoid individual embarrassment. At first the girls flashed each other grimaces of mock horror at Liza's voluminous performance, the power of which was blowing their bangs straight up.

But as Liza roared great, artless lungfuls of lite pop balladry at them, a curious change came over the girls; their opinions shifted, as only the opinions of teenaged girls can, in sudden, collective whiplash U–turns like a school of guppies.

"DON'T CAH-RYEEE OUT LAH-OOOOOUUUD
Just keep it in-sah-eeed
And Learn how to hide your Feelings
FAH-LYYYYE H-I-I-I-GH and PAH-ROOOOUD
And if you should fa-a-a-all
Remember
You almost
Had it
A-A-A-A-A-A-L-L-L-LLLLL . . ."

The girls, who began that day collectively opposed to Liza because they were all vaguely disgusted by her, whipped around in an eyeblink, and were now collectively opposed to Liza because they were all grudgingly *jealous* of her.

When Liza stopped and all of the girls, their lower jaws agape and dangling from their upper jaws by orthodontic rubber bands, actually *clapped* for her, it was the biggest *Ice Castles*-swirling-Olympic-moment of her life. Her eyes went watery from the bright shards of happiness shooting from her heart.

Her glory lasted about six seconds.

The heroic display cracked the code for the other girls, and they all instantly figured out how to sing, or rather, they figured why they should stop *not* singing, and they became ruthlessly competitive. A riot of plastic-braceleted hands went up to sing next when Liza took her seat. From that point on, Lalo's class was all-out, pop-chanteuse-wannabe warfare.

The next day, it was apparent that mothers had been marched to the music store, checkbooks fluttering. Glitter fingernails crammed glossy sheets of new music in front of Lalo's dog-eared fake books. Lalo had to put a sign-up list on the wall; the girls elbowed, cheated, and snaked one another in efforts to get there first. Liza was kicked away from the list like a dog from groceries. The girls fatally attempted "Memory" from *Cats* and "Tomorrow" from *Annie*; they hatcheted songs from *A Chorus Line* and *Evita* into bite-size teen emoto-chunks. As painful as many of the girls were to listen to, Lalo was overjoyed that they had all snapped awake from their dismal comas of peer pressure.

Lalo was accompanying fifteen-year-old Chantal Baumgarten and singing the Barbra Streisand/Barry Gibb duet "Guilty" when Peppy walked by the music room on her way to buy cigarettes. Witnessing Lalo and the underage woman-child trying to harmonize with each other on the wonky, pseudo-operatic lovemaking duet and nearly succeeding, Peppy was stopped cold by a uterine pull of savage yearning. Her black, French-looking "Lulu" wig became warmer as her mind began to ferment with a bacteria of plots.

While the girls respected but disliked Barbette and were perplexed by Lalo, they loved Neville; he was their favorite. They gravitated around him, gushing compliments on him. Many of the girls had crushes on him, knowing little of homosexual lifestyles (only using the words *gay* and *fag* as a means of lite derision). Neville drilled the class through drama exercises of dubious worth and improvisation games, where all the girls crusaded to impress him with their individual wit by making off-color jokes, at which he would smirk and make a "naughty, naughty" gesture with a long finger. He did nothing to discourage their carrying on in this blue vein unless one of the mothers or Peppy was around, because it made him less bored, and, he reasoned, it "loosened them up."

Nobody could say that Neville didn't know where his bread was buttered. He favored Liza shamelessly in class, much to the writhing envy of her classmates, and made it a point to befriend Peppy, watching old movies with her on nights when he was too broke or hungover to go out "whoring in the city." Mike and Ike would often join them, bringing over buckets of chicken.

If Liza could no longer get any solo song action in Lalo's class, Neville was glad to give it to her after hours. He made her watch old Streisand films and listen to Julie London, Shirley "Goldfinger" Bassey, Cher, Nancy Sinatra, and Eartha Kitt records, teaching her all the grotesque showmanship affectations he so loved.

"Raise your hand when you draw out a long note with your fingers splayed out, like you're pulling a baseball-sized wad of gum out of the audience's hair," he'd crow, and Liza would do it, to Mike's and Ike's laughing approval.

". . . and when you sing the word *'love'* flip your hair around like you can barely stand it."

". . . and when the audience claps, pretend like you're surprised and like they're teasing you, then shoo them away, then throw your head back and stretch your arms out straight like you're trying to hug them all, because you just can't *believe* how much they love you."

Mike, Ike, and Neville would pick up strange, flashy dresses for Liza that they'd find in thrift stores; she was their Barbie doll. It was funny to them to have a girl her age imitate the unintentionally self-satirizing mannerisms of aging show-women on the brink of career death.

Peppy, being a very literal-minded person, had no gift for irony and was just delighted that the boys had taken such a special interest in Liza's burgeoning talent. It was Neville who taught Liza to say strange, showbiz things, during nights in Peppy's living room, drunk on jugs of Gallo table wine. Noreen didn't like it.

"They're making Liza grow up too fast," she'd whisper to Peppy.

Peppy was mildly worried that her daughter was becoming a "junior-high fag-hag," but then again, the attention was wonderful, and everyone was having relatively innocent performance-fun, and it was, after all, a theatre, and they were "theatre gypsies," in Peppy's romantic mind. Eventually Peppy would pour herself another goblet of wine, abandon all hope of moral quality control, and shoo her mother off to bed.

The giddy nights when Liza would don a powder-blue chiffon gown, false eyelashes, and one of Peppy's long wigs, and belt out "Gypsies, Tramps and Thieves," standing on the coffee table while Mike, Ike, and Neville laughed, smoked, drank, and deliriously yelled out new, over-the-top performance tips and absurd stage patter were some of the Normal Family's happiest moments. Liza was dizzy with joy from the attention, absorbing all the boozy input like a sponge cake.

All of the camp classes were dominated by the talented Baumgarten sisters, Chantal and Desiree, the only children of one of the county's richest orthodontists. The remote, demure sisters, both svelte beauties, were classically trained dancers who had recently quit the Marin Ballet Company (and its annual production of the *Nutcracker,* where Chantal had locked up the role of Clara two years running) in order to more seriously pursue acting (their mother, the elegant Serena Baumgarten, had found the Normal Family Dinner Theatre "wonderfully bohemian," imagining that its low-rent qualities suggested an uncompromised devotion to pure thespian artistry). Liza was half-wild with jealousy over them; she couldn't understand how any benevolent God could let the exquisite Baumgarten sisters exist in the same world with her, exposing Liza, by comparison, as a loud, inferior clutz and dooming any chances she had to be singled out for starring roles, even at her mom's theatre.

.   .   .

Peppy, through Serena Baumgarten, arranged for Liza to meet Colette Whelan-Zedd, the local children's casting agent for commercials, TV, and film in the area. The Whelan-Zedd casting office was in the quaint top floor of a small clapboard Victorian on one of the small commercial streets in Sausalito. Its floral chairs were cobwebbed with the sheddings of two white Persian cats.

Colette, a zaftig "Giorgio"-perfumed woman in a yellow bouclé suit, burst out to meet Peppy and Liza like a large, blousy tea rose. Then she took one look at Liza: her padded-shouldered bolero jacket, fuchsia eye shadow, aggressive lip liner, fishnet tights, black miniskirt, and white pumps that she couldn't quite walk in, and her whole body snapped into a disproving pucker.

"Wow, if this is you at 9 a.m., I'd love to see your night look."

"That can be arranged," said Peppy, smiling, missing the vibrational shift.

"Roman Polanski's not casting around here, as far as I know," Colette cracked, her eyebrows arch and high. The comment sailed over Peppy's wig.

"Liza's got a great singing career ahead of her. Would you like to hear her do 'Diamonds Are Forever'?"

Liza shifted her weight uncomfortably, looking at the headshots of thirteen-year-old girls framed on the wall. Unlike her, they were all wearing coveralls, smiling guilelessly with daisies tucked behind their ears, cuddling puppies. There was an especially precious shot of Desiree Baumgarten, her collarbones framed by a white leotard, smiling prettily at the camera, sunlight pouring through her teeth. Peppy pulled a small tape recorder out of her purse, and the speaker fritzed out Lalo's twangy piano arrangement. Liza snapped into action, spread-eagled on the Berber rug, wailing extremely in the little room. One of the cats leapt into Colette's lap in fear.

Colette opted not to represent Liza "at this given time" but offered to clue Peppy in to a few upcoming commercial auditions that Liza could try out for, "Just so Liza can get her feet wet." Colette provided this service in exchange for Peppy agreeing to give "special consideration" to the Whelen-Zedd agency kids when casting productions at the theatre. Peppy didn't bother to tell Colette that the Baumgarten sisters hardly needed this extra push.

.   .   .

Peppy drew the instructors together for a meeting about the full-production musical. Neville, who had been thinking a lot about a production that could best serve his own whims, suggested a musical version of *Hush . . . Hush, Sweet Charlotte* with Peppy playing the decrepit Bette Davis role, incorrectly assuming that Peppy would, at first, be flattered and agree, then abandon the role when she figured out it had no sex appeal, and then *he'd* have to step in heroically and play Charlotte himself. Neville had no idea how misguided his plan was. Peppy rejected *Charlotte* outright for being "camp trash" and announced that the premiere performance of the Normal Family Dinner Theatre would be "a real family wing-ding, something to give the *Nutcracker* a run for its money . . . ."

They all thought for a moment, then Peppy's face popped into brightness. "I know, I got it, it's perfect . . . you ready? Brace yourselves. *The Sound of Music.*"

Everyone looked at Peppy, who was suddenly varnished with satisfaction, and realized she was not joking.

"May I ask who you are thinking of getting to play Maria?" asked Neville, suspecting the worst.

"*Me,* dummy," Peppy said sternly. "And Lalo? You're gonna be Captain Von Trapp!"

Peppy turned to Lalo, her eyes twinkling with anticipation at the thought of kissing him every night onstage while people clapped. Lalo smiled weakly, being hungover and sexed-out from the previous night, in which he had been voraciously entertained by two EgyptAir stewardesses. He had no idea what Peppy was talking about; her coral-painted lips were moving, but all he could hear was the warm buzz saw of sleep in his toxic blood.

Peppy was delighted by her plan, and with her own strain of pathological single-mindedness, lock-clamped on it.

"The only way you'll get her to drop that idea is to hit her in the head with a brick," moaned Barbette, later.

Neville secretly hoped that Peppy would realize she was not cut out for the demands of Maria and he'd have to step in, heroically, and play the Julie Andrews role himself, and kiss Lalo every night onstage while people clapped.

"*Innocent fancies can become sick delusions,*" Neville said of Peppy, with a sigh, quoting his favorite line from *Hush . . . Hush, Sweet Charlotte.*

PART II

I,

THE CHEESE

(A Depressing Young-Adult Tale)

HE DAYS OF THE CAMP were drawing to a close, and the girls were beginning to get excited about auditioning for the musical. Chantal Baumgarten, everyone knew, was a shoo-in for Liesl, and Desiree for Louisa, the next sister down; Liza, because of her loud voice and nepotistic connections, would probably be cast as Brigitta. Smaller girls would play Kurt, Friedrich, Marta, and Gretl, the younger Von Trapps.

Neville, disappointed by being unable to play Maria, busied himself by inventing directorial privileges and casting himself in various walk-on roles: the Von Trapp family butler, the Mother Abbess, and Herr Zeller, a monacled and codpieced Nazi. He ran out immediately to buy his costume at the Army Surplus store so that he could admire himself in uniform.

"That thing . . . ," said Peppy, puzzled, pointing to the codpiece over Neville's jodhpurs. "Isn't that from, like, the Victorian era or something?"

"Just trust me," said Neville, with a slitty-eyed grin.

Neville convinced Mike to play Uncle Max Detweiler.

"What the hell! I'm practically the weird gay uncle of all these kids anyway," responded Mike.

"Aren't we all," said Neville.

The only actual teen boy suddenly became a viable commodity.

It was no surprise to anyone but Ned that he was drafted to play Rolfe, the Hitler-youth boy who sings "You Are Sixteen Going on Seventeen" with Liesl.

"But I'm not really a singer," Ned pleaded with Peppy.

"You will be in a couple of weeks. Sink or swim."

"But I'm only fifteen."

"You're big for your age. You think you've got problems? Where the hell am I going to get a wig as boring as that 'Maria' helmet? And all those lederhosens? We've all got sacrifices we have to make, around here."

Peppy resumed scowling her way through a "Frederick's of Hollywood" catalogue, dismissing all of Ned's further efforts to weasel out of the role as "stage fright."

Lalo had been living in the Royal Buccaneer, a men's residence hotel in Corte Madera. He was convinced, after two schnapps-injected hours of Peppy billowing at him over her kitchen table about "conserving creative energy," to move, for the duration of the production, into a windowless room behind the theatre basement that Peppy preposterously dubbed her "in-law unit." Since there would be no rent, Lalo reasoned that he would be able to buy a lot more weed.

Lalo had never seen *The Sound of Music*; its twee, colorized aura of exuberant chastity disturbed him as he viewed the Betamax tape in Peppy's living room, stoned. Liza and Ned watched with the weary faces of children accustomed to hardship as Peppy snuggled against his thigh in a pair of saffron-colored sateen pajamas, conscientiously refilling his glass of Harvey's Bristol Cream. Mike, Ike, and Neville were conspicuously not invited; Noreen was safely down the street at a Presbyterian bingo game.

During the "Lonely Goatherd" number, Lalo began to fidget from the richly hellish psychic discomfort that only a stoned man can experience when his wilting Venus Flytrap of an employer/landlord is showing him a G-rated musical with lascivious intent, her fingernails are slowly stroking his lower spine, and she is whispering hair-raising propositions in his ear, in front of her staring children.

"Oh, I don't know, Paippy, man, these guy, the Capitan . . . how you call it, when singing OOOO-LEEE-EO, he has to do it? I cannot do that theeng," Lalo would mumble, his forehead suddenly sweating like picnic cheese.

"The Captain doesn't have to yodel, Lalo."

"Oh."

Lalo sunk back into the couch in defeat.

While Christopher Plummer and Julie Andrews were singing starry-eyed pledgings of troth to each other, Lalo was inventing a bookshelf of excuses to get out of sleeping with Peppy, knowing that he would need an excellent lie virtually every night of his stay.

"You kids go to bed," Peppy slurred as Lalo bit his cheek.

"It's not even our bedtime," Liza glowered.

"We don't know if the Nazis win or not," Ned pouted.

"You've seen it a million times. They skippety-shkip away to Switzerland. Good night!"

"Paippy, man, I gadda go too." Lalo sighed, yawning dramatically.

"But I was hoping we could block out a couple of the songs . . . ."

"No, no, thenks, eet's late, I gadda get some slip."

"Boy, you wear out early, don't you."

Peppy punctuated her dismay with a double-barreled nostril-blast of cigarette smoke. Lalo practically stepped through the coffee table trying to escape, knocking over the near-empty bottle of Harvey's, and a lit candle shaped like a Siamese cat that Peppy had owned but not burned since 1979 for purposes of decor. The burning cat head indicated that the night was special to Peppy in a way that Ned and Liza assumed from experience would probably fuck up their lives, somehow—it was only a matter of degree.

On the night of the last day of the theatre camp there was a party.

Parents and brothers milled around in attendance, giving the girls something to scream and giggle over.

There was a small performance for the visiting families wherein the kids, in cheap costume top hats and white-tipped canes, sang the song "One" from *A Chorus Line*. Liza did the performance fuming with the acrid smoke of jealousy, because while she was shouting to the music from the far right of the stage, wearing a fake mustache, Chantal Baumgarten was dancing a solo, center stage, wearing a white dress and toe-shoes, having been cast as the "One" in question. Everyone else was reduced to the sorry status of Dancing Boy except for Desiree Baumgarten, who got to wear a black wraparound skirt and do a featured solo in high-heeled silver tap shoes.

After the performance, Liza went to congratulate Chantal and Desiree, who were standing with their movie star–like parents.

"Good job, Chantal," Liza stammered.

"Thanks." Chantal offered a clammy handshake and smile that turned down at the edges.

"You too, Desiree."

Desiree pretended not to hear her; she was busy talking to the cutest boy in the room, a French foreign-exchange student who had come with one of the other families.

"So I guess I'll see you guys in the production."

"They cast you?" Chantal asked, looking genuinely shocked that anyone would want Liza for any reason.

"Well I guess, I mean, I live here."

"Oh! Right," Chantal corrected, remembering who Liza's mother was. She turned her back on Liza abruptly to be congratulated by some of the other parents.

Liza, in bed late that evening, decided to finally write in the pinkly padlocked unicorn diary that Ned had given her for her twelfth birthday.

> Dear Diary:
> Hello. I am Liza Normal, age 14.

(Anne Frank possibilities swirled through her head; she saw her diary published in twelve languages and English teachers everywhere extolling the depth of her youthful prose. "A literary power and wisdom well beyond her years," they would say.)

> Chantal Baumgarten is the biggest bitch in the world. If success is the best form of revenge then I'd better get famous real fast and the only way to do it is to go to the High School of Performing Arts and <u>really nail</u> the audition. Also it would be great if there was TV involved. Hopefully I'll be famous

within 8 or 9 months. That would be cool. Because the
Baumgartens suck so much.
   I HATE CHANTAL BAUMGARTEN AND ALL
BAUMGARTENS!!!!! FOREVER!!!! FUCK C.B.!
   GOD PLEASE MAKE ME FAMOUS.
   Love,
   Liza Normal, Singer, Dancer, Actress
   Lizette Normale
   Liza LaNorm

Ned's and Liza's audition pieces, Peppy decided, would be *Sound of Music*–based, since she was damned if she was going to pay for more sheet music.

Ned began studying for the role of Rolfe. His acting was relatively OK, for a kid, but in his tone-deaf singing, he felt he should imitate Liza, compensating for what he lacked in ability with sheer, yowling volume.

> *YOU WA-AAIT LITTLE GIRL*
> *ON AN EMPTY STAGE*
> *FOR FATE TO TURN THE LIGHT O-ON,*

"Oh shit, Naid." Lalo would laugh, lighting another Camel short. "You sound like some donkey get his balls catch in the Nazzi war machine, man."

The dancing section, for Ned, was the worst nightmare: twenty minutes alone with Barbette, daily. The first week, Barbette worked through clenched teeth and Ned was sullenly obedient, to the best of his abilities. On week two, Barbette could resist her natural cruelty no longer:

"Ned, if you keep bouncing on your toes like that, you're going to need a brassiere." Ned was morbidly sensitive about his pudgy boy-mammaries. The low blow shamed him so deeply he momentarily lost his mind. Ned was slow to anger, but when it came, it was of the shrieking, breaking objects, and locking-self-in-bathroom variety.

Lalo and Ike, who were smoking a joint in Lalo's subtheatre cave, heard his cries and ran upstairs. They soothed him through the door with tender words. Ned finally emerged twenty-five minutes later, red and damp with mortification.

"Don't tell your mom I say, but Barbate is really mean beetch, man," whispered Lalo.

Ned's wet eyes looked at him gratefully. Ike gave him a manly hug around the shoulders.

"Yeah. Screw her," he said, bringing Ned great comfort.

Peppy greeted the news with an exasperated "What now?"

She knew she couldn't afford to let go of Barbette; she was already too enmeshed in the production. Peppy ran to Barbette to apologize for Ned's behavior and gave her the rest of the day off.

"He's going to have to learn how to take criticism if he wants to be an artist," Barbette said. She shrugged, her lizardine eyes half-open.

"You're going to need to be able to dance," Peppy told Ned, sternly.

"I can't do it. I *hate* dancing, and I *hate* Barbette. Look at me! I'm not the dancer type!" Anguished tears sprang into his eyes again.

"What are you going to do, *give up?*" Peppy heard the TV-movie of herself asking, in appropriate cliché-speak. "If you can't pull your jazz shoes back on and march right back onto that stage and give it your *everything*, what kind of hero will you be when *meow meow meow (ad nauseum)*." What she actually said was: "Ned, nobody's asking you to be Rudolf Nureyev, all Barbette wants to do is give you a little bit of movement—"

"I'm NOT DOING IT!!" Ned yelled, blood pounding in his neck.

"So you're *quitting*, then? Is that what my son is? A *quitter?*" said the TV Peppy, tapping her foot, trying to get Ned angry so he'd *dig in and fight* while the real Peppy struggled with feelings more complex and less virtuous.

She looked her miserable son over and tried not to reveal her cold disappointment. Peppy had been so taken with her vision of the vital young *danseur* trapped inside Ned's blobby adolescence, she could not forgive him for willfully sabotaging the future Christmas she envisioned wherein he was a tin soldier in the *Nutcracker*, with round red cheeks, and she sat proudly in the audience in a fur coat, smugly grinning at the other mothers.

Peppy left the room. Ned could hear the suction of the freezer door in the kitchen, the crack of the ice tray, the *tlink* of cubes bouncing in the tumbler.

"I'm throwing my tights into the alley!" Ned yelled through the wall.

"You do that," murmured Peppy.

Ned heard pouring liquid cracking ice, Peppy swirling the glass, *schlick*.

He stuck his tights on a protruding nail in the wall and ripped them into cobwebs, feeling a sick hole of shame over being graceless. Who doesn't want to dance? He cried again, soundless and exhausted, deeply suffering his incurable lack of talent.

"You're out of the production," Peppy yelled abruptly from the kitchen.

"Good. Thank you," Ned yelled back, regret crushing his chest.

"And I guess you're not auditioning for the High School of Performing Arts," Peppy yelled back.

"I guess not," shouted Ned, sensing for the first time, from the pain in her voice, that the whole *Fame* fantasy was more about Peppy than it had ever been about him or Liza.

Noreen was broilingly furious at Peppy for trying to bully Ned into being something he wasn't. There was a loud fight, after which Noreen stormed down the street and bought a local newspaper, then got on the phone and immediately signed Ned up for the first summer course she could find at the local community college, in order to get him out of the theatre and redirect his energies toward something she knew he'd be good at.

"Glassblowing for two weeks, then welding." Noreen was firm.

"Glassblowing?!"

"Then welding."

"Nobody every won a Tony Award for welding," said Peppy.

Ned began his summer school course the very next day. He went every morning on the bus and found within a few days that he liked glassblowing a lot.

Peppy, in the meantime, went into overdrive trying to find a replacement Rolfe. She placed an ad, offering a "Featured Role for Talented Boy 16–18."

They were auditioning a lusterless collection of weedy, sebaceous youths when Roland Spring came in.

Roland was a fifteen-year-old half-black kid, with big black nerd glasses and a pilly hand-knit stocking cap. His general dishevelment and concave posture suggested an unusually vibrant intelligence. Liza glanced at him and didn't smile or say Hi; his shabby brown pants, shredded deck shoes, and unspecified race placed him even lower on the teen totem pole than she was (and as you well know, Reformed Teen Reader, no juvenile of low status misses an opportunity to flaunt their position at someone perceived to be even lower).

Roland came by himself, with a large plastic putty-tub and some drumsticks. Peppy, Lalo, Neville, and Barbette watched him from behind a foldout table as he took a smaller putty tub out of the larger one and sat on it.

Then he began. He wasn't a drummer so much as a human beat-box; his act had been honed in front of movie lines all summer and involved singing, mouth noises, and agile finger gymnastics with the sticks. His head began to nod, his eyes rolled up into his head. His mouthful of large teeth began smiling hugely as he warmed up; raw joy began to spill from his heart in wild currents, filling the room, as he sang:

You got shoes!
I got shoes!
All God's children got shoes!

Liza was nailed to the floor; watching Roland Spring, it felt like all of her hair was being pulled out slowly and easily, like worms from holes; her stomach caved in with something like starvation; it felt like she would simply die of deprivation if she could not eat Roland Spring's real and unquestionable talent, gyrating like a top on its own inexhaustible power. Roland Spring's drumming was the most singular thing Liza had ever witnessed; a world-shattering miracle under the lame, staple-gunned proscenium. Liza knew immediately that Roland Spring was rare, supreme, and without context; a zebra born in an abandoned grocery store, King Tut's golden head suddenly materialized on a rec room ping-pong table. He was, as her mind spelled out in miles of bursting neon, the REAL THING. She couldn't even look at him, his presence was so euphorically blinding. When he finished, Lalo gave him a standing ovation. Liza, unable to breathe, slipped out of the room.

She ran into her bedroom, locked the door, and cried in gasping, appalled sobs. She could not articulate why, but the feeling was one of resentment that she had, all her life, been deprived of something more important than food, love, or breathing. Roland Spring had shown all the frayed holes and cheapnesses in her, like direct sunlight through bad curtains. He was undeniably *special* in a way that impaled her, and she could feel all the cells in herself grasping hopelessly at his divine quality. In the Normal family lexicon, she had just glimpsed her Golden Stag.

"What about Roland Spring?" Liza asked later, when Peppy and the instructors were reviewing the candidates.

"Well, I don't think the audience will buy a mulatto Hitler Youth," scoffed Neville.

"You mean we're not going to use him??"

"Liza has a crush on him," Ned smiled.

"I do NOT!" she said, but she knew it was true the moment Ned said it with the clamor of a thousand anvils being dropped. She didn't have a crush on him, she was consumed by a bonfire of love for Roland Spring that approached holy reverence.

"Maybe you let heem make some music wiz me," Lalo suggested.

"You're going to be *onstage*," Peppy reminded him.

Over the next week, the Normal Family black box was transformed into Salzburg, Austria, in the last Golden Days of the 1930s. Roland Spring, who had called the theatre repeatedly, hoping for any part in the production, was finally assigned to the lowly position of set painter. Liza thought this an outrage, but at least he'd be around for her to stare at. She was already jealously plotting, trying to figure out how to keep him hidden from the Baumgarten sisters and, more crucially, the Baumgarten sister hidden from *him*. The thought of Roland Spring approving of Chantal and Desiree or God Forbid *liking* them was too dismal to bear. Liza's mind roamed unbridled through romantic fantasies; she concocted three main scenarios that were almost plausible enough for her to believe that some strange turn of fate might let them happen. Liza rolled these over her brain like lumps of mental ice cream:

A. SCI-FI: The entire theatre suddenly vanishes, leaving nothing but an oily black rectangle on the charred lot. Roland and Liza, absent at the time of the theatre's sinister demolition, are now primary suspects and forced to flee. Their love erupts over a period of weeks as they realize that they "only have each other now." In the zenith of this fantasy, they are sleeping safely in each other's arms on a Greyhound bus to Mexico. The plot, though unclear in Liza's mind, involves their love being the force that keeps a nebulous paranormal evil at bay.

B. SUSPENSE: Liza is abducted by a traveling gypsy circus when they hear her singing and decide to exploit her talent for their own gain. Roland, the only witness, tracks the caravan relentlessly, trying to save her. After a whip fight with a swarthy snake charmer for whom Liza nearly develops a Patty Hearst–like affection, she is rescued. In the end, Liza and Roland make a deal with the gypsies and become hugely successful international circus stars, traveling Europe in a colorfully decorated private train-car with Lady, their trained ocelot.

C. ACTION (The favorite): Peppy is murdered. Liza emerges from her room after the funeral a changed girl; her hair seems longer, and she wears only black leather. Her sadness has given her a savage, catlike beauty. Liza purchases weaponry and embarks on a quest for Revenge. When Roland sees how dangerous the undertaking is, he insists on accompanying her. Their love germinates as Roland is more and more impressed by Liza's fearless passion for justice and deadeye marksmanship.

In real life, Roland watched the rehearsals longingly while slathering green tempera paint onto cardboard hills, with which *The Sound of Music* would eventually be "alive." Since it was too big a job for one kid, Peppy took a suggestion from a parent who worked as a juvenile correction officer, and got her theatre chores dubbed "community ser-vice" by the local juvenile court system. This way, she gained the slave labor of two delinquents: Misty-Dawn, a girl who, the theater girls were quick to comment, dressed "like an even bigger hosebag than Liza," and Barren, a boy from the all-black side of town who had the blankly terrible, violence-deranged eyes of a hurt shark. The girls quickly redubbed Misty-Dawn as "The Mastodon"; Barren, they de-cided, had a mother that couldn't spell *Baron* and that's where his trou-bles began.

The girls naturally assumed that Roland was also a juvenile delin-quent—"the nice fuck-up," they called him. Liza didn't correct them; in this way she hoarded Roland's golden identity for herself.

Nobody besides Liza seemed to notice Roland's burning to participate onstage; Lalo, Roland's other ardent supporter, had his own problems.

Lalo's English, which was interpretive and impressionistic in the best of times, proved to be a hefty obstacle when it came to memorizing his part. The line "There are rooms in this house that are not to be disturbed" became, in Lalo's sensuous Brazilian mouth (which slurred everything, as if he was oozing out each word like a wet mango pit), "There some room in dez houze to please do not desterb."

"Orderliness and decorum" became "Odorynez and decoral."

He and Neville began to clash on issues of personality and professionalism.

"Lalo, do you *really think* that Captain Von Trapp would wear a midriff T-shirt with parachute pants?"

"Iz not dress rehearzal, OK?"

"And truthfully, I wouldn't care that you're stoned, but would *Captain Von Trapp* be stoned? A very serious, retired officer of the Austrian Imperial Navy? On pot? In the thirties? I just want you to bring the character some *truth*."

And so Lalo stopped coming to rehearsal stoned, and started coming drunk.

To his credit, Lalo did try to employ some method-acting techniques after reading a Marlon Brando profile in a Brazilian magazine. Near the end of the play, after the Anschluss, he would gaze at Peppy, scratch his stomach and drawl, "We gadda get oud of Owstria, man."

"Stop calling me 'MAN'!" screeched Peppy.

Barbette, due to her regal and condescending demeanor, was cast as the glamorous Baroness Schrader, to whom Captain Von Trapp is engaged, previous to falling in love with Maria. Peppy couldn't stand to watch the two of them in rehearsals. When Lalo was sweet and courtly to Barbette, even in character, Peppy would stomp and fume.

"You not going to have de goberness no more," Lalo announced magnanimously to the Von Trapp children, placing a warm arm around Barbette. "Zhou're going to have some new Mother. We oll going to be bery hoppy."

"All right, everybody on your feet," Peppy shouted. "We're having a fire drill."

"What, *now?*" Barbette whined. Lalo's teeth could be heard grinding.

"Yeah NOW." Peppy rose from her folding chair, clapping. "Fire drill! *Ding ding ding ding ding!* Everybody outside! Let's go!"

Liza's one consolation for the fact that *The Sound of Music* was becoming a Baumgarten-showcase vehicle was the dorky freak-boy that was eventually cast as Rolfe. Brigham Hamburger was a six-foot, 119-pound ectomorph whose parents were Christian Evangelicals from the Tiburon seminary. Brigham had been a featured singer in his church's "upbeat" teen group, The Jesus Christ Experience. Chantal Baumgarten took one look at Brigham—the concave chest, body odor, food-filled braces, oily, bumpy forehead, knobby white arms five inches too long for his armpit-stained shirt, and the cheap, drugstore sneakers generally worn only by people with Down's syndrome—and pretended to be sick for the rest of the day.

She's going to have to kiss him. Liza wriggled with ecstasy, listening to Brigham Hamburger belt out "You Are Sixteen Going on Seventeen" with all the formal, nasal resplendence of a young Jim Nabors.

As Liza kept wandering over to the set painting to try to be near Roland Spring, the Mastodon looked at Liza's orange spandex pants and halter top and thought she saw a friend. Nobody had ever gone out of their way to befriend Liza so sweetly: "You sing real nice. I wish I could sing pretty like you," the Mastodon shyly confessed to Liza.

"What were you in juvie for?" Liza replied, asking the one question about Misty-Dawn she had any interest in, and cringing internally at the inevitable coldness she was going to have to employ to freeze the Mastodon's unwanted friendship like a growing wart.

The Mastodon recited her oft-told tale in a run-on sentence of select highlights:

"Me and my ex-boyfriend stole my stepdaddy's Trans Am and took it to Oxnard and when they pulled us over there was two Walther PPKs in the trunk but they didn't belong to us they belonged to my stepdaddy but they put Thumper on trial as an adult coz he had a juvenile record for possession and I was strip-searched twice."

"Your boyfriend's name was Thumper?" asked Liza, when she was really wondering, *You call your mom's husband your stepdaddy?*

"He's Mexican," said the Mastodon, by way of explanation. "Do you like REO Speedwagon?"

"No," said Liza.

Ned, in the meantime, found he liked welding even more than glass-blowing. He loved the welding pit, the smithy, all the macho rudiments of hard matter. The chemicals and tools possessed superhero qualities— a hydrogen flame was *invisible,* an oxyacetylene cutting torch could *slice steel*—yet they were controllable, if one was careful and had the know-how. He fancied himself a Hephaestus–like figure: soot blackened, a lit-tle tragic—fatness and a lazy eye having the same alienation quotient as a clubfoot among teenagers and show people, who always demand per-fect beauty from their ranks. Escape from the feathery, jealous, and fickle world of the theatre was a great relief.

Peppy had her work cut out for her as the "black sheep of the nun-nery." She obtained, from the Montgomery Ward's catalog, some rather shapeless dresses, but she immediately browbeat one of the sewing moms into giving them plunging, cleavage-fructuous necklines.

The wig she chose, one of the more conservative hair-mounds from the Eva Gabor Collection, was a short platinum flip with spit curls and a row of plastic daisies stapled behind the bangs. Behind the daisies, the hair boosted upward in an aggressively teased look, which required that the nun's wimple be bobby-pinned precariously on top. It made Peppy's head look curiously oblong, but she liked that it added considerable height.

Since Liza's tiny role as Brigitta Von Trapp was dumb and thankless, she concentrated mainly on perfecting her High School of the Performing Arts audition piece, deciding on a bossa nova version (with Lalo's taped accompaniment) of "Climb Every Mountain." Barbette gave up trying to get her to do a ballet piece and decided to work with Liza's natural movement abilities, which fell somewhere between modern jazz, dodgeball, and stripping. Neville backed out of coaching Liza, citing his numerous directorial responsibilities.

"Just sell it, honey, sell it" was his only contribution.

The play began to take shape, as plays miraculously do over a period of weeks, like a poster of chaotic squiggles that eventually reveals to the viewer, due to some trick of depth, color, and cross-eyedness, a 3D rabbit on a unicycle.

At first, Neville had been sweating bullets, trying to figure out how to make Peppy, with her cigarette-trashed voice, seem like a plausible nun.

"I can't seem to stop singing wherever I am!" Peppy-Maria complained, in her 3 a.m. Reno rasp.

"Could you do that line, maybe, a little more *falsetto*?" asked Neville.

"It is what it is, fancypants," said Peppy, irked.

Neville eventually gave up. "You can't rebuild virginity with a vinyl repair kit." He sighed.

Peppy had always considered herself musical, but she was actually tone-deaf and incapable of hearing musical cues such as the beginnings and endings of choruses or bridges. Forgoing melody completely, she would shout out lyrics tunelessly, and in a random tempo, but with knee-slapping, beer-stein-waving enthusiasm:

I HAVE CON-FI-DENCE
IN CONFIDENCE ALONE!
I HAVE CONFIDENCE IN ME-E-E!

Lalo, the first time he heard it, turned visibly pale. Neville was open-mouthed.

"You might try doing the song that same way every time, at least," suggested Neville.

"Talent is consistent, genius is inconsistent," argued Peppy (who heard Neville say that once). "And by the way, I think I could be juggling in this number."

Neville spluttered. "You're a NUN! What are you going to be juggling? Bowling pins?"

"What about crucifixes?" asked Peppy, innocently.

Neville looked at her for a moment as if the top of her skull had swung open on a metal hinge, and a metallic claw holding a live eyeball had craned out and stared at him.

"Woman, if you can juggle four crucifixes, what kind of fool director would I be if I tried to stop you?"

"*Meu deus*," moaned Lalo, clutching his head.

. . .

Lalo's heavy drinking began to infuriate Neville.

"Lalo! If you're going to wear those horrible sandals at least don't shuffle across the stage like you're going to vomit all over Gretl."

Lalo exploded, finally. "Fock you, man! You are not *arteest*! You are not a *men*! You wear the dress for *nuns* and these faggot theeng on you pents!" (He was referring to Neville's controversial codpiece.)

"Lalo, if you're too stewed to act professionally—"

"You don't *look* at me!" Lalo stuck an outstretched finger threateningly close to Neville's eye. "You are s-s-some kind flat *worm* that suck blood out of *shit!*"

"Go to bed! If you ever come to rehearsal drunk again you're out of the production!"

"*A puta que pariu!*"

"*Heeeey!*" shouted Peppy, establishing the theatre hierarchy with a mighty bray.

"You can work with this?" screeched Neville, pointing a shaky finger at Lalo, who was hiding behind Peppy, grabbing his pants-crotch and jiggling his privates toward Neville in an offensive manner.

Peppy thought the whole thing was outrageously funny.

"OK, we'll stop for today," she snorted, advancing to her nylon cigarette pouch.

"You guys don't get it! This scene is a mess!"

"Quit worrying," Peppy said, grabbing Neville's lapel. "We're all going to go upstairs and have a nice little drink, smoke some herb, whatever, and make nice. I know my lines."

"*He* doesn't!" Neville shrieked.

Lalo wagged a long red tongue at Neville.

"He's a natural." Peppy beamed, looking lovingly upon the booze-flushed Lalo as he lurched upstairs, cursing and swinging his arms at invisible gnats.

Forty-five minutes later, the three could be heard singing "My Favorite Things" with filthy lyrics in Peppy's kitchen.

The Whelan-Zedd Agency notified Peppy of as many as two "cattle call" auditions a week. Liza would groom herself outrageously beforehand, spending hours with her crimping iron, Aqua Net, and eye shadow palette, always hoping to emerge from her room and totter down the theatre stairs at the serendipitous moment when Roland

would happen to be walking by. When he saw her Olivia Newton-
John-in-*Grease*–like transformation from Mere Young Girl to Ravish-
ingly Sophisticated Woman, Liza knew that Roland's jaw would drop
and their lives would braid into each other's.

The day of the OtterWorld Fun Park spokes-child audition, Liza's
stomach was throbbing with comets, because Roland, Barren, and
Misty-Dawn were right in her path, stapling yards of cheap black fabric onto scrim frames. Liza, surging with the power of spangled fem-
ininity, floated down among them in a sinus-conquering mist of
Jontue.

"Woah," said Roland, looking up with a smile. "Whatcha lookin' like
that for?"

"I'm going out for a gig," Liza said in a casual voice throatier than
her own, her heart hydroelectrically feeding lightbulbs for Ferris
wheels and boardwalks.

"Whatchu auditioning for? Miss Universe?" Roland teased. Barren
giggled, a strange, girlish giggle.

"Oooh! You look *fine!*" gushed the Mastodon.

"You should take some of that makeup off," Roland told her, not
unkindly. "You're a young girl, you don't need all that."

"I like a girl don't have all that shit in her hair," Barren told Roland,
staring disapprovingly at Liza's shellacked canopy of crimp-ripples.

Roland nodded. "Yeah. All soft and blowy."

Liza stood like the remains of a sand castle after a fatal wave, silently
chastising herself for not predicting that Roland would be a fan of the
Clean and Natural Look.

"Liza!" Barren called to her as she slunk away.

"What?"

"You look like Brooke Shield."

"I *do?!*"

"*Psych*," Barren hissed, then giggled.

"Aw, that was cold." Misty-Dawn laughed, high-fiving Barren. Liza
noticed ruefully that Misty-Dawn had instantly abandoned any solidar-
ity with her to suck up to Barren, her new crush.

As Liza slunk into Peppy's Honda, punctured by her failure to hypno-
tize Roland Spring, her feminine guile did take one victim, skewering

his good Christian heart like a shish kebab. Brigham Hamburger was parking his moped and removing the white plastic football helmet his mother insisted he wear when the cosmetically amplified vision of Liza torpedoed his repressed hormones, causing that biochemical system to gush its special poisons and set off submolecular chain reactions throughout his entire nervous system. As the Honda drove away, Brigham Hamburger had to crouch down and put his head between his knees, for he felt the same palpitations, sweatiness, and dizziness that had always previously meant he was about to faint from exertion. When the blood slowly returned to his extremities, he knew he was In Love.

All of the nuns in the production ended up being men. Neville, who eschewed color-blind casting but had no problem ignoring gender, recruited several drag queens; the nuns soon had a great deal of Three Stooges–esque comedy "business"—Nun A would crouch down behind Nun B, and Nun C would shove Nun B backward over the bent body of Nun A, all with a lot of black sleeve-flapping and polite falsetto "Ooofs!" and "Eeeks!"

"This isn't exactly what I had in mind as a religious community," Peppy remarked with distaste.

"You ain't exactly Julie Andrews, Miss Snuffleupagus," countered Miss Vonda Pleasance, a six-foot-four transvestite with shaved eyebrows who had been cast as Sister Margaretha.

"Let's just not get too koo-koo with the slapstick, ladies."

"*Ma-ria's not an asset to the a-a-abbey,*" the sarcastic men would sing.

There has never been an opening of any production without panic. The moment the ads came out in the paper, everyone writhed under the sudden knowledge that the flailing and bleating they had been doing in a half-assed manner was going to be starkly judged by an audience of strangers in just a few days. At this point, a stage production quickens and takes on unplanned flavors of its own; the latent idiosyncrasies of the cast and crew suddenly surge into growth from seedlings into prehistorically huge, steaming jungle plants—these can end up wholly obscuring the landscape of whatever text the group is abusing in the name of art.

Barbette, who wanted to focus exclusively on her role as the Beautiful Baroness (feeling sure the role would earn her a few dates with wealthy divorced fathers), was engaged in a new hell: getting Brigham Hamburger to dance was exponentially worse than trying to bully grace out of Ned; Ned, at least, had some pliable sensitivity to exploit. Brigham was intractably pious, thickheaded, and possessed of jerky, primitively bolted erector-set limbs. No amount of shame Barbette could dish out had any effect on Brigham. He would simply look down at her, smiling with the infinitely smug, pitying look of someone who knows that he is going to heaven, and you aren't. Ned, catching sight of Barbette biting through the filter of her cigarette as Brigham made his palsied stork-hieroglyphics across the stage, felt gratified.

Liza began to rejoice in her tiny role, solely because she didn't have to do any scenes with Brigham Hamburger. Chantal Baumgarten had been forced to buck up with a level of professionalism well beyond her years; Brigham's breath was apparently so unbearable she had taken to buying him cartons of Velamints. "My father gets them free," she lied.

Liza sat in the back of the theatre near Roland, Misty-Dawn, and Barren, who were hot-gluing fabric remnants as Chantal and Brigham rehearsed "You Are Sixteen Going on Seventeen." Liza silently gloated to herself, watching Chantal squelch all of her revulsion and act madly in love with a boy who was an icon of world-class dorkery, taking his hand and flirting desperately with him while he chastely sidestepped her romantic zeal. It made Liza alive with a burning sensation of wrongful happiness.

"It would't *never* happen like that," Barren muttered as he looked on. "No girl that fine would have no problem gettin' *that* motherfucker's attention."

Misty-Dawn's shoulders bounced as she laughed noiselessly.

The rehearsal ended abruptly when Lalo's accompaniment tape spit in squealing loops out of the aged reel-to-reel. Brigham turned toward Liza from the stage and gave her a terrifying metallic smile.

"Oooh. He like you," whispered the Mastodon, who had recently taken to speaking like Barren.

"Shut up. He does not."

"Look. He comin' this way."

Roland and Barren stifled snorts of hysteria and looked down at their work, so as not to interfere with the flow of whatever Brigham intended to do, now that he was advancing toward Liza, blazing with some sort of naked intention.

"He *want* you," giggled the Mastodon.

"Shut up!"

"Liza?" squeaked Brigham, with a frightfully assured look on his face. "Would you come outside with me for a second, please?"

"Why?" asked Liza, horrified.

"I've got something for you."

Roland, Misty-Dawn, and Barren were barely containing geysers of hysteria.

"I don't want to go outside."

"Just come with me a minute. I think you might like it."

"Don't leave the man with his ass hangin' out in the air, shit," encouraged Barren.

Liza shot a look of fury at Barren, who widened his eyes and gave a dramatic, deadpan shrug.

"I'll come outside with you for ten seconds, but that's all."

"That's all I need," Brigham intoned with an excess of courtly confidence.

Liza shuffled out the door with Brigham, who seemed to be seven feet tall at that moment, such was his enthusiasm. As soon as they were on the other side of the doorjamb, Liza heard the set builders splutter into floor-beating hilarity.

"I noticed you leaving in the car the other day, and I thought to myself, wow, who is that beautiful lady? And then I was like, no way, that's Liza," Brigham confessed with the pride of someone convinced that what they're saying is exactly what the listener is dying to hear.

"Thanks," said Liza flatly, trying to come up with her escape route.

"I got you this." Brigham reached into his backpack and pulled out a small porcelain teddy bear in an angel costume, the stand of which read *Bless You!* in cursive.

"Oh, God, Brigham," Liza moaned, trying to impart to him in the least hurtful way that he was an Olympic-level dork, light-years beyond anyone's wildest imaginings of purebred, championship dorkhood, but that she did not hate him for it.

"I know you're hurting," Brigham began emotionally, taking hold of Liza's shoulder. "Your mother . . . I know this is going to sound weird to you, but her vanity and lust are bringing you down, but you deserve better—"

"Oh, for fuck's sake, Brigham," Liza spat out, beginning to hate him.

"No, listen, I'm totally sincere, I wouldn't be asking you to go with me if I didn't think that you were the type of girl I'd want to marry someday . . . ."

Liza was seized by the image of herself in a white bridal gown, age eighteen, advancing down the aisle of an ugly modern church to organ music, toward an unthinkably terrifying future as Mrs. Liza Hamburger. She aggressively pushed from her mind the nightmare of Brigham's trembling virgin dork-fingers exploring her nudity on their wedding night.

"I'm not taking this," said Liza, handing the bear back to Brigham as if it was teeming with bacteria.

Brigham looked shocked.

"But I got it for you."

"I don't care. I don't want it. Take it," Liza said, holding the diabetically cute thing out at arm's length.

"Are you gonna go with me?" Brigham kept at her, unable to realize he was being shot down, such was his faith in prayer.

"No!"

"Wait, wait, wait, let's talk about it. I don't think you know what I mean when I say 'go'—"

"I don't *care* what you mean when you say 'go,'" Liza stammered, suddenly aware that Misty-Dawn and Barren were watching them with glowing eyes through the slits in a rotten clapboard.

"Just get to know me—"

"I don't *want* to know you! Take this goddamn thing!" The noxious figurine began to embody all of the cooties of a nude Brigham Hamburger. "*TAKE IT!*"

". . . come to my church with me, and I'll . . . ."

Liza wound up and slammed the china animal with great force onto the sidewalk, where it crashed satisfyingly at their feet into several dozen shards, one of which ricocheted off the concrete and lodged itself in Brigham Hamburger's right eye.

Peppy, alarmed by the sounds of pain, hustled her fleshy legs past the painting crew as fast as she could motor them; Barren was flat on his back, laughing so hard his limbs were twitching like a bug.

"Yuk it up, Barren. That act will get you a one-way bus fare back to junior jail."

"Bitch," Barren whispered, his face downshifting to its usual wrath.

.   .   .

Peppy looked at Liza with eyes of purest freon as they drove the sobbing Brigham to the emergency room.

"Hold his hand," Peppy hissed with layers of threat.

"I don't want to," muttered Liza.

"Jesus let me not be blind in this eye," gasped Brigham.

Liza felt the stone-deep feeling of time, in a horrible circumstance, becoming composed of heavy individual minutes that one must chain-drag over one's shoulder alone. She noticed, out of the car window, something darkly ironic that would tattoo itself on her mind forever: an aged and peeling mural from a defunct drive-thru of an anthropomorphic hamburger with a talk-balloon that said, in letters nearly too faint to read, "BITE ME!"

Brigham's punctured cornea meant that Roland Spring was immediately installed as Rolfe, to the overwhelming approval of everyone but Liza. Chantal's portrayal of Liesl's puppy love became thrillingly believable. "They've got some chemistry, those kids," chuckled Peppy, watching Roland make Chantal blush.

Barbette pronounced Roland "a physical genius" and rechoreographed the number into an adorable modern pas de deux. Roland turned out to have the silky, relaxed vocal quality of a young Nat King Cole; "You Are Sixteen Going on Seventeen" became the high point of the entire production.

Liza's intestines twisted into sausage links. Her worst fears had come to pass; the blood was on her hands. This turn of events in no way resembled her wish-mantra, in which Chantal and Desiree Baumgarten both broke legs in a car wreck (Desiree being Chantal's natural understudy, by birthright) and Liza took over the role of Liesl. As the final cherry-on-the-insult, Liza was forced to send a get well card to Brigham.

Heartfelt Wishes . . . for a Healthful Recovery

"You bet your ass you're going to be sweet to that boy. His people could sue our pants off. Good thing they're Jesus freaks or we'd be living in a bush already," Peppy said irritably while cutting Maria's wedding gown so that the long skirt could, via Velcro, tear away to a minidress (a last-minute suggestion of one of the mustachioed nuns).

. . .

And suddenly, like a beast in a tree, it pounced upon everyone:

OPENING NIGHT!

A spirit of high frenzy possessed The Normal Family Dinner Theatre; trembling hands drew on liquid eyeliner, dogs barked, things fell down and were hurriedly righted. Hems were stapled, furniture duct-taped. Scenes were cut at the last minute (the "Lonely Goatherd" number, among them—Peppy's take on yodeling evoking crude disembowelments to the human ear), eleventh-hour decisions were made by any available human, and projects were carried out unsupervised.

In answer to the main question that ticket buyers had been asking over the phone, a cardboard sign with adhesive vinyl lettering was thumbtacked to the door reading:

TO NIGHT
THERE WIL L BE NO DINNE R SERVED
AT THE NORMAL FA MILY D1NNER THEA TRE
S Or r Y FOR THe INC0nVENAinCE

(The sign would never be removed.)

"We'll give them popcorn and beer," Peppy reasoned, that particular menu being dinner enough for her, most of the time. Neville realized that there was some wisdom in filling a hungry audience with booze.

Everyone at the theatre was punchy and sleep deprived from the ten-hour cue-to-cue two nights earlier, during which Ike and Ned designed the lighting.

Ned was exhilarated by the emotional power of lights—a blue wash plunged the stage into mystery and spookiness, pink brought actors vigor and beauty, green inflicted disease, a red gel created heat and sin. It was perspective-altering, and Godlike.

The doors were opened. Seats filled with parents and a few denizens of the local press. The apiarylike noise, to the actors, was nerve-racking but euphoric. Girls kept peeking into the audience to glimpse how many people there were; Misty-Dawn saw Brigham Hamburger arrive in an eyepatch.

"Look," she whispered to Liza, beckoning her over to peer through a hole in the backdrop. "There go your boyfriend."

"Shut up!" Liza yelled through gritted teeth.

Backstage, everyone wished each other Broken Legs. Peppy glued on two sets of false eyelashes, donned fishnet tights, and rouged her cleavage. Neville and the nuns did bleating vocal warm-ups. Chantal and Desiree Baumgarten arrived at the theatre with their hair professionally salon-curled into perfect ringlets, which gave them otherworldly, nineteenth-century naiad looks.

Liza was so jealous she attacked the crimping iron with renewed fervor and made herself up, despite her role as an eleven-year-old, utilizing the full weight of Peppy's makeup box.

"I didn't know children wore aquamarine glitter eye shadow in prewar Austria," Desiree Baumgarten sniffed.

"Now you know," Liza spat.

Roland was wearing his lederhosen in the hall, joking with Barren and the Mastodon, who were teasing him for resembling an "alpine faggot." Liza walked up under a patio umbrella of kinked hair.

"You don't look like a kid!" squealed Misty-Dawn.

"This is how they told me to do it," Liza lied. "Break a leg, Roland," she offered, smiling bravely with her shiny purple mouth.

"Thank you," he said, his teeth dazzling. "You too."

"You're not wearing your glasses," Liza gasped, noticing that Roland's eyes were an unlikely greenish color, adding extra torture to her longing.

"I can't see shit, either. I'm probably going to fall on my ass."

"They have to airlift you to Faggot Mountain Hospital," said Barren, laughing.

At that moment, Ned walked by carrying a mostly dead ficus tree (to add to the "hills") and a large flashlight, by which he and Ike would read their lighting cues.

"What are you juvenile delinquents doing?" joked Ned with a cop-like shout, shining the light on Roland.

Liza saw the flashlight's beam illuminate Roland Spring with the ficus tree casting a shadow on the wall behind his head—for a heart-stopping split second, Roland had a perfect set of radiant antlers.

Backstage, everyone held their breath, preparing to plunge into the hallucinatory waters of focused group attention. The music came on (from a new reel-to-reel machine, purchased by Noreen with her meager pension check as an opening-night gift, because she couldn't stand the idea of the old one cacking out midnumber), the lights came up, and the stage effloresced into bright life. The chords swelled, and Peppy jogged out onstage, wig bouncing, breasts heaving. The eyes of the audience grew wide. Husbands and wives nudged each other.

THE HI-I-I-ILLS ARE ALI-I-IVE!
WITH THE SOUND OF MU-U-U-USIC!

Thighs were grabbed in an anguish of vicarious embarrassment.

(Peppy's slummocky nature simply did not lend itself to the sexually astringent role of Maria, a role more suited to actresses like Julie Andrews or Sandy Duncan, whose panties naturally seemed to be full of Borax.)

When the enormous nuns appeared onstage, the audience of parents began to get the idea that the show was not the standard young-adult vehicle they thought it would be. Nonetheless, they were Marin County-ites and thus sophisticated (or so they told themselves) when it came to a little harmless decadence.

How do you find a word that means Ma-riaaaa
A flippety gibbet, a willow-o'-the-wisp, a cloooown,

. . . the nun-boys trilled.

"I'm afraid you don't look at all like a sea captain, sir," Peppy yelled when she had arrived at the Von Trapp family mansion. Snickering was heard in the audience because, in fact, he didn't. Nobody had gotten Lalo the proper shoes, so he wore rubber flip-flops; he still had his handlebar mustache and shoulder-length blond hair, his jacket was buttoned incorrectly. Plus, he was visibly drunk.

"And I'm afray zhou don't look bery mush like a *goberness*." A wave of giggles escaped from Neville's friends, because indeed, Peppy's Maria looked like the kind of governess who would get the children really loaded and let them watch late-night softcore on cable.

. . .

The Baroness Schrader was supposed to be a dazzling creature; a stylish Viennese beauty. Ike looked the other way while Ned designed her lighting—he backlit and underlit Barbette in the starkest way possible, creating a Bride of Frankenstein–type effect. When Barbette delivered one of the Baroness's sarcastic lines, the audience, feeling thus cued, actually hissed at her. Barbette, unaware she was a villain, was shocked to the roots. Her voice cracked, her hands shook. She looked old, frightened, and ghastly.

Ned and Ike high-fived each other silently in the lighting booth, but Ned vowed to himself that he would change the lights the next night; his revenge had been too easy and too damning. It took so little to reveal her pitiable frailty, Ned couldn't believe that seconds previously, he had thought Barbette such a powerful foe.

Mike's star turn as Max Detweiler, with pencil-thin mustache and Tyrolean hat, added a much-needed anchor of intelligence and relative maturity: "I must explore this territory," he exclaimed, happily. "Somewhere, a hungry little singing group is waiting for Max Detweiler to pluck it out of obscurity and make it famous at the Salzburg Folk Festival."

(*This,* **Critical Reader, is one of the criminal bits of logic that corrupts mankind's expectations. How simply Max throws around the idea of bestowing Fame upon those who charm him. How easily these drab, voiceless children will leapfrog into being prodigy songbirds, capable of bursting into spontaneous, complex, Mills Brothers–style harmonies. The children are** *passively led into instant celebrity.* **This is the necrotic root of the prevailing dead-end dream:** *If only the right mentors will produce me, direct me, refine me, and discover me!* **Many a starry-eyed girl or boy would climb into the back of a mysterious big black car for the promise of adequate pop "coaching," because such wishful egoporn has always been tossed into screenplays without caution.)**

Roland sang, like sweet coffee:

Your life little girl
Is an empty page
That men will want to write on . . . .

Women swooned, men admired him.

I'm GLAD to GO-O-O, I cannot tell a LIE-I . . .

. . . bellowed Liza in her power-voice during her one big solo moment, as audience members wondered why she was wearing high Lucite heels with her nautical infant dress.

I flit, I float I flick-I-flee-I fly-y . . .

. . . purred Desiree Baumgarten, adding a ballet stag-leap to her pretty exit as Liza clomped offstage.

"You were blushing in his arms tonight," remarked the Baroness, after Maria and Von Trapp are caught doing an Austrian folk dance.
(*Hisss*, went the audience.)
"I was?!" screamed Peppy, grabbing her cheeks.
(Cackles.)
"Goodbye Maria," sneered Baroness Barbette, "I'm sure you'll make a very . . . *fine* nun."
(Howls of mirth.)
Maria's return to the abbey was the cue for Neville's big scene as Mother Abbess, during which he sang "Climb Every Mountain" in an unctuous pseudo–operatic falsetto. Audience members found themselves checking the program:

```
Neville Vanderlee (Mother Abbess, Herr Zeller,
Franz the Butler) is the last of the living
castrati tenors, his testicles having been removed
in the service of the Royal Latvian Boys' Choir at
the age of nine. His precious instrument has since
been destroyed by cigarettes.
```

After marching down the aisle to "How Do You Solve a Problem Like Maria (Reprise)," Peppy ascended to the altar (a podium draped in gold lamé) and tore her wedding dress down to a white micromini. Gasps were audible. As she began to juggle four sizable wooden crucifixes, the audience sat in goggle-eyed shock. Several parents pondered lawsuits, others considered storming the backstage and rescuing their teens from Act II.

Brigham Hamburger stood and exited, nostrils flaring in outrage.

Peppy threw a wild cross, tripped over her dropped skirt, and sprawled onto her stomach, inadvertently exposing the hygienic cotton crotch of her nylons to the aghast spectators as crucifixes bounced and smacked to the floor.

Ned and Ike wisely plunged the room into total blackout.

~ INTERMISSION ~

("This is the best thing Neville's ever done! It just *pees* all over everything sacred!")

("Should I go backstage and get Tiffany?")

("Can you believe that all they have is generic beer?")

Somehow, the parents were too intimidated by the magical "Fourth Wall" to disrupt the proceedings, and the rest of the show came off without incident. Perhaps, for the actors, it was muscle memory that brought it off. More likely, it was the well-known story itself that insisted on being told, as it was lodged midsneeze in everyone's mind at that point.

Lalo, who had been fortifying himself throughout the night with a bottle of Bacardi 151, had worked up a lather of self-pity. It was with raw feeling that he delivered the Dramatic Pivot Point, when Georg Von Trapp is "requested," via telegram, to join the Nazi Navy: "To refuse them would be fatal for all of us. And joining them would be unthinkable," goes the line.

"Refuse these is to be fate for uz . . . to join the . . . unzirgismol," Lalo moaned, dropping the telegram to the floor, plashing large tears to the stage as Peppy vigorously stroked his chest to comfort him.

He was in such an ecstasy of grief by the time the Von Trapps performed at the Salzburg Folk Festival that before singing "Edelweiss," Lalo struck a few aggressive gypsy chords and emitted a wild flamenco cry like a murderous orgasm. Several of the mothers in the audience felt a dizzying larceny in their hearts as they crossed their legs. A few imagined a mirrored-ceiling's eye-view of their fingernails plunging into Lalo's naked buttocks. Several of the men liked it too.

The show ended, and the audience clapped, breaking up the dream-time and returning all participants to Fairfax, CA.

As Chantal and Roland held hands and advanced downstage for their curtain call, the applause explosively quadrupled in volume. The whistles and *whoooo!s* shot like poisoned blow darts through Liza, making her wonder: *Why can't I stand here in a prom dress, covered with blood, and burn this place down with my mind?*

Her throat filled with the Drano-sensation of repressed sobbing. As she watched Chantal Baumgarten casually hijack every life dream she possessed, Liza got the overwhelming impression that the Gods that ran this Popsicle stand of a fucked-up universe just might be trying to tell her something. A *message.*

And that message was: "Ha ha ha ha ha. *Psych.*"

The parents collected their children quickly afterward, not wanting to let them steep in the weird, electric aftermath of such a depraved opening night—everyone was light-drunk and giddy with the ancient powers of stage energy. A few of the kids, bewildered by the audience response, felt like they were in trouble for something they didn't understand; others felt a vague, blurry sense of having been morally tarnished by their affiliation with something they now understood to be somewhat raunchy. Kids are naturally prudish, and a few of them cried that night. Their mothers would have long discussions with them the next morning about how "The Show Must Go On," all the while having whispered phone conversations with other mothers discussing what, if anything, should be done.

The Baumgartens gave Roland a ride to the bus station in their black Mercedes. Liza watched, waving goodbye as they drove away, their laughing, beautiful heads elegantly framed by the chrome windows of the shiny black diplomat car, the luxury of which seemed to transport Roland to another, better world as surely as a spaceship.

As the taillights glided away, Liza caught her own reflection in the window of a parked Dodge Omni. Under the streetlights, she realized she looked ridiculously trashy; in her quest to look more glamorous, she had inadvertently made herself into a kind of underage sex clown. She shuddered with self-loathing.

Peppy and Neville were extremely hopeful. They went out drinking with Neville's friends after the show while Ned, Ike, and Noreen cleaned the theatre and replaced all the props.

The next day's afternoon paper yielded their first and only review (page eight of the Weekend section of the *Marin Gazette*, no photo):

'SOUND' OF TITTERS AT 'NORMAL' THEATRE

Cabaret Review by Pat Morgenstern

In a production that might be obscene if it were not so clearly inept, the recently opened Normal Family Dinner Theatre has unintentionally shown Fairfax what Rogers and Hammerstein's 'Sound of Music' would look like if it were performed by criminally insane prison inmates under the direction of the Marquis de Sade.

(That was a pull-quote that Neville would put at the top of his résumé for years to come.)

In the words of Susan Sontag, "Camp taste . . . relishes awkward intensities of character, finds success in certain passionate failures." This failure might be considered a little *too* passionate, by some, but it is unquestionably entertaining, if for all the wrong reasons.

" 'Unquestionably Entertaining' is what we'll put on the posters," said Peppy.

Director Neville Vanderlee (who also plays a screamingly funny Mother Abbess) seems to be exploiting the inexperience of his 'actors' to facilitate his own twisted prank. Maria, played by Peppy Normal, would be more appropriate covered with boiled eggs in a John Waters movie. One of the Von Trapp children looks as if she should be soliciting tourists in Times Square. Lalo Buarque's Captain Von Trapp seems to have fallen prey to the alcoholism that has tarnished many a naval career—method acting? I doubt it.

"Who the hell is this 'Pat Morgenstern'? I'm gonna cut his ears off!" shouted Peppy. " 'Screamingly Funny' is what we'll put on the posters," glowed Neville.

The sole redeeming element of the show was the charming "Sixteen Going on Seventeen" number, played by the poised and luminous Chantal Baumgarten (no stranger to the Marin stage—she was a favorite Clara in Marin Ballet's 'Nutcracker') and the wildly talented Roland Spring, whose name we will surely see in lights someday . . . just as soon as he gets out of this tawdry production.

On night number two, as everyone nervously prepared themselves for some unforeseen doom (there had been phone calls; a "meeting" was scheduled for that Monday with a group of parents—an ugly crackdown was anticipated), the cast was amazed and delighted to see that fifteen minutes before the box office opened, there was a thick queue so long it wrapped around the corner, composed primarily of gay men and college students, all carbonating with glee and anticipation. Several of the men were dressed like Peppy.

"It's a smash hit!" exclaimed Peppy, unable to believe her eyes.
"You did this," Neville lied, wrapping an arm around her shoulders.

Liza had an entirely different makeup scheme the second night—she put her hair into two tight braids, eschewed eye makeup entirely, and wore sensible shoes; she looked the part. Neville was disappointed. "No, no! Go back into the dressing room and do that fabulous Francesco Scavullo disco nightmare thing you did last night!"
Liza sadly complied.

Neville quickly located all of the possible innuendi in the script and instructed his actors, as they prepared, to "punch 'em up." That night, lines that weren't supposed to be funny had a new sleazy tinge to them:

Nun #1: "Maria is missing from the abbey again."

Nun #2: "Have you checked the barn? You know how much she *loves* the animals."

The Peppys in the audience made barnyard noises, *baaaah*ing and oinking enthusiastically.

. . .

When Neville, as Herr Zeller the Nazi, came onstage with a codpiece twice as large as it had been the previous night, shaped like a giant erect fang, the parents in the audience who had any doubt whether or not to shut down the production were firmly convinced.

Lalo was furious to be, what he considered in his Latin mind, the laughingstock of the area homosexuals. After the intermission, he refused to come out of his dressing room.

Ned was dispatched to plead with him; he could hear Lalo angrily mumbling to himself as he knocked on the door.

When Lalo finally kicked the door open, Ned was hit by a rolling cumulus cloud of pot smoke; the smell of toasted skunk wafted into the audience and alarmed several parents who were intimately familiar with the aroma.

Lalo was stripped to the waist and had painted large, black, Uncle Fester–like circles around his eyes with a stick of greasepaint. He was staring hauntedly at himself in the dressing-room mirror and mashing a black, Manson Family X in the middle of his forehead. Ned was frightened.

"You have to get dressed and get onstage, Lalo, please," he begged.

Hearing Lalo's cue, Ned threw the captain's jacket over Lalo's shoulders and hung a pair of sunglasses on his face, concealing the blackened eyes but not the X. There was no time to button the jacket; he wrestled Lalo out of the dressing room. Ned noticed as he shoved Lalo onstage, where he lurched and staggered in his war paint like a dying Zulu, that there was a bullwhip in his back pocket (a gift Neville had received the previous night). Lalo glared at the audience and hollered a spit-drenched hail of Portuguese invective at them; some laughed nervously.

Forty minutes beforehand, behind the theatre in the backyard, Love had flourished. Misty-Dawn and Barren, who had been growing closer over the last three weeks, were making out with famished teen intensity, pawing at each other's bodies in a spray of hormonal friction-sparks.

"Let's go upstairs," panted Barren.

"Where?" whispered the Mastodon.

"Peppy bedroom." He smiled.

The wrongness of the idea felt vastly erotic. While the backstage was swirling with chaos, they snuck up the stairs and stole through the door to Peppy's room. The waterbed and its poly-satin sheets stretched fantastically before them like the moonlit Nile.

"I think we bein' watched," giggled the Mastodon, referring to the dozens of staring wig-heads as she struggled out of her airtight pants.

During his rant, Lalo glimpsed Neville's blurry black-and-white nun form creeping onstage from the wings.

"*Bem chato*, you faggo bidje mozsherfugge," Lalo growled, shoving Peppy away from him. He grabbed the bullwhip, let out a fearsome battle cry, and began trying to crack it at Neville; the tail flapped around in harmless loops. Everyone watching made a mental note: *the best weapon for a really fucked-up man to have is a bullwhip.*

Neville's brawny convent shuffled onstage, trying to gently corral Lalo like a spooked horse. Ike, unsure of what else to do, dimmed the other lights and bewildered Liza by suddenly illuminating her in a full spot. Liza gaped for a moment in starkest terror, thinking she might have forgotten a major cue. The bossa nova accompaniment for her High School of Performing Arts audition began to blare over the main speakers.

Oh God. This can't be happening.

"*Liza! DO IT!*" Neville hissed in his loudest whisper, shielding himself behind the wide shoulders of Sister Margaretha.

In a daze, Liza walked to center stage. She took a deep breath, and unleashed her loudest, biggest, most vibrato-heavy voice . . .

CLI-I-I-IMB EV-ERY MOUNTAI-I-I-N
FO-R-R-RD EV-ERY STREEEEEAM . . .
FO-LLLLOW EV-ERY RAINBOOOOOW
'TILLL YOU FIND YOUR DREEEEAM . . .

Her volume nearly drowned out the "Ooofs!" and *whomps* of bodies hitting the hollow wooden stage behind her. The audience was baffled. Liza began fearlessly ripping into the number with a confidence and majesty she only prayed she could summon for the audition.

A DREEEAM THAT WILL NEEEEEEED
ALL THE LOVE YOU CAN GI-I-I-I-IVE . . . . YEAH!
EVERY DAY OF YOUR LI-I-I-I-IFE
FOR AS LONG AS YOU LI-I-I-I-IVE . . . . EVERYBODY!

Liza shimmied her shoulders, stalking the front of the stage. A surge of happiness engulfed her when the audience began singing exuberantly along with her:

CLI-I-I-IMB EV-ERY MOUNTAI-I-I-N!
FO-R-R-RD EV-ERY STREEEEEAM!!
FO-LLLOW EV-ERY RAINB . . . .

Everyone stopped as a great spinal *FFFFZZZZZSSSST* and spray of sparks made all of the lights and music electrically short out, plunging the room into total darkness as a cascade of warm, plastic-scented water began sluicing down from the ceiling, into the lighting booth and onto the petrified audience.

Queen-size waterbeds contain approximately 160 gallons of water; Barren and Misty-Dawn were amazed, in their postcoital exuberance, at the sheer amount of liquid they could force out of the long slits that Barren had gleefully carved into the mattress with a kitchen knife, as revenge for his various grievances against Peppy.

When the fire trucks came, Liza wandered outside, her makeup in streaky lines down her cheeks. Misty-Dawn was being pointedly asked by two cops as to the whereabouts of Barren, who had bolted into the night. Von Trapp children stood on the sidewalk with their coats over their shoulders and expressionless, traumatized faces as their parents hollered at Peppy, who looked small and meek. Ned appeared next to Liza; she grabbed his elbow and held it.

Chantal and Desiree had collected all of their belongings from the backstage by flashlight and were loading them into their parents' car. Roland Spring jogged out of the theatre in his street clothes, past Liza, to hug the sisters. Liza watched as Mr. Baumgarten held Roland warmly by the shoulder and presented him with his business card.

"Let's say goodbye," Ned said, nudging Liza. "We probably won't see them again."

Liza began to cry.

Ned shuffled up to the Baumgarten contingent and began shaking their hands.

Liza waved goodbye at them, unable to move from her spot. Chantal and Desiree barely glanced at her; their parents shot Liza looks of pity.

Ned returned a minute later, bringing Roland Spring with him. Liza thought she might swallow her tongue.

"Hey, you brought the house down!" Roland teased gently, making Liza cough through snotty tears.

"Here," he said, producing a folded handkerchief from his pants pocket. "I didn't use it, it's clean."

Liza accepted it, smearing it with her runny face.

"Thanks," Liza forced out, wetly.

"You shouldn't sing so loud, next time. You could have killed every-one," Roland joked. Liza tried to laugh.

"Well . . . I guess I'll see you around," Roland said, sticking out his hand.

Liza flung her arms around his neck and clung to him direly.

"Woah!" Roland exclaimed, suddenly supporting her whole weight.

"You're *amazing*," Liza choked, wishing she could chain herself to Roland Spring forever.

Roland gently pried her off of his chest. "Thanks. You too, Liza. You're . . . truly unique."

Liza stared at him, her eyes bleeding moons of wretched love.

"Bye."

"Bye."

And Roland Spring, Golden Stag nonpareil, sprang past the twirling red lights and away from the Normal Family Dinner Theatre.

"You told him I liked him, didn't you?" Liza cried, turning viciously on Ned.

Ned stared at the rubber toe guards on the front of his sneakers.

The thought of never seeing Roland again was molten torment. Liza ran into the backyard and grieved in hard, hyperventilating sobs, clutching the stained hanky, its sweet laundered Roland-smell cracking her heart in half.

* AFTERMATH *

Two weeks later, Peppy was still "sleeping it off." She rarely emerged from her room; Noreen brought in bowls of canned soup. She refused contact with everyone, even Mike and Ike, who offered again and again to work on the electrical box and restore basic light to the house. Since "the disaster," the family had been living by candlelight, cooking on the gas burner and keeping things cold in a Styrofoam cooler.

Lalo had been picked up by cops that fateful night and put in the drunk tank; it was discovered, while processing him, that he'd been in the country illegally for the last six months. He was deported back to São Paulo.

Neville was gone—he and his nuns became a cabaret show in the city entitled *Neville on a Sunday*. Barbette quit; she wouldn't be associated with what was now considered, around town, to be the lowbrow and hazardous nature of the theatre. Liza practiced her audition routine in front of the mirror, with no accompaniment, alone in the dark theatre on the sticky floor.

Liza was watching *Brady Bunch* reruns on the TV in a local electronics store when the ad for the OtterWorld Fun Park came on. Desiree Baumgarten was laughing, holding a handful of Mylar balloons. "Come join the fun!" she beckoned, smiling at Liza in a boundlessly friendly way she never had in real life. Liza left the store and slowly walked home, feeling like a mugger had just taken her lungs at gunpoint.

The school year was quickly approaching. Liza knocked on Peppy's door.
"Mom?"
Silence.
"Mom?" More knocking.
"*Whaaaaat*?!"
"Can I come in?"
"Do you have to?"
Liza opened the door. The place was a shambles—Noreen had been picking up the food trays, but clothes and wigs lay everywhere in dark piles, like melted witches. Peppy had been sleeping on a heap of blankets inside the empty waterbed frame ever since her bed was "murdered." Liza sat on the edge of the frame and looked down at her. A brimming ashtray sat near Peppy's head.
"Did you get the tickets yet?"
"What tickets?"
"For New York. For my audition. For the High School of Performing Arts."

Peppy started laughing an awful, cracked laugh. Then she started coughing. Then she lit a cigarette.

"Oh. That."

"Yeah that," said Liza, her stomach filling with hot tar.

"Ah, Liza . . . you're too much, baby. You're a real killer."

"What do you mean?" Liza asked, knowing but refusing to know.

"Look around you, kid." Peppy gestured to the dark walls with her cigarette. "What more could you ask in the way of theatre experience?" Bitter, sick laughing again.

"Where am I supposed to go to school?!"

"You and Ned will go to that school over there, whatever it is . . . you know."

"Miwok *Butte*?! *Oh, GOD!* I can't go to *MIWOK!!*"

"Oh, come on, it's just a high school. How bad can it be? Maybe next year, we'll get that New York thing together."

"I hate you," Liza curdled, looking down at the dark, polluted trench her mother was coiled in and having a vivid idea of *exactly* how bad high school could be.

"Yep, I suppose you do."

Liza felt a rising disgust; the smell of unlaundered nylon, old cigarette butts, and beer-marinated carpet made her suddenly gag. She ran from the room.

"Close the door," Peppy grunted from her floor-nest.

It slammed, leaving Peppy in the dark.

A hole the size of a garbage-can lid had just been blown out, below Liza's rib cage. She wandered zombielike onto to the abandoned stage. The late, cold afternoon gloom tinted the mess a dead blue, making it look even filthier. Liza shivered. An intact can of generic beer lay on its side near a pile of waterlogged and mildewing curtains; Liza opened it and took a sip. It was warmer than she was.

"Liza?"

Ned's voice came from what used to be the lighting booth.

"What?!" She expected her brother to hassle her about the beer.

"You're perfect there. Stand up."

"Why?"

"Just stand up!"

"Why?" Liza rose to her feet. "Are you going to throw something at me?"

She heard a *pouf* and found herself in a blinding flood of sharp, greenish white light, the color of glow-in-the-dark bones on Halloween skeletons.

"Ha HAH!" cackled Ned, delighted.

"Whooo!" Ike's voice came from the back of the theatre. "Man! Is that beautiful! It's looks like she's standing on the moon!"

"Liza! Do you know what you're standing in?"

Ned was tickled.

"A light?"

"A *limelight*. A *real* one . . . I made it! You look amazing!"

"Sing something!" enthused Ike.

(It should be explained that Ned did make an actual limelight, with Ike's help and resources pilfered from the community college glassblowing and welding departments, based on this diagram of "Mr. Goldsworthy Gurney's Blow-Pipe," from *The Boy's Playbook of Science* by J. H. Pepper, London 1860:

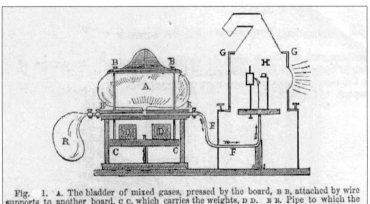

Fig. 1. A. The bladder of mixed gases, pressed by the board, B B, attached by wire supports to another board, c c, which carries the weights, D D. E E. Pipe to which the bladder, A, is screwed, and when A is emptied, it is re-filled from the other bladder, B. F F F. Pipe conveying mixed gases to the lantern, G G, where they are burnt from a Gurney's jet, H.

Ned was able to replace the "bladder of mixed gases" with a decent oxygen/hydrogen welding torch; for the lime itself, which in the olden days was constructed like a spool, Ned covertly chiseled a small chunk of limestone off of the staircase to the community college admissions office. From there, all that was needed was to empty the scorched bulb out of one of the blown-out PAR cans, fashion a wire holding-device for the limestone, and shoot the oxy-hydrogen flame through the can at the rock-chunk. "The hardest part," Ned would say later, "was stealing the gas tanks from the school.")

Liza's pale face squinted. She looked at her arms; it was like being a ghost, or in a black-and-white movie.

"You've only got about one minute to do your thing," said Ned.

"Yeah, make the most of it!" yelled Ike. "You're probably the only person you'll ever *know* who's been in actual limelight!"

As if the glare had bleached out all of the color contrast inside her skull, Liza's mind drew a complete and total blank, like the joke about the "drawing" on a white sheet of paper—*it's a polar bear, standing next to an igloo, in a snowstorm, eating marshmallows. See?*

PART III

PUPPY SQUEEZIN'S

(A Teen Sex Farce)

*In whych Liza suffers the Paynes of an Horrible Hiye School
Experience, sacrifices all Virtue on the Pyre of her
Selfe-Esteeme, and is Generally Humiliayted for being
A Pathological Liare and Slut Alsoe.*

 Y THE BEGINNING OF SEPTEMBER 1981, Liza was
firmly embittered. She had been running into ex–Theatre
Camp girls who would ask, with mendacious semisweet-
ness: "You mean you're *not* going to the High School of Performing
Arts after all?"

"My agency didn't want me to leave town," Liza lied, inspecting her
chipped glitter nail polish. "I have too many commercial opportunities
coming up."

"Oh really? What kind of 'opportunities'?"

"*You'll see,*" Liza snarled.

What Liza hadn't counted on was her level of celebrity even before
the first day of school. Her reputation preceded her as the daughter of
Peppy, who was by now a Town Character. Girls she'd never seen be-

fore walked up to Liza in the 7-Eleven to ask, "Your mom is that lady with the wigs who wears, like, those really low-cut pink pantsuits, right? You live in the scary old firehouse, right?"

You will all pay. I am Liza Normal. I am more talented than you. When I am famous, you will come to beg autographs from me, and I will remember this day. My bodyguards will drag you into the alley where I will look at you coldly, and spit.

"... And you did that really weird, gay version of, like, *Sound of Music*, right? And then your house burned down?"

"It didn't *burn down*." Liza would grab her Slurpee off of the counter and stomp out, giggles searing her back.

She was not greeting the prospect of four years at Miwok Butte High School with unbridled enthusiasm. Ned was equally reluctant. He dreaded the idea of having to rely on the maturity of his classmates to be treated decently—the odds were that they would be just as assholic and insensitive as the other local teens. Peppy's game plan of having Ned conceal his freak eyeball by never taking off his sunglasses probably wouldn't fly too well in the classroom proper.

"We may be screwed," Ned said glumly.

"Every man for himself," said Liza.

Cloaked in these perilous doubts and presullied reputations, Ned and Liza stepped out of the filthy Honda and stood before the flagpole of Miwok Butte for the first time, amid the squall of voices and faces that would be their peers. Cliques had already been established among those who had endured local grade schools together; drifts of teen girls jounced by in matching tightnesses of pants, their hair identically tormented. Elite jock-boys flaunted the latest incarnation of pricey running shoes. Rich kids of the nonathletic variety wore the signifiers of the Ivy League: khaki pants, penny loafers, plaid scarves, French ski-sunglasses. Heavy-metal burnouts displayed long-handled plastic combs in corduroy back pockets. There were stray teens, belonging to no group, and no fashion—concave girls who looked as if they'd suffered low birth weights or family shame, and boys angry at being adopted or dyslexic, feeling the first tugs of crime's undertow. They haunted the undersides of stairwells and various campus no-man's-lands, sometimes binding together in subgroups of two or three. Ned was dismayed to see no malformed potential allies—even the rejects in this teen society looked too cool for him.

The Miwok Butte High School campus was a grim bunch of concrete cubes, a 1960s architectural vision of fascist-modern offering no beauty and inspiring no hope.

For Liza, the only thing to recommend Miwok was that the Baumgartens weren't going there; they had been accepted at the Eiderdijken Preparatory Academy for the Arts, in the posh Pacific Heights neighborhood of San Francisco—an elite private school with connections to the nearby ballet, symphony, and opera houses. Chantal and Desiree were to receive a rarefied education from the finest instructors of dance, theatre, music, and film: culture heroes taking time out from their brilliant careers to raise the next generation of supertalent in a Romanesque Revival showplace with stone archways, polished wood floors, and leaded-glass windows framing views of the bay. In the local interest section of the *Gazette,* Liza read an article headlined "Sisters in Success," featuring a flattering picture of Chantal and Desiree arabesqueing in front of the Academy.

Liza gathered from the article that Eiderdijken was essentially the *Royal* High School of Performing Arts. Liza thought she would vomit.

Miwok Butte posed one particular problem for the average teen. The kids who went there were generally one of three types: either the children of very rich Marin County parents who were too selfish and/or degenerate to try to get them a better education; rich kids who had been kicked out of better schools; or lower-middle-class kids that lived with single parents in boxlike apartments near the freeway. There was an unbridgeable gulf between the rich and not-rich, creating a distinct aristocracy among the kids who drove to school in BMWs with artificial tans and limitless supplies of the latest fashions, and a leper caste of bus-taking average kids for whom designer anything was beyond reach. The kids that weren't insulated by cash fell through the cracks socially and often (perhaps due to the disenfranchisement they felt) academically as well.

The first day of school was an extended sort of pep rally and orientation, wherein robust sophomores and juniors and wholly adult seniors sashayed around the campus greeting friends forgotten during the summer with joyous shrieks and teasing; the freshman class, knobby, brace-mouthed, frightened, hypersensitive, and in many cases as personally unformed as larvae, crept around, clinging to the walls for comfort.

Liza was still heartbroken over Roland Spring, who had vanished from the earth. (She had tried calling his home number a month after the theatre disaster; it was disconnected—she called the Miwok Butte administration office, but they could find no Roland Spring listed among the incoming freshmen), but until some miracle drew him back into her landscape, she felt wholly entitled to appraising all Cute Boys, as her small consolation prize. As much as Liza hated Peppy for failing to deliver her to New York and Fame, she was still privately excited about going to *any* high school; high school held promise and mystery. According to the films she'd seen, it was where a girl found deep friendships and countless flirtations—perhaps even Actual Love. (The messy affair of "womanhood" held zero fascination for Liza—the signifying, Judy Blume–worthy event had already happened, in eighth grade. Peppy tried to congratulate her and offered to take her out for a "woman to woman" dinner at The Sizzler, but the idea of celebrating puberty with her mother over a sirloin was, for Liza, revolting on innumerable levels.)

Liza's first-day-of-school outfit, one she thought was fetching, instantly branded her as socially undesirable. She wore a diagonally striped minidress, high, white ankle-boots, and a braided metallic headband, having assembled the components at a strip-mall store named "WOW! EVERYTHING UNDER $10!" that Peppy had taken her to for back-to-school clothes.

Noreen shuddered when she saw Liza at breakfast.

"Oh, you don't wanna wear that," Noreen said, passing Ned a bowl of oatmeal.

"Why don't I want to wear that?" Liza sassed.

"The kids'll think you're something you're not."

"What am I not?" Liza asked, pushing it.

"You know what I'm talking about."

"Oh, I forgot you know everything about the latest teen styles from reading *Reader's Digest*."

"Be nice to Gramma," said Ned.

Liza liked the outfit because it made her look like a Solid Gold

Dancer (*Solid Gold* being the #1 rated, Top 40 music TV show, hosted by Andy Gibb—the dancers were false-breasted amazons in lamé G-strings who would writhe spread-eagled on the stage, as if they'd been driven into sexual fits by the unrelenting fever of Lionel Ritchie numbers. "When I was a girl, shows like that were for bachelor parties," Noreen lamented.)

In the main building, Liza could hear girls giggle as she passed by. A pack of preppy boys stared at her with their mouths open in cruel mock-shock.

"Catching flies?" Liza snapped.

They laughed heartily.

"Want to bob on my knob?" one of the boys yelled as she clicked away on her heels. Liza had no idea what he was talking about but flipped him the finger anyway.

Liza's homeroom was her English class, which was taught by a species of woman indigenous to Marin County: a fading beauty-cum-rich-ex-hippie clotheshorse, partial to flowing "art to wear" garments of hand-painted silk with bleeding color patterns that resembled magnified bacteria. Mrs. Gubbins—"You can call me Kay!"—had married well, divorced well, and married so well again that she was at leave to pursue her altruistic mission of teaching high school English as an aside to her real "life goals," which were apparently proselytizing for a certain faddish, Marin "self-actualization" cult known as everBest™. Her mediocre, uninspired English teaching was peppered with shrilly enthusiastic everBest-ial axioms and smug truisms.

"Let's situate the desks into a circle so we can all monitor each other's eyes, shall we?" Kay trumpeted to her class of miserable, pocky fourteen-year-olds, all craving invisibility. Kay had all of the students go around the circle and say their names, their nicknames, and what they'd "rather be doing other than being responsibly here, now, in the present."

The average offering was a pained, deliberately boring monotone: "Um, I'm (Michael or Jennifer) (Last name), my friends call me ('Jenny'; 'Mike'), and if I wasn't here I'd rather be (sailing, skiing, or some other affluent sport that required a lot of pricey gear and the kind of status-conscious parents that would encourage it)."

A striking, skinny boy with sardonic eyebrows and a crooked red mouth sat next to Liza. He had long auburn hair pulled back into two Willie Nelson braids and slouched angularly in his seat, his eyes barely open. When the circle came around to him, a few other boys in the class started snickering before he even said anything.

"Uh, my name is Anton Grosvenor," he drawled in a hoarse voice that sounded hungover. "But my friends call me Kay."

At this several boys in the classroom fell over with hysterical laughter. A couple of them mumbled, "Go, Tonto . . ."

"And, actually, I feel totally actualized, here. I don't want to be anywhere else. Ever."

The kids became alert, watching to see how the teacher would handle such scorching insincerity.

Kay looked at him with a tight-lipped smile.

"Kay? Shall we call you Kay?" she asked with no humor at all.

"That'd be great."

Kay opted to ignore the fact that she had just been successfully undermined.

Liza was next.

"Elizabeth Lynn Normal," Liza mumbled. "I've always been called Liza. I'd rather be at the High School of Performing Arts in New York, which is where I'll be next year."

"Are you a dancer, or an actress?" Kay asked.

"Mostly a singer," said Liza.

Liza felt a bump near her leg—Anton Grosvenor was handing her a note. She unfolded it carefully in her lap.

IF YOU ARE A "SINGER" WHY DO YOU DRESS LIKE A WHOARE? ARE YOU A WHOARE, ALSO?

Liza had never even kissed a boy and was shocked by the visceral power and violence of the word *whoare*, even while misspelled. She ignored him.

Another note came banging against her knee:

HOW ABOUT MY UNIT DEEP IN YOUR FACE FOR $6?

Liza got out her pen and wrote back:

FUCK YOU

The note came back:

OK HOW ABOUT $7

Liza ignored it. Another note came:

OK $7.35 THATS MY FINAL OFFER

Liza wrote back:

I HAVE A BIG BROTHER A-HOLE SHUT YOUR FACE

Anton smirked. He wrote for a while, as more students droned their least thoughtful answers to Kay's questions while nobody listened.

The note came back:

CHANGED MY MIND YOU HAVE TO I. GIVE ME $8 THEN 2. WRAP YOUR LAUGHING GEAR AROUND MY SNOT STICK.

The bell rang. Liza got up and moved away from Anton Grosvenor as quickly as possible.

A set of two matching girls, dressed and lip-glossed identically but clearly unrelated, approached Liza after class.

"Hi," the skinnier one said to Liza. "Were you passing notes to Tonto?"

"Who?" Liza asked, trying to de-code the class schedule that had been printed for her.

"Tonto. Anton Grosvenor. That guy."

They pointed to the note giver, who was striking a criminally suave posture near the bulletin board with several of his male groupies.

"Yeah, I guess," stammered Liza.

"What did he say?" the slimmer girl asked, clearly burning with self-interest.

"Not much," Liza sidestepped, unable to figure out where to go for her history class.

"You should stay away from him," said the girl, suddenly turning ugly. Liza now noticed the large, carefully drawn "Nikki + Tonto" tattooed in ballpoint on her new denim binder. "Nikki" dotted all of her *i*s with fat hearts.

"That guy is totally disgusting, I wouldn't go near him if he paid me," Liza blurted out. Her brain was still so infected by the notes, she realized, too late, that the "Liza + Money = Sex" equation was a bad thing to put into the minds of her classmates.

"You look like you'd go near anyone that paid you," sneered Nikki.

"Yeah, *pardon our mistake*," condescended Nikki's chubbier accomplice.

Liza reddened, then purpled.

"*Fuck* you skanky-ass bitches!" Liza shrieked, rearing back into her past when she was a minority in a Reno junior high, and remembering that the best way to frighten white girls was to act nonwhite. "Bes' get the fuck out my face 'fo I kick both yo asses!"

Liza could hear Anton "Tonto" Grosvenor and his minions giggling down the hall at her display.

"Oh, you're *black*, I get it now," sneered Nikki, derisive but clearly nervous.

"Thass right, I 'mo kill your bitch-ass ugly face, too, skeezah!" Liza shouted triumphantly, sensing that her foes were on the run. "Don'tchu fuck wit' me, bitch, I been jumped in wit' the Nevada Queens!"

Liza had never been "jumped in" with the Nevada Queens, an ethnic high school girl-gang she had heard of once, but it seemed to intimidate Nikki and her friend enough to make them leave her alone, after giving her penetrating looks of disgust.

Enough other students witnessed that first-day-of-school display that Liza was instantly branded as feral, trashy, violent, and suffering a racial identity crisis by her peers. They didn't think of her in those words—"gross" was all they were able to articulate—but the girls gave Liza a wide berth, and the boys opted to openly deride her, since they found her outfits sexually intimidating.

(It should be said here that Liza, for all of her faults, wasn't bad-looking—were it not for her unfortunate fashion handicaps, she might have passed for a basically cute, average teen girl. While no raving beauty, she did possess a symmetrical, if angry face, a "decent rack," average height, and a proportional set of limbs. Her hair, if she had stopped perverting it with the crimping iron, would have been shoulder length, light brown, and pleasantly wavy. Her eyes, a viewer might have noticed if their lids weren't plastered with iridescent peacock hues, were the gray-blue of a choppy ocean shot in 1950s film stock.

Her mind, though stunted from years of television, was actually quite good—her indifference toward academia had never given anyone cause to suspect it, but Liza had an above-average IQ and could learn certain things quickly, e.g., sitcom theme lyrics. Unfortunately, her emotional development was mired in the tar pit of her chronological age, so while her intellect may have been capable of absorbing fashion magazine articles several years beyond her grade level, she was still prone to childishly bad decision making, tantrums, and poor impulse control, and sadly devoid of the poise and coolheaded self-possession so evident in the infuriatingly mature Baumgartens. This lopsided inner development would forge Liza's character in crude and painful ways.)

It became clear, in Liza's first few days at Miwok Butte, that socially, the entire school was held hostage by members of the extensive Grosvenor family: six exceptional teens born to the famous identical twins Radcliffe and Horatio, partners in the thriving Grosvenor and Grosvenor law firm. Their wives, wealthy southern debutantes, were also identical twins—hence, the Grosvenor offspring weren't so much a batch of double first cousins as an obnoxiously attractive race unto themselves, raised en masse in adjoining Tudor mansions on an enormous lot in prestigious Kentfield.

None of the Grosvenor kids would have been attending public school were it not for the political aspirations of their fathers, who considered it important that their children mingle with the Great Unwashed during their preuniversity years, just in case they ever wanted to be mayors or assemblymen or even Governor Grosvenors. Teachers fawned over them, seduced by the glamour of such a healthy, wealthy, intelligent, and beautifully toothed army of teens; the Grosvenor presence leant dignity to their second-rate teaching jobs in the way that fine china can dignify a modest meal.

Miwok public opinion set as hard and instantly as epoxy—one was either in or under the Grosvenor vanguard. Because there were so many of them, the deadly Grosvenor gaze was virtually omnipresent and held the entire school in its crosshairs.

Radcliffe ("Rad") Grosvenor IV, a senior, was the school king; he boasted a 4.0 GPA and was quietly, fiendishly excellent at everything he put his mind to, most notably the Miwok Butte Coyotes water polo team and Keynesian economics. He maintained a professional level of distance from everyone, even his demure, fearfully submissive girl-friend, who rarely troubled him by speaking. Rad's popularity was etched in stone, despite the fact that he was an exceptionally repressed, conservative, boring, and judgmental teenager.

His cousin Kensington ("Kenzie"), a junior, was "the hottest girl" on the entire campus: a tall, auburn-haired racehorse with TV teeth, a fig-ure built for *Penthouse,* and unusual tequila-gold eyes. A vivacious, brainy, and limber cheerleader, Kenzie always seemed to have a Harvard man, an Olympic contender, or a professional race-car-driver trailing after her, salivating. In short, she exposed all other girls as inferior in looks, intelligence, cash, and connections but had a wonderful act of seeming blithely unaware of her terrible power.

Rad's brother Dean ("Dino"), a sophomore, was the teen-angst-pinup Grosvenor—a foul-tempered loner whom his grammar-schoolmates remembered as an emotional problem-child who cried and hit people. He had tousled black hair, dark circles under golden eyes like Kenzie's, and an aura of existential turmoil. He appeared to hate everyone, espe-cially his family—nonetheless, he was the school heartthrob, looking, as he did, like a depressed young Alain Delon. Other boys tried to imitate his sexy exile from the world of sunlight and happiness; lovestruck girls quoted Camus in bored mumbles like him and dressed in black cash-mere turtlenecks (Dino's signature "look") to underline their grievous desire to gnaw on him.

Kenzie's sister Anastasia ("Tayzie"), a sophomore, was a Valkyrie, the best female lacrosse player in the state: a paragon of rude health, with big, tanned, muscular legs, golden-blonde hair that was twice-washed daily, buttonlike bunny eyes, and the simple, disciplined brain of a great athlete. She had no cavities in her teeth, no blemish on her skin, and no malice in her soul; she was therefore too freakishly well adjusted and fortunate to relate to as human.

Tayzie's fraternal twin Destrey ("Dezi") was the social Grosvenor. Sharing a womb seemed to rub all of the sharp edges off of both Dezi and Tayzie—Dezi was blithe, charming, and silly. An average student, he would surely become a lawyer someday by coasting on his family connections—in the meantime, he was a social magnet with the singular distinction of being invited to every party thrown by Marin County youths during his entire four years of high school.

Anton ("Tonto"), the youngest Grosvenor, was the filth-scrawling hooligan tormenting Liza. His debut with the rest of the freshmen was something of a legal miracle—he had been busted during the summer with over $6,000 worth of stolen Blaupunkt car stereos hidden in his closet, shortly after being fired from his summer job as a car alarm installer. The Grosvenor clan pulled many strings to settle out of court. Legend had it that when the stereos were found, he had been asked why he'd done it—his family lacked for nothing, he could have had any stereo he wanted—and had replied casually, "Car theft is an art form."

One would think, given Liza's hapless high school debut, that she would scuttle down to join the lowest dregs of the sub-staircase-dwelling teens and live out her next four years suffering quietly beneath the Grosvenor boot. But Liza, as we know, is not a girl ruled by the logic of self-preservation.

High school girls, whose hormones outweigh their brains, generally fall for the worst, most abusive male louts available, out of some DNA-throwback, chimpanzee fealty to the Alpha Male. Over the first few weeks of high school, the felonious visage of Tonto Grosvenor began to creep into Liza's subconscious and create a Feeling that Liza thought she recognized as Mild Hate—a safe and comfortable feeling, with which one can have a laugh and a beer, then forget about moments later.

But Liza's Mild Hate for Tonto Grosvenor, once it had gotten safely under her skin, shed its Wicked Wolf suit and revealed itself, when she was utterly defenseless, as the Deadly Lamb of Love.

Cupid has rarely been so cruel. The romance continued thusly:

YOU ARE A SPUNK-DRENCHED BAG OF USED SLUT-MEAT,

Tonto wrote as Nikki and her chunky friend Beth watched the transaction with furious eyes. While part of Liza was stung by Tonto's notes, another part of her was impressed with his flair for writing them. The verbal section of her mind began inadvertently developing as she wracked her vocabulary sheet and pocket thesaurus to come up with a laudable insult.

You are a jejune, lice-infested pariah, she wrote hopefully.

LAME THESAURAUS WORK YOU CUM-SICK HOSE MONSTER

Liza dissected Tonto's notes during class, trying to reverse-engineer them and determine the reasons for their toothsome violence and shock power:

MODIFIER (Somethinged-up/out/on)—NOUN (weird receptacle), PREPOSITION (of) ADJECTIVE (weak/small or sexual), MODIFIER (suggesting gross sex/disease), NOUN (food/weak/ugly thing).

Using this as a model to respond to Tonto's notes, Liza began to "A.A.I.: Apprehend, Adapt and Improve," as Kay had been sanctimoniously harping upon them to do:

Eat yourself, you piss-stained prison puppy

AWESOME ALLITERATION, ASSHOLE

So many rules! Liza fumed. Nevertheless, spurred by this wretched correspondence, she was doing well in English.

Ned's schedule caused him to suffer a morning square-dancing class, which was grudgingly attended by the broody Dino Grosvenor. Ned invariably found that whatever unlucky girl was limply holding his hands in the Allemande Left was staring over his shoulder at Dino, who was James Dean-ing his way through the class by expending the least amount of energy possible to animate his limbs. Girls trembled in his casual dance-holds, pollinating with blushes.

It was here, do-si-do-ing across from the satanically beautiful Dino, that Ned grasped with brute force something he had only tacitly realized before: he was physically repellent, and it was unlikely that he'd ever have a "normal" sexual encounter, at least while in high school.

Ned began to isolate himself even further and read alone in the marsh behind the campus parking lot whenever not in class.

While Liza's history and math classes were uninteresting, drama and aquatics presented stark personal challenges. The "experimental" drama class was run by a couple who called themselves David and Yvette Running-Drum. David had come from a conservative Jewish family in Queens but had spent several weeks with the Lakota Nation and "gone native" for life; Yvette, his young wife, had been an impressionable senior drama student at Miwok Butte just four years previously and was now working as David's teacher's aide after getting a BA in developmentally disabled studies at the local city college. Yvette fancied herself a playwright; she and David liked to flex their spiritual largesse by dragging "special" citizens into her productions. Each of the drama students, after a week of "trust exercises" (leading each other blindfolded and stumbling across the baseball field; falling stiffly backward onto each other's crossed forearms), was assigned a disabled or retarded partner with whom they would work in the upcoming production, *Searching and Seizures*. "Liza, I'd like you to meet Deenie," Yvette announced with cloying altruism. "Deenie" was a four-foot-seven, 180-pound woman with thick plastic glasses and a stained terry cloth jumpsuit.

Deenie smiled outrageously at the air behind Liza's left ear and took Liza's hand in both of her own.

"Pleashe to meet you Li-zha!" Deenie shouted warmly.

"Nice to meet you, Deenie," Liza said, trying not to visibly recoil.

"I am wearing a mackshi-pad," Deenie confided with delirious joy. Liza, for whom such topics were so embarrassing as to be physically painful, winced.

"That's just great," she said, wishing to let go of Deenie's tiny, sticky hands.

Girls in Liza's locker room gave her arch looks when she opted to change into her swimsuit, daily, in one of the tiny, dank toilet stalls. Liza overheard conversations speculating that she was tattooed, a burn victim, or hermaphroditic.

Liza, not a natural swimmer, was jealous of tawny blondes like Tayzie Grosvenor, who had big shoulders, small hips, and muscled thighs, who could spring off of diving boards and spear into the turquoise like sexy javelins, then undulate speedy and eel-like at the bottom of the pool. Liza's lungs, perhaps from a lifetime of secondhand Peppy smoke, felt like greasy balls of newsprint that collapsed into damp wads as soon as her face met the water.

One wretched, gray, fifty-two-degree morning, when the gym teacher humiliated Liza by having her paddle on a foam kickboard while other girls swam elegant laps, Liza noticed a redheaded girl with a pink bandanna around her neck, wearing a men's overcoat and dirty red leather skirt, sitting in the bleachers above the pool, painting her fingernails. Some girls got out of swimming for monthly bleeding or illness; this girl didn't appear to be sick at all but had sat out of class for two full weeks, scowling at the water, *never even bothering with the locker room.* Liza was famished with curiosity as to how the girl pulled it off.

Liza saw the girl later that day in the "smoking section" of the outdoor amphitheatre.

(Yes, Young Readerlings, California high schools once had smoking areas. It was rather civilized, if deliriously irresponsible ... society had more latitude then; people were at leave to entertain filthier habits. For all the cheap drugs, insincere bisexuality, and hair spray, the 1980s were an innocent and clever time, and compared to the 00's, fairly *creative*. By the 1990s, all such whimsy was quietly beaten to death by the new executive guard of MBAs.

The gravestone marking the end of the amusing 1980s, in this Author's opinion, is the movie *Working Girl,* starring Melanie Griffith. "If you wanna be taken seriously, you gotta have serious hair," says Tess, the plucky protagonist, right before hacking her large Jersey-girl perm-with-Niagara-bangs into a tidy office-helmet. Tess, a lowly temp secretary, lies, sneaks, and identity-robs her way into a better social stratum, executive position, and True Love with Harrison Ford; hence, the thesis of the film, which informed the remainder of that decade, arguably read: "Corporate conformity can be sexy, rebellious, and personally fulfilling! Relax, and let the moral

ambivalence of Free Trade work wonders for you, at the office and [wink] in the bedroom."

But back to Liza, in her school's official smoking area:)

"Excuse me, um, can I ask you something?" Liza stammered, approaching the redhead.

"What?" asked the girl, lighting a Marlboro 100.

"Um, how did you get out of swimming?"

"Oh, that was totally easy. I said I had hep."

"Is that like a school credit?"

"No, it's *hepatitis*. A disease. If you have it, they worry you could give it to everyone in the pool."

Liza shifted in her pumps, wondering how close you had to get to somebody with hepatitis to catch it in the open air.

"I don't actually *have it*," continued the girl.

"Then . . . why did you say you did?" asked Liza. The girl gave her a look.

"To get out of swimming! This is Northern California! Nobody should swim here! It's too fucking cold!"

"O-o-o-oh. That is so, so true."

"I'm Lorna," said the girl, holding out a hand with bitten red fingernails, then pulling it back when she remembered her fresh polish was still tacky.

The next day, Liza forged a note from Peppy.

> *Please excuse my daughter Liza Normal from aquatics since we think there is a possibility she might have Hepatites. We'll update you when the tests come back from the hospital. Thank you,*
> *Penelope Normal*

Now Liza Normal and Lorna Wax both sat out of aquatics, and this way they became friends. Lorna, a sophomore, was a font of experience.

"Beware the goddamned Grosvenors," Lorna warned, after unfolding a terrible story about her unrequited lust for Dino the previous school year, which had culminated in a disappointing bout of drunken fellatio that sealed Lorna's reputation as a "Campus Slut" for what would surely be her entire high school career.

(**Dearest Readers:**

Since you are a vast repository of stories, I only need to toss out a select handful of hoary chestnuts to suggest certain templates, and you will start filling in the blanks. So far, you have been introduced to Liza, A Young Adult, learning important lessons in the midst of a Generation X laundry list of nostalgic consumer objects. This is intended to create, in you, a comforting recognition and therefore earn your trust. The keynotes of this chapter suggest, at this point, that it is evolving into a Saga of Hard-Won Teenage Triumph: Liza, Misfit Underdog, Rises-Above-the-Cruelty-and-Emerges-Victorious. If this format has worn a sufficient groove into your mind, you may crave a campus class-warfare wherein Poor Liza Overcomes Persecution by Rich Grosvenors, Liza and Tonto undergo startling personal transformations, and at the end of the chapter end up kissing with their eyes shut during a homecoming slow dance as Lorna applauds and Nikki cries in the parking lot. I give you fair warning: you might end up feeling cheated out of the familiar satisfactions of that classic storyline, because Liza's fate is to be dragged down harsher and sleazier terrain.)**

Lorna had also had an unconventional childhood. She lived in Sausalito, in a cluster of ramshackle houseboats made locally famous by a legion of hippie squatters who fought off gentrification (and subsequent eviction) in the 1970s by staging a riot. Long-haired men shouting in rubber dinghies were teargassed on the news; braless mothers hit police with oars. Finally, after months of bloody foreheads and pro-bono legal wrangling, the houseboat community was written off as an intractable nuisance by the city and left to fester. Dead, rusty cars filled the unpaved parking lot; children with dirty mouths and no pants ran barefoot on splintering gangplanks. Lorna's houseboat, named *The Amnion* by Lorna's Wiccan midwife mother, was a rotting geodesic dome on a plywood platform, which floated in the murky bay on barnacle-crusted blocks of orange polystyrene. Inside the dome, the triangular ceiling panels were strung with dusty crystals and fading piñatas. Lorna's father, like Liza's, hadn't been in the picture for years and was, said Lorna, "probably in jail." Her mother, Sky-Rose Wax, was a pot dealer in addition to her midwifery. Liza felt comforted that Lorna had never fit in with the local rich kids, either—whatever social cachet Lorna was able to cobble together came from stealing buds out of her mother's stash and selling them to her classmates. Lorna herself abhorred pot; "It makes my mother so fucking stupid," she would say.

It was Lorna's reluctant pot-sales that got her and Liza invited to a party with the inner sanctum of popular kids. It was the end of October; the sudden, crisp smartness of the air and the thrilling pine and sea atoms in the sprinting wind made everyone hopeful and ambitious, except Liza and Lorna, who had spent every recess since they had met in the outdoor amphitheatre, huddled around the lit ends of Marlboro 100s.

Dezi Grosvenor walked up to the unhappy girls in a red plaid scarf, his strawberry-blond hair sticking straight up from the wind. Dezi was clearly in a different life-movie than they were—he looked like he should be whistling bird calls and carrying armfuls of Christmas gifts to bouncy violin music, while Liza and Lorna evoked an exhausted, soup-kitcheny desolation.

"Hullo! Lorna Wax?" asked Dezi, twinkling, holding out his scrubbed pink paw.

"Huhn?" mumbled Lorna, momentarily unable to process this cheerful apparition.

"Dezi Grosvenor! Glad to meet ya! Hey, it's kind of OK over here in the smoking section, isn't it?" Dezi surveyed the amphitheatre and its shivering teen clientele, braving a miserable chill for the comforts of Mother Nicotine.

"I guess," Lorna muttered, nonplussed by the invading Grosvenor.

"Smoking is what brings me here, actually," Dezi segued, his eyes alight with Claymation mischief.

"Oh?"

Dezi sidled up next to Lorna.

"I hear you sell a little you-know-what every now and then."

Lorna gave Dezi the fish-eye. He leapt to recover.

"I hear you only do it occasionally, but that your stuff is the *best*."

The compliment fell like sweet rain on the desert of Lorna's soul. She snorted and rolled her eyes to mask her pleasure. Liza twisted with jealousy.

"Here. Why don't you guys come to this little Halloween party." Dezi handed Lorna a square of slick paper. "Annabella Sorkin's parents are out of town for the weekend. You know Annabella?"

"No," said Lorna.

"Well, it doesn't matter, I'm sure she'll be glad you showed up. So come, and bring as much you-know-what as you can, I'm sure you'll sell it all."

Dezi flashed a dazzling smile and sauntered away.

"What the fuck was that?" Lorna asked.

Liza's eyes spun in her head.

"Our *big chance*," she said, breathily.

On one side, the pricey, color Xeroxed–invite had a picture of a winking supermodel, over the caption:

When the Cat's Away, the Mice Shall Play . . . .

On the other side, it read:

Your presence is requested at Annabella's
Grand Masquerade Bash
HALLOWEEN NIGHT
9 PM—Whenever
BYO—Whatever
Serious Costumes Required!!

Liza was obsessed by the flyer, which seemed to be an invitation to excellence, sophistication, and social dominance . . .

LIZA'S DIARY: KEEP OUT MOFOS!
Maybe now me and Lorna will have a chance to get in with the Front Lawners (as the affluent In-Crowd was known, at Miwok Butte).

They will have to talk to Lorna if they want smoke.

Maybe I will look really hot and when T.G. is stoned he won't be such a dick. Then maybe I'll get to suck on his big lower lip . . . AAAUURRGGGHH!!!

He is SOOOOO FIIIIINE.
Why do no boys like me?

They will regret it when I am a singer/dancer/actress.

High school, for most people, gets boiled down to select formative experiences that can still make the person writhe like a cold ball of worms, twenty years later. The agent of Liza's demise, what the Greeks would call *ate*—the "blindness of folly" that led our hero to her destruction— was her unwillingness to accept, during the first two months of high school, that she would be reviled by the popular kids *forever*. Something had to give, she thought. There had to be an "Ugly Duckling" moment that would subvert her lowly status: a new haircut, or a talent contest, or maybe just the right animal-print spandex unitard. This delusion, brought on by rapt consumption of certain films and sitcoms, would be her undoing at Annabella Sorkin's Halloween party. Lorna, having lived through her own Great Death of Hope the year before, warned Liza to no avail.

"We're just going to be, like, delivery people, like pizza guys. They're not interested in us, they just want drugs."

"But maybe they'll decide we're cool and then we'll get to go to more parties."

"I don't understand why you want to hang out with them *anyway* . . . Oh wait, yes I do, oh *fuck* Liza."

"What?!"

"You're going to throw yourself at Tonto." Lorna's tone was mournful.

"No I'm not," said Liza, hating herself for her ecstatic dreams of devouring his sinister mouth.

"Yes you are," said Lorna.

Liza desperately wanted to stay away from Tonto Grosvenor, but her hormones fizzed and popped like bacon grease every time he slipped her another well-turned character assassination:

. . . FIST IT UP YOUR CAKEHOLE, YOU SPIT-SHINED
DISCO PIG . . .
. . . YOU CHEAP RENTAL BACK-HO . . .
. . . YOU DOUCHE-HUFFER . . .

Halloween had always been an incriminating holiday for Liza, whose mother had curious ideas about what constituted "dress-up." While other schoolchildren arrived at Halloween parties wearing handmade panda suits, faerie princess gowns with yards of pink tulle, or respectable, store-bought Superman or Wonder Woman masks with printed nylon coveralls, Peppy had always dug into her box of sequined Reno finery and tarted up Liza in cocktail dresses, wobbling lines of liquid eyeliner, and a long black wig. "Tell people you're a gypsy fortune-teller," Peppy would slur. "Pull up your bra strap."

"I can see your future, all right," a smirking mother once said to Liza while dropping Tootsie Rolls into her plastic pumpkin.

Liza and Lorna rooted through a Hefty bag of Peppy's old outfits, considering what to wear to the party, taking occasional breaks to smoke cigarettes in the backyard.

"That's a horrible habit!" Noreen yelled down at them from the kitchen window. "You look ridiculous smoking with those young little faces! You should stop trying to be things you're not!" Noreen slammed the window shut.

"I like your grandma." Lorna laughed.

At Peppy's urging, Ned had gotten a driver's license at the beginning of the month. Peppy had taken to getting drunk so early in the day she was rightfully worried about her ability to steer to and from the supermarket, and was sick of being berated in the car by Noreen. For Liza and Lorna, this meant that Ned was their chauffeur, by right.

"You're coming to the Halloween party with us," Liza informed him.

"No I'm NOT." Ned was petrified at the idea of being in an unstructured environment where teens would be making out.

"You'll be in *costume*," Liza begged.

>>FF

("Get on with the horrible life-altering Incident of Shame already," you're thinking at this point. To soothe your impatience, we Fast-Forward: Liza and Lorna, moving in kung fu blurs, compose costumes. Lorna steals a bag of pot from her spaced-out mother, and Ned is bribed with a promise of $20 in after-pot-sales. Tonto passes more hair-raisingly rude notes to

Liza. Liza and Lorna consume five more packs of Marlboro Lights. That is all, and now it is The Night.)

The Honda wheezed up the driveway of an enormous modern stilt house perched on a hill in Belvedere. The Sorkin home was exquisite: long and spacious with walls of polished Carpathian elm burl, a Japanese garden with koi-filled Zen pond, enormous picture windows and a wraparound balcony with a view that stretched and rolled like a beautiful nude over Angel Island and Alcatraz, the marinas and dark green hills of Sausalito, the black satin sheets of the bay and the twinkling Golden Gate Bridge, finally meeting the horizon in the sparkling tiara of San Francisco, city of jewels—a soul-stirring luxury view that made those fortunate enough to be standing on that balcony, hanging over the fog as it poured like steamed milk down the hills, intoxicated with a feeling of owning the world.

The house hurt Liza, it was so beautiful.

"I never want to go back to my shit-hole of a room," Liza said to Lorna as they threw their coats on the pile on Annabella Sorkin's nineteenth-century four-poster bed. "Me either," said Lorna. "Me threether," mumbled Ned, looking at Annabella's sleek personal home entertainment setup.

Lorna and Liza looked fairly wonderful in their mermaid ensembles. They had hot-glued glitter and shells to bikini tops, and cut and stapled two of Peppy's old sequined dresses into remedial fish-tails. The crimping iron was used to excellent effect; Lorna's hair was big and purple, Liza's huge and green with food coloring and glitter. Liza's ordinarily vulgar makeup looked appropriate and whimsical. Together they were snazzy and fantastic; they felt full of the strange power of new personalities (as a successfully transformative outfit will do) and strong hopes of a fabulous entrance and subsequent social improvement. Ned, likewise, was happy to be seen in his Long John Silver costume, and proud of how well the components had come together at the Salvation Army. Ike had rigged him a fake peg leg with Ace bandages, big pants, and a toilet plunger. The eyepatch hid his small deformity, and his portliness was in character. "Arrgh, ye swabby," he said happily, waving his hook at the moth-eaten stuffed woodpecker hot-glued to his epaulet in lieu of a parrot.

Most kids at the party weren't Miwok Butte students, but private and prep-school types who knew one another through country, yacht, and ski clubs. They seemed to be a whiter, shinier race of superior young humans, dressed in movie-quality French Court ensembles with powdered wigs, Sherlock Holmes tweeds, and die-cast metal armor.

"Shit, those are the best costumes I have *ever seen*."

"Moneymoneymoney," Lorna murmured, watching a girl (who must have been Annabella Sorkin) in a huge, satin Scarlett O'Hara hoop dress swan over to the doorway to kiss a seven-foot tennis ball can.

Dezi Grosvenor waddled up to Lorna wearing an adorable penguin suit, fanning his face with $300 in twenties.

"You look great! You bring it?" Dezi squealed.

"I don't know if I brought *that* much," Lorna said, suddenly self-conscious.

"Meet me in the master bathroom. It's the big black one with the Jacuzzi and the palm trees!" With that he wobbled down the hall. Two attractive cat-girls pounced up against his plush breast with meowling delight.

"LOOK! IT'S CAPTAIN QUASIMODO AND THE SEA-WHORES!" shouted Tonto's familiar voice. Liza felt goose bumps spray from her knees up to her shoulders. Tonto was dressed like an Indian—he had, in fact, dressed like an Indian for nine of the fifteen Halloweens of his life. Each year, his schtick had gotten a little better. The long, feathered headdress, fringed buckskin pants, beaded accessories, and hairless, painted torso, along with his customary long braids, was more than Liza's young lust could bear. Behind him, Dino Grosvenor (Lawrence of Arabia) was chatting intimately with Chantal Baumgarten, powdered and sublime in a vintage silk geisha ensemble, fresh from rehearsals for the Eiderdijken Academy production of *The Mikado*. Liza looked down at her hot-glue mermaid outfit, which was leaving a snail-trail of glitter and escaped sequins, and the old leaden feeling of inescapable trashiness settled into her stomach, ruining her mood.

"Look, Ned," Liza moaned, rolling her eyes. "It's Chan-TALLLL."

"Where?" asked Ned brightly. Liza couldn't understand Ned's lack of hatred for the Baumgartens.

Liza and Lorna proceeded to the bar, which boasted an impressive alcohol selection.

"I'm going to drink heavily, like I've never drunk before," announced Liza.

"You're the one that wanted to make friends with these people. Don't make it your personal Waterloo." Lorna sounded ominous.

"Whatever that means!"

Liza poured herself an extra-large glass of triple sec.

Ned spent a minute generating courage, then limped over to Chantal and Dino, happy to have a connection at the party, however distant. Chantal's white face, slinky eyes, and puckered red mouth turned to Ned like a perfect Kabuki mask.

"Ned? My God! What are you doing here?" she asked, as if asking a pygmy how he'd manage to ride his zebu into the embassy ballroom.

"Hi, Chantal. Hey Dino, I'm Ned, I'm in your square-dancing class," he said bashfully, offering his hook for shaking.

"I don't remember you," Dino said in his sexy whisper. "Do you always have a dead woodpecker on your shoulder?"

"It's *not dead*," Ned quipped bravely, remembering a familiar British comedy routine. "It's *resting*."

Dino and Chantal gave Ned patronizing half-smiles.

"Remember that fleabag theatre I told you about?" Chantal asked Dino. His eyes widened. Ned, suddenly ashamed, looked down at his shoe and plunger-peg.

"Nice to see you, Chantal," he said, and hobbled away.

"I'm gonna go find Dezi," Lorna said, watching Liza watch Tonto. "Try not to do anything you'll regret later, OK?"

"How will I ever know what I regret later if I never do anything, ever?" Liza asked loudly in a perturbed tone.

"That's one way of looking at it," Lorna said doubtfully.

"I'm not going to be around these assholes next year," Liza said upon espying Tayzie Grosvenor, muscular and divine in a Statue of Liberty costume with illuminated crown. Liza's inner disgrace-generator picked up speed. "I'm going to New York. *To the High School of Performing Arts.*" She made this announcement with belligerent denial; she and Lorna both knew that dream had shriveled on the vine. She downed the rest of her glass of triple sec, slammed the glass down, and mock-gagged. "Jesus, what was that stuff? These people obviously don't know their liquor."

"Next year's a long way off," Lorna cautioned, her monotone implying she knew it would do no good.

. . .

As Lorna went off in search of the master bathroom, Liza remained at the bar to watch Tonto and his boy sycophants play mumblety-peg in the kitchen, stabbing a paring knife between their splayed fingers.

"Liza!" Tonto shouted. "Come here! Lay on this butcher block and we'll amputate your upper half so you can be all fish."

"Yeah RIGHT," Liza brayed artlessly, her head suddenly glowing like a kerosene lamp. She tottered over to Tonto, her legs pinned together by her tight tail.

"Want to make a movie?" Tonto asked. "I've got a camcorder and a cot."

His groupies laughed.

"It would depend on the role," Liza said, not getting it. "You have to call my agent."

(The only thing worse than this naive and grandiose comment was the Taser jolt of embarrassment Liza felt, eleven years later, when she finally realized what Tonto actually meant.)

Liza leaned heavily upon the butcher block, trying to look seductive. The staring boys made her feel energized and naughty.

"Will you be needing a fluff boy?" Tonto asked, to the delight of his crew.

"I need a LOT of things," Liza spoke in truth.

"You need another drink!" Tonto playfully grabbed Liza around her neck and dragged her back to the bar, much to her euphoria.

As Liza downed two shots of Kahlua, Tonto unfolded his wallet. There was what looked like a small white coffee-ring pressed into the leather—the imprint of a condom that had lived, sandwiched between Tonto's money and his ass, for months.

"Do you know what that is?" Tonto asked.

Tonto stared hard at Liza with expressionless eyes. Liza stared back, giggling.

"Is that the circumference of your brain?" she asked in a flash of drunken inspiration.

"I bet you'd like a tour of the house," said Tonto.

"You bet I would," slurred Liza, with what she thought was sophisticated flirtiness.

And within fifteen delirious fucked-up minutes, Liza's maidenhead was unceremoniously given over to Tonto Grosvenor in the walk-in utility closet of the Sorkin garage.

(Sexually Intelligent Readers: there is no escaping the clumsy adamance of new hormones. Since the dawn of creation, teenagers, civilized or no, have been humping badly and tackily and causing outrage among their parents and peers. This is a natural and inevitable fact of life that is *not going away*. And why shouldn't one perform these wretched experiments when one's emotions are young and rubbery? No compassionate person could support imposing irreversible consequences on such innocent, human bungling.)

Tonto would have been genuinely surprised, given the abusive nature of their correspondence, to find out that Liza, a sweet girl encased in a deceptive exoskeleton of slut cues, had any tender feelings for him at all—Liza, fool as she was in her boozy and inexperienced Scorpio hot pants, once kissing the long-sought-after lips of Anton Grosvenor, thought they were In Love. In her blotto state, she could not differentiate between her dream of a splendid and mutually passionate deflowerment on silken sheets, and an awkward rutting on a linoleum floor with her head wedged between an ironing board and some skis.

Lorna had been waiting in the master bathroom for Dezi and was surprised to discover that she was only one of several drug carriers designated to peddle their wares in this hot spot. Lorna sold badly rolled joints to the teen menagerie, in-between the Coke Guy (appropriately dressed in white plastic as a *Star Wars* Stormtrooper) and the Speed Guy (in the form of Ace Frehley from KISS). All were doing excellent business over the onyx double-sink counter, and Lorna, after only twenty-two minutes, swished away a full $140 richer.

Upon leaving the bathroom, she found Ned, who was uncomfortably alone, reading the titles on the Sorkin bookshelf.

"Where's Liza?" Lorna asked.

"Tonto dragged her into the garage," Ned said with annoyance.

"Uh-oh."

There was a whoop and a loud, ululating scream as Tonto suddenly burst into the living room, holding two fist-fulls of long, sparkling green hair.

"Oh my God," Lorna gulped.

Ned's face froze; he wombled over on his peg-leg.

"What have you *done!*?" Ned demanded, staring aghast at the hanks of his sister's hair.

Tonto looked at him with funny eyes, wide and fey.

"I scalped her," he said simply, with a shrug.

Ned had never hit anybody in his life, and never intended to, but he suddenly found the door of The Past locking behind him, and The Future likewise slamming its gate in his face—this left Ned in a cold, clear pinspot of *NOW HIT TONTO OR SPEND THE REST OF YOUR LIFE REGRETTING IT.*

Moving with dreamy inevitability, Ned belted Tonto as hard as he could, in the mouth. Tonto jerked back slightly, holding his lip with a quizzical expression. Ned felt his hand become three bright and separate sparks of pain.

"Ow! Jesus!" Ned swooned, clutching his fractured hand as Dino, Dezi, Batman, Groucho Marx, and Hitler jumped him simultaneously. Groucho hit Ned in the cheek with a full beer can, which dented open and sprang a white arc of foam. Ned whimpered and crawled, his bound leg ripping through his pants and Ace bandages unfurling shamefully on the rug. Tonto, unhurt, leapt soundlessly in his moccasins to kick Ned in the chest with such force it flipped him onto his back. The sight of Ned wallowing in terror made Dino and Dezi hold Tonto back from dishing out further, unnecessary abuse.

Lorna, in the meantime, had run through the garage, following the trail of sparkling hair to find Liza in the backyard greenhouse, wearing a men's yellow raincoat and vomiting extremely onto a two-hundred-year-old-bonsai tree. Lorna did not recognize Liza at first, because she now had a Mohawk.

"Oh, Liza!" Lorna cried, her heart torn with pity and outrage.

(For logistical reasons, it should be explained that Liza's advanced drunkenness caused her to forget her painful modesty and become sufficiently undressed for her unfortunate devirginating; immediately afterward, she had passed out cold.

While looking through the hardware cabinets for something interesting to steal, Tonto had found an instrument of fate: the Sorkin family poodle-clippers. Hopped up on an assortment of white powder stimulants and feeling very much the Indian Brave, he plugged them in and counted coup on Liza—a whimsical atrocity appropriate to his costume.)

Now she turned to Lorna with her eyes lolling around under glitter-smeared lids.

"Weshooooould maybe go-o-o-o," she managed to blurt before getting sick again on a prize-winning orchid.

Lorna, after stashing Liza into the back of the Honda (where she promptly passed out again), stormed back into the party and wedged herself between Ned's quivering form and the dangerously adrenal Grosvenor boys.

"I'm calling the cops, you fucking assholes!" Lorna screamed.

"Are you, Miss Drug Dealer? Shall I find you a phone?" asked the penguin with toxic politeness.

Lorna looked at the hateful wall of handsome lads staring down at her and realized that the Grosvenors were, for someone like her, as untouchable as the ceiling of City Hall. The best course of action was to flee with the Normals, quickly, before they opted to torture them again.

"Fine, fuck off, we're leaving," Lorna said.

"Give us all the money you made, first," Tonto said with a leer, looking at a tiny spot of blood that he'd wiped off his otherwise unharmed lip. The other boys appeared to mull this idea over. Lorna, tensing herself to fight, shot a look toward Dino. *We had something like sex once and therefore, you should help me now* . . . .

"Oh *God*, just let them go *away*," said Dino, turning his back and stomping down the hall in a billow of white Arabic robes. This broke the gravitational threat-spell; Ned's assailants dispersed, slightly abashed, having been reminded of their superior place.

Tonto gave Lorna a villainous wink, which made her twitch with rage. Ned wobbled up from the floor, trembling and gray. Way worse for him than the beating were the calligraphic eyes of Chantal Baumgarten, clearly embarrassed that she'd acknowledged him earlier. Lorna helped Ned out the door amid arch whispers and exaggerated looks of revulsion. Someone threw an olive at them.

Ned pulled it together enough to drive, although he couldn't stop shaking. Lorna bravely tended to Liza in the backseat.

"Liza, can you sit up? SIT UP. Don't lean like that, you could choke."

"How can she go back to school like *that*?" Ned asked, anguished.

"She doesn't even know yet, that's what freaks me out!" Lorna yelled. "Tell your grandma Liza's spending the night with me, and drop us at my house, OK?"

Ned's throat burned as he silently cried, trying to fix on the double yellow line. His ribs were throbbing, his hand was purple and aching up to his shoulder, his sister was sick and shorn. He remembered Noreen's old poster of the abandoned *Babes in the Woods*; he thought of Hal Normal, his worthless father, and Peppy's hell-bent, showbiz delusions. Ned felt like he'd been beaten up by a forest of mean trees, particularly as he watched Lorna walk-carry Liza through the jagged darkness between two tilted, sinking houseboats. Driving away, he felt his heart dangling from the lowest rung of sadness he'd ever known.

Liza's sleep was hot and fitful with terrible dreams of the theatre being burgled. When the sun irradiated Lorna's dirty window the next day and woke Liza, her eyeballs felt hickory smoked, her headache was knitting needles buried to the hilt up each nostril. Her head felt wrong; too unweighted. When she touched the sides of her head, her empty stomach plummeted; she had dreamt that her hair was gone—to wake up and find herself so vandalized was like waking up next to a corpse. Rewinding her spotty memory of the night, she realized she was changed in more ways than one.

"OK, we're going to have to discuss plans of action," Lorna said, bringing Liza a glass of orange juice and a Pop-Tart. Liza sniffed; her wet raccoon eyes looked at Lorna gratefully. Her throat was a hot drain of tears; liquid shock seemed to run from her nose. "But you don't have to decide anything right this second," Lorna added with a gentle tone.

"My hair was *long*." Liza choked, feeling sick and hopeless.

"Go take a shower and I'll make you some eggs," said Lorna, reaching over to rub the fresh, hamstery stubble on Liza's head. "My mom isn't here, thank God. She must be delivering a baby."

Lorna's kind touch made Liza's agony more excruciating; a new batch of tears rushed up from her throat. She picked up one of Lorna's many bandannas and tied it tightly to her head. It felt soothing, like it helped to strap her loosened self back into place.

. . .

In the shower, the water seemed to penetrate her nude scalp and press, like hot fingers, all the way into her throbbing brain. As the green and glitter rinsed from her remaining swatch of hair and swirled down at her feet, Liza felt she was watching all of the magic of childhood bleed away. She dried her sore limbs and her aching nether parts, with a sense of having been abruptly divorced from Innocence: Never again could she afford to believe in the flight of plastic ponies with long, combable hair, or the trainability of Sea Monkeys, or that the wind flapping loose tar paper on the roof was the light footsteps of Christmas reindeer. *I am fifteen and neither an Olympic gymnast nor a blind figure skater,* Liza realized with acute gloom, *and that sure as fuck wasn't true love.*

Squarely facing the terrible moment, she swabbed the steamed bathroom mirror with her towel and surveyed the damage.

It was bad, but slightly less bad that she had imagined. She had a nicely shaped head, at least. The stubble was only a quarter-inch long on the sides of her head, but the jagged hair-strip across the top was long enough to cover one side down to her ear.

I look like a farm boy, she thought, and cried. Then she thought of Tonto, and threw up again.

The idea of wearing hats twenty-four hours a day, Liza and Lorna decided, was absurd, and Liza was dead set against wigs—she had always thought they looked medical and wrong on Peppy—she would only feel more tragic with prosthetic hair.

"Go to sleep again, if you can," Lorna said, putting her coat on.

"What am I going to *do*?" Liza sniveled.

"Just . . . just, shut up for now, OK?" said Lorna, nervously biting skin off of her thumb. "I'll be back in a couple of hours."

Liza didn't think she would sleep, but the second she shut her eyes her pained consciousness bolted like a shoplifter.

Meanwhile, Ned was at the hospital with Noreen, getting his hand set into a cast. Peppy had been unimpressed, at breakfast, by Ned's bruised cheekbone and purple, swollen hand, saying only "My foot looked like that once," before staggering back to her room with an ice tray and a family-size can of Clamato juice.

"How could you get into a brawl?" Noreen asked, with a worried face.

"I don't know," Ned said darkly, wincing as the doctor tried to move his fingers.

"That's not like you."

"The guy was a total bastard," Ned murmured.

"Didja teach him a lesson?" Noreen asked, trying to cheer Ned up.

Ned looked at his grandmother with eyes that reminded her of a basset hound she'd seen once. "No," he said. The doctor slathered cold plaster onto his wrist.

While Liza slept, Lorna went shopping with the $120 she still had from the pot sales. (Twenty dollars went to Ned—he had stared at the bill ruefully, like he'd sold his soul for it.) When she returned, she dumped the contents of the plastic bags onto the bed:

1. One bottle Lady Lee 40-vol. peroxide hair bleach
2. One Plasmatics LP, *Metal Priestess*

(Item 2 the result of stopping by Paramecium, a popular, subversive record store, to ask the poxy clerk for "any albums where there are girls with mohawks on the cover." Wendy O. Williams came to mind. "She's a total beast," the clerk said with admiration.)

3. One choke chain (dog variety)
4. One pair combat boots (used, from the "Free Box"—a plywood holdover from the hippie era in the houseboat community parking lot, where residents dumped unwanted clothing and invariably saw it the next day, unwashed, on some other resident)
5. One pair plaid golf pants (also from the Free Box)
6. One package safety pins
7. One can Aqua Net hair spray (Ultra Hold)
8. One bottle black nail polish
9. One black eye pencil
10. One black Magic Marker
11. One long needle (sewing variety)
12. One bottle hydrogen peroxide
13. One bottle rubbing alcohol
14. One bag cotton balls

"You're going punk," Lorna informed Liza.

"No I'm *not*! I can't listen to this shit!" Liza yelped, staring with horror at a screaming Wendy O. Williams, wearing nothing but what looked like black electrical tape. "I like Neil fucking *Sedaka!*"

"You have no choice," Lorna said, leveling her gaze.

"But . . . everyone will *stare at me.*" Liza sobbed.

"They already do."

"They'll think I'm a scagged-out *freak.*"

"They already do," Lorna said, seriously. "Plus also a slut and a whore and an exhibitionalist."

"But . . . *I'm not any of those things!*" cried Liza. A lifetime of injustices rose up in her like a tidal wave, a glassy black wall that blocked out the sun, then roared down with unthinkable weight . . . roofs were swallowed; horses were drowning in treetops . . . .

"I know you're not those things. Big deal. They're assholes."

"But what about all my *commercial auditions?!*"

Lorna just looked at Liza. Both knew that in all the time they had known each other, even though she talked about her career constantly, Liza had gone on exactly zero auditions. The Whelan-Zedd agency never returned Liza's calls.

Lorna handed Liza a glass full of ice and a washcloth.

"I want you to ice down your nose," said Lorna.

"Why?!?"

"We're going to pierce it."

"Fuck NO! My *nose!?!*"

"I thought about it all morning. You need to make the mohawk look like it was *your idea,*" Lorna said sternly.

Though deranged by her trauma, Liza could see the wisdom in this. She coughed down another sob and dropped ice into the terry cloth, wondering how much more this episode could possibly hurt.

"We should sue him!" Liza screamed, before she was suddenly filled, as Lorna had been, with the laughably futile image of herself, Ned, and Peppy cowering in a courtroom in shabby, patched clothes with pieces of dry straw fringing their necks like scarecrows, as Teflon-suited, Grosvenor lawyer-kings roared blue flames at them.

Lorna took her Bic lighter to the needle in an effort to sterilize the tip.

"I think we should do the right nostril," Lorna said with doctorly confidence.

Seagulls flitted around *The Amnion,* shouting *wok wok wok wok wok wok,* and *ear!*

. . .

And so it came to pass that Liza Normal reluctantly became Miwok Butte High School's first hardcore punk. In truth, the tall, bleach white mohawk, black lips, ripped plaid pants, and safety-pin-in-the-nose were a vast improvement on her previous style. The safety pin was a real commitment for a fresh nose piercing, which was unhealed and slightly infected. Liza had to pull it out every night and put in a hypoallergenic stud to keep the hole from closing, then flush the hole with rubbing alcohol, which stung so much it brought tears to her eyes. Then she'd wrangle the pin back in her face the next day. Though painful, it was no more annoying a beauty regimen than the blow-dryer had been. Lorna had intuitively grasped that this transformation was the only possible way to give Liza, whose reputation was a lost cause, any power or choice. It rendered all further derision redundant (e.g., "You're trashy!") and liberated Liza's possibilities for "fun," given the bounty of misconducts that punkhood implied: swearing, drinking, drugs, petty crime, truancy, staying out late, picking fights, etc.

Liza knew it was a boldly intelligent stroke.

Naturally, with her new look, there were hurdles to overcome.

Noreen: "Oh, honey, why'd you do that to your pretty looks? Hair grows back, but you're not going to like that hole in your nose when you get a cold. Oh, Jiminy. I hope you don't get a tattoo."

Peppy: "What happened? You try to give yourself a permanent? I did that once. You stay away from my wigs."

Ned was the lone voice of approval.

"Short of killing Tonto, I guess that's about the best way you could have dealt with it," he told her, quietly. "Actually, I think you look kind of radical."

Liza had never loved her brother more.

Ned had changed; his will to thrive seemed to have been broken along with his hand. He hid in the burned-out lighting booth of the theatre for the rest of the long weekend, dragging up blankets, flashlight batteries, comic books, boxes of crackers. He wouldn't look at or speak to anyone.

His first morning back at Miwok Butte after the ill-fated party would be his last; square-dancing did him in.

In the middle of a Triple Scoot, the walls began shimmering. The girl standing opposite Ned began to look at him nervously. His face was red; his hands were suddenly drenched with sweat—the girl dropped them and wiped her fingers on her pants. Ned began hyperventilating.

"Um . . . Mr. Deitch?" the girl yelled over the music.

With wide eyes, Ned began to feel for the floor, since his legs had gone soft and tingly. His heart was pumping foreign toxins into his body with violent jerks; specks of light shot into his peripheral vision. All the students stopped dancing and stared. His hand-cast smacked the parquet floor with a loud *thwack* as he went down. He felt like a huge sturgeon suddenly dropped onto the basketball court; a flapping, stinking alien, unable to breathe or escape.

Ned's moan of fear ricocheted around the gym. Then, for the second time in his life, he fainted.

While unconscious, Ned dreamt of a beautiful sunlit meadow, where a Chinese child-prince in an embroidered silk gown was sitting on a log. Ned sat with the child—it was divinely peaceful. The grass was light green, soft and new, birds were making songs, sunlight glimmered in prismatic beams through dewy leaves. The child turned to Ned with deep black eyes and a spiritual smile, then put his small hand on Ned's shoulder, and whispered with infinite pity and compassion, "You know, there are only thirty-six cycles in the Universe, and they're *all* corrupt."

At this Ned abruptly awoke on the gym floor with the alarmed eyes of his classmates boring into him.

"It's OK, son," said the gym teacher's oversize face, full of veins.

Ned shook like a maraca, dry beans rattling in his skull.

After a visit to the school doctor, Ned was shunted off to the school psychologist, who determined that he had had an acute panic attack.

"You'll feel better tomorrow, Ned," Peppy said unconvincingly, when she came to pick him up. Ned's nerves felt frayed as an old toothbrush.

113

Colors Insulting to Nature

He visibly jumped in the car seat when the lunch bell rang, petrified that students would file out of the buildings and see him, stupidly huge as a parade float, smelly and hideous.

"....... Just .... DRIVE!" Ned commanded. Peppy was frightened and obeyed. After driving several blocks, Peppy looked at Ned, clammy and jittering in the seat.

"You're really sick, aren't you," Peppy said, worried. Ned glared at her with his good eye.

"When do you think you can go back to school?"

"Never," said Ned, with such finality that Peppy realized he was serious.

"How are you going to get an education?" Peppy asked.

"*How the hell should I know*?!" Ned shouted.

"Don't get snotty."

"Take me home, just please, please, *please* take me home."

Ned bit his lip and started to cry, realizing that "home" was not something he ever felt at the theatre, or at any of Peppy's previous apartments, either. Noreen's little Reno house was the only safe haven he had ever known, but she had sacrificed it to live in the wake of Peppy's narcissistic tailspin.

"Talk to me that way, you can start walking," Peppy snapped, more interested in her own feeling of having been insulted than in Ned's real crisis.

Ned took off his jacket, zipped it up, and pulled it over his head. He could breathe and see partially through the neck hole as the car moved through town.

Facing Tonto the following Monday was Liza's biggest challenge; she had fretted all weekend about the monkey knot of conflicting emotions she would suffer on seeing him. Surprisingly enough, despite her nearly fanatical abhorrence of nudity, she wasn't particularly bothered by the fact that they'd had sex (it was dark, she couldn't remember it, and she had no use for the weird, overrated preciousness surrounding virginity, anyway—she had already been planning, with clinical detachment, to unload hers at the earliest possible opportunity), but she was really freaked out that Tonto was the first guy she'd ever *kissed*—the impassioned willingness of the kissing having exposed her as being madly and stupidly in love with him. This felt more like being caught with her pants down than the fact of her pants actually having been down.

. . .

Despite this turmoil, Liza could not help noticing that the stares she ordinarily got walking through the halls were qualitatively different; *there
was no casual disdain in them.* The eye-energy had changed—Liza realized
in a rush what the new ingredient was: *Fear.* Fifteen minutes after arriv-
ing on campus in a heat cloud of self-consciousness, Liza was unexpectedly stoned on the power of visual intimidation. Her oversize boots
made resonant slaps through the halls, as opposed to the dainty *clic clic clic*
of her stiletto heels. It felt good, this stomping—an energizing balm!

"Halloween was days ago," some joker dribbled in the hallway.

"Fuck your mother, dickweed."

So easy! So *effective*!

The worm was turning. The Fear felt like something Liza had always
craved (Fear is, after all, the cheap, ugly twin of Admiration).

Ten feet from the dreaded homeroom door, Liza paused and felt a truth
embrace her. She recognized the mohawk and its accoutrements to be
a *costume,* nothing more. She had, after all, been disgraced *many* times in
her life, and even though she couldn't remember anything specifically,
she'd *surely* been humiliated by bigger, better, and more important assholes than Tonto Grosvenor. She breathed deeply, fully assuming her
new role with depth and conviction. Her lip curled into an Elvis-sneer.
She suppressed an urge to spit.

Finally she launched forward and crashed into the room, bruising the
sleepy air with noise, leaving all doubts, shame, and foreboding behind
her.

I, The New Improved Liza Normal, am someone not to fuck with.

Tonto couldn't bring himself to look at her.

The vile exuberance of his assault had passed, and he knew he was
going to have to see something when her head came into view, but he
didn't know what to expect. If she skulked in, cowering and defeated
under a baseball hat, he would have made a point of ripping it off of
her head and laughing, to distract himself from any possible feelings of
guilt. When his eyes finally darted her way and he saw that Liza,
through her drastic transformation, had effectively reclaimed her scalp,
he was stupefied.

Liza turned to Tonto with black-lined cat eyes set on Ultra-Hate. He
glanced back.

"Woo-boo-boo-boo-boo-boo-boo," Liza said with bored sarcasm, tapping her hand against her lips in a derisive Indian war whoop.

"Nice haircut," murmured Tonto.

"Some faggot gave it to me," said Liza.

No more notes were passed between them; it was the end of the affair.

Liza knew she had handled the situation admirably, but her heart felt like it would drop out of her body and explode into rotten black juice like a bad tomato.

There's something really wrong with me if I still love that motherfucker.

Throughout the day, Liza found silver linings to the punk persona thrust upon her. For once, her alienated outsides matched her insides. She had never fit in, but that wasn't the hardest part of living in the world with other teens; it was the trying-to-be-accepted-and-constantly-being-rejected loop that was most demoralizing. There was liberty and relief in looking like you didn't give a fuck what people thought of you anymore.

"You know, I might even get to like this haircut," Liza told Lorna during the lunch break, after a handful of stoners reverently touched the spiky top and marveled nicely at the pin in her nose.

"I'm beginning to almost want one myself," said Lorna, running her fingers across the soft side-stubble again.

Liza was asked to leave her drama class when Deenie, her *Searching and Seizures* partner, took one look at the mohawk and safety pin and began to scream and cry inconsolably.

"Deenie, it's just a haircut," Liza said, feeling a little guilty but also secretly thrilled by this reception. "You want me to take the pin out? I can take the pin out!"

"No! No! *No! No!*" bellowed Deenie, who was shaking her head back and forth and punching her own abdomen with little fists.

"For this project, it's very important that we have a *nurturing environment*, Liza, and I think that you're trying to say to the world that you are a very *angry person*, right now," Yvette Running-Drum said with smarmy condescension later in her office. A deal was struck in which Liza would get drama credit for spending the class period in the library. She was only too pleased not to have to endure long hours of playing Twister with persons of questionable hygiene, but her dismissal from the class still smarted. Being kicked out of any production was not in keeping with a Broadway-bound trajectory, but Liza's goals, unhampered by reality, remained ruggedly intact.

They can't kill my dreams, Liza told herself, feeling secretly heroic.

Over the next few weeks, Tonto Grosvenor tried to take credit for Liza's new look, but for the most part, everyone thought him to be merely boasting. Liza didn't deny that he had cut her hair but enjoyed fabulizing how it actually went down: "I begged him to do it. He begged me not to. He was practically crying. I said, *Shave my head, already, you big pussy!* And he was all, *No, no, your hair is too beautiful* . . . So I slapped his bitch-ass face, and then he was all cowering, like *OK, OK* . . . ."

Since Liza and Tonto were both flagrant liars, there was no divining the truth (Lorna was an excellent secret-keeper—a tomb), but most students tended to believe that Liza had volunteered for the makeover, however it had come about. This take was reinforced when Liza proudly reshaved the half-inch of growth on her head a month later.

By April 1982, Liza and Lorna were both full-blown, hardcore punks, entrenched in San Francisco's thriving underage scene—a niche where both girls fit in easily for the first time in their lives. Punk had gathered all of the misfit youths of the surrounding areas and given them a rallying point: fierce, idiot freedom—and several venues in which to flaunt this new ethos—Club Foot, The A-Hole, The Tool and Die, and a Filipino restaurant called Zamboanga Gardens. All were crumbling bar/cabarets that had succumbed, through mismanagement, to the terminal social disease of eighteen-and-over shows. Lorna cut off her long red locks and now had matted blue-black hair buzzed around the neck and ears, filled with plastic children's barrettes. All of their clothing came either from the Free Box or the Salvation Army; all of their money came from pot sales.

"You stay out of my stash!" Sky-Rose Wax would yell at Lorna. "Get your own goddamned weed!"

"Get me a goddamned college fund!" Lorna would yell back. "You owe me!"

Liza and Lorna openly hated their mothers and the lifestyles they embodied. Liza barely looked at Peppy anymore—Peppy had packed on an extra forty pounds during her bedroom days of gin and Chips

Ahoy!, and made no effort to connect. Sky-Rose Wax was dissipating from underemployment, due to a dip in the popularity of natural, drugless childbirth: "Man, all you really need to do is put a plastic shower curtain on the living room floor and let God and Gaia do the rest. All this white-medicine, epidural shit has gotten wa-a-a-ay out of control," she complained, expertly sucking down fragrant, hybrid pot-buds so dense and sticky as to cause major "I'm having a heart attack" freak-outs in any but the most experienced career stoners and Rastafarians.

"If I ever have a baby, you can bet your ass I'm not letting that woman *anywhere near me*," Lorna would say to Liza, loud enough for Sky-Rose to hear.

Ned had stopped leaving the theatre altogether, except to go to psychiatric appointments. Even then, he had to be picked up at the curb directly in front of the house and deposited right in front of the doctor's office, and he kept his head and face entirely covered by a T-shirt or sweater. Ned was pronounced "severely agoraphobic" and "prone to anxiety and panic attacks," but nobody knew exactly what to do for him; he test-drove new drug combinations that invariably treated some symptoms but caused others to flourish. School was out of the question, but Ned liked information, so through Noreen he established a relationship with the driver of the local bookmobile, requesting books on certain subjects, which the bookmobile lady would provide and Noreen would pick up in bimonthly stacks. Ned had dragged his mattress up to the lighting booth, and now left it only to go to the bathroom.

Liza chatted with him in his booth infrequently, since she was usually partying in the city or crashing at Lorna's. Besides Noreen, the only other human with whom Ned continued to have any vital exchange was Ike, who gave him small electrical repair jobs, usually clock radios or tape recorders. Sometimes a burning smell would come from the booth—Ned would be carefully bending tiny diode wires and soldering them into place. In exchange for his work, Ike brought Ned comic books, tools, gum, clip lights, bits of hardware. Ned perked up a lot when he saw Ike—they had amusing, esoteric conversations—then he would leave, and whatever dark mood Ned had been momentarily relieved of would settle on him again.

.   .   .

Liza and Lorna were having a great time venting their aggression in the rampant punk scene. There was good fun to be had: unlimited beer and blue cream soda, public urination in alleys (girls too!), Vespa motor scooters and late-night wanderings through the dirty yellow esophagus of the Broadway tunnel, to read the graffiti, finger-drawn in the exhaust-grime:

BOB IS UNCOUTH

JAKS TEAM SKATES ON YOUR FACE

STUNT COCK!

New bands seemed to be sprouting up every weekend, among them "His Holey Wounds," with lead singer Brigham Hamburger, who was now going by the punk moniker of Hammy Christ. Stigmata was his gimmick; during such numbers as "Gallo, Galilee, Galileo" (Gallo being the cheapest fortified wine available at that time), he would gouge a corkscrew into his palms and twist until they bled, to the delight of all. It was, in fact, Liza's previous acquaintance with "Hammy" that gave her and Lorna instant popularity backstage at the O, Columbus! club, a rotting theatre smack in the middle of a row of strip joints and peep shows that disgraced the otherwise quaintly Italian neighborhood of North Beach. Brigham Hamburger had undergone a startling transformation from the Christian zealot he had been—now he was an anti-Christian zealot. His hair was buzzed to the length of mildew; an upside-down cross was tattooed between his eyes—the horizontal line connected his tear ducts across the bridge of his nose (a tiny red spot in the white of one eye was all that remained of the ceramic bear incident).

"Liza? Oh, shit. . . . look at you! Little hardcore princess, you're so hot!" Hammy had yelled, when Liza first reintroduced herself to him, after a particularly bloody concert. His hug covered her ripped X-ray Spex T-shirt with sweat and red smears (which she later took pains not to wash out—"Yah, Hammy *bled all over me*," she'd say proudly to other jealous punk girls).

He dragged Liza to meet his drummer, all the while trying to palm her ass. Liza couldn't believe that she'd ever be delighted to see Brigham Hamburger again, or flattered by his compliments, but times had changed. Lorna even thought he was kind of sexy.

Liza enjoyed hanging out backstage at the O, Columbus!—it was an airless, vandalized box with low ceilings, broken mirrors, and a filthy yellow couch, on which somebody would usually be unconscious. She and Lorna would drink Hammy's beer and draw band logos on the unfinished Sheetrock, ignoring Hammy's endless, half-drunk, nonlinear rants about his childhood:

"The Book of Revelations—who really came up with that shit? Was John the ancient Greek Stephen King? Hey! Thy God is a vengeful and jealous God, but Jesus is Santa Claus, vice president, and general manager of all human beings! It's Good Cop/Bad Cop! You guys want more Burgie?" he would ask, holding out cans of his favorite cheap beer.

Liza liked how Hammy had willfully transformed himself. He brought her furious feelings about her own childhood into sharper focus. Lorna was taken by Hammy's intense stage presence. He sang with drastic, frenzied abandon, like he was trying to cough his condemned heart out into the flailing mosh pit.

In an effort to get Lorna hooked up with Hammy, they accompanied him one night to his "squat"—an abandoned schoolbus parked outside of the abandoned Hamms brewery, which had come to be known as "The Vats."

Many homeless young punks squatted in The Vats—it was a huge, three-story industrial building deep in the City's no-man's-land, South of Market Street. The floor was indented with huge dry tubs, fifteen feet long and ten feet deep, where beer once fermented. What had once been offices were now illegal apartments; fifty or more punks lived there at any given time, and countless more streamed through the cavernous, tiled hallways, horsing around, getting in slap fights, trading amusing stolen objects—salon hair dryers, stop signs, dachshunds—for drugs. There was electricity, but no plumbing—a designated passageway lined with plastic garbage bags between two of the vat-tubs was covered with human shit.

"Drugs are the American teenage adventure," Hammy said, handing Lorna and Liza two tabs of acid—tiny pieces of paper with pictures of Saturn on them. "Apart from bar mitzvahs, there is absolutely no mystical, teen ritual experience of Welcome to Adulthood. Which is why we now use Microdot," he said, crossing himself with the tab and placing it under his tongue.

Lorna and Liza looked at each other and braced themselves for the new experience.

"Am I gonna freak out?" asked Liza.

"I've never seen anybody rip their own eyes out, except in that drug education film they showed us in sixth grade," said Hammy.

Hammy, who had been institutionalized shortly for a faith-based nervous breakdown during his sophomore year, was now eighteen and living on SSI—a welfare income for those who succeeded in convincing the State of California that they were mentally unfit for the workplace. Hammy had blocked out the windows of his abandoned bus with pages torn from Bibles and Hello Kitty stickers. Large mobiles made of chicken bones twisted from the punctured metal ceiling on strands of monofilament—these were Hammy's "art." As the drugs came on, Liza noticed the geometric designs on Hammy's tattered bedspread locking and unlocking themselves like automated Chinese wood-puzzles. She sensed a vibe of attraction flowering between Hammy and Lorna, who were playing with the feathers in a ruptured pillow.

The Vats were lit up like a many-eyed jack-o'-lantern, and Liza suddenly felt her personal being rise with new juice and vigor, coating her limbs with impenetrability, making her shimmer with power. She wanted to perform; to be seen by people and test-drive this potent new charisma.

"I'm going to go walk around in The Vats," Liza informed her friends, who were now staring at each other in an open confession of mutual interest.

"Be careful," said Hammy. "There's a lot of violent people in there."

"Yeah, you gonna be all right?" asked Lorna.

"Oh yeah. I'd like to see somebody *try* to fuck with me, right now." Liza giggled, overflowing with a tingling, adrenal desire to pounce on whoever might be foolish enough to pester her.

"Uh-oh. Maybe you should stay," said Lorna.

"You guys have fun," Liza said, stepping out of the bus with what she imagined was a casually superhuman fearlessness.

Liza had never seen so many tattooed necks before, let alone tattooed faces. A hostile tapestry of punks hung on The Vats fire escape, their green skin-inks growing and winding into one another like kudzu. Inside, Liza stalked around the tubs with sure gravity, throwing back her shoulders, simmering with brave defiance, sparkling like a bomb fuse.

There was a huge bull dyke she knew slightly, a burly, six-foot surfer girl from Huntington Beach who always wore a nun's habit. Liza watched with interest as she drunkenly beat up a junkie named Patto in what looked, to Liza, like slow motion. Liza's mind felt fast and excellent—Patto and the nun were moving through muscular tar with unpupiled eyes; the punches came from minutes away, and her fists sunk heavily into him like he was wet cement. All the while they were slipping, due to tractionless old boots, in a pink mud made of (probably) beer, blood, urine, jism, and industrial detergent. Two skinheads had been thrown down into one of the deep, slick-walled beer vats. A crowd fringed its rim. One of the skinheads had a skateboard and was trying to escape the tub by using the vertical walls as a half-pipe, but with no luck—there was no means for getting the ugly boys out of the modern pit.

Cacophonous rumbling bounced and echoed off the high tiled ceilings, the aural landscape making Liza think of an underwater earthquake.

Liza stared through the kaleidoscopic and crawling hallways toward a glow at the end; her heart jerked to attention. She was sure she saw an enormous set of golden antlers, their shadow cobwebbing the scribbled wall. *Roland?* She began to walk quickly, then began running. *Lead on, Roland,* she thought to herself in what amounted to a little prayer.

The hallway abruptly stopped at a door covered with slitty holes made by throwing knives, and the door opened. It was the squat of a speed-freak boy that Liza had met a few times who went by the name of Creature; Creature had been waiting for his speed-delivery.

"You're not Stan Rancid," said Creature, disappointed.

"You're not Roland Spring," said Liza, equally disappointed.

"Oh well. You want to come in, anyway?" said Creature, who was always happy to show people the bizarre magazine-photo collage that occupied every inch of his wall space and all of his amphetamine-powered productivity. The wall of faces beckoned to Liza; she thought she could see the Golden Stag moving and hiding behind the model-heads; antlers camouflaged behind manicured fingers. *If I just look past the pictures*, she thought, entering the room.

While scanning Creature's wall and squinting, trying to see the primeval forest she knew lurked behind the waxy red lips and pulsating gemstone eyes, Liza was unpleasantly stunned to see a picture of Desiree Baumgarten in an ad for a moisturizing facial soap.

"That girl is so fully cute," said Creature in a tender voice.

Oh for fuck's sake, not HERE, TOO, Liza fumed, having thought she had finally escaped into a different world, away from where the Baumgartens had such smothering leverage. As she looked at the photo, she was mesmerized by the soap in Desiree's hand: a rounded pink bar of perfect smoothness, a magic stone of peace. Liza wanted to lick the soap, to absorb its beautiful, radiant color and feel its silky texture on her tongue. In staring at it, her eyes crossed involuntarily and the picture blurred.

In this blur, Liza saw a vision of herself: cool and perfect, in a spangled white dress, walking toward herself in a bright spotlight, with her hair grown back, shoulder length and blonde as sunshine. She was singing a simple, beautiful love song into a silver microphone, a song she had never heard before. Her eyes were bright and unclouded by nerves—she was relaxed, open, nothing to hide, uniquely lovable and pure. Skies flew past her, an eternity of mornings. The rebirth of spring hummed with deafening force through her bones. A waterfall, filling all space, smashed all filth away.

Purity. And the pink disc of soap swam back into focus.

The concept hit her in the head like a diamond bullet, exploding on impact into a chandelier of intense and brilliant clarity. It was the dawn of Liza's first philosophical revelation; a new perspective:

That's what's always been missing from my life—INNER CLEANLINESS.

A shattering discovery. Suns erotically swallowed suns.

"You got any soap?" asked Liza, who was going to ceremonially eat a small piece.

"Nope," said Creature, who was burning warts off of himself with a piece of dry ice.

Liza rose, queenly and serene. A decision was made: she would no longer frequent the habitats of anyone who did not possess soap, the key to spiritual excellence.

"Thank you for the hospitality," Liza said, in a posh tone.

"You wanna have sex?" asked Creature.

"No thanks," she said, escaping into the hall.

Liza left the loud world of The Vats and retrieved Lorna, to start the long urban hike to where the first Fairfax bus of the morning stopped.

"Come by anytime," said Hammy, his head and skeletal chest emerging white and wormlike from a musky sleeping bag. Lorna bent over to kiss him, hard and playfully sloppy.

Once outside of Hammy's domicile, Lorna sighed happily, her cheeks chapped from whisker burn. The darkness in the east had cracked open; the red predawn was oozing over the black rectangles of the industrial neighborhood.

On the bus ride home, as Lorna slept, Liza struggled to retain her great epiphany as the acid wore off, trying to capture the last straggling sparks of enlightenment before they flew up her mental chimney, or chilled down into the ash of humdrum reality. *It's a lonely world*, Liza decided, looking through the rippling drops of bus-window condensation into the foggy white-noise beyond. *One should strive to be pure and clean.* She stared for a while at the black muck under her fingernails.

Punk rock and its big Fuck You to the system was great, but in her heart of hearts, Liza still felt that famous people were famous for a reason; their incredible luck could only be the result of an unsayable spiritual something. You got famous because other famous people noticed that you, also, had that Thing. If you didn't have it, and wanted to get it, it was very difficult, but there were clues, like Liza had seen—the Holy Antlers and other great signs would appear, to guide your evolution, if you were constantly alert. Liza vowed to watch for these clues very diligently. She knew that deep within herself, there was a better, smarter, cleaner, more talented *über*-Liza that was dormant for the time being but would awaken, given the right set of external cues and circumstances, and burst forth like Superman from his phone booth chrysalis.

Her eyes involuntarily crossed again, and a throbbing circle of cartoon snowflakes swirled stupidly on the seat-back in front of her.

Several days later, Liza, still technically enrolled in the drama class, had to attend the performance of *Searching and Seizures*. At the climax of the show, the earnest group of retarded citizens (Deenie included), with feathers sewn to their shirtsleeves, were onstage performing a "Healing Ritual" where they had to "fly" around a circle of seated, tom-tom–playing drama students. The innocent pleasure of the guileless performers was moving as they flapped around; they clearly loved being in the show. Liza and Lorna, drunk, were thrown out of the theatre for laughing their asses off so hard they couldn't breathe.

"That was so 'tard-sploitational!" Liza yelled, once outside, in mock outrage, but secretly, she was suffering terrible spleen, not being in the production. She badly wanted to play the tom-toms while Deenie stomped around the circle, flying with her dumb little wings and a face of total happiness. Liza felt she'd been cheated out of a crucial step on her road to pristine glory.

Over the next few days, Liza hatched a plan for a dramatic healing ritual of her own. Ideally, it was going to make Tonto Grosvenor not just love her, but, moved by her greatness, break down, weep before his peers, and reform. Her mind churned with power-fantasies. She wanted to terrify Miwok Butte by unleashing the raw, spectral inner might she knew she possessed.

"Forget that guy! He's an asshole!" Lorna nagged wisely.

But Liza didn't listen and began to prepare herself for a metamorphosis, from which she would emerge spectacular.

RITUAL——NEED TO GET:
A sheet? Big white thing
Some whiteface mime makeup?
Knives
Cow heart? (butcher?)
Gasoline/flammable whatever
blowtorch (Ned?)
metal tray thing (not flammable)

There was going to be a dance held, shortly before the end of the school year, with a "Surf's Up!" theme. While other girls bought bikinis and lay in tanning beds around town, Liza gathered props.

"You have, like, this driving need to make a spectacle of yourself, don't you?" Lorna asked as Liza rooted through the Free Box in the houseboat parking lot.

"Success is the best revenge," Liza replied. "But since I don't have success, I'm going to have to do something totally fucking weird and *intense*."

"Don't make me be a part of it, OK?"

"You're not, but believe me: you'll want to see it. Can you set nail-polish remover on fire?"

"I don't think so. Hair spray, maybe."

"Oh my God, check this out, it's so perfect," said Liza, finding a stained, abandoned wedding dress and tattered veil.

"Eeeu," said Lorna.

The school year was ending. While both taking an "incomplete" in aquatics (they would have to take it over again, in order to graduate), Liza and Lorna managed to fudge through their other classes with Cs and C minuses. Kay Gubbins, Liza's English teacher, had taken a personal interest in Liza, whom she perceived to be coming from a truly unfortunate and possibly dangerous household. Liza did not disabuse her of this idea. "I'll bump your grade up to a B if you write me an essay," Kay informed her. "I want you to write and tell me exactly why you chose to look the way you do. I want you to look deep inside of yourself and give me the *real reasons*. I promise you, complete confidentiality—nobody will read it but me."

Liza could smell the cheap psychotherapy and smug desire to "make a difference in a child's life" wafting off of Kay's scarf-garments like a noxious eau de cologne.

"Do you absolutely promise and swear you will never, ever show it to anyone else, or tell anybody anything that's in it, Kay?" Liza asked with earnest and grateful eyes.

"I give you my word, Liza," Kay said with authoritative warmth, pressing Liza's hand.

After two days of deliberating whether or not to tell Kay the truth (and thus implicate Tonto in a way that might earn her a grade boost out of pity, if not actually instigate an official punishment), Liza turned in the following:

WHY I LOOK THE WAY I DO NOW,

by Liza Normal, Abused Child. Kay Gubbins—English Rm. 143

"Girl you better wake up and gimme what I want before I beat you with this crowbar," said the loud, drunk and mean voice of "Uncle Brock," a fat, mean pervert who was wearing my mom's only nightgown. Brock was just another one of my mother's countless lowlife lovers. He, like many, many others, had finally gotten tired of my mother's fatness. He had staggered

drunk into my room wanting sexual favors. He smelled disgustingly like Old Crow and strawberry massage oil.

"Oh please no, sir, I am but a child," I said, clutching Mr. Bunny, my only friend.

Boy, was my life terrible. Beatings with blunt objects and kinky sex with ugly men old enough to be my father were my daily bread and butter. Then, one day, an angel appeared in my room as I was cleaning the butter off of my toe-shoes (don't ask).

The angel was dressed just like Wendy O. Williams of the Plasmatics, in fine patent leather. Her hair was golden and in a large, spiky fin at the top of her head. I had never seen such a stylish hairstyle.

"Alas!" I said to the Angel. "How might I relieve myself of these terrible woes?"

"Lo, Liza, I am the Angel of Punk," she said to me as I shook with awe.

"Go, ye, and shave the sides of your hair, and lighten the rest with Lady Lee 40-volume peroxide hair bleach," she said to me. "That will make thee so ugly that thy mother's obese and fetid companions will bother ye no longer."

"Hallelujah!" I shouted, running to the bathroom to fetch the buzz-clippers.

And ever since that day, whenever a fat, scab-covered ex-con wanders into my bedroom in the dead of night, instead of kinkily violating my young body with his scabby loins, he says, "Jesus Christ, what the fuck did you do to your head?"

And he goes away. All thanks to the Angel of Punk.

THE END.

Kay was very disappointed in Liza and did not raise her grade.

"Sorry, Kay," said Liza with a shrug.

"That kind of thing isn't funny at all," Kay said, hurt that Liza had derailed her act of mercy.

Liza didn't want any official interference in her handling of Tonto Grosvenor.

. . .

Liza almost freaked out when she saw a musty deer-head hanging above the cash register of the butcher shop. *A sign!*

"A whole beef heart?" asked the butcher.

"Yeah. Do you have any extra blood?" asked Liza.

The butcher looked Liza up and down with distaste, with particular attention to the nostril pin.

"What for? You gonna drink it?" he asked.

"Har, har, har, meat-man." Liza scrunched her nose and crossed her eyes at him. The butcher was faintly offended.

On her way out of the butcher shop after securing her purchases, Liza noticed a pile of flyers by the door for the Eiderdijken Academy spring production: *A Midsummer Night's Dream.* The photo, unsurprisingly, was of Chantal Baumgarten (as Titania, Queen of the Faeries), in flowing golden gown, butterfly wings, and a wreath of wildflowers atop her pre-Raphaelite waves of hair, smiling rapturously, dancing with arms outstretched toward a boy . . . Liza's heart twanged like high voltage through a piano wire . . . the boy dancing with Chantal, wearing what looked like a Peter Pan suit, returning her look of giddy, whirling love, could be no other—nobody else had such velvet skin and phosphorescent eyes, such a wide and true smile, such waves of hot life pulsating around him: it was Roland Spring. At the Eiderdijken Academy. Dancing with Chantal, as if their ecstatic moments on the Normal Family Stage never ended, but were *amplified,* snowballing into a rich and ideal partnership, in a wondrous, high-art context too beautiful for Liza to look at without wanting to hurl herself through the glass wall of the refrigerated delicatessen case and lie bleeding with the cutlets. She took several flyers and shoved them into the bag. This surely augured something.

Do whatever you have to do, said a dirty, thrilling little voice from deep in the liquor of Liza's spine.

There was something wild-making about seeing the high school lights on at night; kids who were invisibly shy and boring by day were capable of totally different behavior in nightclothes. Latent pheromones filled the air; potential makeouts transfigured the gym into a bordello lantern; the teens wore the casino-game-faces of inexperienced people trying to locate and inhabit their secret cooler selves.

Lorna pulled Peppy's Honda into the back of the school parking lot, passing boys with surf shorts and Long boards, and girls in grass skirts, leis, and bikini tops, smelling deliciously of cocoa butter.

Lorna looked toward the passenger seat at Liza, already in whiteface and wedding dress; a pale, hugely pregnant bride.

"I'm *so* not being seen with you."

"You'll be sorry you missed it, it's gonna be legendary," Liza replied, trying to hide a large carving knife in her bodice without stabbing herself.

"I wish you hadn't gotten kicked out of drama," Lorna groaned. "You know, I hate to say it, but you're probably still coming here for sophomore year."

"So what. Help me tape this Aqua Net to my leg. Oh shit . . . where's my lighter? Do you have a lighter?"

Lorna pushed the car lighter into the dashboard with a click.

"No, don't you have a lighter-lighter?! You have to find me a *lighter*, a real one, or I'm completely *fucked*," Liza screeched, in panic.

"I'll see what I can do," Lorna said, rolling her eyes and slamming the car door, leaving Liza in the dark to fumble with the pop-top on her Hueblein "The Club" Brandy Alexander: courage in a can.

"This is all you could get?!" Liza asked when Lorna came back twelve minutes later and presented her with a cardboard book of matches. The plastic bag with the beef heart in it, which was wedged inside the control-top of her panty hose, had begun to bleed cold pink juice down her legs.

"I asked and asked, and nobody had a lighter," whined Lorna, clearly just wanting the whole thing to be over. "Maybe it's for the better. They have laws about setting stuff on fire, on campus."

"Fuck their stupid laws made for ordinary people," Liza said, para-phrasing a line from *Valley of the Dolls* that Neville used to quote often.

"That's not a healthy attitude."

"I'm not a healthy girl," Liza growled with hot metallic breath.

"Maybe you're a little *too* healthy," said Lorna, throwing Liza's empty cocktail can over the chain-link fence, onto the baseball field.

"Did you see Tonto? Where is he?"

"When I left, he was at a table with Nikki and some other cretins near the stage. You don't have to do this. We can go back to my house. We could change, and go into the city."

"Quit worrying! It's ART. That's what's so great about this stunt—

if they try to bust me, I can just say they're *repressing* me." Yvette Running-Drum had spoken to her class at length about the repression of females, artists, and female artists. It was a concept that occasionally came in handy.

"I don't think that would do you any good," groused Lorna, lighting a cigarette.

"I'm going. Tell me to 'break a leg.' "

"I'll pull the car around. We're probably going to end up spending the night in juvee."

• • •

Liza waddled through the gym clutching her leaking abdomen, occasionally tripping over the tattered lace hem of the dress in her large combat boots. From beneath the veil she had a pixilated view of students jabbing and whispering to each other, turning to stare at her with chiaroscuro faces of disbelief, amusement, and disgust.

Liza chose a route directly through the middle of the dance floor—the incongruity of her gothic whiteness formed an aura of creepy insanity around her. Dancers in flip-flops and smears of fluorescent zinc pushed back to give her a four-foot radius. Liza became fiendishly aware that she was making people nervous. The remedial disco lights were red, then blue, evoking police cars. "Walk Don't Run" by the Ventures sloshed in muddy, beatless echoes around the bad gym acoustics.

Liza saw the spinning disco ball reflected in Tonto's Vuarnet sunglasses and knew he had seen her. Every heartbeat bashed in Liza's skull; cold sweat ran like tiny snakes down the small of her back. Holding her unborn assault, she stood before Tonto's table, ablaze with terrible intention. His friends, openmouthed and spooked, backed up a little. Liza pulled the large kitchen knife from her cleavage, held it up and let out a savage wail.

Kids stumbled farther away from her; Tonto didn't move.

Liza stabbed herself repeatedly in the large abdomen, brutally ripping at the wedding dress with funereal shrieks until there was a large, tattered hole, through which she was able to push, with yowls of atrocious labor, the bloody, punctured cow heart, which fell with a satisfying wet smack on Tonto's table.

Liza then lifted her skirt (school security was by now alerted and walking quickly toward her) and ripped the masking tape holding the Aqua Net can to her leg. Tonto remained seated, having not so much as flinched through the entire display. Liza lit a match and poised the hair spray; Tonto, seeing the flame, leaned slightly away.

In planning this performance, Liza had envisioned a flamethrower effect: she would hold a lighter with a tall finger of fire under the stream of Aqua Net, the spray would ignite, and she would train an apocalyptic, tube-shaped inferno onto the bloody meat. Instead, she couldn't get the match and hair spray to cooperate—the hair spray kept putting the match out. Liza eventually sprayed down the meat, dropped the hair spray can, and tried to ignite the beef heart manually. But every time Liza lit a match, Tonto leaned over and blew it out. She lit five or six matches, then lit the whole book—he blew that out too, easily, with a wide smile.

"I thought I ordered a baked potato with my Satanic fetus!" cracked Tonto, eyes shimmering. He lost it, laughing so hard at his own joke that his eyes streamed. His friends were equally slayed. Hysterics spread like brushfire through that corner of the gym.

All of the potent, scary shock-energy Liza had entered the gym with was suddenly spitting out of her like the vulgar air from an untied balloon. She didn't know how to deal with her Moment of Power being hilarious. It was paralyzing; her limbs went noodly.

Come up with a comeback, quick, she screamed to herself, but her mind stalled stupidly in the middle of the combat intersection and no words came.

Oooooooooh, Wipe-Out, mocked the Ventures.

Liza snatched her knife, turned, and stormed out of the gym.

Tonto and his people were still laughing, each laugh a mortal blow to her sense of magnificence. *So much for theatrical healing rituals. I need a fucking healing ritual to heal that healing ritual.*

The dance security squad (namely, Mr. Dietch, Ned's ex–square dancing instructor, and two other male teachers) had been watching Liza intently up to this point, unsure as to whether she was pulling a prank or having an actual psychotic episode. Since they would do nothing that might incur a potential lawsuit, they didn't advance toward her until she was steaming toward the exit.

Liza was taken into the gym office, where she petulantly explained her artistic intentions with eye-rolling and pointed exhalations. Her kitchen knife was confiscated. She was let off with a "warning."

"I should have poured the Brandy Alexander all over the fucking thing and drank the hair spray," Liza complained as Lorna drove. Having struggled back into her pants, Liza pulled off the stained wedding dress and tossed it out of the car window, watching through the rearview mirror as it billowed backward into the dark marsh by the road.

"Dude, you're out of your mind," Lorna admonished. "You're just like your mom."

"Don't you *ever* say that!" Liza was suddenly vicious. "How would you like it if I said that about you? You and Sky-Rose are fuckin' *twins.*"

"You have to admit, there was something very Peppy about that whole thing."

"I don't know what the fuck you're talking about."

"Oh my God! The fact that you don't know what I'm talking about is so totally Peppy!" Lorna laughed.

Liza felt her self-hating fang bite into herself and suck.

"You'll probably end up a midwife," Liza grumbled.

"You'll probably end up onstage," said Lorna, knowing that it was what Liza craved most, yet least wanted to be reminded of at that moment.

Liza put her feet on the dashboard and lit a cigarette with the car lighter that had been the harbinger of her evening's failure. As an afterthought, she tossed the car lighter out the window.

"That was dumb," said Lorna.

Liza sighed.

"Pull over."

The Honda swung to the shoulder, popping on loose rocks.

Liza got out and ran back into the chirping night, trying to see the orange coil on the ground before it cooled to black. *Stay hot*, Liza prayed to the lighter. *Just for another minute, please, just stay hot.*

✷ (FADE TO BLACK.) ✷

• • •

For the few days remaining before summer vacation, Liza was something of an antilegend. News of her stunt had traveled; the general consensus was that her unrequited love for Tonto Grosvenor had caused her to completely lose her mind, which was more or less true.

Surprisingly, Yvette Running-Drum somehow received the full, desired effect of Liza's performance; she cornered Liza in the hallway.

"That was incredibly powerful feminist imagery," gushed Yvette, with direct eye contact and a straight face. "It reminded me of the earlier works of Carolee Schneeman. Liza, I'm sorry this year didn't work out. I hope you'll consider being in drama next year."

Liza, wholly stunned, looked into Yvette's face, open and sincere.

"You wish. Fuck your pathetic retard sandbox, you bogus Indian slag," Liza spat, feeling immediately proud of the horrible chain of words she had clicked together, so quickly. Her dealings with Tonto had yielded, finally, one resonant Good: the ability to draw her stiletto tongue and cut people into dice-size cubes with whiplash speed. She fancied herself a rogue samurai of verbal abuse, with one of the most lethal mouths ever to insult the land. Yvette Running-Drum reeled from the blow; her eyes clanged with betrayal. She stiffened and walked quickly away.

Liza suddenly felt so guilty she wanted to cry.

Tonto made the news two days after the dance when he was caught trying to steal a live puff-adder from the reptile wing of the Steinhardt Aquarium. Somehow his previous record was ignored, and the offense was shrugged off as a "boys will be boys" hijink, but rumor had it that he would not return to Miwok Butte; he would be sent away, in the fall, to a boarding school in the Colorado Rockies that had an emphasis on ice climbing. Despite their appalling history, Liza felt like the exposed nerve of a monstrous cavity when she heard the news.

Liza had thought she'd have three more years to cook up a better revenge; after hearing that Tonto was leaving town, she couldn't shake a morbid compulsion to attempt a last-ditch parting shot. The avant-garde abortion gambit might have blown up in her face, but she had a Plan B. It would be fast, scary, and brutal: on the last day of school, she would spray-paint Tonto's face with flat black Rust-Oleum—a hit-and-run attack.

I'll de-face him, she thought, *just like he defaced me*. It would be a serious offense and potentially harmful; Liza was fatalistically resolved to suffer the consequences, whether expulsion, juvenile detention, or both. Lorna knew nothing of the plan; Liza didn't want to risk being saved from herself before she carried it out.

On the last day of school, Liza made her mohawk very tall and very hard, using blow-dried egg whites, the stiffest fixative. She wore a large, off-white men's dinner jacket and hid the spray can in the breast pocket. She lurked the last twenty minutes of the lunch period, hidden near Tonto's locker, her anxious stomach simultaneously nauseated and starving.

Tonto had changed, in the aftermath of the bust—his swaggering cockiness had given way to the broody self-loathing and sickly, insomniac pallor that made his brother Dino appear so elegant. He walked slowly, hunched over, as if weakened by recent surgery. Liza's predatory eyes watched as Tonto removed the papers, binders, and books from his locker and dropped them listlessly into the hall trashcan. More students filed in. As Tonto pocketed his combination lock and started for the double exit doors, Liza materialized in front of him, her hand inside her coat. She was shaking. Her sweaty finger found the button on top of the spray can.

To Liza's complete shock, Tonto ran up and abruptly hugged her, tightly. It was a long, emotional hug filled with terrible regret. Liza heard a faint hiss from the can, where his chest was crushing her trigger finger.

"I'm sorry I fucked up your life," he said quietly in her ear.

Tears threatened to charge up Liza's throat; she swallowed them.

"Don't flatter yourself," she managed, with an artificial lip-curl. "My life was fucked up way before you."

Tonto released his grip, looked at Liza, and gave her a bitter half-smile before merging into the now crowded hallway, where a bustle of last-minute yearbook-signings was taking place. Liza watched the back of Tonto's head bounce among the other heads until she couldn't see it anymore, the way she once watched the white spark die on the family's old television as the tube blinked off, leaving a faint ring of ultrasonic lint in her ears.

Liza looked down at the front of her jacket. The black paint stain soaking outward from her breast pocket was an interesting Rorschach blot: an Arabic numeral that had yet to be invented. She looked intently at it, trying to see (as a hopeful fortune-teller might cheat the interpretation of clumped tea leaves) if there was any way of looking at the stain that might suggest an antler.

PART IV

PYGMALIENATED

Fairfax, California, June 1984

FTER THE DEPARTURE OF TONTO, the star villain, Liza's sophomore and junior years were chapters (like those in most of her schoolbooks) that she skimmed but mostly skipped, and would remember almost nothing about later in her life, apart from a few clutzy, off-campus promiscuities, jealousies, rejections, and embarrassments (all of which the mind recalls with greater ease than moments of boredom or mild pleasure). Liza and Lorna were a clique of two, and like proper outcasts kept a snobbish distance from the rest of their schoolmates, enjoying their social activities and occasional gropings in the alleys of North Beach and Chinatown. There were arguments at home and in parking lots, and the usual monetary anxiety chewed on everyone (Noreen wisely applied for food stamps). Lorna graduated, being in the senior class of 1984; Liza was her prom date. They both wore black plastic garbage bags with holes cut out for the head and arms, making a statement about "how bullshit the whole spend-a-bunch-of-money-on-a-dress-that-looks-like-a-fucking-wedding-cake-thing is."

Liza was unable to cope with the idea of high school without Lorna, so she opted to take the GED (or "General Equivalency" exam) and skip her senior year altogether; there were always classes available at the community college, in the unlikely event that she decided to get serious about higher education.

After various psychiatrists made it officially clear to the school authorities that he was incapable of returning to class, Ned was free to become a hermit. He worked long hours with scraps of colored Mylar and a slide projector. With a razor blade, tweezers, and vast patience, he would glue confetti-size specks of the plastic film to blank slides, then shine the abstract designs on the theatre wall, for his own amusement.

Ike liked these little creations a lot and insisted on paying for a few of them—he and Mike hung them over their oven on the fan hood, with magnetized clips; every time their burner light was on, the slides came awake like little stained-glass windows. They got a lot of compliments on them; Ike always passed the praise along to Ned, even though he knew Ned would just blush and change the subject.

Peppy had an awakening, of sorts; she got bored with her unchecked indulgences. The allure of sucking down whole packages of Marshmallow Pinwheels in the dark finally wore thin. She began venturing further out into the theatre than she had in months, and began drinking coffee in the morning again, instead of generic beer—a baby step toward actual motivation. Noreen saw her chance and recruited Peppy to help mop the theatre floor; this task evolved into a major spring-cleaning. Curtains were opened and light was allowed into the big room for the first time in ages; dusty cobwebs and creeping molds were exorcised with Lysol, refreshing the soul of the theatre.

"Ow," said Ned, when muddy windows were pried open near his lighting booth and squeegeed. Unaccustomed to brightness, he stuck his head in a pillowcase, his nose smarting from chemical Lemon Freshness.

Mike and Ike always came over on Wednesday nights, to watch cocktail-addled TV with Peppy. The first week of summer, *My Fair Lady* was on, and Ike was able to convince Ned to come upstairs to witness "Audrey Hepburn—arguably the most beautiful movie star ever."

Even Liza and Lorna, who ordinarily shunned family events, eventually slunk into the room, when they heard Mike and Ike laughing at a few of the more misogynistic Bernard Shaw lines. Noreen was delighted to see all the family and friends in the same room again; she made popcorn and instant pudding.

The Cecil Beaton costumes rebooted Peppy's imagination and soon had it swarming with fancy possibilities. Beauty, Peppy had always remarked, was "fifty percent attitude and eighty-five percent artifice." Given the right hat at Ascot, anything was possible, even the resurrection of her own cremated self-esteem.

"I'm going to reopen the theatre," she announced at the end of the film, before the orchestra had played down all the credits.

"As what?" asked Mike.

"As a *theatre*," said Peppy, with some defensiveness.

"What about Ned?" Ike asked, knowing that tromping tap-dancing girls through the same room where Ned jittered in his booth-nest wasn't going to work out.

"You could get him to rig up the stage lights again," Peppy said. "You like projects, don't you Ned."

Ned got up with eloquent silence and started back down to the stage area, to hide in his booth. Everyone stopped to listen to his heavy feet carefully creaking down the stairs.

"Why don't you have Ned be a nude trapeze artist, while you're at it?" Liza asked, puncturing the worried hush. "He could just fly around, in front of crowds of people, naked. He'll love that."

"Reopening the theatre is a good idea," said Noreen, quietly.

Peppy's reborn theatrical ambitions made her reevaluate Liza with fresh eyes. "If you're going onstage again, you'll need to wash some of that crap out of your hair," Peppy remarked. Liza had allowed her mohawk to grow out, but her head now resembled a spiky pink sea anemone. Lorna's blue-black hair had matted into dreadlocks, into which she twisted small fishing-weights and bits of broken silver jewelry. The girls were in the Normal family kitchen, dribbling undiluted bleach onto their new jean jackets. "Fix your hair and maybe I'll let you be in the show," Peppy said in coaxing tones.

"*Let me*? You couldn't pay me to be in that shit, Wigwam," Liza barked. ("Wigwam" was Liza's new name for Peppy, since she wore wigs and had become somewhat conical in body-shape.)

Liza was dead set on refusing participation in any further Normal

Family productions; the last one had been so emotionally excruciating it practically killed her.

Shortly after Lorna's graduation, Lorna and Sky-Rose had a falling-out. Lorna had seduced her mother's pot connection one afternoon while Sky-Rose was out, according to Lorna's description, "yanking a baby out of some masochistic hippie." The pot dealer, Clive, was an amusing, leather-jacket-wearing, twenty-nine-year-old ex–music critic who used his faded 'zine articles to lure young rocker chicks into his houseboat and "photograph" them in various stages of undress. Lorna had always had a little thing for Clive, and her wayward, punk-rock cheerleader outfit was more than he could resist; Clive agreed, with panting complicity, to provide Lorna with all of the superior marijuana she thought she could sell, provided she came through with the cash up front.

Shortly thereafter, Sky-Rose found Lorna's stash of profoundly debilitating Humbolt "heroiuana" (which was of a considerably superior quality than the weed that Clive had been selling to Sky-Rose), and accused Lorna of trying to usurp her drug business altogether. An epic battle culminated in Lorna dragging an overstuffed, plaid nylon suitcase down the creaky gangplank of *The Amnion*.

"Your karma's gonna bite you in the ass, kid," Sky-Rose hollered.

Lorna kicked her heavy bag toward the parking lot, away from the moldy dome, screaming horrible epithets at her mother, most involving the female anatomy with which Sky-Rose was so familiar.

"I swear, that woman makes me want to have my crotch sealed up with cement," Lorna seethed, hurling her suitcase into the theatre vestibule; the cheap nylon burst open like the skin of a baked potato, spilling out her clothes.

Lorna stayed with Liza in the theatre for a few weeks, until, feeling the power of financial independence that arose from selling pot to a discreetly expanding clientele, she moved into the Lucky Drive trailer park in Greenbrae, renting a small camper from an ex-girlfriend of Clive's.

"It's a fucking crash-pad paradise," said Liza, admiringly.

"You know it," Lorna said with pride.

At one end of the trailer was a built-in couch; a Formica dining table jutted out from the wall. There was a tiny closet and bathroom with a shower stall, separated from the minuscule kitchen by a vinyl accordion door. In the back, twin beds were clamped to the walls. The tawny faux wood-grain veneer over everything was leopard-spotted with cigarette burns, but it was a totally serviceable, compact home. Within two weeks of Lorna's moving into the trailer, Liza, who had lately been frothing into a rage merely by being in the same room as Peppy, moved most of her stuff onto one of the twin beds. Lorna didn't balk; they were together all the time, anyway.

"This is the beginning of a whole new era of greatness," Liza said, opening a plastic bag of campfire marshmallows and spilling them all over the couch.

Though Liza was still crusading for the same mystical television-glow that had been the revelation of her acid trip, it had been a long time since she had seen any divine antlers. She still washed her hands more than usual, in an effort to purify herself with the immaculacy of soap, and she still wholly intended to be famous, but her lofty intentions of Spotless Inner Radiance were giving way, from lack of outer nourishment, to her usual sullen and rebellious teen affect. She had heard some interesting news about Roland Spring: the Baumgarten family had helped Roland obtain a large scholarship to the prohibitive Eiderdijken Academy (who were grateful to add a person of color to their rosters, thereby proving their liberalness), and underwrote the remainder of his tuition as a testimony to his rare talent. He was living, Liza knew, with his mother in Marin City, a one-square-mile indentation in the Marin hills near the Sausalito houseboats, where shipyard workers had lived during World War II; their barracks had become subsidized housing for the black community, which was segregated from the rest of Marin County by freeways and a swamp. White people generally didn't have any business in Marin City, except at the bus station hub, and at the flea market, a vast bazaar of human refuse that covered an unpaved lot the size of a football field every weekend. Liza would roam through it on hungover Sundays, searching for divine clues and hoping to run into Roland.

(Flea markets, the Bazaars of Human Refuse, can work as psychic axis points for a kind of gestalt-object-summoning-geomancy. They are the Twilight Zone between being and noth-

ingness, where inanimate things irrevocably lost in the past materialize anew, as if resurrected by sheer sentiment alone, and things only half-dreamed-of emerge fully formed from the back of unlikely vans:

That is the one Bill Cosby album that completes my collection. I just found the glass part for my grandmother's broken percolator. That's the Holly Hobbie lunch box I had when I was seven. That trivet has the exact same heraldry symbol as my linoleum. And that is the most wonderful pair of silver leather pants I have ever seen.

There is always the hope of finding a buried treasure or rich archaeological artifact: a stolen Picasso, a necklace of human teeth. Given the rich bounty of possibilities, a visitor might have luck finding long-lost people, as well as things, for who can resist the unanswerable, Zen-koan-like questions that the weird jetsam of our collective consumerism inspires?

Who would ever take a bad gold statue of two people fucking, seal it in a Lucite block, and call it a "coffee table"? How could anyone just "casually" collect Nazi war memorabilia? Why does that filthy, eyeless Snoopy cost $300? And aren't we all through with redwood burl by now?)

So far, Liza had accumulated several old girdles and an occasional churro at the flea market, but no sight of Roland Spring.

Lorna now had an actual job, to supplement her pot income and give some semblance of respectability to her cash flow. The Fotostop was a quick film-developing joint in a strip mall in San Anselmo. The manager felt that Liza did not exactly exude the cheerful competence expected of a Fotostop employee, but Lorna gave him three thumb-size Indica buds in exchange for Liza's gainful employ.

The Fotostop was more interesting than what the girls had expected. San Anselmo was home to a large and affluent bondage scene that had no compunction about photographing each other *in flagrante perverto*, then dropping the film off at the cheapest local processing joint. Liza and Lorna began looking forward to these rolls—there was always a good surprise or gross-out in them—people entirely mummified in black rubber with only snorkels to breathe through; scrotums with so many clothespins attached to them, they resembled porcupines. All the young Fotostop employees, including Liza and Lorna, made duplicates of the hairier photos and tacked them to a large bulletin board near the processing machine, out of sight of the customers. Though many of the bondage enthusiasts in the photos wore black leather half-masks, they were still mostly recognizable.

"*Look,*" Liza once whispered fiercely as she and Lorna were buying cans of chili in the supermarket. She pointed at a man who looked like a company executive, striding through the meats section in a navy blue blazer. "That's *Donkey Kong!*"

It was astonishing to the girls that anyone with such intense personal proclivities could walk around, in the daylight hours, doing anything so ordinary as selecting ground chuck.

A black bodybuilder, naked and dwarf-size, started showing up in a lot of the photos. The girls couldn't believe their luck. In one, he sported a powdered, French court wig; in another, he was wearing what looked like a chain mail bib and flexing his well-defined abs and biceps, standing with one boot on the head of a groveling blond man. They began to live for pictures of the flamboyant "Power Dwarf."

While Lorna was in the back of the Fotostop one afternoon, packing shots of a truly ugly baby into a paper envelope, Liza ran to her, squiggling with excitement.

"*He's here, Ohmigod,*" Liza gushed. "Come *quick!*"

Lorna scurried to the front.

The Power Dwarf, dressed in tiny Dr. Martens boots, a small motorcycle jacket, and a black leather cap with a chain slung over the brim, looked like the smallest leather-daddy the girls had ever seen.

"What are you staring at?" he asked in an insouciant voice. "Watch yer manners!"

"You just look really familiar," said Lorna. Liza nearly died.

"I should look familiar, I'm sure you've seen about a million pictures of me," the dwarf admitted, matter-of-factly.

"Are you Gary Coleman?" Liza asked, deadpan.

Lorna tried to disguise the hacking laugh that escaped her for a cough.

The dwarf raised an eyebrow.

"Don't tell me you haven't been staring at my beautiful black ass, I know you have," he said with what struck Liza and Lorna as an egomania as oversize as he was undersize. "Go get my pictures."

"No really, you're a movie actor, aren't you?" Liza asked, trying to get the dwarf to aggrandize himself more.

"Actually, yes!" he said brightly, flashing a magnificent set of white teeth. "I have been in several made-for-television movies."

"Would you like to make a contribution to Jerry's Muscular Dystrophy kids?" Lorna asked, holding out the slotted can of change that had long since become the girls' private beer fund.

The Power Dwarf sniffed. "I know you ain't giving that shit to Jerry. You best get my photos, now, before I come behind that counter and spank your fanny."

It was the best thing to happen to them in weeks.

The girls, through a barrage of questions that set the dwarf up to brag about himself, got him to hang around the shop for over an hour. His stories about the foot-worshipping scene in nearby Cotati were hilarious, and the girls were delighted with him. Later that night, Liza, Lorna, and their excellent new friend, DelVonn D'Shawn, found themselves traveling to a bar in the city in Lorna's recently purchased (used) Plymouth Duster.

"What's your middle name?" Liza asked him, thrilled to have such an exciting new person around.

"Chaka Khan," DelVonn purred, turning the rearview mirror toward himself to comb his invisible eyebrows with a tiny brush.

DelVonn brought the girls to his habitual hangout: a bar covered with Christmas ornaments all-year-round, known for its trans-gendered clientele, called Cape Horn. Cape Horn was host to the third-sex community in San Francisco's squalid Tenderloin district, where most of the bad habits of the city circled the drain. Home to hardcore sex clubs, methadone clinics, and the attendant glamour of these walks of life, the Tenderloin held a vast bohemian fascination for adventuresome young people and was usually an easy place to drink without ID. "FUCK SEX, LET'S PLAY DRESS UP" was the largest graffito on the unisex bathroom wall of the bar, right over a mothball-filled trough that men hiked up their dresses to urinate into.

A stage was set up in the back of the bar, for lip-synching shows and midnight productions by a theatrical troupe known as the Cock-a-Zoids, run by two of San Francisco's premiere drag queens, LaTuna Canyon, the "Drag Queen Private Dick," and Her Highness Ragina Victoria, a 380-pound black she-male who favored tiaras, tea cozies, souvenirs of the Prince Charles/Lady Diana wedding, and/or anything else that smacked, however tackily, of British royalty.

Style-wise, Lorna and Liza had abruptly dropped punk, since the scene was dying off from a combination of neo-Nazism and heroin abuse, and embraced a more ethnic phase. Three hit movies came out the summer of 1984 that informed the girls' new trend-phase: Prince's *Purple Rain, Beat Street,* and *Breakin'* (the progenitor of the more popular *Breakin' II: Electric Boogaloo*). These, like *Fame,* were Victory-Via-Uninhibited-Song-and/or-Dance-template-movies targeting a young, mostly nonwhite demographic, which brought a new kind of mating dance to the silver screen by saying to the adventurous young girls of America, *poor brown boys are filled with sex, rhythm, and music, such as you are unlikely to find in the suburbs. Their hips are snakier and their eyes are dark and wet from volatile sensitivities (and eyeliner). Can't you just feel your foot-less lace tights melting off your little white legs on the dance floor?*

These films invented a phenomenon loosely referred to as "The Street"—a multicultural, utopian zeitgeist built around the welding of inner-city dance-club music to New Wave Eurotrash hair and fashion accessories. The "latest sensations" in dance, music, style, and graffiti-art came from "The Street"—if you expressed yourself better than anyone else on the highly competitive "Street," there was the promise of not just fame on your own terms, but also a supercharged, Hot Cherry, ultrasexual Love; the desperate rhythms of your fight for survival would naturally evolve into a steamy carnal slow-dance in lingerie. (What a blessed "Street" it was! Oh, to redon those studded plastic pants of Hope!)

. . .

Liza loved *Breakin'* and saw it four times in one week. As outrageously dumb as the movie was, she never wanted it to end; if she could have walked out of her life forever and into the lives of "Turbo" (played by Michael "Boogaloo Shrimp" Chambers, whose genius for the folk art of break dancing turned his skinny body into an astonishing, rubbery machine) and "Ozone" (played with a minimum of acting skill, but a maximum of Clark Gable-y charisma, animal magnetism, and Zoot Suit panache by Adolfo "Shabba-Doo" Quinones), Liza would have done it gladly.

The plot of *Breakin'* involved Turbo and the handsome Ozone transforming Kelly, a privileged white jazz dancer, into a ghetto Street Dancer, over several sweaty afternoons. It was the blackification of *Rocky II,* for girls—A *My Fly Lady,* if you will, wherein the Henry Higgins trains Eliza to mimic the ways of the socioeconomically underprivileged, that she might be admitted into low society.

There is an obligatory "Big Dance Contest," but for reasons of racism, dance-establishment snobbery, and a dress code disallowing torn T-shirts and spiky wristbands, Turbo, Ozone, and Kelly, the best "Street" dancers in LA, aren't allowed to compete.

In the climactic scene, Kelly finds Ozone at the beach, angrily throwing rocks into the water with several bandannas tied around his ankles.

"We don't fit into your world. Because we don't have the right *credentials,*" Ozone snarls, his voice full of minority pain. "You don't know how I *feel!*"

"You know what your problem is? Your problem is *you*. You're a Quitter!" yells Kelly. (Roses fall from heaven. Red carpets ejaculate out of a golden volcano. The Format-God is sated, and there is rich bounty for all men.)

"Come on," sneers Ozone. "I want you to see what real dancin's all about."

Ozone leads Kelly farther down the beach, and there, on the sidewalk, are a bunch of breakin' street dancers, one of whom is a paraplegic who spins on his head and crutches, swinging his small, atrophied legs in the air like a windmill.

"You see his face?" Ozone says somberly. "That's dancin', Kelly."

.   .   .

"That's *entertainment*," Liza whispered to DelVonn, on her third viewing of the film.

"Bring on the gimps!" DelVonn said, in full voice.

"Sssssssshhhhhh," said the people behind them.

There was a melancholic, carnal starvation in Liza that *Breakin'* tantalized—as well as she could define it, it was a hunger to dance with a feral brown man who had the kind of undeniable talent and rude will that makes dreams come true against impossible odds. Liza had never had a fan-crush on anybody before, but midway through *Breakin'* she felt the same insuperable, Roland Spring–like pain in her chest cavity—like somebody was scraping out her insides with a vibrating melonballer—over Shabba-Doo, the actor/dancer playing Ozone. Fan-love was qualitatively different in that requital was exponentially more hopeless than an unreturned crush on a nonfamous boy. This frustrated love crawled into Liza and magnetized her limbs; it made her wear spandex dance tights and extra belts, and compelled her to dance like Madonna.

It infuriated her that Ozone and Kelly never kiss in the movie, despite a heady current of attraction—they're "just friends." Presumably, the producers thought the interracial makeout would be too controversial, but Liza felt the kiss to be a glaring omission. One morning when Lorna was out, she began to write what she felt was the missing scene:

BREAKIN'
THE MISSING SCENE

By ~~L. Normal~~ Liz Lamron

Ozone leads Kelly through the door of his place, after the big contest. They are both still totally high on the energy of winning the biggest dance contest!!

He looks her over and his eyes start filling with smoking passion. "Girl, you know what I'm gonna do to you now?" he asks, a sly smile crossing his full, Latin lips.

"No, what?" asks Kelly, starting to feel hot under her leotard as slow, sexy music comes in over the radio (El DeBarge?). It is a hot night and the sea breeze is blowing

through the window. Kelly's spandex leaves little to Ozone's imagination, but he wants to see what's under it anyway, and BAD.

He steps up. She stares at him, standing still. He gently pulls down the suspenderlike straps on the top layer of her leotard outfit and she gets goose bumps that make her turned on even more.

Ozone stares at her hungrily. He then grabs her backside with his strong hands and digs his fingers into her fleshy womanlyness. Her head tips back as she takes in a gasp of excited air. He tears the other part of her leotard top off with his teeth as she moans with pleasure ~~and is topless~~.

They take each other's many belts off for a long time, gazing into each other's eyes with animal heat and total tension!

Ozone is totally out of his mind with anticipation as his strong, muscular, brown body hurls the dancer/gymnast to the bed. She wriggles sexily out of the rest of her dance-pants and shows herself to his pleasure. He loses his mind, practically, it's so hot staring down at her total nudity. His shiny, brown biceps and shoulder muscles flex as he powerfully grabs her hips and takes her with a dancer's tender brutality.

That's good, Liza thought. *"A dancer's tender brutality." I write my ass off.*

Her body arches back and makes erotic dance-shapes as she backbends with passion. He licks her unclothed torso hungrily. She claws at his gyrating Latino-muscled back and backside, crazed with satisfaction. Thigh and ab muscles grind sweatily, wet lips part in extasy. Their faces are shown in sillowette with the sun rising between them and it is clear they have been at it all night!

In the morning they are tangled in sheets together.

"I love you, Special K," says Ozone, looking like he's almost about to cry.

"I love you too," she says back.

Liza felt extremely proud of herself; she knew the scene was hot. It worked for her. She closed her diary and rebuttoned her pants.

• • •

It pleased Liza that DelVonn was an actor—"talking shop" with him made her feel more actress-y. Aside from sporadic TV work, he had also been in Cock-A-Zoid productions at Cape Horn, such as *Caligula Goes West,* where he played a shepherd in assless chap-pants. One night at the bar, he introduced Lorna and Liza to LaTuna Canyon and Ragina Victoria.

"Liza's an actress! She worked with Neville!" DelVonn shouted. The Cock-A-Zoids naturally knew of Neville Vanderlee and respected his work.

"Can you sing?" LaTuna asked loudly enough to be heard over the disco anthem "Born to Be Alive."

"She totally sings!" yelled Lorna.

"We need a Christina Crawford!" Ragina exclaimed, grabbing Liza's arm as if she had no intention of ever letting her leave, nearly spilling her frozen green cocktail.

Thus, Liza was absorbed into the Cock-A-Zoid production of *Beneath the Valley of Mommie Dearest.*

The theatrical conceit was that Joan Crawford (played by LaTuna) was a nymphomaniacal motorcycle-hellcat not unlike Tura Satana in *Faster Pussycat, Kill! Kill!,* who sexually brutalized big Hollywood moguls in order to secure film roles. As Crawford's adopted child Christina (DelVonn was playing the role of her brother Christopher), Liza's mandate was to act like she relished being beaten by her famous mother. "Look, Mommie Dearest! I used a wire hanger to hang up my beautiful clothes *again*," Christina would provoke, writhing with perversion.

The whole show was a vehicle designed for LaTuna to make heavily lipsticked, kidney-shaped grimaces and fly into campy fits of psychosexual wrath while Virgil Ortiz, the synthesizer accompanist, played Hitchcock violin-shrieks from the classic shower scene : *Yite! Yite! Yite! Yite!*

At Cape Horn, Liza and Lorna found a play zone in which everything ordinarily considered to be depraved, criminal, or depressing was hysterically funny, including them. The Cock-A-Zoids were loud and tragically amusing people, who lived action-packed, crisis-fueled lives filled with squalor, drugs, betrayal, mild violence, evictions, injustice, promiscuity, theft, and vermin, glossed over with cheap makeup and clad in loud, oversize banquet-wife finery from Thrift Town. The tiny backstage area was a breeding ground for the most hair-raising gossip Liza had ever been exposed to, either in life or on television: a nonstop Tijuana opera of jealous rage provoking hypodermic stabbings, perpendicular "T-bone" auto collisions, cosmetic surgery malfeasance, and sectional couch arson.

The production, while impoverished, had some good moments. LaTuna, six foot three inches of wiry enthusiasm, made great hash of Faye Dunaway's strange, dramatic line-deliveries (ten pregnant seconds of crazy-eyed staring beforehand, for extra *oomph*). Liza and DelVonn looked naturally hilarious as brother and sister, fidgeting in cheap blonde wigs and matching nautical ensembles.

In one scene, Christina provokes Mommie by refusing to eat the hard, green petrified rabbit on her dinner plate (They borrowed the dead rabbit from the Catherine Deneuve horror movie, *Repulsion*; dramaturgical potluck), so Mommie gives Christina a Flowbee Precision Vacuum Haircut, as punishment.

Ragina found emotional peaks in the *Mommie Dearest* text that naturally suggested a burst into song:

"DON'T FUCK WITH ME, FELLAS! THIS AIN'T MY FIRST TIME AT THE RODEO!" LaTuna would shout, climbing on the PepsiCo boardroom table in a pair of black vinyl over-the-knee boots.

"Mercy!" the executives would shout, groveling on their knees.

The ensuing original song, *I'm a Bigger Monster Than You*, was Liza's favorite.

The play ended with a nice piece of minor pyrotechnics, in which Joan Crawford, before her death, booby-traps her casket so that it explodes when Christina and Christopher put a flower in her dead hands, killing them both.

"You know, it's actually kind of moving," said Ragina Victoria at the technical rehearsal, munching Scottish shortbread cookies out of a tin.

The girls were leading a late-nite life, sleeping most of the day in Lorna's trailer and rising at one to three in the afternoon, when their Fotostop shifts began. Rehearsals for *Mommie* four nights a week meant a lot of bus trips with no reimbursement, but Liza felt the "exposure" would be worth it. Besides—transferring buses meant stopping in Marin City and a possible glimpse of Roland Spring, so the journey always inspired wiggly feelings of hope.

Liza went home to Fairfax one Saturday morning to retrieve some old clothes and found Peppy and Mike embroiled in preparations for *My Fair Lady*.

"Oy, Ayeee, Oye, Ower, You," Peppy was yowling in a deplorable take on cockney vowels.

"Better," said Mike, who, in addition to directing the production, was also going to be playing the role of Henry Higgins, since ninety percent of the cast (all paying "moderate fees" to be in the production) were unfulfilled Marin housewives. Many of the lesser roles needed to be gender-reversed; Peppy and Mike had to search high and low for a Captain Pickering. Finally the local mailman, a short Chinese guy named Earl Tang, plucked the flyer off the door, confessing that he "always wanted to be an actor." In terms of "experience," he told them he had once been a card counter in Las Vegas. "Watch: poker face!" Earl said proudly, then gave them a squinty, tough-guy expression, with his thin mouth turning down at the edges.

"That's pretty convincing," said Mike.

Earl Tang had smiled, winking at Peppy.

Ike, after several days of intense negotiations, had finally convinced Ned to vacate the lighting booth and move back into what had once been his bedroom. Liza's remaining things were packed into a large cardboard box.

"You want to take this, or should I give it to the Salvation Army?" asked Noreen. Liza snatched the box out of her grandmother's hands.

"I want it! God! You were just gonna give it all away?!"

"Nobody thought you wanted that stuff," said Ned. "It's been lying around for months." Liza had semiofficially "left home" but was secretly hurt that the bedroom to which she had assumed she could always come back was now being taken over (she half-imagined the mess she left behind remaining forever unchanged, in her honor, and eventually glassed-in, so that fans might view her humble beginnings). It was obvious that Ned, who had taken to wearing knit ski masks even in the house, could no longer share a room with anyone—his anxiety around other people, even his own family, had only grown more intense.

Liza tried to connect with him in her usual sisterly fashion.

"Ned, lemme see your face!" she yelled, trying to yank his mask off.

"DON'T!" he shouted, pulling away violently. "Leave me alone!"

"I'm doing a play, in the city," Liza told Peppy, handing her a mimeographed flyer for *Beneath the Valley of Mommie Dearest,* featuring an image of LaTuna screaming in a blue-clay complexion mask. Liza was proud that the production was in "The City" (which sounded professional and made Peppy's theatre seem hopelessly provincial).

Peppy read the flyer carefully.

"Do you strip in it?" Peppy asked.

"No!! Jesus!" Liza hollered in outrage. "Why would you even ask me that?!"

"I know about that bar."

"You've never been there!"

"It's drag queens," said Peppy with a snobbish air.

"So!?"

"So you can't say it's serious theatre."

Liza thought she would leap across the table and start bashing Peppy's head against the wall.

"And YOU'RE doing *serious theatre*?" Liza fumed.

Peppy sidestepped the character assassination by becoming even more haughty, as if Liza was too low for her opinions to have any value.

"I do legitimate family entertainment. If you'd rather do campy, gay bar crap, that's your business, but I think you're making a mistake, if you want a career in the performing arts."

Liza blazed out of the room, telling herself that she was *glad* that Ned had taken over their bedroom; now, she had to "face up to the reality" (romantically amplifying the drama of the situation) that she had "no home to return to."

"Liza!" Noreen croaked as Liza was stomping down the sidewalk toward the bus station, awkwardly shouldering the large box (filled with trash she would never use).

Liza stopped and watched her grandmother, who seemed pale and smaller, jog up in a wobbly way. Liza's soul clenched when she noticed that Noreen was wearing cheap shower shoes and was also holding an orange and a banana.

"I thought you might want snacks for the trip," Noreen said, feeling bad that she couldn't have produced something more substantial.

Liza didn't want to cry—she furiously resisted crying, but her little grandmother harpooned through all her layers of defense.

"I'm not hungry," said Liza, swallowing a sharp tangle of emotions. She didn't know how to cope with an orange or a banana on the bus, and felt disgusted by her own powerlessness against life's indignities.

Noreen sighed. "Well, I'd like to see that play you're in, anyway." She stuck the fruit into the front pockets of her zippered sweatshirt.

"You can't come to that play, Gramma. It's too late at night."

"Past ten?" asked Noreen.

"Yeah. It starts after midnight."

"That's too late for me."

"I know."

A loud van went by.

"You should try to get along with your mama," said Noreen.

Liza could not, for the life of her, imagine calling Peppy anything so benign as "Mama."

"I can't," said Liza, feeling wretched.

As Liza watched her reflection crying in the bus window on her way back to the trailer, she imagined herself sitting in the audience, watching the movie of her life, and feeling moved by her portrayal of herself. Her crying redoubled, but with more beauty, dignity, and pouty French lips. The bows of sad violins sawed across her heartstrings. She envisioned Roland Spring watching her too, his heart also breaking from the depth and purity of her performance; she established the shot in her mind, the flattering angle at which he would see her, the way his teary eyes would look, illuminated by her forty-foot face.

Liza walked down the red carpet to receive her Academy Award.

"I want to thank Roland Spring, most of all. I never could have done it without you, Roland." She kissed the statuette. Liza also thanked her grandmother, but not her mother. She couldn't decide whether or not to thank Ned. As an afterthought, she thanked Lorna.

Beneath the Valley of Mommie Dearest got off to a nice start. DelVonn sometimes appeared in low-level bondage films, locally produced by Centaur Productions, a small company that also put out smutty newspapers such as *Heft* (for gay men) and *Sorority* (for straight men) that could be found in coin boxes in sleazy, touristy, or businessman-heavy parts of town. Both papers were primarily devoted to ads for sex shows, outcall massage, escort services. Due to DelVonn's long affiliation with Centaur, *Heft* sent out a "reviewer," who praised the show generously and gave *Mommie* a full-page ad, featuring LaTuna smiling while strangling DelVonn with one hand and Liza with the other. Because of this nice plug, Cape Horn was packed to the rafters with demimonde types, come showtime.

Since Liza was the only organic female on the stage, the rare occasions in which a straight male drifted into the club (curiosity seekers and junkies darting in to use the rest room, usually), she looked, by comparison, to be the daintiest, smoothest-skinned young beauty in five states. The irony was not lost on Liza that the one venue in which she looked like a normal, cute, teen ingenue was a context in which men were transforming into women.

One night, a beautiful, young, light-brown man came into the club, in a white suit, white cap, white leather tennis shoes, and white V-necked T-shirt. Liza felt her entire field of vision squeeze into a laser point and bore into him, captivated. He had such satiny thin skin and pronounced muscle, his body looked tongue-sculpted from a block of butterscotch toffee. He was accompanied by a B-rate actor Liza recognized from small roles in several teen pictures—Liza knew his face but not his name.

"Do you know who that guy is?" Liza asked, panting.

"That's that movie star, *M———*. He's a big queen."

"No, not him, the guy in white."

"Oh! That's ChoCho!" said DelVonn. "He's fabulous. He knows lots of famous people."

"What's his deal?" asked Liza, totally transfixed.

"He sells coke to celebrities," said DelVonn, with an admiring sigh.

"He's really good-looking," Liza gaped.

"So? He's *straight*."

Liza couldn't take her eyes off of ChoCho. She asked everyone about him—Ragina, the bartenders, anyone, triangulating her information.

ChoCho Santocha was one-quarter black, one-quarter German, one-quarter Thai, one-quarter Bolivian; all silky slickness and infectious charm, having seemingly inherited the best aspects of each of his backgrounds. He had a pantherine way of moving, flirted with everyone equally, and gave big tips. People thought he was gay when first meeting him, since he was gentle and sweet and had no aversion to gay bars (homosexuals bought drugs like anyone else), but behind his graceful manner and pretty, expressive hands was the threat of a quick, deadly ass-whomping; he was reportedly a gifted Muy Thai boxer. His car, a 1982 Nissan 280ZX, had been detailed and customized to Lowrider show perfection: everything—the hubcaps, the door handles, the velvet diamond-tuck interior, the windshield wipers—was "coke white," in the patois of his auto-subculture.

Liza could barely concentrate on her role in the show, she was so distracted by ChoCho. During Act III, there was a rolling catfight between Mommie and Christina. LaTuna and Liza grunted like a Wimbledon death-match. Ragina cued a tape recording of glass breaking, furniture splintering.

"You love it! Don't you! You LOVE TO MAKE ME HIT YOU!!" LaTuna howled, shaking Liza until her head was a blur, then giving her a juicy sock in the jaw (Ragina loudly whapped a belt, backstage).

"YES!!" Liza screamed with delirious lust.

Liza heard ChoCho burst out laughing.

"Ho! That shit is dark!" she heard him say.

I made him laugh!!!

Aside from ChoCho's guest, the audience raptly enjoyed the show. The movie guy was too busy chain-smoking, sniffing irritably, and creeping into the bathroom every few minutes.

At the curtain call, the nicely drunk audience gave a semi-standing ovation. Ragina picked up her heavy skirts and rushed onstage, shouting, "Author, Author!" for herself; the clapping resurged.

"Ragina, you gotta introduce me to ChoCho!" Liza whispered.

"Why, you wanna get some gack?" Ragina asked, using the prevailing cocaine slang.

"No, I just think he's *hot*."

Ragina's fat face, blooming out of a starched, linen ruff collar like a chocolate gardenia, gave Liza a theatrical wink.

"Liza, this is ChoCho, the *man* of your *dreeeeams*," Ragina teased, after they all emerged from the dressing room.

Liza rolled her eyes and snorted involuntarily, holding out her hand to shake ChoCho's, which was cushy and hot, like the paw of a big puppy.

"You sang so well," ChoCho said with hair-raising direct eye contact and apparent sincerity.

"I could see you when I was onstage," said Liza. "You were like a ghost."

"Thank you," said ChoCho, with a lazy smile. "Would you like to dance?" he asked, giving her the sweet wet stare that had surely seduced countless long-haired, Aztec princesses from the Mission District. Liza realized nobody had ever asked her that question before.

The Cape Horn dance floor, its ornaments and disco balls, suddenly became a hazy bubble of encapsulated euphoria. Postperformance endorphins and cocktails fused in Liza, who found herself weak with pleasure in the midst of the heavenly prom-moment she'd never had . . . .

You . . .
Are in my System . . .
O-o-o-oh, you are . . .
You're in my System

(*ch-changchangchang,* went the cowbells)

"Can you breakdance?" Liza asked, hypnotized. ChoCho obliged her with a few laughing shoulder-pops. Liza suddenly understood why teenage girls screamed until they fainted when the Beatles disembarked planes.

"You're a foxy little thang," ChoCho purred.

Liza reeled. "Hnggguh," she blurted, swallowing unwanted giggles.

"You're quite a little actress," he said, laying it on thick.

"You wanna make me a star?" Liza whispered to him hotly. She felt like Lynn-Holly Johnson in *Ice Castles*, going for championship with gusto, despite all personal handicaps.

Liza couldn't know it, but her request hit a nerve bull's-eye in Cho-Cho: he aspired to be more than a drug dealer. His association with celebrities was giving him pretensions; he fantasized about using these connections to jockey himself into a position of legitimate power. He wasn't sure what he wanted to be, exactly, but he felt strongly that he could be some kind of Player in the entertainment industry. Liza, he thought, was a trashy little slice of semitalent, but she could act and sing adequately enough and was obviously ambitious. What if he could sand her rough edges off? ChoCho had long maintained that any halfway-decent-looking girl could be a starlet with the proper grooming, makeup, clothes, and half-gracious, half-snotty attitude. He'd hung around bars at 4 a.m. with enough Hollywood actresses to identify and replicate the currency of their physical presentation—their artifice, their expensive beauty tricks.

Making over Liza was a project that interested him in the same way that customizing cars did: ChoCho liked throwing his easy money at things and reupholstering them. Plus, he reckoned, if he could success-fully remodel a girl as thrice-removed from the A-list as Liza, he could easily elevate *himself*. Liza was an ideal test subject: she was young and raw, and she seemed to believe everything he said—furthermore, unlike ninety-nine percent of the girls he came in contact with, she didn't seem interested in him because he was synonymous with cocaine (ChoCho himself took a sniff or two very infrequently; only to satisfy famous and insecure clients who needed to feel that they were being "partied with." He was, at this point, still two years away from the kind of drug habit that would eventually ruin his life).

ChoCho smiled and grabbed Liza around the hips. *He could enslave me,* she mused.

"You like sushi?" he asked, his lips brushing her ear. Liza had never eaten sushi, and didn't want to, but she agreed enthusiastically to dinner with him the following Monday.

"Very nice to meet you, Liza," he said, taking her hand and kissing it with an effeminate limpness that suggested surplus masculinity.

As soon as he left the club, she began jumping up and down. She couldn't *believe* that anyone that flashy and exciting would be interested enough in her to ask her on an actual *date*. From that moment, Liza could think about nothing but ChoCho; her skin was crawling with an electric lust akin to fire ants; the thought of kissing him made her salivate. She wanted to eat him.

"You have to help me get a nurse uniform," she told Lorna, as they were lying in their trailer beds.

"Oh, God, here we go," moaned Lorna, anticipating another stunt.

"No! It's just the only white-clothes look I can think of, apart from, like, country-western shit!"

"You fall too hard, too fast," said Lorna, wisely. Lorna was "Off Love" these days, following the demise of her affair with Clive the Pot Dealer (which, fortunately, did not end their "business arrangement").

"He knows *movie stars*," Liza whined, in an anguish of longing.

The next day, Lorna drove Liza to a uniform warehouse, where she was able to buy a nurse dress several sizes too small, and a little nurse hat. Liza spray-painted a pair of pumps and bought white fishnet thigh-highs. She bleached her hair as white as it would go. In place of her safety pin, Liza stuck a small silver ring in her nostril.

"Is it pretty?" asked Liza.

"It's perverse," Lorna yawned. "You'd better not drink any red wine."

Liza couldn't stop looking at her white self in the mirror.

Liza met ChoCho at his favorite sushi bar. Liza beamed and spun around, showing off her outfit.

"Ooh, nursey!" ChoCho said with a sly smile. "Help me out, I'm sick!"

Liza admired his expensive white cable-knit sweater and felt out of her league, though in a different way than she had once felt outclassed by the rich Baumgartens and powerful Grosvenors. ChoCho, in Liza's heat-vapoured eyes, was self-possessed in a way she had always craved: there was nothing ironic or quirky about him. He was boy-king of the underworld and possessed of the rare, cabalistic secrets of "coolness" and ethnic street credibility.

ChoCho made a point of ordering everything by the Japanese names.

She made a point of trying all the sushi; she didn't like any of it.

ChoCho fed her things that nearly made her gag; she swallowed as much as she could without chewing, flirting the whole time. ChoCho knew she was faking and liked it; it meant she really wanted to please. Other patrons in the restaurant stared, wondering at their bleached-out apparel. The attention made Liza feel onstage and giddy; something like famous.

ChoCho name-dropped in a conspiratorial way that made her feel the reflected heat of the celebrity world. Liza had never felt like such a giggling bimbo. It was not unpleasant, fawning stupidly and fluttering over such a magnificent specimen of male.

By the time they left the restaurant, ChoCho was charmed by her goofiness, convinced of her mutability, and intoxicated by the notion of renovating her. Liza was starving, wasted on *sake,* and messily in love.

ChoCho's apartment opened before Liza in a riot of whiteness. An eight-foot polar bear was stuffed in attack pose in the entry hall. There was barely any furniture or personal touches—a couch here, a coffee table there; a white heavy-bag hung on a chain from the ceiling. Liza remembered her fantasy album cover from childhood and swooned; she felt as if Providence had read the back chapters of her unconscious mind and granted her part of a sacred, buried wish.

"Here I am!" she smiled to ChoCho, wobbling on one foot.

"Here you are," he said, smiling back.

Making out with him, she was very happy; his kisses were big, wet, and smashing. He had nice sheets. His brown body was so muscular it was uncomfortable, like having sex with a leather armchair, but she wanted to possess him, and it made her feel gratifyingly pummeled. When she woke in the middle of the night, a white moon was flooding through the vertical blinds into the luminous room. The mysterious phosphorescence reminded Liza of Ned's limelight, eerie old magic shows, glow-in-the-dark planet stickers. She was discovering a new dimension of herself in this controversial place. Having always been essentially loud and feral in character, any genuine catcalls she got usually came from elderly drunks. She considered ChoCho her biggest sexual conquest to date. She felt sly and proud in a new, naughty, superfeminine way.

When Liza woke in the early afternoon, ChoCho was already dressed and on the (white) phone, running a small, quiet vacuum cleaner.

Liza noticed that her clothes from the night before had been hung up, her shoes were aligned under a chair. Liza watched as ChoCho finished the call, Windexed the phone, put the vacuum away in its special cabinet, then walked to the sink and brushed his teeth very intently. When he was finished, he rinsed and blow-dried his toothbrush.

"Why do you blow-dry your toothbrush?" Liza asked, still half asleep.

"Germs," he said with a wink, handing her a cup of light coffee and kissing her on the mouth.

He is Mr. Cleanliness!

"Put your clothes on. Let's go shopping!"

Liza's mind couldn't process such astounding luck.

ChoCho really enjoyed spreading money around. He made regular commando raids on the shops of Union Square: Saks Fifth Avenue, Neiman-Marcus, all of the places that old white women and international rich people shopped. ChoCho loved to seduce department store employees into his ever-expanding, coke-addled retail army; an underground network of boys and girls who would casually clip security tags or provide ChoCho with alarming eighty percent discounts on designer merchandise. Liza found ChoCho's outlaw economy thrillingly romantic.

ChoCho wisely began Liza's overhaul with shoes, for no women can resist them; brazen moods sculpted in fragrant leather, begging the question: who is the wanton man-eater who would endure such retrograde, counterfeminist foot-agony, just to disguise her feet as sex bait?

Bah ha ha, it is I.

After dozens of boxes lay eviscerated on the floor, ChoCho selected for Liza a pair of tiny white stilettos with ankle straps thin as braided dental floss.

Liza had essentially grown up in high heels, so she stomped around in them the same way she did at thirteen. "Walk softer, and more with your hips more front instead of back," ChoCho said, squinting. Liza tried to mimic a model-runway, catwalk-bounce, the way she'd seen LaTuna do once. "There you go. Yeah girl," ChoCho encouraged. Liza felt pleasantly obscene, for once, as opposed to unintentionally vulgar.

. . .

"I want something sexy yet demure," ChoCho said to the stylish girl working in the pricey dress section, turning on his X-ray charm, making her feel naked. The willowy shopgirls all looked so perfectly colorized, bronzed, and airbrushed to Liza, she felt like she'd been clumped together out of damp grits by an uncaring God.

The salesgirl was kind to her, if aloof, and gave her tips in the dressing room, such as, "That's a strapless dress. You don't put your arms through those ribbon things, those are just for hanging it up."

"O-o-o-oh, right," said Liza, cowed.

Once the dress was on correctly, Liza thought back to her acid trip, and the inner and outer cleanliness she aspired to. It was almost like a planned déjà-vu, seeing herself cloned to infinity in the four-sided mirrors, so blonde and shiny in a white dress made of fabric so superior, Liza thought she'd snag it with her dry fingertips. *Now I'm getting somewhere*, she thought. With a sudden jolt of gestalt-giddiness, she saw her multiple reflection as her eternal, spherical being, willing itself toward the ever-improving Ideal Future-Liza, who was now staring at her own shimmering eyeballs. *Zoinks!*

"That's viscose," said the shopgirl.

"Thanks. So are you," said Liza, thinking she was getting a compliment in French.

"Now, that's looking a whole lot more like it," said ChoCho, sitting on a bench outside the dressing room, watching Liza twirl in wonder like a falling snowflake, abandoning herself gladly and utterly to his vast collection of white things.

"Good God," said Lorna, when Liza had finally stumbled across the gravel lot back to the trailer, her feet bleeding from straps that cut through her skin like piano wire through cheese. "Who died and made you Frosty the Snow Queen?"

Liza liked the comparison. She remembered the Snow Queen as a sophisticated, if villainous, character, and Liza desperately wanted sophistication now that she knew she didn't have any.

Beneath the Valley of Mommie Dearest became a minor cult hit. The run was extended after a local interest piece about the show appeared in the city's afternoon paper. Liza felt vindicated.

"Ha!" she screamed, reading the review to Lorna.

She mailed a clipping of the review to Peppy, to rub her nose in it, outlining the quote about herself:

".... Liza Normal, appearing as the luckless Christina Crawford, brings a fresh face to lewdness...."

Hi Mom:

I thought you might be interested in this press I got. I guess it isn't what you would call "legitimate family entertainment" but that doesn't seem to matter to the City papers. Hope things are going well over there for you and your "legitimate family entertainment." We have packed houses every night but I guess it doesn't count because it's only drag queen crap after all and you're so legitimate and everything. Please show the article to Ned and Gramma.
Love, Liza

Between the hit play and her ongoing, if somewhat irregular, romance with ChoCho (who dutifully came to see her perform every weekend, bringing fresh daisies backstage before going off on his club rounds), Liza was better dressed and more full of herself than she'd ever been. The only fly in the ointment was the sudden loss of her Fotostop job; now that she was thriving, she felt too fancy for it. She started showing up later and later until the manager finally had to fire her. She wasn't surprised, but she was forced into the position of looking for another job with flexible hours and relaxed expectations.

"Do you think you could get me a job at Centaur doing something non-naked?"

"I dunno. Can you write pornography?" asked DelVonn, when they were at Happy Donut at 3 a.m. (the regulars of the establishment, at that hour, were such human shipwrecks—substance-addled, pockmarked, crazy—that the Cape Horn kids called it "Unhappy Donut").

"I sort of wrote some about Shabba-Doo, once," Liza said, popping pink sprinkles between her teeth.

"I can show it to Butch Strange, if you want. He might be able to use it."

.   .   .

Butch Strange was the senior editor of Centaur's paperback book division. Under his tutelage, an anonymous klatch of hacks put out such smudgy, misspelled classics as *She Licked Them All, A Sailor Hung for Justice, Two Spunky! (Parts I & II),* and *Black Bottom Pie.*

Liza borrowed a typewriter from the trailer park office and typed up her Shabba-Doo diary entry and a job résumé exaggerating her importance at the Fotostop.

"It'll probably be weeks before Butch reads it," said DelVonn, accepting the manila envelope. Liza shrugged. She was in no real hurry. Lorna pulled in enough pot money for the two of them to live; Liza's job hunting was more or less a ceremonial gesture to Lorna to show that she actually was trying to support herself.

"If we were trapped in the mountains after a plane crash, would you eat my body if I was dead?" asked Liza, after she and ChoCho had exhausted three condoms in a particularly sweaty and athletic romp one Monday afternoon.

"Absolutely," answered ChoCho. Liza felt it the most romantic, lovely thing she'd ever heard. It was intoxicating to Liza that someone who was the cannibalistic equivalent of the buttery, syrup-wet center of a stack of pancakes could possibly find her comestible as well.

"Are you gonna introduce me to J——?" she asked, referring to another Face of Young Hollywood who had called, wanting to "party" that weekend.

ChoCho looked at her with his sad eyes.

"No."

"Why not?"

"You're not ready. When I introduce you, it should be like . . . nobody will believe it. They'll be all, 'Damn, who's *that?*' "

Liza was annoyed. "What do I need, still?" she asked.

"You just need to carry yourself a little more mature. It'll come," ChoCho said, being almost encouraging.

He had been wondering how he was going to alter her character. There were things he didn't want her to do anymore, such as talking and laughing too much, walking too hard, eating and drinking too enthusiastically, being too impressed by money and fame, and generally being Liza-like. Since ChoCho was primarily Latino in his sexual politics (his Bolivian grandmother had exerted a particular influence on him), he had an impression that rich, high-class women should be beautiful, mysterious, and above all, *quiet*. Liza was loud and far from mysterious. What she did have, however, was a certain cockroachlike resilience: you could put her in the ring with anything, knock her block off, hit her with sticks, drive over her face, and she would *never completely go down*. Being a fighter, ChoCho knew that this in itself was a kind of star quality—many celebrities had gotten where they were mainly because of an abysmal capacity to suck down rejection. Cho-Cho had noticed that Liza was capable of absorbing humiliations that might drive a more fragile girl insane. This, conceivably, was a talent that could be exploited.

"I really wanted to meet J———," Liza said, hurt, J——— being somebody she had secretly lusted after in several B-rate teen films.

"There's time. We just gotta work on you a little more, first."

This pissed Liza off. "ChoCho! I'm sick of this 'later-later' shit. Show me everything *now*. Today. This week. Just tell me how you want me to be, already," said Liza, who didn't mind the idea of her personality being retooled, since she had always felt completely at sea when it came to how to behave in public. She impatiently wanted to be *envied*.

"Oh, you think you're ready, huh?" ChoCho smiled, with cocked eyebrow.

"I can do it. I want to be a cool-ass mofo, like *you*." Liza pouted. "And I want to meet J——— this weekend!"

Tick, tock, tick. ChoCho, who enjoyed the stress of a challenging deadline as much as anyone else in our studio audience, took the bait.

ChoCho liked being thought of as a mentor. His own personality, constructed piecemeal from movie roles (Humphrey Bogart's limp-handed smoking and sad smile, James Bond's cocked eyebrow, James Dean's vulnerable stare and tough-guy slouch, Mickey Rourke's girlishly soft voice), was mainly the result of being a lonely and racially confused kid with no father around, and a mother, aunt, two older sisters, and a grandmother who spoiled him like a young pasha. During ChoCho's teen years, his insecurity begat bombast, and the artifice he'd culled from male screen idols soon became his full-time, larger-than-life character. The people drawn into his orbit—biggish drug dealers, smallish celebrities, and the most beautiful girls in his Latin-American neighborhood— were proof that his jerry-rigged personal magnetism worked, at least for short bursts of time. Liza, his first white girlfriend who'd been raised in a middle-class neighborhood, was proof that his hi-gloss charisma could be sustained indefinitely, over days and nights, in front of people with better educations than his. For all his gorgeous bravado, ChoCho was still somewhat ashamed of being from the "Streets" (*ch-chang chang ch-chang*) and was afraid his persona might just wash off someday like a cheap paint job.

After a morning of serious consideration, ChoCho handed Liza a small gun.

"This is a shortcut to feeling confident in a room," ChoCho said, divulging one of his bigger secrets, sticking the small, unloaded automatic into the front of her new white jeans.

Liza immediately felt a rush of barbarian power.

"Take a walk down to the delicatessen. But *don't you pull it on anybody*, I don't care what happens," said ChoCho. "Just keep it in your pants, don't let anybody see it, and see how it feels."

Liza put on a new white jacket. She felt an urge to flip the collar up. The gun was cold against her navel, humming with fearful might.

She felt herself prowling on the street, looking at people with an eye toward shooting them. She imagined every other pedestrian she passed for two blocks attempting infractions against her person.

"Hey, watch yourself, bitch" she imagined a pudgy, bearded man with a grocery bag saying.

Excuse me? Liza imagined herself saying, softly, musically, withdrawing the gun from her pants and scratching her nose with it. *I believe you need to learn some manners.* Liza pictured the man groveling and felt a noble clemency arise within herself. *I'll let you off with a warning this time, but remember: politeness is a virtue.* She imagined all the people in cars showing her timorous respect.

She was ice-cold and hard as granite by the time she got to the deli.

"Just give me some Kool Filter Kings," she meant to say; she surprised herself by pronouncing it "Kool Filtah Kangs." She pictured herself being recruited into a lethal crime syndicate, as their deadeye femme-fatale. She would sit at expensive restaurants in a white fur coat, surrounded by beautifully dangerous-looking black men in snap-brim fedoras, double-breasted suits, and wraparound shades. She would have "seen too much," and this heaviness would make her sad, beautiful, and terrifying. She would leave a single white rose on her victims. "Real class," the police would say reverently, secretly seduced by her extraordinary, hot dangerousness.

When she got back to ChoCho's, she realized with embarrassment that she had left the cigarettes on the counter at the deli. ChoCho wouldn't let her take the gun with her when she went back.

"If you're going to make me an actress, I need some headshots," said Liza.

"Fair enough," said ChoCho, enjoying the lopsided power dynamic of the relationship more and more.

ChoCho had Liza go down to the South of Market area and visit a brick warehouse that had once been a plastic bag factory. The photographer, an acquaintance of ChoCho's named Winston, was a gray-skinned, furtive, adenoidal rat of a man, who agreed to take Liza's headshot for two grams of coke.

Winston unrolled a large, gray paper backdrop under a row of muddy skylights. Liza looked through Winston's "book," a leather binder stocked with prints of his favorite photos.

"What are you trying to be, an actress or a model?" Winston asked, snorting up a finger-size line of blow on his light-board, and not offering Liza any.

"I'm too short to be a model," said Liza.

Then Liza realized that the word *model,* in Winston's world, had a rather open-ended definition—most of the girls in the book were topless and sprawling suggestively. There was a series entitled "Stigma II" featuring naked girls coated with black motor oil in poses of lesbian passion. A leggy, dark, African girl, in a photo entitled *Devil's Food,* was coiled like a donut and appeared to have been sprinkled with powdered sugar. *Aspic* featured a backbending nude, coated with a snotty, gelatinous mucilage. The shots were black and white, which made them "artistic," but it was clear that Winston's love of art was not nearly so great as his love for rolling young naked females in various icky substances.

Nevertheless (beggars can't be choosers), Liza had her photos done that day. She did her own hair and makeup. Carried away by possibilities of high fashion, Liza eventually allowed Winston to soak her hair in vegetable oil until it dripped down her face in strands; Winston, gacked out of his mind, camera chattering like a pair of joke dentures, had kept saying, "Sexier! That's good! Oh, that's hot!" every time Liza loosened her jaw and puffed out her lower lip.

When Liza picked up the proof sheets a few days later, she looked drowned, raccoon-eyed, and mildly brain damaged, because her mouth was always open. She tried to select the one that looked the least (in ChoCho's words) like she "just gave somebody an underwater blowjob."

A long white stretch limo pulled up in front of ChoCho's building; ChoCho knew that it was going to be, effectively, the bar exam, in terms of Liza's behavior studies. Liza walked out into the evening light and yelled, "Oh my GOD!!" jumping up and down in her tiny white shoes.

"No, no, no, just get in like it's what you expect every day," ChoCho whispered in her ear.

"But it's NOT!" squealed Liza, wriggling with joy. "I've been wanting to ride in a limo since I was *six years old*! Fuckin' A!!!"

"It's not that big a deal," said ChoCho, faintly embarrassed. "It's just a big-ass car."

Like Eve in the Garden after her discussion with the snake, Liza realized she was emotionally naked before the limousine, and felt shame.

The driver came around and opened the door for her.

"Hello," said the driver.

Liza made a point of snubbing him and sliding into the backseat without a glance.

"Hey man," ChoCho said to the chauffeur, with his usual amiability, before sliding in next to Liza.

"You can be nice to people, you don't have to act like a bitch. Just be cool," said ChoCho, once the doors were shut. Liza was hurt and puzzled by the fine line between coolness and bitchiness.

Once the car was moving, Liza had an uncontrollable desire to stand up through the sunroof, have the wind blow in her face, and yell, "Whoooooo!"

"Get down," said ChoCho.

"Oh, this is so FUN. I'm like, having such a *blast* right now." Liza sat heavily back into the plush seats.

"It's not really supposed to be fun. It's just transportation. What, you think every time you're in a limo it should be prom night?" ChoCho asked with infuriating superiority, clicking on the television. Mention of proms always gave Liza a painful twinge of alienation.

Liza was now nervous, uncomfortable, pissed off. "You're the party king. Whoooo. No wonder the stars all come to party with you, this is such a party riot," she sneered, eyeing the wet bar.

ChoCho laughed at her. Liza crawled over and punched him in the stomach as hard as she could. He laughed harder. She tried to bite him on the face. He wrestled her into a playful choke hold.

"You gonna be good?" he asked.

"No!"

"Be good or I'll make you unconscious."

"It would be more fun than hanging out with you."

ChoCho throttled her and she laughed and coughed simultaneously. He pressed the intercom button to speak to the chauffeur.

"We're stopping at this dry cleaner's, bro."

Liza picked up Lorna's phone one morning. It was Peppy.

"I'm going to come and see you in your play this Saturday. Will you put me on the guest list, plus one?"

"One what?" asked Liza.

"I've got a date, for your information."

"A *date*?"

"Yes, as a matter of fact. He's playing Captain Pickering in our play. His name is Earl. He's a mailman."

Liza was torn: ChoCho would be there—the thought of introducing him to her unsightly mother and someone bizarre enough to be her *date* made her nervous—but she also knew that there would be a full house and itched to rub Peppy's nose in it.

Peppy, who stood out even in a Cape Horn audience, was spotted by LaTuna first.

"Did you see that alky mama with the Loretta Lynn wig? She looks like she just escaped from the International Halfway-House of Pancakes."

"That's my mom," Liza said, half-ashamed and half-proud to have evidence of her impressively low origins in a crowd that thrived on competitive squalor.

"Woo-eee," hooted LaTuna. "No wonder you're the most fabulously Problem Teen."

A tall transvestite was leaning heavily against the bar in a honey-blonde flip-wig, smoking. This wasn't exactly unusual, but Liza thought she recognized something about the figure, especially in regards to the way she shifted her weight, favoring her lower back. She was bowlegged; her low, square-heeled pumps were modest and had been carefully selected for feet more knobby that most. The ruffled prairie dress was on the frumpy side; this was clearly a utilitarian transvestism, one designed more for comfort and regular use than flamboyant, drag-queen show costumes, or the stretchy Day-Glo clothing worn by tranny hookers.

"She's opening the show tonight," said Ragina, pointing with a red cocktail straw at the cross-dresser.

Liza opted to watch "The Groovy Gun Show" from behind the curtain. "Groovy," the transvestite, strapped on a white cowgirl holster containing two air-pistols and ascended to the stage. She was tattooed; Liza saw, on one arm, a fading Yosemite Sam. Looking closer, a horse head appeared, with a familiar banner. On her back, just above the boat-neck collar of the prairie dress, Liza could just make out the letters ". . . EELIN' GROO . . . ." Under the lights it became abundantly clear that underneath her thick veneer of orange-tinted Max Factor pancake makeup, the transvestite was none other than Johnny Budrone.

Liza swallowed her gum.

Panicking, she peered out into the audience: Peppy looked so stricken, bats might have come streaming out of her mouth.

Slow down, you move too fast
Got to make the mor-nin' last!

Peppy left her date, a short Chinese man in a blue polyester suit, and went to the bar. Without taking her eyes off "Groovy," she slugged down a shot of clear fluid, then signaled the bartender for another. It came, she shotgunned it back, and signaled for another. The third shot hit the back of her throat to a serendipitous *Pop!* of one of Groovy's balloons. Liza watched the slurry of sugars and alcohols engage Peppy's bloodstream; Peppy laughed a very tragic laugh that trailed off at the end and signaled the bartender for yet another. Groovy shot the mass of balloons down to a large, betesticled phallus. Peppy started clapping very slowly and loudly. *Clap. Clap. Clap.* Ragina walked onstage and shot a can of Reddi Wip from the end of Johnny's sculpture, to resemble ejaculation. The crowd hooted and whistled. Liza couldn't watch Peppy anymore.

Groovy's props were brought backstage, and the overture for *Mommie* kicked in over the speakers. It was a good night—the audience was big, drunk, and rowdy. ChoCho snuck in with J———, intentionally late, after the show began, to attract less attention. The Movie Star's opinion meant the most to Liza that night. The alternating current of nerves emanating from her mother, the freak advent of Johnny Budrone, and the sudden pressure of having a celebrity in the house gave Liza a nauseating head rush. She stuttered her way through Act I, barely conscious of what she was doing, nearly missing several cues.

In Act II, Louis Mayer cancels Joan Crawford's contract and asks her to leave his studio, because she is "box office poison." Mommie orgiastically chain-whips Mayer, climaxing loudly at the moment of his death.

The chain-whipping was Liza's backstage cue to change into a particularly complicated dress with an annoying pinafore. She was struggling with a row of tiny, square buttons when she felt a blast of greasy, schnappsy breath on her cheeks.

"Where is he?"

Peppy was vibrating eerily. Liza noticed that her mother had loud stripes of fuchsia blush on her cheeks and half-moons of white eye shadow caked beneath her eyes; the effect was savage and warlike—a rabid toucan.

"Mom! I have to get this dress on! Go back to the audience!"

Peppy bared her oversize, yellow tooth caps; her voice was full of threat. "I saw him come back here. *Where is he?*"

"Shhhhhhhhhhh!!!!" DelVonn interjected, scurrying up to them.

"Get back to your seat! We have a cue!" Liza said as quietly as she could, taking Peppy by the elbow and noting that she was wearing a clingy polyester blouse that had been recently unbuttoned to midsternum, in order to better reveal an industrial-strength bra and her Johnny Budrone–inspired horseshoe tattoo. Peppy stood firm, yanking her arm out of Liza's grip.

Liza and DelVonn heard their cue; DelVonn bolted onstage, giving Liza an anxious look.

Liza tried to follow him but Peppy held her. "Tell me where he is!"

"Mom! Let GO!"

To Liza's vast relief, Ragina Victoria snuck up behind Peppy.

"Mrs. Normal! I've always wanted to meet you," Ragina whispered, distracting Peppy long enough for Liza to scoot onstage in the nick of time, semitraumatized.

Shortly before the end of the scene, Liza saw Ragina escort Peppy back to her bewildered date, where she remained, staring at the stage with disconnected eyes.

Rushing backstage to blot her sweat-pouring face, Liza saw Johnny Budrone leaving through the club's alley door, aluminum gun-case in tow.

"Are you leaving?" Liza asked him, pointedly. She knew it was semi-irrational, but she was suddenly furious at him. The part of her childhood that had suffered under Peppy's abandonment meltdown was at least partially his fault.

"I got another gig tonight, Darlin'," he stuttered, wondering why he was being grilled by this pretty little guy in a starched pinafore.

"You don't want to say Hi to my mom? Peppy Normal? She's in the audience."

Johnny Budrone's eyes widened and skittered around Liza's face, trying to recognize the little girl he'd once known in this angry adult perversely dressed like a little girl.

"You tell her Howdy for me," he said, after a thickly uncomfortable moment, and turned to leave.

He doesn't even fucking remember my name, thought Liza. Rage drenched her brain.

"I'll be sure to do that, *'Groovy,'*" Liza said viciously, grabbing a piece of ice out of his hastily abandoned bourbon, and hurling it at the back of his head.

Johnny turned slowly. His whole painted face went slack, like a burning wax clown; his skull seemed visible; and his haunted black eyes froze Liza with a look of such frightening, unimaginable pain, Liza almost cried out in alarm. He turned and scuttled out the back door like a hermit crab.

Liza shakily downed the rest of his bourbon.

Liza could hear ChoCho whistling during the curtain call. The trill of it partially revived her, but she knew she still had more flaming tunnels of unease to crawl through. She couldn't believe she'd have to introduce ChoCho and J———to Peppy on this dark night of all nights, when her mother was so flipped-out and plastered. After changing into a ChoCho-generated outfit (and taking several deep drags of a borrowed cigarette) Liza crept over to Peppy's table as invisibly as possible and introduced herself to Earl the Chinese Mailman. Earl had a round face, several silver molars, and graying black hair, greased into a combover. He fawned over Liza's performance with such boisterousness, it was obvious that he too was completely hammered.

Peppy's catatonic, melancholy drunk had turned 180 degrees into spooky sentimentalism. "My baby! Lookit my beau'fullest baby girl!" Peppy squealed in her baby voice. "Izzunt she gorgeous?" Peppy asked a nearby cluster of young men in sailor dresses who were trying to ignore her. Peppy clung to Liza, stroking her face and hair in a way that Liza had never previously experienced and therefore had no idea how to handle. Peppy whispered in her ear, "I said to myself, Li, I said, *my daughter is a woman* tonight." Liza was repulsed to her soul to be any such thing.

"Ma'am?" said ChoCho suddenly, emerging splendid and heavenly cool from the crowd with J——— in tow, not noticing Liza's vigorous head wags imploring *No, no, go away, not now* . . . "I'm a friend of Liza's," he said in his whispery voice, offering his limp hand.

"Oh, lookit you!" Peppy slushed. "Where'd you come from, TV Land? I know you from the *television* . . . ," Peppy cried happily, ignoring ChoCho's hand and reaching past it to grab J———'s face and smush it. Terrible shame washed over everyone in a five-foot radius, because Peppy had violated the unspoken but ironclad Never-Touch-the-Celebrity rule. Most denizens of Cape Horn wouldn't even acknowledge celebrities, on the rare occasions that they came in; it was way too gauche.

"We'll wait for you at the apartment," ChoCho told Liza, extricating J———'s cheek from Peppy's damp fingers. "Take a cab."

He slipped a twenty-dollar bill into Liza's palm, kissed her mouth lightly and winked, then hurried out with J———.

This was a big deal. Even after meeting the horror that was Peppy, ChoCho was still inviting her over, on a business night, with a celebrity. This was a breakthrough—it meant Liza had somehow graduated, in his estimation, into presentability.

Liza was relieved that ChoCho had left, but for a wholly different reason than she thought she would be: she couldn't believe it, but she was actually *slightly embarrassed to be affiliated with ChoCho around Peppy*, even in Peppy's near-blackout state. The very thought was outrageous; if Peppy had dared say anything even vaguely negative about ChoCho, Liza would have reached into her mother's face and yanked out her tongue, but it came about a different way—Peppy had just *looked* at ChoCho—Liza watched her study him drunkenly for a moment—and Liza *knew* that Peppy could *smell* that he wasn't a kosher, law-abiding citizen. Peppy was too fucked-up to count to twenty, but *not too drunk to feel superior to her boyfriend*.

Infuriated by this insight, Liza refreshed her commitment to Cho-Cho and his pedantic, distant affections. She tried to be proud and excited about her invitation to his late-night get-together. When Peppy and Earl got up to leave the club and drive back home across the Golden Gate Bridge, Peppy nearly fell down going through the doorway.

"Are you all right?" Liza asked, gripping her mother's arm harder than she needed to.

"Yes I'm all right," Peppy slurred. She grabbed Liza's neck and pushed her mouth almost inside her ear. "Johnny was always a cross-dresser," Peppy whispered, with solvent-strength breath.

"Good night!" yelled Earl, saluting to the entire bar.

Liza watched them putter into the middle of the street; a car honked at them. Earl waved at it.

"Those motherfuckers gonna end up wrapped around a pole," said Ragina, with wide eyes.

Liza took a cab to ChoCho's house, filled with ideas of how she was going to act. For example, she was going to say "Hi-How-AH-you," with no question mark at the end, in what was the prevailing Eurotrash accent, and drape her cold hand limply over other people's hands, like she was handing them a little dead snake. Everyone would notice her, for Was She Not All in White? And Was She Not Filled with Secret Television Powers (however latent they might be, at the moment)?

All was dark, save for a few candles and a string of clear Christmas-tree lights that ChoCho had carefully wrapped around a tangle of white twigs in an alabaster urn. The music was low and bass-thumpy. There were approximately twenty elite people in the room: a tiny starlet with a surprisingly large head, a few models, unsmiling and whippet-thin, and a bunch of young club guys with triangular jackets and multicolored hair. Everyone turned with a twitchy, paranoid glance toward Liza when she walked in, then turned back to their talking and cigarettes. There was a huge spiral of drugs in the middle of the coffee table, which people were taking turns snorting to the limits of their nasal capacity. Everyone in the room seemed to be morbidly high and urgently trying to express their manic revelations to whoever was nearest.

Liza was amazed by how unimpressed she was. There wasn't a single person, J——— included, that seemed very *interesting*. Though everyone was unreasonably good-looking and well dressed, they seemed hollow and desperate. These were Lost Children of Easy Glamour—young people too rich and too pretty for Life to have made many demands on them. There was a clingy sense of tribalism; they seemed to travel in packs for safety and reassurance. Liza thought, in a moment of imperiousness, that none of them had substantial *character*; they all seemed to be adrift, flitting in the breeze, fickle and insecure, coddling themselves by burning money up their nose holes and talking frantically about themselves.

But despite all that, Liza wanted to be one of them, because they were in the hip, young, famous, elbow-rubbing cadre, and she wasn't.

"All right Liza!" said J———, walking up to her with ChoCho in tow. Liza's ears lit up with starstruckness; she checked herself. *Not too excited, now.*

"Hi-How-AH-you," she said, thrusting her lifeless hand into his. ChoCho smiled weirdly. Liza had never seen him stoned before.

"Can we interest you in a proper blast?" J——— asked loopily, the cocaine careening around in his skull like a glitter in a snow globe. Liza looked to ChoCho for approval.

"Go 'head, baby," he said, clearly not himself, massaging his jaw and licking his dry lips in a geckoesque fashion.

"What the hey," said Liza. She took a rolled twenty-dollar bill from J———and knelt before the coffee table. She snorted a small pile up each nostril and coughed.

The coke dripped down her throat in bitter chemical globs. Her nose became numb, and a kind of cheerful agitation possessed her, making her itchy to smoke, flirt, and move around. Suddenly these lost and empty people seemed terribly interesting, and she was positively thrilled to be sandwiched on the couch between ChoCho and J———.

She began jabbering irrepressibly about how *embarrassed* she was about her mother and how she nearly *died* when Peppy grabbed J————'s face and how *interesting* it was that people feel like they can just *do* things like that to famous people because they feel like they already know them or something!

"Yeah, your mom was a trip!" J———— said, grabbing Liza's knee in an unexpected burst of intimacy. Liza rolled her eyes, tingling with pleasure.

"Liza wants to be a movie sta-a-a-a-a-ar," said ChoCho, dragging the word out with weary condescension.

"Really? Hey, Liza should meet Dennis! Maybe he can use Liza in that shoot!" said J————, winking at ChoCho.

ChoCho gave him a Mona Liza smile, his epicanthic eyes slitting. He had been looking at Liza extra critically all evening, due to the self-conscious energies of his celebrity-drug-babysitter-persona, and the cocaine brain-chewing that made him obsessively compare himself to other people. That night, his prevailing opinion on Liza was that she was too young and too rough, and who knew how far she'd go for self-exposure?

"You wanna be in a movie, Liza?" J———— asked sweetly, turning toward Liza with the toothy, ultrabright eye warmth that captivated teen girls and casting directors.

Liza perceived no sinister nuance; she was delighted to be acknowledged by the scintillating likes of J———— and was already replaying the conversation for DelVonn and Lorna in her mind.

"Well . . . . . yeah." (She bit her tongue instead of saying, *I'll have to talk to my agent.*)

"Hey, Dennis! Bro!"

Dennis, a pudgy, ponytailed frat boy wearing Ray-Bans, architectural shoes, and a Yale baseball cap, pogoed to the couch and kissed J————'s ring. Liza loved these vivid, rambunctious people.

"You need another girl for your sports movie?" asked J————.

"Always!" shouted Dennis. The boys laughed.

"This is Liza. She's an Actress," said J————.

Liza fizzed with pride.

She shook Dennis's sweaty hand; Hi-How-AH-Yous were exchanged. Dennis had been "directing a series of independent films"; the new project, which Liza understood to be a "meditation on sports, games, and athletes," was being shot in a downtown warehouse. "Come on down sometime tomorrow evening!" Dennis told Liza while smiling at ChoCho.

Liza felt so lucky she thought she'd explode like an M–80 and whirl into flaming magnolias.

ChoCho grabbed her playfully around the neck. "She's a good girl," he said.

"You're eighteen, right Liza?" asked J————.

"Oh sure," she said, lying easily. She'd been sneaking into Cape Horn with her bad fake ID for so long, she'd completely abandoned all truth about her age. *Thank you God. Thank you, thank you. A movie!!!!!!!* She enjoyed several moments of undiluted bliss. Then it went away, and she got cranky, so she did another line.

The party got weirder. ChoCho ceremoniously spiraled another huge bag of coke onto the glass table, and the party frenzied onto it, reminding Liza of a movie she once saw, in which piranhas swarmed on a bloody horse. A minute later, nothing was left but a smoky white film on the glass; fingers were licked and run on the table, the dust wiped onto gums. There was a general gnashing of teeth, and everyone's monster face was visible—greedy, edgy, buzzing with inner violence. People got restless with one another and engaged in little slap fights. One of the models was sick in the bathroom; the club boys argued about guns and motorcycles. The starlet was walking around in her bra, tongue-kissing boys and girls indiscriminately.

Liza was unable to fully abandon herself to the depravities, and it made her feel like she lacked guts. She didn't have the vital chromosome necessary to "Party Like It's 1999," i.e., hopelessly, and without regard for tomorrow. She didn't really like cocaine; it was too manic and agitating. She was too happy and excited to be at the party to be jaded; she didn't want to get too fucked-up to fully *experience* it. Liza wanted to be *more* present, more alive; these "beautiful" people of the alleged In Crowd smoked, drank, and drugged to oblivion, like they'd had too much perfection and needed to be dead.

One of the club boys was out of his head, obnoxiously demanding that ChoCho lay out another line for him.

"Gimme some money, I'll give you whatever," said ChoCho, steely browed. The boy tried, through sweaty weaseling, to get "credit"; ChoCho refused. Other guests began to watch, hoping ChoCho would entertain them with some fluid Mui Thai moves.

"I'll give you a quarter gram if you let me try this on you," said ChoCho with a fiendish grin, pulling a black electrical stun gun out of a cabinet drawer.

"Shit," said the club boy, looking nervous. The compulsive insect-pull of the drugs was visible on him, overriding self-preservation, self-respect. "OK. What the hell. Gimme the quarter first."

Liza couldn't watch. She bolted into ChoCho's bedroom and shut the door. The sun was crawling up, looking bloodshot and weak. Through the thin wall, Liza heard the *clackclackclackclackclack* of the stun gun, and heard the club boy's body hit the floor, and the muffled flutter of limbs on carpet. People were gasping. There were sounds of concern and panic, the words *seizure* and *cardiac arrest* drilled into Liza's ears above the murmuring. She was too afraid to open the door; twenty endless seconds passed in fear.

Hey! There he is! He's all right. Ayyyy! Y' OK? Oh God, dude, that was intense! After peeking out and ascertaining that the asshole was not dead, Liza slammed the door, dove into the bed, and tried to sleep, wishing everyone would go away. Her ears were ringing; she felt as ashy and dry as if she'd crawled out of a volcano. In place of sleep, there was gritty exhaustion, eyes closed, wide awake and irritated, for what seemed like hours.

"Well, how was I? Did I pass the special personality test with your fancy friends?" Liza asked the next afternoon, with some sarcasm, when they were both awake enough to empty ashtrays.

"You were all right," said ChoCho, drinking orange juice out of the box in hard glugs.

"*All right?* I only got offered a *movie role*," she said, trying to put an empty beer bottle on each finger and thumb to carry ten of them to the trash bag.

"By who, Dennis? You gonna go to that thing?" asked ChoCho. Liza couldn't figure out if his tone had a tone on it.

"Hell yeah!" said Liza, amphibious green and brown fingers clinking. "I just hope he'll let me sing!"

"Maybe you should skip it," said ChoCho.

"Why should I?"

ChoCho looked at her. He felt desiccated and nasty. "Whatever. Go on down and see for yourself."

"You coming with me?"

"Nope."

"What's with you?"

ChoCho didn't answer; he got out the vacuum cleaner.

"You love that vacuum cleaner so much, why don't you buy it a bunch of little white outfits?" Liza yelled.

That evening, Liza walked into Dennis's warehouse wearing a new white tennis dress, with a strip of four pictures from a photo booth (she hadn't printed her headshots, they were too gross) and her theatrical résumé. Two other girls were there, smoking; they were taller and skinnier than Liza, with bleach-fried hair. Dennis said something to them, and they both began to nonchalantly pull off their jeans. Liza was shocked to see they weren't wearing underwear, and that they had no pubic hair save for thin lines shaved to resemble the tops of exclamation points. They kept talking to each other as they stripped off their shirts; one girl poked at her breasts like she was trying to see if they were fully cooked. The other fastened a garter belt on, then began to pull a pair of stockings over her knees, not caring who saw what of her. They were so unself-conscious, doing what Liza considered to be intensely private procedures, that it made her afraid.

"Liza, right? Hey! So! You want to be in the movie?" Dennis asked Liza.

"What would I have to do?" Liza stammered.

"Whatever you want." Dennis shrugged, tearing the wrapper off of a piece of spearmint gum and cramming it into his mouth. "Take that stuff off and go on up there." Dennis pointed toward a large wrestling ring that had been erected in the center of the space; two bare mattresses sat behind the ropes.

Liza felt her bile rise.

"Is this a *porno movie*?!" Liza screeched. The blonde girls turned around to stare at her with tough, disaffected faces. "No way! I'm not taking off anything! I thought this was a movie about *sports*."

The tough blondes emitted *tsssss* noises. One cackled.

"Sorry to disappoint you," said Dennis. "It's kind of about sports, if you think about it." He thought himself quite clever.

"Yeah, well . . . ," said Liza, turning her back to leave. "No thanks."

"It's three hundred dollars a day, if you're really cooperative," said Dennis.

"Oooh, great! Fucking people I don't know, all day, on film, for a whole three hundred dollars?" flamed Liza. "Gee, why didn't you say so before, Satan? What a great offer."

"How about three hundred and twenty-five?" asked Dennis, with gleeful frat-boy offensiveness. "And who said anything about fucking people? I was going to give you this," said Dennis, picking up a football that somebody had jokingly covered with a condom.

"Yeah, well, fuck your own football," said Liza, turning to leave.

"*Ooooooooooh*," said one of the hard blondes, without any feeling.

"Lemme know if you change your mind!" yelled Dennis, cheerfully. Liza walked out the door without looking back.

Fuck your own football, Liza thought. *What a stupid line.* Liza felt like the movie of her life had just been demoted to the TV movie about her life. Worse yet, the cable TV movie about her life. *A "stag" film,* she thought with murky irony. The disappointment was piercing.

"Thanks loads for setting me up with Dennis! What a valuable opportunity! You scumbag! Why didn't you tell me it was porno?!" Liza yelled into the pay phone, her eyes filling with tears. People on the street watched the hysterical girl in the tennis costume, screaming and stomping her white heels on the corner in front of a liquor store, and wondered if she was a hooker.

"I wasn't sure if you'd care," ChoCho said honestly.

Liza called ChoCho every horrible name she could conjure, her face and scalp flashing red against her white hair. She hammered the phone back into the cradle as hard as she could, trying to break the Bakelite receiver. It was too hard. She gave up and walked to the bus stop to begin the journey back to Lorna's trailer. She was sobbing.

"You need any help, Miss?" asked a scabby, grime-caked old bum.

"No!" Liza shouted, wetly.

"OK," the bum said in a tone of apology.

The following day, at the Normal Family Dinner Theatre, a new drama unfolded with the morning newspaper's Arts & Entertainment section.

THEATRE OF CRUELTY

'Normal Family Theatre' Punishes
Lerner and Loewe's 'My Fair Lady'

Cabaret Review by Pat Morgenstern

Somewhere in hell, there is a village peopled by the chimney-sweeps of *Mary Poppins,* Eartha Kitt, and the cast of *Hee Haw.* Judging by her accent, it is where Eliza Doolittle came from, in the Normal Family Dinner Theatre's new production of *My Fair Lady.* Perhaps the only thing more execrable than Eliza's accent is her singing, but neither are the worst aspects of this show. The true horror comes when you realize, as an audience member, that *My Fair Lady* is lost to you forever, because you will never be able to shake Peppy Normal's performance out of your mind.

Ms. Normal, the founder and self-proclaimed star of the Normal Family Dinner Theatre (which has never actually served dinner), has returned to the stage after a 2-year hiatus. It was not a long enough break for some of us to recover from her last production.

There is no appropriate reason for a woman of Normal's age and girth to play Eliza Doolittle—one can only assume that her need to perform a starring role outweighed any need for self-preservation. Her director and supporting cast, indeed, must be partially blamed: any human being with a shred of decency would have convinced Ms. Normal not to spring this show on an innocent and unsuspecting public.

Still, there is much that is compelling about this doomed production. Watching this show inspires the viewer to take up an instrument they've never played and try to sit in with the philharmonic, or perhaps don a tutu and crash onstage with the Royal Ballet. Most people try to avoid such ill-advised forays into reckless self-exposure; one must hand it to Ms. Normal for her bold disregard of common sense.

Perhaps shamelessness is the key to happiness, and Peppy Normal knows something that the rest of us don't, displaying herself in these excruciating productions.

But that is no reason for the rest of us to have to watch.

Peppy read the article slowly, picking up a head of steam. Noreen had hidden the review in the paper that was delivered to their door, but Peppy had gone out to a newspaper box and stolen a large pile in anticipation of the press.

"Where are my car keys?" Peppy asked, unscrewing the top on a bottle of gin, her face contorted and veined with rage.

"Oh, don't you do anything!" Noreen shouted, trying to pry the bottle away. "That's just one little critic! Ned! Help!"

"That wasn't criticism," Peppy brayed in a cracking voice. "That was *assassination*."

Ned ran down the stairs in his ski mask in time to see the last flicker of Peppy's caftan as she slammed the front door.

"Can't you get her?!" screeched Noreen.

"She's already across the street," said Ned, his woolen face peering out at a handful of pedestrians, with stark fear.

The police report described Peppy as having lied her way into the offices of the *Marin Gazette,* wanting to give a "flower" to Pat Morgenstern (the "flower" in question turned out to be a handful of leaves she had picked up in the parking lot). Morgenstern, a blond man in his forties with tortoiseshell glasses and wide-wale corduroy pants, was called out of his office to meet "a fan," and was "terrified" when Peppy Normal lunged at his face with a cluster of leaves that concealed the points of her car keys. Morgenstern's glasses broke on impact; other employees of the *Gazette* office called the police and helped separate Morgenstern from his assailant, who was "difficult to restrain" and "issued death-threats."

An assault charge was filed against Peppy, and a Protective/Restraining order (stating that she was not allowed within 150 feet of Morgenstern or the *Gazette*) was granted by the presiding municipal court judge. Peppy was taken by two local officers and detained in a holding cell overnight until her preliminary hearing; afterward, Earl bailed her out and drove her back to the theatre.

"Your mom got into some trouble," said Noreen, telling Liza the story over the phone. "You'd better come over and show her some support."

"Support for *what?*" asked Liza. "Her decision to stab some guy with her keys?"

"You just come on and be here with us, please," Noreen asked patiently.

Liza was loath to go anywhere; she hadn't left her twin bed in the trailer since the Dennis incident. ChoCho had called, several times, but Lorna was under orders to say Liza wasn't home.

· · ·

It was clammy and colorless outside. Standing at that particular bus stop, a D-shaped growth on the gray arm of the freeway, Liza always felt the most desolate; the *whussshh* of passing cars seemed to echo her feeling of nobody caring about her. The world was cold and speeding past her, and there was nobody glamorous or exciting in any car she saw; no chance of being seen or discovered by rare persons, no reason to be dressed in good clothes (the only ones she had, now, were white and overpriced)—except to collect black flecks of damp exhaust grime. She thought she felt her glands swelling in anticipation of a cold.

When she got to the theatre, Peppy was secluded in bed. Earl was helping Noreen sort out and read the various citations and court appointments. He had already cancelled all future performances of *My Fair Lady*—the rest of the cast complained bitterly, having paid "production fees" to be onstage for what they hoped would be a minimum of three weeks. There were requests for refunds and the use of threatening words such as *actionable*.

"Why am I here 'supporting' her if she's all zonked out?" Liza asked Noreen.

"Go in there and talk to her. Be nice, she's had a tough time."

I've *had a tough time*, Liza thought but didn't say.

The room had the hopeless vegetable scent of health abandoned to the whims of Devil Booze. Liza saw one eye looking at her through an alien mass of strings that Liza realized was Peppy's actual hair—ignored and sickly white, like asparagus grown under a basket, deprived of sun.

"Why're you here?" asked Peppy. "She tell you to come?"

"How can you lock yourself in your room again and make Gramma do everything?" asked Liza.

"You don't need to get down on me too. I've got enough of that shit coming from all directions, lemme tell you."

Liza sat down on the side of Peppy's mattress and extracted a cigarette from Peppy's pack, defiantly smoking it in front of her mother as a demonstration of her Adultness.

Peppy looked at her.

"Why are you dressed like that?" Peppy hit the question with a certain back-spinning English.

"I'm selling my body on the street."

"You'll be nice and easy for cops to spot."

"If I were you I wouldn't be talking about *cops*." Liza blew smoke near Peppy's face.

"Don't yell at me today, kid," said Peppy, suddenly feeling luxuriously victimized. "I've been through enough."

Liza's throat burned with frustration—it was the same communication-stalemate that always happened with her mother; both of them compulsively participating in what they both knew was a hopeless, degrading mud wrestle.

It was Liza's birthday the next day. She was thinking, with great satisfaction, that Peppy had forgotten. Liza planned to be very stoic and say nothing until the day after, when she would call up and blister her mother with the failure, and hear Peppy scramble to make amends.

"I put something on the dresser for your birthday," said Peppy. Liza resolved to be disappointed with whatever it was. She walked to the dresser and found two pairs of coffee brown nylons, size Extra Tall.

"These aren't my size," she said.

"Those aren't for you, those are for me," said Peppy.

"Since when are you Extra Tall?"

Peppy, with a grunt of effort, got up from her mattress as slowly as if she had been hospitalized for weeks. She stumbled over to the dresser and found a small red plastic bag.

"I didn't have time to wrap it. But these are good, they weren't cheap. And they weren't on sale."

Liza opened the crinkling red bag and extracted a pair of large silver and turquoise earrings in the shapes of dolphins. Liza knew in a flash that Peppy had bought them for herself in a fit of impulse shopping, then changed her mind about them.

"Ooh. Thanks. Native American hippie crap. Just what I always wanted."

There was a price tag on the back of the earrings: $24.00.

"They're sterling! And turquoise!" Peppy shouted in her defense.

Liza became infuriated to the edge of tears.

Her mother had let her grow up without providing any clues as to how to develop a concrete sense of *self,* let alone self-respect; no hints on how to grab an inner roothold. Liza felt half-baked; she was a girl who looked for answers to *really fucking important questions*—like, Who She Was, and Where Her Potential Might Lead—in the false confidence of flashy hustlers like ChoCho Santocha. Peppy had tragically failed her as a mother, and she was just lucky not to be a cringing invalid like Ned . . . .

. . . This all hit Liza as a complicated emotional fastball into her chest as she looked at the earrings. Not knowing how to articulate any of it, Liza coldly remarked, "I really, really hate dolphins," and believed she meant it.

"Look at the grotesque hippie crap she gave me," Liza said, once she had finally talked Ned into letting her in his room.

"Mom loves dolphins," he said.

"Yeah. *She* does. But I hate them. If I had a dolphin right now, I'd beat a Duraflame log right down its blowhole."

"Dolphins are beautiful and smart. If I had a dolphin, I'd have him tow me around in warm water."

Liza looked over Ned's current projects. Since the theatre had reopened, Ned and his activities had been confined to his room. The Mylar mosaics on slides had evolved; now he had constructed a large light-box and was painstakingly gluing the tiny squares and triangles of colored plastic into a big, quasipointillist design, resembling strange, geometric flowers flocking together in night skies. All the tiny, fitting pieces represented a staggering amount of patience—hours upon hours of razor blades, tweezers, glue, toothpicks. When it was plugged in, the piece looked like stained glass pirated from a temple built by tiny Moorish sorcerers; gem-speckled pinwheels; the secret watch-jewel machinery of flying carpets.

"Jesus. That's really gorgeous, Ned."

"Heh!" Ned laughed nervously. "It's just how I stay out of people's way."

"Are you all right?" Liza asked, trying to get the masked Ned to look at her with his good eye.

He avoided her searching gaze. "Oh, probably not very," said Ned, trying to sound cheerful.

"You sniffing that glue?" Liza asked, looking at the pile of small, mangled tubes.

"Nothing gives me any relief," Ned said, finally locking her eye with chilling, simple honesty. Liza felt afraid for him and found a reason to leave. She didn't know what else to say.

Back at the trailer, Liza was so unhinged by her family visit, she actually picked up the ringing phone, knowing it was ChoCho.

"Girl, why you gotta do me like this?" ChoCho apologized vociferously for his behavior; Liza more or less accepted, out of loneliness and a stinging need to escape from her own skin through any available distraction. Liza knew that ChoCho didn't really love her, and the energy he was expending toward getting her back was really just another aspect of his control-freakyness, but she craved something or someone, and he was the only volunteer.

"So what do you want to do for your birthday tomorrow?" he asked in his seductive Let's-Go-Shopping tone.

"I want you to take me to the Marin City flea market," said Liza. She was sick of watching ChoCho get his ass kissed by Union Square coke-groupies.

The next morning, at 10 a.m., ChoCho pulled up to the Lucky Drive trailer park in a white limousine. Liza threw on some of her finest ChoCho regalia—a tiny white dress, white stiletto boots, white leather bolero jacket. In the strip of mirror she looked at herself and felt powerful, if not actually happy.

"Knock him on his ass," Lorna mumbled in half-sleep.

. . .

ChoCho was leaning against the limo in a vintage gabardine suit, white tie, and Panama hat. He had obviously done himself up especially fancy on Liza's behalf, but Liza found the overall effect garish and sleazy; too *Miami Vice*. In his Sunday best, ChoCho, though inarguably handsome, was unmistakably a ghetto drug lord. Liza stepped into the limousine, thanking the chauffeur politely. ChoCho handed her a single white rose.

The flea market teemed outside of the smoked limo windows; corn dog stands, a large old truck crammed with antique telephones, wooden fruit crates filled with rusty tools, an old woman in a strange hat sitting behind a folding table, covered with statuettes of the Planter's Peanut man. Liza spotted a western saddle draped over a car door and a large tarp shingled entirely with burgundy eel-skin wallets.

. . .

Liza and ChoCho zigzagged around the market holding hands, examining dusty objects. Liza became conscious of the way that ChoCho carried himself, staring back at people who stared at the young criminal couple in white. ChoCho would occasionally give them a specious smile—*yes, thank you, fuck you, I know I'm fabulous.* Her feet began to ache in her inappropriate footwear.

"Go wait for me in the limo," said ChoCho's sly face. Liza figured he'd seen something he was going to buy for her. She hobbled to the limousine, illegally parked in the bus stop; the driver opened the door, and she sat in back with the door open, removing the torturous boots and massaging her toes.

Out of the corner of her eye, Liza saw an energetic figure begin to move toward her; she felt her atoms exhilarating like iron dust in thrall to an electromagnet, scurrying and climbing into ecstatic pyramids toward the pull, seconds before her brain even realized that it was Roland Spring. With a shiver up her thighs she realized her Impossible Luck: she was dressed to the nines and sitting in a limo. *This is probably the coolest I have ever looked in my entire life.*

"Liza? 'Zat you?" Roland asked in a merry way, seemingly delighted. Liza blushed to her core, and got up to hug him.

They chatted. Yes, he had graduated from Eiderdijken, yes, he was still in touch with the Baumgarten family. He wasn't going to college, he was currently in the corps of a small modern dance company. Liza could barely absorb what Roland was saying, she was so fascinated by his perfectly articulated sense of antistyle; his clothing was old and very worn—small holes, frayed edges—but somehow more beautiful and dignified for the repeated washings: all of his items were visibly *loved*; well cared for and well used. Through his virtuous antivanity he had organically achieved the kind of antique patina that designers often attempt to simulate through sandblasting; he was like beach glass, gently sucked and tumbled by the ocean to perfect, gemlike smoothness. He was carrying his purchase of the day, a cast-iron frying pan—it matched him, as if it was just another physical emanation of his preternaturally superior taste, economy, utility. Liza noticed that his hair, ordinarily very short, was longer—and in wild ringlets. He wore the same black glasses; Liza noticed that one of the arms was held onto the frames with a bent staple.

"Man, where'd you get those crazy threads from?" Roland asked. His big, gap-toothed smile rocketed like wet sunshine through Liza's veins and suddenly made her acutely self-conscious. His gaze, though completely friendly, yanked the rug out from under the slick persona she'd been inhabiting for months, and something she'd been in willful denial of hit her like a brick: hanging out in a white limo, wearing a $450 white leather outfit at the flea market . . . *I must look like a TOTAL WHORE.*

ChoCho materialized, in his pimp hat and suit, returning from his foray into the flea market with a zebra-skin rug. The wonderfulness of Roland made Liza feel completely *busted*, mid-drug-lord lifestyle. Until that very second, she hadn't consciously figured out that ChoCho lacked all the humble virtue that made Roland Spring starlike and exceptional.

"Roland, this is my friend ChoCho," she said, trying to sound as unenthusiastic about the word *friend* as possible.

"S'up, blood," said ChoCho, suddenly amplifying the black-eighth of his multirace background and going for an ethnic hand-grab.

"Peace, man," said Roland, in a lower vocal register than Liza had ever heard him use before, taking hold of ChoCho's thumb. She was aghast that Roland was compelled, by ChoCho, to use a deep-guy voice. The subversive, criminal "flava" of the "Street" she had so savored and envied in ChoCho was suddenly stripped of its Hollywood veneer and revealed for what it really was: corruption, addiction, moral squalor, violence, desperation, sleaze, and despair. ChoCho looked like an illness, next to Roland Spring, some opportunistic virus that turned everything malevolently white, like dry rot; and there he was with a zebra rug—an extravagant, tasteless, murderous object. As Roland hugged her, Liza felt so ashamed, she couldn't bear the thought of inflicting her tainted presence on him further, so she didn't ask for his number or offer her own. As he smiled and waved goodbye, walking off to resume his noble, magnificent life, Liza's heart snapped like the ankle of a racehorse in slow motion. She wanted to crawl into Roland's frying pan and die.

ChoCho dropped her back off at the trailer. The limo was coming back for her, late that night, to bring her back to his apartment for a "private party" with some "surprise guests"; Liza knew that there would be some token celebrity, and a lot of drugs, a repeat of the wretched scene she had already witnessed. This was supposed to be a big birthday treat.

Her phone rang.

"Happy fucking birthday you motherfucking jailbait bitch!" screamed DelVonn, with unmistakable affection.

Liza felt rotten, restless, and belligerently entitled to some unspecific form of savage self-expression; it was a destructive itch she had felt before and one she would surely feel again. She knew, like she knew in worthless detail the constellation of blemishes on her own face, that she was going to Do Something.

"What are you doing tonight, DelVonn?" she asked as she clipped on the large dolphin earrings. She knew ChoCho would hate them even more than she did.

"I'm getting really shitfaced with you?" he asked.

DelVonn could be a world-class sidekick; he had no shame. If Liza wanted to make a spectacle of herself, DelVonn would enthusiastically egg her downward in unregenerate spirals, see her wildness and raise her ten, especially if they both were drunk.

"Bring your bad self on over," said Liza.

Liza laid out on her twin bed all the expensive white clothes that Cho-Cho had bought for her. She didn't want to put any of them on, any more than she wanted to cover her body with live snails.

Lorna had left half a squeeze bottle of blue-black hair dye on the sink; Liza selected an especially pricey white wool minisuit and squirted black stripes all over it. Then she drenched various strands of her hair at random and wadded them in tinfoil—in an hour, her head would have black stripes as well.

She stuck the safety pin back in her nose hole, and it felt like victory; a dog flouting all its training, willfully dragging garbage through the house.

DelVonn showed up with a bottle of Crown Royal, and the two of them did several shots in rapid succession.

"To burning bridges," said Liza, toasting DelVonn.

"To me helping you burn bridges!" he shouted.

"To fucking up potentially valuable opportunities," said Liza.

"Fuck valuable opportunities!"

"Tonight, I do everything wrong," said Liza.

"You owe it to yourself."

"That's right. To fucking up royally."

"And we are the Royal We," said DelVonn, "and we wear the Royal Crown!"

DelVonn took a mouthful of liquor from the bottle and sprayed it at Liza in a cleansing, celebratory raspberry. Liza laughed her most raucous and abrasive laugh, one she had been politely suppressing for months.

By the time the limo showed up at the trailer court, DelVonn had been striped with thick, crusty lines of Liquid Paper; Liza's face, arms, and legs had been blackly striped with a waterproof El Marko, to match the dripping black stripes on her white suit; her hair was black in patches and battleship gray where she had sloppily rinsed the dye over her bleach job.

Liza had sawed a hole in the middle of the zebra rug with a pair of scissors; DelVonn now wore it as a poncho with nothing but a G-string underneath.

ChoCho answered the door with two glasses of champagne in his hand. His face fell.

"Oh boy," he said, quietly. "What is *this*?"

"We're *zebras*!" Liza shouted.

DelVonn muscled past ChoCho and went galloping into the living room like an avenging pygmy warlord.

A couch full of sleek people jerked to attention at the sight of DelVonn; he scowled back, an aboriginal skull-negative with glowering white eyeballs.

"Whatssamatter, ain't none of you bitches ever seen a motherfucking zebra before?! Moo!" he shouted in his shrill voice.

"Moo," said Liza, taking the glass of champagne from ChoCho and swilling it in several fast gulps.

The celebrity guest-stars of the night, Liza noticed immediately, were S———, a young man in his twenties who had virtually grown up on various television sitcoms (and, Liza knew, had a pop recording career in Japan), and D———, the suave host of a nationally syndicated dance party show; both were clearly high. Two girls in matching stretch-velveteen pantsuits with identical D-cup breast implants had been provocatively mock-wrestling on the carpet when DelVonn rudely upstaged them.

"Shit-howdy! Drugs!" shouted DelVonn, spotting a tidy mound of white powder on the table. "Zebras love drugs!"

Liza lunged for S——— and D———. "Oh, lookie! Celebrity cokeheads! Tell me, what was it that first attracted you to ChoCho? Was it is his incredible *personality*?" she shouted, staring at ChoCho with cold fury. ChoCho turned a shade of olive Liza had never seen before; for a second, she felt afraid.

"Don't look at me like that!" she shrieked. "You know what you are, ChoCho? I figured it out: You're *Joan Crawford*! Behind the super-clean, fluffy-white-ChoCho show, you're just a mean, scared bitch!"

"You're an *Unhappy Donut*!" shouted DelVonn, getting in on the act. S——— suddenly began laughing uproariously and crawled over to give DelVonn a "high-five."

"You're awesome, little man! You're funny as shit!"

DelVonn took this as his cue to stick uncut drinking straws up each nostril and inhale as much cocaine as he could. There was a fast series of *schluck*ing sounds, then DelVonn coughed loudly, pounding his fist on the table. S——— went into giddy hysterics, inspiring D———, and the velveteen girls began to laugh as well. DelVonn had won the room with pure dazzle.

ChoCho lit a cigarette; his eyes were black and dull. "We're going to Alias tonight," said ChoCho, referring to the city's newest, hottest floating nightclub. "We're on the guest list, so, uh . . . Liza? You'll be leaving now. Goodbye."

Oooh, this was it; the cold breakup-face.

"Guest list? Who cares!" screamed DelVonn. "Liza and I are on the *endangered species* list! So much for your tired-ass plans!"

"Let's take Zebra-man with us!" shouted S———.

"Let's not end it bad. I'm sorry things didn't work out, all right?" ChoCho whispered to Liza, with the dulcet undertone which had said to dozens of girls *I'm dumping you, but you won't call the cops on me because I'm too sweet, right?*

Even in her drunk and inflamed state, Liza knew that there was really nothing more to say. Her anger dribbled away, transforming into the anticlimactic understanding that ChoCho was ChoCho; she had finally awakened from the enchantment and could see into his dismally crippled soul, and what more could be done? Like a novelty cartoon made to look like one thing right-side-up and another thing upside-down, the trick really only worked once; after seeing the submissive image the first time, you could never be blind to it again. The instant of minor magic became just another piece of disposable information, another sad piece of carnival debris.

"OK. No hard feelings," she said, offering her striped hand for shaking. ChoCho took it with warm relief, guiding her softly but forcibly to the door. There had been some good times, and each felt a flash of poignancy as Liza fidgeted with her short skirt in the doorway for what they both knew would be the last time. (The feeling would vaporize the second the door clicked shut with Liza on the other side; they would both realize, simultaneously, that they were delighted to be rid of each other.)

"I'm leaving!" Liza shouted to DelVonn.

"I'm staying!" DelVonn shouted back; by now he was riding S———— like a pony, kicking his thighs as he crawled around the rug on all fours.

"Happy Birthday," said ChoCho, giving her a chaste farewell kiss on the cheek.

"Tssk," said Liza.

The door shut, and that was it. Loud laughter erupted behind the white door.

As Liza began to walk toward the bus stop, she stopped to stomp and lean on the tall heels of her $70 pumps until they snapped; she aggressively twisted the heels off and dumped them into the nearest mailbox. She tried to feel powerful, but as she hobbled along on the shanks of broken shoes, she was left mainly with a lonely, hollow, Unhappy Donut–like sensation.

The next afternoon, back at the trailer, still covered with ghostly, semi-permanent ink stripes that no soap would remove, Liza held one of the old Fotostop prints of DelVonn in a powdered wig. It was the photo that started her whole trip down the Cape Horn rabbit hole.

In the kitchen sink of the trailer, Liza's white clothes were being dyed black in what looked like an oil spill. Everything Liza wore would look smeary and tie-dyed, for a little while, until the flea market replenished her wardrobe with plaids and color.

The worst part of the whole episode, for Liza, was the rotten realization that Peppy was right, even though she'd never said a word—she had seen through ChoCho right away. *Add to all of my millions of defects that I am a shitty judge of character*, thought Liza.

"Hey," said Lorna, emerging from the back of the trailer with a small cake. "Congratulations."

"On what?"

"Well, Happy Birthday, a day late," said Lorna. "Also, you got a call from Butch Strange. He likes your porno stuff. He wants to give you some work."

It was October 26, 1984. Liza had just turned seventeen. She was grossed out by the idea of doing anything even vaguely smut related for a living, but glad for a chance to make money again.

"That is so nice of you," said Liza. It was a chocolate-frosted cake in a cardboard pan, with three lit pink candles.

"I'm a nice person," said Lorna.

"You're the only one I know," said Liza.

"Oh, come on. You have to figure out what you learned that was positive from all this," said Lorna, the true (if estranged) child of a New Age marijuana mom.

A flash-edited blur of after-school specials, tender sitcom moments, teen public service announcements, and needlepoint wall plaques cavorted in a circle around Liza's mind like trained pigs in embroidered vests and Tyrolean hats.

"Are you actually telling me that I shouldn't have tried to be somebody else because I should always BE TRUE TO MYSELF?" Liza yelled, pretending to slit her wrists with a butter knife while making choking sounds.

"No," said Lorna. "I was thinking more along the lines of something my grandmother always used to say: 'Pit Elegance Against Despair.' You thought you were pretty hot shit for a while, in those white clothes, right?"

"Not exactly."

"Oh, come on, you thought you were Little Miss Celebrity-Pants. So, now, if you're feeling bad about yourself, you know it helps to dress up and look good."

"Fuck Sex, Let's Play Dress Up!" said Liza, quoting the Cape Horn bathroom wall, partially regretting that she was dyeing all of her best clothes in the sink, badly.

"You're my best friend," said Liza, right before she blew out the candles.

"What did you wish for?"

"I can't tell you, or it won't come true," said Liza.

God, please let something cool and special happen to me this year so I am not a complete fucking loser. (Preferably singing/actress related.) Help me be true to myself yet be more Roland Springish at the same time. And thanks for Lorna. Amen.

PART V

EXILE ON

PHANTASY ISLAND

(A Judeo–Christian Rock Opera)

San Francisco, Fall, 1988

 QUANTUM THEORY once described by UFO conspiracy figurehead Bob Lazar paraphrased something like this: space is pliable. How does one travel millions of light-years in the blink of an eye? One generates autonomous gravity, and the result (he said) is "kind of like putting a bowling ball in the middle of a waterbed." Time and space, if you have the technology, can be warped to order.

We are dropping such a bowling ball on Liza, bringing her instantly and traumatically to the age of twenty-one.

Liza was now a scowly, suspicious, and feisty girl with damaged hair and a nasty temper. Things were not working out. Despite what she perceived to be grueling effort, she had not been Discovered or made Connections with the Right People, and she did not seem, in any way, to be advancing down the golden path. Still, she ached to be an internationally beloved chanteuse, and for the redemption it would bring her from a life tarred by unjust humiliations.

The girls had moved out of the trailer and into various temporary roommate situations in the Haight-Ashbury district of San Francisco, birthplace of the hippie, flower power, and psychedelic movements. In the late 1980s, the Haight was teeming with panhandling punk teenagers, speed freaks, stylishly ragged poseurs on vintage motorcycles, damp and dingy bars and cafés, counterculture shoe shops, and liquor stores. It was where young people in their twenties, after dropping out of state universities, went to boldly experience drug consumption, casual sex, and menial jobs. Generations of young people had come to this cosmic whirlpool, ingested strange substances, and found themselves sucked through interdimensional wormholes into alternate universes, paranoid schizophrenia, and Nietzsche-delic spin-cycles of Eternal Return that sucked away all their money and sent them back home to live with their parents. Decade by decade, kids tuned in, turned on, and flipped out in Icarian bouts of consciousness-expanding that crashed and burned. Today, you can tell how long a girl has been on Haight Street by the tattoos and other body modifications, which date her like forest fire rings on a tree stump: *Look, there's the 1983 Black Flag tattoo, and the 1985 anklet-rosary tattoo, and the 1988 Rockabilly cat tattoo . . . there's the pock from the 1992 eyebrow piercing . . . that's the 1997 ritual scarification . . .* now, of course, she is wearing a little bridesmaid's halter dress, and the permanent accessories of her past are clashing, sore reminders of a world she never thought she'd outgrow.

For money, Liza was working for Centaur Productions, and Butch Strange.

Butch was a short, pudgy man in his forties, who many of his employees suspected had been born a woman. He had small hands, a thin mustache, and always wore a baggy black horsehide vest.

"You know what Slash Fiction is?" Butch asked Liza when he hired her, jettisoning a black wad of juice through the gap in his teeth into a mason jar.

"Nope," said Liza.

Butch tossed a handful of cheap, mimeographed booklets onto his desk. One was entitled *Battlestar Gaylactica*; its cover featured a pencil drawing of Apollo and Starbuck locked in a shirtless embrace. Another was entitled *Very Happy Days* and featured a pencil drawing of the Fonz and Richie Cunningham kissing passionately, Fonzie reaching authoritatively down Ritchie's pants. Another booklet featured Captain Kirk and Mr. Spock staring into each other's eyes, horizontal, Spock on top.

"Slash fiction is homoerotic, usually," Butch explained, sucking his cheek. "It's fan fiction for people who want to read about Starsky fucking Hutch and stuff like that."

"Wow," said Liza, fascinated, leafing through the stack.

"I want you to try something else. I want to try to aim this stuff at young women. Heterosexual, softcore slash. More romantic."

"Uh-huh," said Liza, transfixed by an image of a naked Erik Estrada being straddled and handcuffed by his partner from *CHiPs*.

The prose was purple and wishfully overwritten; Liza liked the "literary" pretensions—it made the smut seem more emotionally sincere. It was mysteriously easy, Liza noticed, to imagine the characters in a hardcore gay context.

Liza's new job consisted of watching movies and TV, manufacturing fairly tame, "vanilla" sexual fantasies about the male leads, and typing them onto an old IBM Selectric II that Butch let her take home. Hurling herself into fantasy scenarios with handsome actors was one thing, but projecting her mind into fictional constructs in order to have sex with fictional characters was time-consuming, libido-warping and, she thought, pathetic. But it was easy, Butch paid her eight dollars a page under the table, and she was able to produce anywhere from seven to ten pages a week, if she could latch on to a movie stud she actually had the hots for. Butch was willing to buy everything she could crank out, once it met his criteria.

At first, Butch brutally edited her pieces and handed them back to her covered with red pen; finally, Liza was so sick of rewriting things she learned to adapt to a fail-safe structure that she wrote and stuck on the wall in front of her typewriter:

1. Describe show environment + intro characters

BABERUNNER by L. LaRoman
(Or: Do Androids Sleep with Electric
Sheep?)

Decker sat in his dark apartment and
drank his whiskey, one of the few comforts
left in the urban chaos of New Tokyo, and
watched the geisha winking on the thirty-
foot billboard outside of his window. Air
transports hummed through the crowded
skies. Rachel, he thought. She is probably
dead by now. . . .

2. Set up the horny feelings

. . . . and that's too bad, because I
wanted to fuck that beautiful Replicant into
a hundred spare bio-parts . . .
The door burst open. Decker's arm swung
under his leather chair and found the laser
gun. The red dot found Rachel's forehead as
she entered the room, the slats from the
window shades casting neon stripes onto her
angular cheekbones, cold and perfect.
"Rachel," Decker gasped, lowering the gun.
Her high-collared fur coat fell open,
revealing a silky, champagne-colored slip
underneath, clinging to her classically
engineered bio-physique . . .

3. Set up place they finally do it (NOT BEDROOM)

(Tearing her black hair down from its stiff
chignon, Decker pushes her onto the steel lid
of his orgone accumulator and leans heavily
over her superior form; is she breathing
harder? Is her heart beating faster? Do
Replicants feel physical pleasure?
If she's anatomically correct, she can

learn, Decker thinks, ripping a long black
stocking down her flawless, ivory thigh . . .

4. *Everybody has screaming O. by page 4–5 with
many adjectives.*

(. . . she whimpered, her eyes rolling
back in a program-overload wholly resembling
bliss—This is a woman, I don't care who
invented her, Decker thinks, clasping her
Dermostyrene breast and shuddering his hot
animate being into her invisible diodes and
gears . . .)

Soon Liza had written quite a collection of slash booklets and was
thereby keeping body and soul together with basic necessities.

The Normal Family Dinner Theatre was having its share of difficulties.

Peppy's life was a nerve jungle of court appearances, after the Morgenstern incident. The assistant district attorney of Marin County
opted to arraign Peppy on an aggravated assault charge—a felony,
which, if she was convicted, could hold a jail penalty of two years.
Peppy became hysterical at the news, despite her public defender's repeated assurances that he could get the charge lowered, since her car
keys hardly classified as a "deadly weapon." During the arraignment,
the public defender wheezed bravely about her "contributions to the
community," the "devastating blow" the review meant to her professional and personal life, and the brave home-care she had undertaken of
her "mentally incompetent son." There were titters among the lawyers
and families of the other arraignment cases on the calendar as the Morgenstern review was read in its entirety. Peppy, who attended court in a
powder blue pantsuit, was zombified on Valium, staring vacantly forward with heavy blue eyelids over bloodshot slits. Eventually, Peppy
pleaded no contest to a charge of simple assault and battery, and received six months of probation and a $750 fine.

Peppy thought the nightmare was over, but two weeks later, a letter arrived on embossed Grosvenor & Grosvenor law firm stationery, announcing that Morgenstern intended to sue Peppy for $2 million, for

having caused him "severe emotional trauma," rendering him "incapable of performing his job at the required level of professionalism." Peppy asked Mike, "Seriously: how much do you think it would cost me to have Morgenstern killed?"

Noreen and Earl plied her with tranquilizers and sweet vermouth.

"You can't kill him because you'd go to jail and I won't marry a jailbird," Earl would say, smiling and vigorously stroking Peppy's cold hand.

Peppy would look at him rudely. "We're not getting married, Earl."

"Says you," he'd say, winking at Noreen.

In the civil case, Radcliffe Grosvenor (III) Esq., representing Morgenstern, was able to obtain a settlement against Peppy for $200,000. Peppy screamed at the judge and was ordered to remain calm. Peppy's hired defense lawyer, Lou Schwab (a dog-hair-covered guy whom Earl found in a Terra Linda strip mall—he had dusty file folders stacked up his walls from the early 1970s, and scabs of dried mustard on his suit), appealed the decision, thus stalling the inevitable, but it was fairly clear that Peppy would lose the battle royale.

She considered filing bankruptcy in order to avoid paying the settlement but was advised that in the case of an intentional tort, such as having physically attacked someone, she would probably be forced to come up with the cash anyway. Either way Peppy was eventually going to lose the theatre.

Liza attended a few of the court proceedings in order to hold hands with Noreen, who was wracked with anxiety. She was surprised, at one point, to see Rad Grosvenor, who was working for his father, assuming the family tradition of lawyerdom. She'd never noticed, when they were in high school, how much his features resembled Tonto's, and she felt a hard pinch of her old longing. She had a *connection* to Tonto; it was inevitable, they had been truly intimate, in an awful, fucked-up way. Tonto, she figured, was probably as scarred by their whole collision as she was. They had a *bond*.

She tapped Rad's shoulder in the cavernous hallway. "Are you Tonto's brother?" she asked.

"I was, yeah," he said, giving her a dry handshake. Rad, who was a virtual adult in high school, was now even more adult than most adults—his blue wool suit, his red tie and white shirt were crisper and pricier than those of most executives twice his age; his hair more conservative, his soapy smell more astringent, his shave closer, his demeanor more clipped and professional.

"Aren't you still?" asked Liza, something in her bowels sensing a rotten thrill.

"He died a little over a year ago," Rad said, his eyes shifting in his head, as if to avoid witnessing Liza's reaction.

"O" said Liza, her mouth making the noise with almost no air, as the vinyl-tiled floor slid out from under her, leaving her legs dangling over the abyss of mortality. "I'm . . . . . I'm really really sorry, I didn't . . . . . . I . . . ."

"Yeah, thanks . . . . You knew him?"

Liza thought back to the notes, the garage, the deflowering among the flowerpots, the mohawk. In a small way, she was relieved that the witness to her shame was gone; a dirty part of her felt strangely elated that her injustice had been karmically avenged; an even dirtier part of her found it thrilling to be connected, in a small way, to this tragedy, death possessing its own potent breed of celebrity; but the sharpest feeling, flooding over all of these, was one of having been *robbed*—Liza felt her story with Tonto *wasn't over*; she wasn't *done with him yet*. Death stole the day she had half-imagined in the future, when she would reel in that long string and pull Tonto's face in front of hers, and she would be famous, and he wouldn't.

"I knew him. I . . . . yeah. He was pretty much the embodiment of high school, for me," Liza managed.

Rad gave her a distant smile with a trace of something almost like warmth, or pity.

"Do you mind telling me what happened?" she asked, feeling creepy the second the question left her mouth.

"It was a motorcycle accident," Rad said in an automatic way, as if this stripped-down, oft-repeated fact were his hole puncher—the ticket, the question, was handed to him, and he would punch in that exact hole, forever and ever.

"What's your name?" he asked.

"Liza Normal. You're suing my mom," she said, feeling she owed him that much honesty.

They said goodbye and didn't speak again.

"Tonto's *dead*," Liza wailed on the phone to Lorna, later that night. She needed a cool, soothing earful of Lorna's sympathies. Tonto's death set off a whole chain reaction of freaked-out feelings; it served as a drain hole down which tears for multiple sorrows could be cried.

Realizing that her remaining time in the theatre was limited, Peppy decided to stall the inevitable by appealing the civil judgment, in order to use the space, in its numbered, final days, to earn as much money as she could. After a night of drunken brainstorming with Mike and Ike, the three of them landed on the concept of exploiting Marin County's enduring self-improvement fetish; they would turn the theatre into a Drama Therapy camp, where repressed and nervous adults could act out in a "safe and supportive environment."

"Besides, if we look like a 'therapeutic community' it might give us a better chance on the appeal," Peppy reasoned.

A New Center
For Healing
Through Self-Expression:
LICENSED DRAMA THERAPISTS
NEEDED!
Send Resume + Credentials
to Dr. Mike LoBato
c/o Normal Family Dinner Theatre

Mike felt mildly uncomfortable about calling himself a doctor, but Peppy assured him people did it all the time, and nobody would find out "unless he traumatized someone."

"Why don't *you* pretend to be the doctor?" Ike asked Peppy.

"Because I traumatize people all the goddamn time," she said with enough vehemence that Ike realized it was a sore point.

Lorna had fallen in love with a tattoo artist named Jimmy "Jimbo" Beaugereaux, and over the past two years had become covered with thick, black, "modern primitive" tribal designs that suggested anacondas squeezing her into submission. Jimbo was only too happy to have a human sketch pad, since he had run out of space on his own body, which had been covered with ink during a particularly Catholic phase and resembled a criminal, Chicano rendition of the Sistine Chapel.

Lorna and Jimbo were renting a room in a somewhat notorious two-story Victorian on Waller Street, the communal home of five like-minded young adults given to the consumption of acid and amphetamines. This group had enjoyed a sudden, collective-consciousness breakthrough in the living room the previous summer, when they realized together, in a swarming night of weeping, synergistic madness, that they were Elves. Since that night, all of their energies had been focused, like those of born-again Christians, toward a new, vibrant, spiritual center of Elfhood.

"Elf House" was run by four emaciated boys with long flowing hair and pointy shoes. The lease holder was a high school football star from Foster City named Greg Coates, who, once his blond hair grew to midwaist and his thick sport muscle melted into lean, speedy elf-strings, had changed his name to Greycoat. His fingernails were long and blue; he jingled with an excess of silver jewelry; his gray overcoat was stenciled with runes.

Greycoat's best friend, Steve Barden, became known as Slipper; he was known for his silver-painted skateboard, outlandishly named TimeRod; he claimed to be able to travel interdimensionally on it, down certain treacherous hills. His longtime girlfriend had recently changed her name to Faun Bell; in her lucid dreams (she said), she was a pocket-size creature who traveled on the neck of a baby deer.

Nodnik and Paisley were two video arcade stoners from Sacramento who had originally just been ancillary roommates, but who had been too weak-minded not to be swept along with the irresistible new group identity.

All of the card-carrying members of the Elf tribe had "remembered" a time and place, a "simultaneous incarnation" in a "separate but parallel astral dimension," where life was an eternal garden of meadows, flute music, and waterfalls, and all beings delighted in the interconnective harmony of nature. Elves and faeries sang as naturally and joyfully as crickets, and slept in the velvet faces of dew-kissed pansies. Love, the true and inexhaustible currency of the universe, zapped in free currents from plant to elf to animal to bee and back around in a dervish circle of ecstatic, honey-drunk rapture.

"It all sounds pretty fuckin' *twee*," sniggered Liza.

"Oh, but it's *sweet*," said Lorna, in a pitying voice.

Lorna and Jimbo hadn't had "The Awakening," but the elves considered them part of their extended "Otherkin" community anyway—they thought of Jimbo as a "living Church," projecting antique divinity through the large, barbed-wire-encircled Sacred Heart tattooed on his sternum—Jimbo had met Greycoat by tattooing Druidic runes on him. Lorna, with her thick stripes, was seen as a primitive shaman-woman, capable of shape-shifting into big cats; the elves all swore they had seen Lorna's "tiger body" prowling the halls on certain stoned nights. This was all fine with Lorna and Jimbo; it was a nice house, centrally located, the rent was cheap, and the amusing scene was not unlike living at the Renaissance Faire all year-round.

Liza attended a party at Elf House with Lorna and found herself drawn in by getting a crush on Greycoat (all girls did, at first, until they realized that his elfin mystique was mainly used to expose an endless parade of giggling new Haight Street conquests to his version of "Sex Magick"). Something about the scene reactivated the tingling voodoo part of her mind that she had first experienced at The Vats; she had to acknowledge that it was *possible* that the elves knew more than she did about other heightened, sparkling dimensions. Or maybe it was all just the acid, but she wasn't sure.

Since Liza wasn't getting along with the other roommates in her Mission District apartment, Lorna petitioned for Liza to move into Elf House. The elves needed another roommate, but they vaguely mistrusted Liza—she had ingested acid with them, a few times, but she had not officially had "The Awakening" and was therefore capable of screwing up the very complicated, invisible web of "Thoughtweave" they had psychically knitted around the household (another way of stating that she was capable of questioning the authenticity of the Elf Experience and/or mocking it). Lorna assured them that Liza was "a benign spirit" and would not interfere with their vibrational frequencies. With some reluctance, Liza was allowed to move into one of the six small bedrooms flanking the dark, narrow halls of the old Victorian, for $280 a month.

Within a few weeks, Liza truly envied the passion and euphoria of the elf bund and longed to participate in their heady collective reality. She craved their sense of grandiose spiritual privilege. There was at least a sense of an important cultural project happening at Elf House; plus, the elves enjoyed a miniaturized version of fame in the neighborhood, and Liza wanted in on it.

Greycoat, Liza, and Paisley were in the living room, doing lines of methamphetamine off of a china plate at 2 a.m. and listening to Eric Satie's *Gymnopédies*. Greycoat took a long, clay gnome-pipe off of the mantel and began stuffing it with marijuana, staring through Liza in his piercing, insecurity-inducing way. The pupil in his left eye was smeared from a childhood injury, so it looked like a tiny black bowling pin, giving him an unnerving, predatory gaze. It was a power-stare; Greycoat knew it made the subject feel like a slug frying under a lens.

Liza, sensing a moment to disarm, confide, and connect, tried with all of her powers of speed-fueled articulation to translate and share her experience of the Golden Stag in The Vats, her lifelong hunt, and its significance to her destiny.

"I can't figure out the specifics but I keep *watching*, and I have this spider-sense that if the exact right constellation of antlers and other stuff lines up around me, then, my true, like, *enlightened* self will come out of its cocoon . . . ."

She rambled for a while, trying to explain it all without mentioning how she thought this True Enlightened Self tied into celebrity. Greycoat and Paisley gazed at each other knowingly through the smoke. A puckish smile curled onto Greycoat's red lips; Paisley gave a kind of snort and shook his head.

"I think your experience was artificial," Greycoat told her with a face of infinite sympathy.

"Whaddaya mean, *artificial?*" asked Liza, hurt and defensive.

"I don't mean to put you down, but that's exactly the kind of psychic . . . uh, *delusion* . . . . that is, unfortunately, the result of doing too much acid with an unprepared mind." Greycoat toked off of the long clay pipe again, two white columns of smoke curling out of his nostrils.

Paisley nodded in agreement. "Yep. Exactly."

"*Ai, camlost Engwar,*" Greycoat said in conspiratorial tones to Paisley.

Liza knew they were speaking Quenya, the J. R. R. Tolkien version of High Elf language, and it annoyed her severely—*Engwar*, she had learned, meant "sickly human." *Fuckers.*

"*Firimar*," Paisley said, laughing.

Their smug condescension infuriated Liza, but she was still jealous, even as she stormed out of the room to their high, whinnying elf-giggles.

In the daylight world, Liza was scrappily doing anything she could to stick herself into the public eye. She had a gig doing cover songs at a juice bar on Market Street, for a while; the sign written on the dry-ink board and posted in the window had read:

> POWER SMOOTHIE LUNCH WORKOUT SPECIAL $2.95
>
> WHEAT-GRASS SHOTS
>
> LIVE MUSIC FRIDAYS!
>
> LIZA NORMAL SINGS THE SONGS
>
> OF LISA LISA & THE CULT JAM
>
> Virgil Ortiz on Electric Piano

Cape Horn had purchased a karaoke machine, which Liza would visit if she was really desperate; the queens were viciously competitive and domineering, and Liza would often have to wait through endless Madonna, Streisand, and George Michael numbers before finally getting onstage, at which point nobody paid any attention to her. Apart from Virgil Ortiz, her accompanist, none of the old crowd from the *Mommie* days was around anymore . . . LaTuna and Ragina had both taken ill and retreated backward into deep midwestern states they had, only a few years earlier, taken great, expressive pains to run as far away from as the continent would allow. (AIDS was prompting a yo-yo snap back into the fold of sympathetic, if not actually understanding, families, for many of San Francisco's brightest stars.)

DelVonn, after the fateful night at ChoCho's house, had really hit the big time. He became part of S———and D———'s general entourage, and the world had cracked open for him and revealed its inner geode. He had recently starred in a documentary entitled *Dwarf: Living*

Large and made guest appearances on two sitcoms; the rest of the time he made a killing working for a Hollywood party company that supplied celebrity look-alikes and other novelty players—jugglers, contortionists, and other performance creatures. DelVonn got paid hundreds of dollars to attend corporate and Hollywood industry functions in a bondage-jester outfit and be his outrageous self. He was a big hit and was now spending half of his time in LA, where he rented a basement studio in Northeast Hollywood, and San Francisco, where he still had a lucrative relationship with Centaur Productions. Liza could barely stand talking to him on the phone, she was so jealous.

"You still shaking your ass over at that juice bar?" DelVonn would ask, in a teasing tone.

"Are you still short?" Liza would snap back.

Finally, through Virgil, Liza met an "agent": Burt Swan was a dandruffy alcoholic working out of a tiny, cluttered office near the Fell Street freeway overpass. His walls were covered with sun-faded pictures of shirtless male models, cut out from magazines. Ancient copies of *Variety* lay about, curling from beverage accidents. His clients were mostly male models too unusual or "exotic" (brown) looking to get into more reputable agencies, but he was alerted to various "cattle calls" in the area—the occasional search for crowd scene extras or fresh commercial faces to dot with acne medication. Burt complained that there was "no industry for cabaret," but he promised he'd keep Liza's number in his Rolodex, just in case any auditions came up. Liza made a point of calling his machine every Monday; he screened her calls, never picking up the phone.

One was easily absorbed into life around Elf House because there were always Big Plans. On the esoteric front, there was big talk about building a gate on the astral dimension, through which they could return to a place they had all "glimpsed with their hearts," alternatively referred to as Aelfheim, Rivendell, or Shamballa; the elves all spoke of returning to this fantastic place with the urgent homesickness of POWs.

"How exactly does one 'build a gate on the astral dimension?'" Liza asked in a snippier-than-necessary tone one morning over breakfast as Greycoat ate his yogurt (since Liza's romantic feelings toward Greycoat were ignored, their roommate relationship had devolved into a pitch of constant, nattering antagonism).

"*Belethin*," said Slipper. Faun Bell giggled. The brass bells tied to her ankles tinkled as she tiptoed to the old refrigerator.

"We create a bridge, a *yanta*, through celebration and ritual," said Greycoat simply and patiently, like it was the most obvious thing in the world. "All time exists simultaneously. We have déjà-vus because our past selves, our future selves, and our parallel selves are all in play at the same time, separated by a sense of 'now,' which is only an illusory part of the space-time continuum-construct which is the burden of three-dimensional life."

Liza did not want to believe him, but something about the conviction with which he said it created a buzzing sensation in her skull that made it feel annoyingly True.

"So when does all this hoop-de-doo go down?" asked Liza.

"*Beltane*. May Day. You don't wake up at the Kinship Gathering, Liza, there's no hope for you."

"Blessed be," said Faun Bell, revealing her most winsome, spiritual smile to the breakfast table before pouring milk onto her bowl of Lucky Charms. Liza regarded her with contempt.

Greycoat was growing increasingly paranoid about the other druggo-mystical subcultures thriving in the Haight. Alien House, a large, purple Victorian on Clayton Street, had started to gather followers when new mutations of MDMA appeared on the street; these were people who believed that dancing around in a circle to European "trance" music, while flying on the new designer drugs, put them in contact with aliens. Several Alien House tenants claimed to be abductees; they had tales of "lost time" on lonely roads, blinking in the light of a particularly bright star, then coming to, hours later, miles away, with strange, triangular puncture marks on their backs. Greycoat believed that the big-eyed, Zeta-Reticuli aliens they obsessed on were sexless intergalactic drones who victimized humans and cows in order to poach their hormones. "They can't breed naturally anymore, so they're trying to kick-start their genetic strain through inter-specific bioengineering."

"Right, gotcha," said Liza, sarcastically. Secretly, she thought the evidence was compelling.

Then there was the clique of vampires; a ragtag band of pathetic, slow-moving Goths whom the Elf House denizens regarded as "dark elves" who'd lost their souls. The vampires liked to cut themselves and bleed each other; several had shelled out to get permanent dental-bonded fangs on their eyeteeth. They were listless bisexuals with bad posture, fucked-up professional lives, tragic romantic histories, and demanding heroin habits, who crept around at night, played marathons of fantasy computer games, dabbled fearfully in Satanism, and cried a lot. The vampires were harmless to everyone but themselves, but Greycoat perceived them as a "cloud of darkness" that needed to be resolutely fought. He wasted a lot of energy antagonizing unsuspecting Goths around the neighborhood.

"What say you, *Dokkalvar*?" Liza heard Greycoat say, menacing a black-haired guy wearing a velvet shirt and a bunch of deconstructed rosary beads in front of the bagel shop.

"What are you babbling about?" the Goth drawled in annoyance, obviously hungover.

"Stay thee weak in thy darkness," Greycoat murmured, making a spooky magickal hand-gesture, his rings clicking.

"Hooo-oo. Whatever you say, Ladyhawke," said the Goth, with a sarcastic eye-roll, returning his attention to his egg sandwich.

"You feel how he sucks at you?" Greycoat asked Liza. "Look at his muddy energy, it's like a black hole, he just sucks all the light in." Greycoat spat three times in the direction of the Goth, with his arms crossed over his chest. "Vampires are like rats, they have no sense of courtesy. Just *Me-me-me. My needs are what's important.* No sense of interconnectivity."

"He's just trying to eat his bagel," said Liza.

"You *would* say that."

Greycoat snapped the end of his overcoat away from Liza, protecting himself from her contamination.

It was April. Cutting winds blew plastic trash down Haight Street that collected in gritty corners and doorways. The attendant squalor of druggy lifestyles was easy to bear in the summer, when one could loiter outdoors, cut the legs off of old pants, and live on cheap Popsicles, but it was depressing toward the end of winter, when light-starvation, the craving for rich, unaffordable foods, and the constant apartment chill was so bone deep, it kept everyone dour in their dirty living rooms, digging black sludge out of bongs with a coat hanger.

Liza was embarking on a new slash booklet for Butch Strange, when she realized there was really no adequate female lead in *Road Warrior* with which to sexually engage Mel Gibson.

"So make one up," said Butch.

"I can do that?"

"Give it a whirl. It'll either work or it won't."

It was a good idea.

Mad Max needs a renegade girl, Liza thought. *Someone cruel and tough and vicious, with her own muscle car. Someone who can terrorize him.*

THE ROAD WARRIOR MEETS THE ROAD AMAZON

Max stood by his smoldering vehicle, the black desert road stretching and vanishing into pinpoints on the horizon, in both directions. Goddamn booby trap . . . . the middle of nowhere. Precious gasoline was hemorrhaging from both tanks. He quickly gathered rags from the backseat, trying to sop up the fluid before it vanished into the dirt. The outback sun was high, the boiling water in the radiator, once it cooled down, wouldn't last him more than a couple of days.

The noise of a distant engine told him he wouldn't be alone for long. A black speck crept into view on the road to the East, shimmering in waves of afternoon heat. The speck grew larger as the engine roared over the flat land in rolling fits of sound.

A car.

Not just any car, but a Grand Torino with a 351 Cleveland engine, fortified with riveted plates of sheet metal. A combat vehicle.

(Liza had asked Nodnik what kind of big, loud car he drove back in Sacramento, when he was still a White Punk on Dope.)

He saw the blonde hair and thought it must be one of Gargantua's boy-slaves until her long, smooth legs swung out of the car. Her pistol was drawn.

"Gimme your gas," she commanded in a harsh voice.

Max couldn't believe his eyes. Women didn't survive alone in this wasteland—they were either raped and flayed on the road or taken prisoner. The lucky ones escaped to the coasts.

Max indicated his leaky tanks with a dirty thumb.

The girl leapt to her trunk and shoved two plastic buckets under Max's car to catch the spluttering fluids.

"Get in the backseat," rasped the girl, keeping the gun trained on Max's head. Max raised a scarred eyebrow.

She gestured to her car. "Strip first."

Max slowly peeled off his dirty leather clothes in disbelief. The blonde, a rapacious, lip-licking amazon-slut of obvious physical strength, seemed sexually drunk on the anarchic violence of the road. She watched Max with a wry smile, wandered over, and slapped his naked ass, hard.

"You're cute," she whispered, tonguing his ear. She took a deep inhale of his gamey stench, and let out a savage sigh. Max noticed her wide backseat was lined with dozens of rabbit pelts . . . .

Butch loved the girl. "She's awesome. You can use her all the time. Just have her show up anywhere you need a female. Have you got a name for her yet?"

"No," said Liza, feeling a small rush of creative gratification. She was so unused to getting praise for anything, she felt almost drunk until she remembered that she hated the job.

Butch looked around his office. There was a small plaster replica of the Venus de Milo that had been pilfered from a local bar.

. . .

Thus was born Venal de Minus, the latex-thonged Moloch who, over the coming years, would throttle Liza like a sacrificial chicken.

Butch released *The Venal de Minus Series*—a batch of select slash fanfiction. Venal, a timeless figure, could waltz into any movie in any era and brutally ravage the male lead. For James Dean in *Rebel Without A Clothes*, she would appear in a doorway with a switchblade, wearing a tight black cashmere sweater, ski pants, and stiletto heels, which would end up making small, semicircular dents in his chest. For Mickey Rourke in *9½ Minutes*, she was a mysterious, crowbar-wielding socialite in a black limousine, who left him weeping in the gutter from pain and unfulfilled longing. She cudgeled the shit out of Judd Nelson in *Breakfast Clubbing* as a nunchaku-wielding ninja-cheerleader, pierced Jack Nicholson's other nostril with a carpet tack in *Venal de Chinatown*, and hog-tied Paul Newman in *tHUD,* dragging him a quarter mile down a dirt road behind her Cadillac before molesting him behind a creosote bush.

Meanwhile, Liza really only wanted to *sing*.

While she really didn't want to give Greycoat the satisfaction, Liza finally decided to ask if she could pay him a nominal fee to make a "spell" for her; an Elfmagick charm that might boost her singing career. ("Why not? What have you got to lose?" Lorna had said, instead of shooting down the idea, as Liza had hoped she would.)

"Oh, fine, whatever," Greycoat groused. "Give me fifteen dollars and I'll make you a bath spell."

"A *what?*"

"Baths are great, you can use them to get rid of daily spiritual detritus and hexes," said Faun Bell.

Liza felt stupid but handed Greycoat a wad of crumpled bills. She was desperate.

A couple of hours later, Greycoat knocked on her door with a mayonnaise jar full of rock salt suspended in a green gel, which Liza realized later was Palmolive. There were sludgy brown chunks around the bottom, and Liza recognized some dry herbs from the kitchen pantry—thyme, oregano. "Here," said Greycoat, handing her the jar. As she leaned in to take it, his hand darted out and wiped something on her throat. Liza flinched and drew back.

"*Aire linde*," Greycoat whispered.

"What are you *doing*?" she barked.

Greycoat held a charred garlic clove out in front of her eyes, with great annoyance. "I'm making a *Dagaz rune* on your *throat-chakra* with this burnt garlic, OK?! God."

"Why? Is it supposed to keep away the wompires?" Liza asked.

"It's for prosperity in work," he said with vast condescension. "You know, it's just a waste of money if you can't open yourself to the Teachings." He glared at her with his weird eye.

"For somebody so enlightened, you're awfully *touchy*," Liza scowled.

Greycoat whirled his back to her and went back down the hall.

"Blessed be!" Liza yelled, sarcastically.

Liza lifted her head from under the lukewarm green bubble bath, her ass gouged by crunching lumps of rock salt and brown sugar, and wondered what the hell she was doing. The pantry herbs made a ring of sediment on her chest and around the tops of her arms. *Pray for prosperity through singing,* she reminded herself, gazing into the green candle she'd lit. Liza didn't really know who or what she was praying to. She'd always believed in some unnamable force that engineered profound coincidences, serendipitous moments, and primal, divine mysteries like the Golden Stag, but she'd never really asked herself if this grand, abstract power could be directly petitioned, in English or Elvish or anything else. She stood up in the tub and then fully submerged herself again (as directed—seven full immersions, including head), the detergent stinging her eyes. *Oh Gods of singing, whoever thou are. Obviously, I am not exactly moving forward career-wise. I hereby take this magic Elf-bath to please . . . um . . . help kick-start my career. Amen.*

She sat back down, feeling slimy, itchy, and stupid.

But strangely enough, she got a phone call the next morning from Burt Swan, her first in months—a minor miracle. "That cop show that shoots here, you know it? Whatsit called . . . *Roman Gunn,*" said Burt's sniveling voice.

Liza knew the show—it was a secondary cop-series on one of the smaller networks, in its third season. The box-jawed male lead had been a promising movie star until a drug scandal brought him low, down to Lesser TV, a leather jacket with padded shoulders, and tall, feminine hair.

"They're looking for a singer for a bar scene—you'd just be in the background, wiggling around, no lines or anything, but I think you should go down there and audition."

Liza looked at her dark television set; the tangle of makeshift wire antennae, which Nodnik had fastened around a candelabra, looked as antler-esque as anything she'd seen in years.

The audition, amazingly enough, was a breeze. She was perfect—the right age, the right height, she had the right subculture-trashy look, a significantly different hair color than the female lead—everything slid and locked effortlessly into place like German machinery. "You want the gig?" asked the youngish male director, with little round glasses and baseball cap, after Liza sang the Lisa Lisa & The Cult Jam hit, *I Wonder If I Take You Home* (with cassette-tape accompaniment by Virgil Ortiz, on electric piano). "It's yours."

It was Liza's very first shoo-in. She was overjoyed until she walked out of the studio office and realized that Greycoat's stupid bath enchantment had been responsible for this sudden bolt of success, as opposed to her own talent or star quality—she couldn't, she realized, take credit.

While Elfmagick had cheated her out of much-needed self-esteem, she could no longer ignore its legitimacy. She was now convinced Elfism was based on some real, paranormal *geist*, which funneled into everyone fortunate enough to have the The Awakening, which she wanted now, worse than ever.

"How many hits of acid were you on when you had The Breakthrough?" Liza asked Faun Bell, as Elf House prepared to host another Friday night of fey psychedelia.

"Some people just aren't meant to have the experience, Liza. If you haven't had it yet, you probably weren't supposed to," Faun Bell said consolingly. "Don't, like, fry your brains out."

This made Liza feel only more excluded and deprived. She decided to take two hits of windowpane and extra speed that night, calculating what she thought might be the perfect ether/hallucinogen combination. *Come on, Aelfheim, I'm knocking on the gate.*

Around 2 a.m., the rest of the house was speaking Quenya. Nodnik was composing medieval odes on a zither, Faun Bell and Lorna were wearing white tablecloths and doing barefoot Isadora Duncan–type dances on the rug, Greycoat was massaging the delicate white feet of a smiling blonde named Vanessa with bergamot oil, Jimbo and Slipper were chiseling runic blessings into Jimbo's new skateboard deck, and Paisley was happily making a chain-mail falconer's gauntlet out of coat hangers with a pair of needle-nosed pliers.

Liza, separate from the group, was in the bathroom, squeezing and inspecting every single pore on her face, a horrific lunar surface contaminated by filth and clotted oils. She felt that she'd never get her face completely clean—the dirt, she felt, was arising from within her (probably as a result of writing smut) and working its way out through her skin, as if to announce her inferiority to the world. She could not, in this polluted state, impose herself on the Elves—she would surely ruin the delicate Thoughtweave. She ran and locked herself in her room, relating to Ned's seclusion in a way she never had before.

"So, how'd you do last night?" Greycoat asked the following afternoon, when Liza finally wandered into the kitchen. He was feeding sections of grapefruit to the newly enslaved Vanessa; both were wearing silky robes. Her eyes never left him, she was delirious with love; her mind had orgasmically opened like a fresh water lily.

"Terrific. So hey. Vanessa," Liza said, trying to conceal the small circular Band-Aid she had been forced to put on her chin. "How did *you* do? Are you an Elf, now?"

Vanessa looked at Liza, joy and wonder wafting out of her like sweet laundry steam. "God . . . ! It was the single most beautiful experience of my entire life!"

Greycoat smiled hugely, his eyes moistening for a moment. He leaned forward, taking Vanessa's small, pearly hands, and kissed the center of her forehead with vast tenderness.

In her agitation, Liza dropped a large knife to the floor while trying to hack open her packet of Pop-Tarts; it clattered jarringly. Greycoat gave Liza a menacing stare, and she scuttled into her bedroom.

Liza began to feel that in order to really succeed in her role as the chanteuse in *Roman Gunn*, having The Awakening was absolutely vital. She needed it, or the opportunity would be a fluke—she'd never have another one. She decided it was prudent—a career investment, even—for all of her discretionary funds to go toward speed and acid, at least until she had her Breakthrough. She sensed that if she could just push her mind expansion a little bit further, on the perfect combination of chemicals, she would emerge on the other side of consciousness into the magical world that seemed to surround her even as it refused her admittance. It was, therefore, with lucid and even noble reasoning that Liza began her big drug binge.

Coincidentally, Peppy, back in Fairfax, was hosting some very powerful breakthroughs into the Land of Oz.

(A small digression, Readers, with your permission.

The Wizard of Oz **has had an inestimably deep effect on the consciousness of our society; it is the rich Grandmother of family viewing experiences.**

The story is a shamanesque journey into altered consciousness. At Dorothy's time of personal crisis, the tornado comes: a malignant brown slinky—catastrophe, wrath, and torment. The house is torn from its roots, the kite of the soul is torn from its string, and the hallucinations begin. Dorothy is coldcocked by a flying windowpane (is it a coincidence the acid of later years was so named?) and is transported from the sienna-tint of Kansas (who hasn't felt that the colors of their lives were washed-out by tedious daily routine?). The house lands and the door swings open to thrilling colors; a heightened, mescaline reality, replete with strange heavenly choirs.

A yellow spiral marks the beginning of the yellow-brick road, the aboriginal dream-journey.

There's no-place like home—**meaning, we're all traveling in a big circle—not an existential circle in which one stumbles through the desert, leaning ever leftward, and dies discovering their own old footprints with nothing but a bovine understanding of Greater Futility, but a Zen-like understanding of the deep and endlessly expanding journey of standing perfectly still.**

"You've always had the power to go back to Kansas," says Glinda the Good.

"If I ever go looking for my heart's desire again, I won't look any further than my own backyard, because if it isn't there, I never really lost it to begin with," says Dorothy, which is quite a subversive and Oriental worldview, considering the Judeo-Christian, God is A-Big-White-Man-in-Space sentimental perspective that was so prevalent at the time. *The Wizard of Oz* suggests that all answers are within; it just takes a good whack on the head to realize.

In the great tradition of all experiential religious tales, nobody believes Dorothy when she shows up back in brown-and-white Kansas, proselytizing to those she loves about the colors she's seen and the places she's been. After the credits roll, Dorothy will, by the constant drip-pressure of everyday life, begin to doubt her own experience, and will eventually chalk it up to adolescent hysteria. If she stubbornly defends the veracity of Oz, she will be sent to a sanitarium. The world, sadly, has little use for minor prophets like Dorothy.

Peppy naturally wasn't interested in any of this.)

Peppy and Mike were not besieged with drama therapists offering their services; there were only four applicants, altogether. The Normal Family Dinner Theatre finally hired Starwoman Klein, an overweight and rudely cheerful woman in her forties in a purple cape and matching hat, whose specialty (in purple script on her pink business card) was Single Women's Actualization and Fulfillment Through Psychodrama. The three other applicants, who worked with ex-cons, juvenile-delinquents, and rape and incest victims, seemed overqualified to Peppy (and therefore potentially capable of bossing her around). " 'Women's Actualization' sounds safer than having a bunch of crackheads in here," Mike whispered.

"Are you a psychiatrist, Dr. LoBato?" asked Starwoman Klein, extending a lavender-scented hand.

"Me? No," said Mike, ruing the day he let Peppy convince him to call himself a doctor. "He's a doctor of Animal Husbandry," said Ike, who was replacing lightbulbs in the studio. Peppy gave him a killing look.

The Wizard of Oz became the healing vehicle through which eight unhappy local women gained a deeper understanding of themselves and
their own fears, needs, and goals for eight weeks.

The ladies began with various organic movement exercises designed
to "release their inner character affinities"; often, more than just affinities were released, during the more strenuous poses.

"This is true intimacy," Starwoman would shout, and the women
would chuckle.

Starwoman found deep philosophical and feminist questions in the
truisms of the script. "Glinda the Good says, 'Only bad witches are
ugly . . . .' What does that mean to you, Barbara?" Starwoman would
ask, Barbara being a 260-pound accountant with a dismal personality
and an omnipresent rash of electrolysis-pox on her jowls.

"What the hell do you mean 'What does that mean to me?' " Barbara barked.

Starwoman's painted head swung around the circle of fidgeting
women expectantly, like an alarmed parrot.

"Do we think Barbara's being defensive?" she chirped.

Starwoman began acting the part of the Wizard (renaming the role The
Sorceress), in order to better lead the group Over the Rainbow to Self-
Actualization. Inevitably, a row arose between her and Peppy, who had
taken to wearing a pigtailed wig to each session and always insisted on
being Dorothy, to the vast annoyance of the other ladies.

"Peppy, maybe you want to let Barbara be Dorothy, for today," Starwoman asked carefully, wearing a purple dunce cap embroidered with
yellow stars.

"Did I die and leave you my theatre? I don't think so," Peppy
sneered. "I think you're getting a little carried away with your Sorceress schtick, there, 'Starwoman.' "

"*Pay no attention to that woman behind the curtain,*" Starwoman
shouted, something she often said as a means of undermining her own
authority, in what was supposed to be a humanizing gesture. "Aren't
we *all* wizards? Operating behind our own curtains? Why don't you
come out from behind *your* curtain, Peppy."

The room fell silent. Peppy glowered poisonously at Starwoman.

"You're the one who wears curtains every day, honey, not me."

Peppy bolted upstairs to unscrew a bottle of sparkling wine for herself. She refused to participate in any more sessions after that, but took comfort in the fact that she was taking the group's money.

* * *

Liza's TV shoot was to take place mere days after Beltane.

She had been crawling around on the hallway floor like a lizard for days, wearing only a long thermal underwear set. It made her feel "grounded," since she had a keen sense of reality peeling away from her with every hit of acid and line of speed, which she abused daily. She'd spent the last three days dismantling her bedroom in an attempt to paste a vast photo-collage on her main wall, resembling Creature's fateful creation at The Vats. She cut out pictures from magazines and advertisements of trees, flowers, shrubs—anything that seemed to evoke the forest lair of the Golden Stag. The speed was enhancing her sense of serendipity; significant coincidences seemed to happen to her constantly. Almost every scrap of paper that fell on her floor seemed to hold an *undeniable indication* that she was speeding vigilantly and productively toward the fulfillment of her dreams.

Word had spread throughout the Haight that there was to be a large gathering of Otherkin on the eve of Beltane; Greycoat had had a revelation that the astral gate-building ritual should, obviously, be held in Golden Gate Park. Creatures of like mind began to crawl out of the woodwork—Hobbits, dwarves, orcs, faeries, and Jedi Knights approached Greycoat and Slipper on Haight Street and earnestly discussed strategies for time travel and astral projection, speculating on sacred geometry and architecture. Several had "channeled visions" of a metaphysical sea-change as planetary changes ushered in the Piscean Age. Others merely wanted to buy drugs.

Alien House had its own agenda for May Day. They thought that a "Crystal Ship" was coming for them and planned to crash the Beltane ceremony in order to use the confluence of psychic energies to summon it. Greycoat was furious that they intended to "metaphysically hijack" his vibrations; the Vampires, for their part, were so sick of being elf-hassled on the street that packs of them threatened to crash the Beltane ritual as well. "We're going to eat you when the sun goes down," one of the larger vampires hissed to Greycoat in front of the head shop. "Get thee behind me, *rauko*," Greycoat barked back, assuming a combat stance and pulling the back part of his coat forward, shielding himself with his protective runes.

"Auugh! Not a rune-stencil! It *burns*! I'm *melting*!" shrieked the vampire sarcastically, clutching at his throat and dropping to one knee. His Goth companions burst out cackling.

At Elf House, preparations for Beltane began to mean not only readying themselves for a Dionysian expression of High Love, which would bring about an interdimensional passageway to Elfish paradise, but also a preparation for psychic Holy War. Paisley made a quiver of arrows and purchased a longbow from the sporting goods shop. Slipper had obtained, from a group of Creative Anachronists in Berkeley, a handcast broadsword.

"What are you going to do?" Liza asked Greycoat as he sharpened a decorative letter opener. "Tune in to heavenly elf-frequencies, dance around the May Pole, then stab some Goths and go to jail?"

"Nothing's going to happen on this dimension," Greycoat scoffed. "When we take out the vampires, it will be on the astral plane."

"Then why are you sharpening that letter opener? Gonna open some really heavy astral-mail?" Liza gloated.

"Why are you gluing pictures of trees all over your wall?" Greycoat asked, with his penetrating spooky-eye. "What you do on this plane is echoed on that plane. If I have this weapon, so does my light-body."

"So your light-body is going to slice up some Goth light-bodies with the light-body of that letter opener?" Liza knew she was being bratty.

"Liza, come in here and eat something," said Lorna, buttering marshmallow Fluff onto oyster crackers, concerned that Liza was cruising wild-eyed and malnourished toward some unspecified calamity.

Liza was half-mad with sleep deprivation. She hadn't eaten properly in weeks; the walls in her disastrous room were now a vast, tangled landscape of weird trees, multiple seasons, and clashing ecosystems—

huge daffodils towered over tiny pines, jungle bananas sprouted from golf fairways. Her floor was a sea of shredded magazines, dried scabs of Elmer's Glue, and Charleston Chew wrappers. Liza stared passionately at her walls, trying to will herself into and through them. Every once in a while, she thought she saw something moving behind the poinsettia leaves, but whatever it was remained aloof.

Beltane fell on a mercifully warm Sunday evening, for May in San Francisco. The boys got decked out in High Elfish lambskin tunics and tall suede boots over women's gym leggings; buckles were shined, they wore their best silver jewelry. Their long hair was blow-dried, brushed, and pomaded to maximum sheen; little leather medicine bags, filled with stones, bones, and herbs, swung meaningfully around their necks. Homemade absinthe had been obtained from a local hippie, and the boys were doing shots out of pewter cups. They were all wearing light makeup, applied by Faun Bell, and wax Spock-tips on their ears. All in all, the boys pulled off a solid effect—they looked like Renaissance rock stars of Middle Earth, sleek and mighty, brandishing ancient weapons.

Jimbo had found, at an antique store, a priestly chasuble, bishop's dalmatic, zucchetto skullcap, and a mitre. He had whittled himself a crosier-staff and painted it gold, and found a large amethyst ring from a Fillmore pawnshop that his friends, when passing, would stop, kneel and kiss.

Lorna leapt into the hallway with a happy "Rooowr!" wearing leopard-skin spandex and a cat-half-mask. Liza scuttled across the hall on all fours in her filthy thermal underwear, her hair matting into dreadlocks, and stared up at Lorna.

"Liza, where's your costume?" asked Lorna, as Faun Bell minced over Liza in a tulle pixie tutu, each hop of her dainty foot emitting puffs of glitter.

"Liza's had a breakthrough," said Greycoat, in a snide voice. "Now she's a *salamander*."

The elf-boys giggled.

Liza, from her vantage point on the floor, hissed at him, imagining a black, forked tongue slithering out of her mouth.

"Come on, let me help you get dressed," Lorna said, prying Liza off the floor and forcing her to walk on her hind legs.

"You've been doing too many drugs," Lorna admonished as soon as her bedroom door was shut.

"Oh *please*, like everyone else here doesn't."

"Everyone else hasn't regressed back to, like, reptile-consciousness."

"What's wrong with reptiles?" asked Liza, her eyes black and glassy. Lorna felt a pang of anxiety as Liza skittered under the bed and stared at her from the darkness.

"Look, let's pull you together. It's Beltane. You want to look *pretty*. It's about Love. It's a bacchanal in honor of springtime and life. We're supposed to dance around in nature and be happy, not tweak around the carpet ripping up magazines."

"I can't get dressed, I don't know what to be," said Liza in a miserable voice.

"Well, that's easy enough. What are you?"

The question hung over Liza like a Test from God. *Failure to provide the right answer will result in instant condemnation. You are what you say you are.*

"*Nothing*, obviously."

"Well . . . what do you want to be?"

"Honestly?" Liza plumbed her depths. "*Appreciated.*"

"Well," said Lorna, snapping on her matter-of-fact voice, "nobody appreciates a weird bummer person who can't accept what they are."

"I don't *mean* to be a bummer," whimpered Liza, starting to cry.

"I know. And you're not, most of the time. Come on. Get dressed. Wear this. You'll look like a woodland spirit-type thing."

Lorna pulled a wadded, ivory-colored antique nightgown out of a bottom drawer. Liza obediently put it on. Lorna threw a lace tablecloth over Liza's shoulders as a shawl. "You're dressing me again. It's like the time you made me be punk," Liza said with astonishment, feeling that she was witnessing a profound, eternal pattern. She could picture herself being friends with Lorna for countless millennia, numberless lifetimes, Lorna forever rectifying Liza's trapped situation by giving her another disguise.

"When we get to the park, we can put flowers and leaves in your hair, OK?"

Liza sniffed. It was a beautiful idea, and in the mirror, after Lorna helped her tease out her hair with Aqua Net, and she covered herself with white face powder and black liquid eyeliner, Liza looked like a ghostly, nineteenth-century doll. She was very grateful. She resolved to take four hits of acid at the same time.

Golden Gate Park was exhilarating in the unusual warmth. Pink cherry blossoms were leaping out of their buds to greet the sun. Evening concerts started happening in the band shell, and hippies played guitars under the magnolia trees.

For the ritual proper, Greycoat had invited three women he knew whose lives were devoted to smoking a lot of crack and playing chamber music. They called themselves The Kräkhausen Trio and were partial to Schubert string trios for violin, viola, and violoncello. Their timing was noticeably off, but they were all accomplished musicians and their formal training leant a cultural legitimacy to the druggy pagan rumpus. They were set up in the moonlight against a wall of sweet-smelling lilacs, surrounded by tall glass candles from the Mexican supermarket. The fact that they played everything too fast contributed to the feeling of frenzy in the chirping evening air.

Elves were squeezing full wineskins, spouting cabernet and port into one another's mouths. Haight Street subculturites were everywhere under the trees, frolicking in fantasy wear, talking metaphysics, slapping gnats, and freely experiencing the warm evening the way their predecessors twenty years ago had done, on acid and other drugs, feeling the chemical interconnectedness of everything in the process of becoming everything, with the geometrical eye-boggling of an Escher lithograph.

Greycoat, Slipper, Nodnik, and Paisley were in their cups, trying to find a way to make a campfire behind a nook of dwarf conifers without the park authorities noticing it, watching, out of the corner of their eyes, for any enemies lurking in the glade.

Greycoat let out a whoop and began dancing a manic jig. He had already appointed himself and Vanessa, his girl-of-the-moment, the May King and May Queen, and they began the honorable task of dancing the ribbons around the maypole to the energetic sawing of the string instruments, much to the secret consternation of Slipper and Faun Bell, who had expected to be the ones to do it, because they had "been a couple way longer" and felt that they "represented the union of Male and Female energies way more."

In truth, the elves were itching for a brawl. Classically, a mock battle between Winter and Spring had taken place on May Day, and the elves, seeing themselves as instruments of nature's rebirth, were dying to beat up the vampires and alien-mongers, to insure the "triumph of light over the powers of darkness" in the coming year. Paisley, having been a parking lot grappler for most of his teen years, was especially keen to start shit and began firing potshot arrows out of his longbow in the general direction of a clot of Goths loitering behind some pyrocanthus bushes.

"Knock it off, cupid," said a frosty voice from the thicket.

Paisley chucked another arrow.

"Next arrow you shoot at us gets shoved up your ass."

"You'd enjoy that, wouldn't you, *Elenserke?*" asked Paisley as he drew another arrow from his quiver.

"Try it and find out, you fuckin' fairy."

Nodnik ran in to hold Paisley back from shooting the next arrow straight at the vampire's concave chest.

"Quit giving them negative energy, man, you're just *feeding* them," pleaded Nodnik, who was extremely high and feeling the need for peace, at least for a few more minutes.

"It wouldn't have killed him," said Paisley as Nodnik dragged him back to the maypole. "Mighta put a little teeny hole in him, is all."

"*Belethin*, dude. Fuck those guys. We're building the Golden Gate."

Lorna had twisted together a wreath of clematis and placed it on Liza's head.

Liza's acid came on, and her head felt like a fly being sucked into a jet engine. At first, she found herself laughing and dancing in a circle with Lorna, Vanessa, and Faun Bell, the four of them holding hands, running barefoot in the wet grass below a yellow moon, orange fog-streaks in the freshly dark sky, black treetops ornamentally framing Liza's vision when she tossed her head back. Then the sky pulled at her, and her body slipped away, no matter how she clung white-knuckled to the grass, she floated upward, the faces of her friends a distant ocean, crashing, as oceans do, as loud as they can, but from so far away, who hears and who cares? Liza climbed over the moon.

She came to, she didn't know how many hours later, in the top of a Japanese maple tree, her consciousness swirling back into her body like food coloring invading a jar of water. She was immediately struck by a feeling of something soul shaking just having happened to her, which she reassembled like scraps of a complex dream from a tingling part of her mind that was immune to memory:

After ascending through harmonic fields of pure color, there was a bright ray of sublime, beneficent intelligence. This intelligence had cared for her; hard layers of negative psychic plaque had been hosed off of her, and she had been returned to a pure, clean, infantile state of awareness: wonder and fascination. There had been some kind of lecture; she had reviewed painful moments in her life but had felt no shame—the Ray was a compassionate entity, which showed her a glimpse of her True Self . . . .

(Here Liza nearly toppled out of the tree and broke her neck . . . .)

She recalled the birth trauma of Everything, energy screaming outward, light ripping open at speeds exceeding itself, profound currents of inexorable attraction clamoring to fuse in rapturous Love to form matter from subatomic stuff traceable to the first silent, violent unfoldings of the universe, blinding heat cooling, freezing, condensing, and newborn stars sacrificing their finest dust to sculpt, through the enormously long, painful, deliberate, and supreme effort of evolution, **LIZA**, from infinite care and eternal patience. She saw that she was, inarguably, through no fault of her own, *indescribably precious*.

"AHHHHHH!" Liza howled, spilling over with superawareness, the tree trembling beneath her in symbiotic ecstasy.

Nobody heard her, because, at the foot of the tree, Elf House, Alien House, and a bunch of assorted ghouls were throwing punches at one another on the grass. Liza laughed until tears rolled down her face— the big celebration of love and creation that Greycoat had gloated about with such lofty expectations had degenerated into a wholesale free-for-all. The *oofs*, swearing, screeches from hair-pulling and muffled sounds of underweight bodies clashing in velvety fabrics were hilarious proof that the elves were caught up in the usual moronic horseshit of the physical world, no matter what transcendence they claimed.

But Liza's Night of Revelation was only beginning. Her limbs were simmering with new juice, glowing an antifreeze green. She felt that while she was rising through the colors and revelations of Ray, she had been weightless, lithesome, *flying*. She had an image of herself as tiny, fluttering with hollow bones and the papery wings of a dragonfly, shooting diamonds sparks that swarmed around her, the *tingle* of tiny bells. . . .

★ *!!!!!! I . . . . AM . . . . . . TINKERBELL !!!!!!* ★

This stunning realization made perfect sense; it was the consummation of her immortal self, her highest unconscious wish-persona and her temporal being. She remembered watching *The Wonderful World of Disney* on Sunday nights as a child with Ned, Tinkerbell swirling around the castle bashing streams of stars out of her magic wand, and wishing, wishing,
  ★ *Wishing Upon STARS* ★ . . . .

Liza had always wished she was Tinkerbell. She wept. It was too wonderful, too rich, too generous a universe. She didn't deserve it. But oh, she obviously *did* deserve it. What was more, each and every human soul deserved this exquisite magical joy; it was the birthright of everyone who wished upon stars. *Everyone should know that they are their ultimate secret fantasy of themselves. This is too beautiful to keep a secret.*
  "Check out Liza. She's so slatched," said Jimbo, suddenly noticing Liza making ballet-arm-movements in her treetop perch as he and Lorna watched the rumble from the sidelines.
  "Liza! Come down!" yelled Lorna.
  "IT'S *HAPPENED!*" Liza shouted, with all of the joy in her magnificent, fresh soul.
  "Uh-oh," Lorna said, grabbing Jimbo's arm as Liza spread her lace tablecloth wide and flew confidently out of the tree.
  The plummet downward visibly surprised Liza, but not as much as her landing on one of the denizens of Alien House, a guy in faded overalls named Robbie Seacroft. He happened to be standing at the foot of her tree in an attempt to ambush Nodnik, who had utterly forgone his peaceful instincts of earlier in the evening and had now joined Paisley full-heartedly in cracking the heads of anyone who wasn't one of their roommates.
  Robbie Seacroft let out a massive yelp as Liza's body landed on him, severely spraining his right forearm and ankle, breaking two fingers, and bruising the side of his face.
  Liza, shocked by her sudden fall, was still processing the disappoint-

ment of not having soared over the treetops when it became apparent that Robbie Seacroft, who was already primed for battle, thought that Liza (a known resident of Elf House) had attacked him intentionally, and, as soon as he evaluated his pain and recovered his wits, was fully intent on mangling her.

Liza, watching Robbie Seacroft's drugged eyes spin with murderous rage, picked up her skirt and ran.

May Day/Beltane, a holiday with many names, is also known as Walpurgis Night. There is a George Balanchine one-act ballet entitled *Walpurgisnacht*, which is set to the music of Gounod's *Faust*. One of the cultural events happening in Golden Gate Park that fateful eve was a timely production in the park band shell by a certain modern dance company, entitled *I Am the Walpurgis (Night)*, a modern reimagining of Balanchine's minor classic, set to music by the Beatles. Roland Spring, now a featured dancer with the company, had just finished dancing the leading role of Pan in the energetically choreographed Mephistophelean romp (to a lovely round of applause) and had jogged a small distance behind the performance area into a dark, unpopulated glade to take a leak, not wishing to use the park's public rest rooms wearing nothing but gold body paint, fur pantaloons, and strap-on antlers.

What happened next can only be described as a Once-In-a-Lifetime moment, a confluence of energies and events funneling into the tangible result of years of ardent cathexis: a phenomenal, wish-fulfilling Event.

Escaping the elf melee and dashing through the glade to elude the wrath of the limping Robbie Seacroft, Liza crashed through a myrtle bush and suddenly found herself face-to-face with Destiny in the glimmering, antlered form of Roland Spring, bare-torso'ed and golden in the moonlit woods, beautiful beyond myth. His back was to Liza, so she couldn't see his face, but there was no question, in her mind, whose back it was, such was its thermodynamic effect.

"Roland!" she screamed, her heart broadcasting zillions of loose-flying gems.

Since it was dark, and Roland didn't have his glasses on, and he didn't know who this breathless apparition was, crashing through the shrubs in a torn white nightgown with flowers and leaves in her tangled hair,

Roland did what any normal boy would do after a successful dance performance when faced with a potentially crazed fan: he ran.

Liza, filled with superhuman Tinkerbell energies, shot after him in hot pursuit. She was a blur; her life had never depended on anything quite so emphatically before, sparks were shooting out of her bare feet. Roland, in peak condition, was merely loping, sailing over hedges with long, gazelle leaps, a child of remote, blazing suns and worlds with less gravity.

Liza summoned her superpowers. She had never had any previous evidence of them, yet she knew they were in her. She called forth her burst of adrenaline, her physical miracle, the one impossible feat of strength or skill that lay dormant in her, inside some mystic casing that read IN CASE OF EMERGENCY, BREAK GLASS . . . . .

Roland, looking behind him, slowed down to a trot, realizing he was probably not in any mortal danger at the hands of this crazed waif, at the exact moment Liza chose to rocket into the air with a surge of divine might and, with a howl of victory, dive-tackle him.

"Woah!" he shouted as they lay panting on the grass, Liza clinging to his spotted faun pants.

"I *caught* you!!!" Liza shrieked, with such sincere joy that Roland gave a puzzled laugh. "Roland, it's *me*, it's *Liza*," she whispered, out of breath. Whacked out of her skull, she was unable to differentiate between her actual time passed with Roland Spring and the timeless relationship she had shared with him in her fertile imagination. She gazed at him with the radiant confidence that this was also the happiest moment of *his* entire life.

"Liza. . . . ," he said, not knowing who this Liza clinging to his legs was, in the dark. "Oh, man . . . *Liza*! Liza Normal! OK! Hello!" he said, laughing. "You look different!"

"I *am* different. . . . .I *ca-a-a-a-ught yo-o-o-o-o-ou!*" she sang, shaking her head to throw off a spiraling excess of mad joy. "Do you realize what this *means*?!" she shouted.

"No!" said the bemused Roland, who had figured out by now that she was high as an escaped balloon.

"You're the most beautiful thing in the world, you're the Golden Stag, and I've caught you, and you're mine, and I love you!" she squealed.

"I want some of whatever you took tonight!" Roland said, gently attempting to wriggle free.

"Oh, don't go away . . . don't go away. Don't you see? If we stay right here, we can bless the whole forest," she said, passionately kissing her way up Roland's golden stomach.

"Whoooo! Hey now! Whatcha doin', baby?" Roland asked, getting slightly nervous but not altogether ready to stop her.

"This is perfect . . . we're alone, there's nobody around . . . this is a magical night, it's Beltane, and we are Male and Female . . . ! It's *perfect*! We can light up the whole *universe*!!" Liza gripped him with her thighs and her enchanted fingertips worshipped him; she was so delighted by him, so deliriously loving (and that glade had been the site of much delirious loving, for decades, the soil was positively tropical with generations of druggy fecundity) that Roland Spring, already a bit stoned from his postperformance endorphins, was swept into her unabashed euphoria, and the moonlit spring night was already so sexy, with the new plants and flowers stretching open and sticking out their tongues, that within a few seconds, he found himself returning the kisses of the most willing, excited girl he would ever kiss, her heart melting and melting all over him. She had never remotely imagined such happiness. "We are flowers," Liza cooed to him, her hand gliding down the front of his costume pants as he shivered. "This is what we are *supposed* to do, now . . ."

"Right on," Roland gasped, surrendering to the spontaneity of the moment. Dionysius collected two more good children into his eternal Love-In. Spring entered Liza's soul. The elysian Golden Gate opened, for a shining moment, and all was natural bliss.

"Oh no . . . leave the antlers *on* . . . ," she whispered.

". . . OK, girl, whatever you say . . . ."

Liza smiled so hugely, two big tears ran down her temples and into the plush and loving earth.

There were sirens heard nearby; the rumble had grown and spilled out onto the roads, inspiring drivers-by to call the cops on the Middle Earth-massacre-in-progress. The police came out in full force, and soon the meadows were alive with hot and cold running Lycra and the rhythmic jangle of handcuffs. Sweet scents of hair products mingled with astringent, trampled salvia, and rosemary. Pointy boots were caught on rocks and striped stockings were snagged on bottlebrush.

Liza and Roland found themselves on the verge of discovery as the tufts of skunk cabbage surrounding them began rustling and swearing, and the thuds of panicked woodland feet vibrated under the grass beneath them.

"Liza, I gotta run . . . ," said Roland, suddenly looking nervous. "Those are cops, and my ass is black and gold."

"How can I get ahold of you?"

Roland had already hopped up and pulled his fur pants back on.

"Where do you live?" he asked, snapping into high alert.

Liza blurted out her Waller Street address.

Roland leaned over and kissed her, then dashed into flight over a large rhododendron, leaving nothing but gold all over Liza, and the memory of a glorious moment that would make her whole frustrating life leading up to it seem worth living over again and again and again.

· · ·

"I had a quantum leap," Liza announced in the living room the next afternoon, still smiling like the painted sunrise on an orange crate. Her announcement was not greeted with enthusiasm. Greycoat lay whimpering on the couch, his wounds being daubed with peroxide by a weepy Vanessa. Several Goths had attacked him, held him down, and gnawed small, bruised holes in his limbs with their prosthetic fangs. He felt violated, sick, and frightened, and was convinced that he was now in grave danger of becoming a vampire himself.

Nodnik and Paisley were also lying around in infirmity—Paisley complained of broken ribs, and his left big toenail was black; Nodnik had two black eyes that made the others wonder if Alien House hadn't infected him with some form of Zeta Reticuli–germ. Slipper had become violently ill in the night from an excess of mead. Faun Bell was also looking significantly the worse for wear and was not the twinkle-toed font of feyness she ordinarily wished to seem; she blasted in and out of the living room on the way to the kitchen, vastly perturbed, gathering cleaning products to combat Slipper's toxic disgracing of their bedroom carpet.

Lorna surveyed the whole scene, including Liza, with deep annoyance.

· · ·

"I saw the universe unfold," said Liza, punctuating her statement with a small hop. "I felt my light-body, and I found the Golden Stag, and it was total *paradise*! I had The Awakening! I woke up like *crazy*!!!"

The battered elves looked at her darkly.

"Whoopee for you," said Nodnik, sarcastically.

"You also fell out of a tree onto some guy from Alien House who wants to sue you now," said Lorna.

"Are you guys deaf? I told you, I had The Awakening! I'm Otherkin, like you guys! It happened!"

Greycoat regarded her with sullen annoyance. "Really," he asked, with no interest whatsoever. "So what are you, now, exactly?"

Liza smiled beatifically at the room; she'd hit the cosmic jackpot and would now generously rain the golden loot all over her friends.

"I'm *TINKERBELL*," she announced, with passion and magnitude, a delighted giggle escaping her lips. She waited for the gasps of awe; she imagined that Nodnik or Paisley might even drop to one knee at the announcement. She wasn't just a faerie, after all, but a *celebrity* faerie. It was a big deal; she felt it was a near equivalent to being born the next incarnation of the Dalai Lama.

"Oh for Christ's sake," said Lorna, in a tone of purest dismay.

Liza was confused.

Greycoat, green and punctured on his couch, began to laugh, a mocking, dreadful laugh.

"What? Isn't it great? It's the most beautiful thing that's *ever happened* to me, and I'm so *happy* I can share it with you guys! I owe it all to you!!"

"Tsss. Don't give me any credit for this, please," Greycoat sneered. Vanessa met Liza's eye for a moment and her expression made Liza deeply nervous.

"Tweeeeeeeaker," squeaked Paisley, using the Haight Street code word meaning "someone who has completely flipped out on speed."

The word hit Liza like a blow to the head. "What do you mean?" she asked, bile starting to churn in her stomach, extinguishing the golden light she was suffused with; she felt all her dirty old misery seeping in, all of the doubt, all of the failure . . . .

"Nobody wakes up as a *Walt Disney character*!" Greycoat shouted at her. "You're fucked up! You burned your brain out! Too bad!"

Liza stood in silence for a moment, paralyzed by the terrible accusation.

"You . . . *evil motherfucker*!" she screamed. "I'd say you definitely *were* infected by vampires, Greycoat, but then again, you've *always* been an asshole!"

Vanessa took in a sharp intake of frightened breath. Faun Bell dropped her can of Bon Ami.

"I had an *experience*. Why the fuck is it any less valid than *your* stupid experience?"

"I don't need this right now," Greycoat moaned, turning to face the inside of the couch.

"You're a drug addict," Nodnik told Liza, simply.

"It's called amphetamine psychosis," said Paisley, in a superior tone. "Maybe you should seek professional help."

"Oh, you worthless sacks of elf-shit," said Liza, before grabbing her purse and exiting in rage.

"We should maybe call her mom," Lorna said with concern when the front door slammed shut.

Liza, marching her way up Haight Street toward the park, was grasping at the very air for any straggling bit of the previous night's happiness that she could recover. She looked everywhere for signs; something Disney in a store window, maybe . . . anything with antlers, preferably Roland. The midafternoon, however, had done its usual dirty trick to the neighborhood—it was overcast, the smutty fog had trudged over from the beach and loitered; the weather of the area, most days, seemed to be as hungover, clammy, and lusterless as its inhabitants.

Somebody must see me, and know that I am changed.

While passing the hippie ice-cream store, Liza noticed looks coming her way from a cluster of pale lads playing hacky-sack—looks that seemed to hold some special, immediate significance. Her metamorphosis and its attendant supercharisma, she guessed, was responsible for this extra attention. She stood up straighter and walked in what was very nearly a ballet-prance.

One of the boys stared openly at her, with a half-smile, as if trying to ascertain if they had once been lovers. This was precisely the cue Liza had been waiting for—her transformation was not in vain—there *were* sensitive people who could see her magnificent, fresh aura, and the love-magic like arcs of fireflies zooming out of her fingertips. *Please, God, let him know me, for I have wished upon a star, and my dreams . . . .*

The boy approached her, with a slight limp.

"Hello," he said. Liza had never felt quite so famous. She turned on her most charming smile, her most gracious posture.

"Do you *recognize* me?" she asked, fluttering her hand into his. She was making a *connection*, this boy would be her ally on the ether plane; it was a spiritual meeting.

"As a matter of fact I do," said Robbie Seacroft, taking her hand. Liza clasped him warmly, with a wide smile, only to have the little finger of her right hand grabbed, wrenched backward, and snapped. Liza screamed and fell to her knees. It was only then that she noticed the swelling on his cheek, and the two splinted fingers of his left hand.

"Thanks for jumping out of that tree at me!" Robbie Seacroft yelled as he and the rest of his posse skateboarded away, leaving Liza both abused and disabused of any notion of luck, spiritual or otherwise.

People walking on the street stopped to try to aid the crying girl, but what was most broken about her, at that moment, was not her little finger, which was hanging backward and purple from her hand like the stick-noose drawn for a game of Hangman.

After two brutal hours in the crowded emergency room, Liza begged the attending physician to make her splint small and unobtrusive, because she had to shoot a TV show in just two days.

"Oh, you're shooting a TV show, huh? OK. We'll fix you right up," he said in a humoring tone in which he might have said, "You're the warrior-Christ of the Apocalypse, huh? OK." His reflexive belief that Liza was crazy made her feel crazy.

Later, Lorna walked with Liza to the drugstore on Market Street to fill her prescription for Percocet.

Liza's finger began to throb so badly that her every footfall made her nauseated with pain. She sat hunched over on a plastic chair, holding her hand above her head, waiting for the pharmacist to bottle the pills, strangely aware that all of the fluorescently lit details of this stupid, miserable moment would be worthlessly preserved in her mind forever, fossilized in amber like the lyrics of an old pop song she couldn't stand. Liza stared morbidly at the collapsed, diabetic ankles, knee-high hosiery, and plastic sandals of the large black woman sitting next to her.

"I really *did* have The Awakening," Liza told Lorna, with an imploring look in her eyes.

"I know you did," said Lorna. "I just think you've been burning the candle at both ends kinda hard. You need to relax, some."

"How am I supposed to *relax*?!" Liza shouted. "My entire world has completely shifted, Lorna. *I found the Golden Stag.*"

Liza told Lorna about her magic Beltane moment with Roland Spring. Lorna pretended to believe her.

"I think you should take it easy on the tweakage for a while," Lorna said seriously.

"I feel fucking horrible," Liza moaned. She would have sensed that something was wrong with the conversation had the pain in her hand not set a chemical fire in her arm that spread its smothering vapors everywhere.

The drugs came, and Liza dry-swallowed two of them. Lorna swallowed one, and they began their walk back home.

When Lorna and Liza appeared back at Elf House, Nodnik mumbled that there was a phone call for Liza. Liza missed the conspiratorial glance between Lorna and Nodnik. Liza rushed to the phone, certain that it was Roland; it was a woman named Amy, calling from the *Roman Gunn* production company, requesting that Liza show up for a costume fitting the following afternoon, for the shoot the day after. Liza tried to take down the information and discovered that writing was extremely painful. She struggled to speak intelligently to the woman through her gummy, barbiturate haze. Liza had to repeat herself several times before hanging up.

Later that evening, when Liza was staring from a fetal cringe on her messy bed into the incomplete forest on her wall, she heard the doorbell, feet shuffling into the living room, and voices trying to remain quiet. *Roland is coming to take me away*, said some overly hopeful part of her mind.

She was unprepared for the sight of Mike LoBato and Ike Nixon carefully entering her disastrous room, and doubly unprepared for the sight of her mother, wearing a black espionage pantsuit, a scarf around her wig, and large sunglasses.

"Jesus Christ, Li . . . ," said Peppy, her voice wobbling with emotion at the sight of Liza's environment.

"How you doing, Liza? Let's see your finger, there," said Ike, speaking softly and moving toward her too carefully, as if she had rabies. Mike seemed to be triangulating Liza from the other direction, their faces too alert, as if they were watching for her to bolt.

"Why're you here?" Liza slurred. "Go 'way. Alien Housasshole broke my finger."

"She said something about *aliens*," said Peppy, alarmed, talking to Lorna through the doorway. "Is she brain damaged?"

"I don't know," Lorna's voice said softly, from outside the room.

"Let's get some of your things together, Liza," Peppy said, picking up some of her underwear off the floor.

"Why?" Liza asked, now feeling distinctly paranoid. Ike picked up Liza's pillow and stuffed it into a plastic trash bag, then began folding her comforter.

"Liza, which toothbrush is yours, in the bathroom over there?" asked Mike.

"What's going on?!!" Liza shouted, now fully convinced she was on the verge of persecution.

Peppy sat down on the bed next to Liza and took her shoulders in a firm grip that intended to hold her in place as much as it did to comfort.

"You're going to the hospital, Li."

"Wha-a-at?? Why??" Mad thoughts ran through Liza's head: *Greycoat is responsible, he's afraid of my new power . . . .* "Tell Greycoat that he can keep his fucking Thoughtweave! I have no interest in being a Tolkien character! I'm a *Disney* character!"

"You see what I mean?" Lorna said softly, to Peppy.

"I can't go to the hospital! Lorna!! *Roland won't know where to find me!!*" Liza broke into tears at this realization, her searing finger externalizing her feeling of inner torture.

"Liza, you're going to be OK . . . . You're going to get a chance to rest . . . ," Peppy said, stroking Liza's matted hair.

"Where are you sticking me? A SANITARIUM?" Liza shouted, having watched *Spellbound* and other films, and having an awful vision of herself getting electroshock under klieg lights in a straightjacket.

"No, no . . . , Liza, you're just going to rehab," Lorna said, connecting with her eyes. "I called your mom because I thought you were tweaking too hard, and I got worried."

"Thanks a *lot*, Lorna!" Liza hissed through hateful tears.

"It's a nice place," Mike said in a plaintive voice, carrying in a handful of Liza's toiletries. "We have a friend named Steve who went there. It's really clean." Ike tweezed one of Liza's black socks between thumb and forefinger and brushed off shreds of magazine paper.

"How long will I be *gone*?" Liza wailed.

"It's an inpatient program. We could only get you four weeks," complained Peppy.

"But I have to do a *TV show*!!" Liza hollered.

"She really is supposed to do a TV show," Lorna told the room, aware that nobody trusted anything Liza said to be based in reality.

"Well. Not this time, kid," Peppy said, with an utterly nonconsoling overtone implying, *You brought this on yourself*.

Liza felt a piano drop through her solar plexus and crash into abysmal darkness with a horrible death-chord; she began to sob.

She was mortified by her perp-walk through Elf House; the roommates watched with red, reflective cat-eyes as the glum procession led her out the door in a custodial fashion.

"If Roland comes to the house, don't tell him where I went," Liza said, gripping Lorna's arm.

"OK," said Lorna, by now crying herself, because she did not believe that the Roland event had actually happened and worried that Liza had gone permanently insane.

"There's some good news, right, Peppy?" said Ike as they crammed Liza, Mike, and all of Liza's bags into the backseat of Earl's borrowed Mazda.

"What good news?" Peppy muttered, trying to remember how to start the car.

"There's a woman named Jacqueline who's been taking the Oz workshop, Liza, and she owns an art gallery. Have you seen Ned's light-boxes?" asked Mike.

Liza nodded her sullen assent.

"Well, she went to use the phone upstairs, and she accidentally walked into Ned's room, and of course he was wearing a ski mask so they both started screaming . . . ."

Liza couldn't listen, her intestines were wrapping themselves into a noose.

". . . but then she saw the light-boxes, and she really flipped out. She thought they were really important. So, she said she was going to try to get Ned a grant and help him put a show together."

"Really?" Liza asked, dumbfounded.

"He won't talk to her, is the only problem," Peppy said, wobbling the hatchback into the fast lane. "He won't talk to anyone but Ike and Noreen."

"What about you?" asked Liza.

"He writes me notes," Peppy said, obviously infuriated by both of her children.

Liza put her forehead against the cold car window. After a while, she noticed that they were driving past the airport. She mercifully blacked out.

* * *

The following three days were a blur. Liza would not remember walking into the hospital, or Mike and Ike carrying her plastic bags of belongings. There was a bunch of blood tests, nurses taking her blood pressure, and endless plastic cups of urine she had to provide. A doctor took away the Percocet prescribed for her broken finger and replaced it with ibuprofen, which didn't help. The room she slept in was always too cold, and the staff was unkind about giving extra blankets, so Liza slept in her clothes. Her roommate was a Stevie Nicks–like woman in her forties who had barely survived two rock marriages; she sobbed at night and spoke often of killing herself. The days were rigorously scheduled. Liza was to make her bed at 6 a.m., shower by 6:20, appear at breakfast by 7:00, and attend in-house 12-Step meetings all day long, with breaks for lunch and occasional visits to the hospital's cardio-gym facility. She always felt she was sleepwalking—the endless, confessional morality tales of drug abuse, invariably ending in humiliation, incarceration, divorce, poverty, and overdose, always felt like the same story, in different hues: alcohol, cocaine, speed, heroin. The drugs were gradually flushed out of her system with countless paper cups of cranberry juice, and Liza became slowly aware that she was the most miserable, foolish, and lonely girl in the world.

Liza was finally allowed to use the pay phone to call Burt Swan—he leapt onto the line at the sound of her voice on the machine and fired her, furious that she had never shown up for the *Roman Gunn* costume fitting.

"I'm in the hospital," she explained.

"Why are you in the hospital? You get in an accident?" Burt asked.

"Yeah," Liza whimpered.

"I just don't feel like there's anything I can do for you, at this point," Burt said before hanging up.

A manila envelope arrived, after ten days. Inside was a card from Lorna, with a pre-Raphaelite picture of a faerie princess on the front.

> *Hi Man!*
>
> *I hope you're doing OK in there. Jimbo and all the Elves wish you all the best for a speedy Recovery! (Oops maybe I shouldn't say speedy!)*
>
> *Don't worry we rented out your room to Vanessa even though she and Greycoat aren't together anymore. It took 4 coats of paint to go over your collage!!!*
>
> *A black guy came by to say hi to you and wanted to know where you were and I told him you didn't live here anymore and he said if I saw you to tell you he's going on tour to Europe for 8 months. He didn't tell me his name, and so I asked, and guess what???? It was Roland!!!!! (I hate to say it but I sort of thought that Beltane story was just tweakage. I'm so stoked for you it was true!!!)*
>
> *Anyway eat all your vegetables and feel better and I'm sure everything is going to turn out OK! Because you rule!*
> *Love,*
> *Lorna*
> *P.S. This letter from Centaur came and looked important so I sent it along. Be good!*

Liza found the letter from Centaur Productions inside the envelope and opened it. Inside, there was a check, made out to her, for $1,600, an unimaginably huge sum. There was a note attached:

From the Desk of
BUTCH STRANGE

```
Ms. Normal:
   Venal de Minus is a surprise mail-order hit.
Congratulations. Here's your 8%. You're the
```

second Centaur author ever to get royalties.
We need you to write more stuff. Call ASAP.
   B.

Liza stared at the dusty IBM Selectric II, with the cord malevolently coiled on top, sitting on the hospital floor with its keyboard facing the wall. Liza hadn't wanted to touch it at all, it felt filthy and sinister. She hated the typewriter. She hated Venal de Minus. Her mind reeled at the insulting idea that Venal de Minus was the only thing about her that had ever been spontaneously rewarded by the world.

Her broken finger, as if recoiling in shock from the very idea of returning to the typewriter, began screaming. Liza began to shudder and hyperventilate.

"Hey. Take it easy. It's all part of the process," said her depressed roommate, laying a dry, nail-bitten hand on Liza's shoulder.

Liza took another look at the check and started laughing a horrible, weeping laugh, like a haunted-house skeleton; the shutters of her unkempt mind flapping open and shut in the gale-force wind. *Oh, Lord, Dear God, Walt Disney, whoever you are: this is not what I had in mind, at all.*

PART VI

THE HORROR

June 1989, Hillsborough Methodist Hospital

EHAB WASN'T ALL BAD. As many celebrities will testify, spending a summer month in a locked hospital ward and detoxing under fluorescent lights with a bunch of weepy, gray-skinned failures doesn't exactly inspire unbounded holiday pleasure, but Liza ate a lot of graham crackers and gained a little weight back in all the right places. Best of all, The Universe lightened the load of her torturous Roland-ache by giving her a hot new boyfriend who had only just stopped being famous.

Bernardo Jones was well remembered among the few other twenty-somethings on the ward floor for having been a member of Guyzer, a commercial, bubblegum-pop boy band that had enjoyed a brief ubiquity.

Bernardo, a tall, skinny black guy, had elegant hands, a sexy, triangular chip in his front tooth, and sensitive eyes that looked too tired and sad for a virile young man of twenty-three. His hair, shaved around the back and ears, had an octopus-knot of dreadlocks sprouting out of the top that made his head resemble a handsome pineapple. It was the coolest hair Liza had ever seen, and magnetic as a cat—Liza couldn't resist squeezing and biting his thick, wooly dreads and taking deep, narcotic inhales of his scalp, the sweet lanolin smell of which made her reel with tenderness. It was a thrill kissing the velvety muscles of Bernardo's exotic face—she found him excruciatingly yummy. Relationships among rehab patients were forbidden by the hospital; this paired with the fact that they had both just suffered tremendous blows to their self-esteem made their sudden union seem boldly romantic. They had to sneak around to make out under desks and in utility closets. Love connections invariably happened in the rehab ward, despite the rules, because of the heightened level of personal intimacy; inpatients revealed themselves in group therapy. The low animal in them came out, along with whatever incorruptible sweetness they had; their fractured pride and hubris, foolish hopes, neuroses, and untreated emotional wounds were as visible as measles.

Bernardo no longer trusted himself; it was the common bond of almost everyone on the ward floor, after a couple of weeks of having their egos beaten down. Everyone was learning to accept that they had fucked up and could not control their various appetites. The patients more likely to recover were ashamed and despondent; the ones who would probably leave the hospital and head straight for the alley where they could score their drug of choice remained sullen and defensive. Liza (according to the counselors) belonged to the latter category. She didn't feel that her "binge" made her any more or less of a drug fiend than anyone else she knew; she was furiously convinced that Greycoat had orchestrated her removal from Elf House because her newly discovered spiritual majesty threatened his authority (while Liza had an idea, at this point, that her Tinkerbell-revelation was probably not literally true, she still firmly believed that she had been blessed with an experience of profound metaphysical importance. She didn't understand it, but she knew it was NOT just tweakage, and anyone who doubted her could go fuck themselves).

Bernardo had been through more life challenges than most of the other inpatients. In addition to having blown all his cash, relationships, and professional reputation on cocaine, he was on the bad slide down from a brief stint at The Top, and the massively addictive privilege, attention, and free stuff that being a star entailed.

Just a few years back, Guyzer had filled stadiums worldwide with hysterical children and ludicrously extravagant production values: laser beams, colorful explosions, and gigantic chrome scaffolding sets that shook from the hugely amplified, groin-thudding assault of Guyzer's sledgehammer bass line. Liza remembered the boys popping and locking their religiously choreographed routine of synchronized dance-gymnastics on MTV; a lethal current of teen heat in silver jumpsuits.

Bernardo fascinated Liza with stories of Guyzer's black limousine pressing through thronging mobs of whorishly dressed, screaming little girls, shocked and deranged by mob-lust. Fans would dogpile onto the limo with no thought for safety; girls splattered against the windshield, yanking stretchy shirts upward and pressing their junior-high breasts onto the darkened limo windows. Bernardo spoke of feeling afraid in these moments. In their carnivorous-bird frenzy, the girls seemed capable of clawing away the car's exoskeleton to devour the soft boy-meats within.

Guyzer was always surrounded by an immense security barricade; armed men in SWAT suits stood shoulder to shoulder, making sure a tsunami of unruly preteen passion didn't macerate the band. Teams of professional assistants wearing wireless telephone headsets stocked Guyzer's dressing rooms with gourmet buffet items and coddled the band like nannies, anticipating the boys' wants and making water bottles, fresh socks, and chocolaty nougat bars materialize in their hands before they knew they wanted them. An avalanche of corporate gifts tumbled upon Guyzer wherever they went: footballs, skateboards, T-shirts, computer games, athletic footwear, Japanese cigarettes—the whole world, it seemed, craved Guyzer's endorsement.

Now, Bernardo had no money at all. Donny Challenger, the band's "creator," made sure the young Guyz didn't think too much for themselves, particularly concerning pecuniary matters. Donny, a forty-five-year-old former bond trader, had found his teen boys at high school talent shows in California's economically depressed Salinas Valley. To be tapped by Donny Challenger was, for all intents and purposes, to be recruited into a pop star military academy; before anything began, the boys had to sign draconian, all-binding contracts. There was a period of intense training with vocal coaches who taught them power vibratos, and street-jazz-dance instructors who drilled them into the regimental alikeness of Rockettes. Donny monitored their diets, bedtimes, and girlfriends, and made them take urinalysis tests once a month.

At first, the band performed in elementary schools, hotel lobbies, and old folks homes. Shortly after graduating to malls, they went straight to big stadium venues in the Philippines, Indonesia, and Thailand, where the boys were all shocked to see how crazy a mass of adoring kids could become. Tawny twelve-year-old girls bloodied their fingers trying to claw through chain-link fences to them. Boys on mopeds drove around town brainlessly waving hand-lettered signs that read "GO GO GUYZER!" These concerts were where the Guyz learned the standard rock star tricks—wading up to the sea of outstretched arms at the front of the stage, taking a hand, accepting a kiss or a flower, singing a solo bit to a young girl while she quavered violently, weeping globs of tarry eye makeup, her mouth a mortified figure eight of wet teeth.

Home, for the Guyz, was their fully appointed tour bus, whipping all night along dark highways during grueling, fifty-city tours. They rarely knew where they were; a glimpse out the window into the pasty night skies revealed nothing but flat lands and telephone lines. They slept, usually with portable headsets on, the openmouthed car sleep of exhausted children.

Donny had supervised Guyzer's clothes and hairdos to coincide with the racial-profiling "images" he'd chosen for each of them: white Anglo-Saxon Douggo was the varsity-quarterback-next-door with the guileless blue eyes. Ginero, a Mexican *suavecito,* was the chain-twirling, cholo homeboy. Jacky-Lee was the Chinese-American kung fu kid, with angular New Wave hair. Bernardo, who had actually enjoyed a solidly middle-class upbringing, was supposed to be the quintessential African-American ghetto boy, sanitized for your protection—a polite gangsta you could bring home to Mom.

Bernardo was an especially beloved member of the group. He would hang weakly off of the mike stand when singing his part of the love-jams, resembling a tender cattail reed in a prevailing wind. Surprisingly, older women went gaga for him as well. Bernardo had received numerous letters from married women, housewives, and mothers, begging for a few seconds of his time, offering him every dark corner of their bodies. Normally he threw those letters away, because due to a touching devotion to his mother, he had an abiding respect for middle-aged women that even their own scurvy behavior couldn't compromise.

One such fan letter disturbed him to the point of obsession. Although the band had been defunct for more than two years, Bernardo still carried this letter with him. He slipped it to Liza one morning in the meeting room while they were supposed to be writing "Self-Evaluations." It had been read so many times, the folded corners of the heavy paper were beginning to shred. The stamps on the envelope were from Zurich.

Dear Bernardo:

I confess that I do not listen to your music, but I have been watching you with interest. I have made a study of you, through all of the available media. The videos, photos, and posters make one feel quite intimate with you; I watch for subtle changes in your mood on different days. It is, of course, a deceptive intimacy.

I will get to the point.

I am a woman of fifty, divorced, well educated. You might recognize my family name, so I won't tell it. Suffice to say that it has been, for some time, synonymous with wealth.

I feel compelled to confide in you, at the risk of shocking you.

I am a specialized type of anthropophagist. My hunger is for the flesh of a living person; a luminous, beautiful star, who I can see afterward on television and in magazines, and know that I have taken part of them into myself, as communion. This, for me, is the ultimate intimacy, the greatest pleasure. Catholics enjoy consumption of the living Christ through faith in transubstantiation; I am not religious and must unfortunately resort to other methods.

If you're still reading, I make this proposal to you.

The removal of a piece of your body is obviously a sacrifice. I offer you the exact sum of eight million U.S. dollars for eight millimeters of your left buttock. These figures are absolutely NOT negotiable. Do NOT answer this missive to bargain with me. An 8mm wound heals extremely well. You would never see it, unless gazing at your backside in the mirror. Your lovers need not know the truth; the scar resembles that of a bullet hole.

Should you accept my offer, I will contact you with access codes to a private bank account. Once you have accepted the money, I will send my private doctor to perform the operation. The recovery is uncomfortable for approximately three weeks. I am thinking of this pain when I offer such a large sum. We will never meet. The removed section of you will be flown to me in dry ice.

I have made this offer to other celebrities, and while I will never reveal their names (or yours, if you accept), I can assure you that they found the arrangement beneficial. They were able to secure greater fame for themselves with the money, by hiring the best publicists and stylists; this naturally attracted better management, who connected them to better projects.

Forgive my bluntness, but I presume you are aware that Guyzer will not last forever. The silly songs are already vanishing from European radio. I believe Bernardo Jones should be known, worldwide, as a solo performer.

Think of my offer objectively, without taboo and childish superstition: I ask considerably less of you than a record company would, and offer considerably more.

If this proposal is uninteresting to you, I only ask that you do not show this letter to the police.

Please respond, if you are interested, at the general delivery address below.

With Adoration,

X.

For Liza, the letter was a riveting curiosity and subcultural artifact—something that should sit in a glass case alongside clown drawings by mass murderers and giant hairballs removed from children's stomachs.

She had to read it over and over again. It was even more interesting than Bernardo—it was a throbbing, living remnant of Bernardo's gilded past, whereas Bernardo was now, sadly, just Bernardo.

"I can't put it down! It's just so amazingly *sick,*" said Liza, on her fourth read.

"What's sicker is that I almost did it," Bernardo confessed.

"X," the author, had correctly assessed at the time she wrote the letter that Bernardo had no control over his future; fame was running through his cupped hands and the tap was about to be turned off. The savvy cannibal knew that momentum was crucial; if Bernardo disappeared from the public eye for too long, he would have to revive a stone-dead career, which was far more difficult than injecting new pep into an ailing one. The intolerable conundrum churned in Bernardo constantly.

He started having a recurring dream: Flashbulbs were surrounding him, burning hot, white oysters into his vision as he shuffled backstage, bathed in sweat and the euphoria of stadium love. A towel would be placed around his neck; he would be handed a cold bottle of water. People would be patting his wet back, but he still couldn't see. Then he would hear a sound above all the others in the backstage cacophony: a scream, a shrieking gasp, a gurgle, then nothing. He was sure it was a girl being stabbed to death, right in front of him, but he was still blinded by the flashbulbs. Bernardo would still be trying to shake the spots out of his eyes when he woke up.

Bernardo developed anxiety and insomnia; his mind became so troubled, he began to seek relief through alcohol, drugs, more drugs, cheating on Donnie's urinalysis tests with cupfuls from sober fans or child relatives.

In the end, Bernardo took too long trying to decide if he should accept X's offer. The girls who formed the band's original fan base had grown up another critical year. Donny Challenger sensed that Guyzer had begun to lose steam, and with no warning at all, he terminated the band outright with four identical, terse letters that arrived by overnight mail—a fifth copy was sent to Donny's lawyer. He offered no further provisions or opportunities to any of the boys; they were yanked out of the Guyzer fairy tale like wiggling baby teeth.

Quite suddenly, it was almost as if the whole thing had never happened. After Donny and the music publisher took their cuts, and tour, recording, travel, and wardrobe expenses were deducted, the Guyz's total earnings, despite the fact that they had sold millions of albums, were barely in the tens of thousands—for most of them, not enough to cover credit card debt they'd accrued while living the high life.

What was even worse, Guyzer, once the most vivid and powerful entity in the commercial market, was by that point overexposed to the point of revulsion—nobody wanted anything to do with them anymore. Guyzer was a punch line on late-night TV; instant has-beens at the bottom of the Where-Are-They-Now deck, victims of the fickle whiplash of faddish consumerism. Now in their early twenties, the boys were international laughingstocks with barely enough cash to rent cheap apartments and look for alternative careers. (Donny Challenger, of course, moved on to greener pastures: a girl group called "Glee Club," which combusted overnight into a mushroom cloud of Top 40 radioactivity, then abruptly died of overexposure, just as Guyzer had.)

The loss of everything all at once—credibility, audience, lifestyle, and A-list status—was too much for all the boys, except for Douggo, who had little creative fire in his soul to begin with. He cheerfully used his experience to launch himself into a future as an assistant A&R guy, "developing new acts."

Ginero segued into a real Chicano car-club community and adopted their feral codes, having the gang symbol of his new neighborhood tattooed on his neck. He seemed to be on a quest to bring retroactive legitimacy to the costume Donny Challenger picked for him by becoming "hard" and "real" (this hardness and realness would put him in jail, soon enough). Jacky-Lee obtained a Dutch girlfriend and moved to Amster-

dam; they lived on the dole, smoking pounds of pot and hashish, prefer-
ring a sleepy dream-world to any further connection to society. And
Bernardo, who had collected some unsavory friends around the edges of
fame, snorted cocaine until his nose bled, then smoked it; soon, the bills
and debt piled up, he lost his apartment, and nobody wanted him on their
couch anymore, including his mother, who forced him into rehab.

Liza badgered Bernardo relentlessly to figure out what his "next move
was." He was deeply divided on the subject. Since he was a child, he
had always been a singer and dancer. A dyslexic, he had barely made it
through high school; Donny Challenger had pulled him out in his junior year, hiring hotel-room tutors to help him cheat his way through a
GED. He was articulate and could read well, but his writing and
spelling was more or less arrested at a sixth-grade level. He hated the
whole Guyzer phenomenon and cringed whenever he was recognized;
he was fearful that he would be forced to resurrect his Guyzer persona
in order to rebuild any sort of career.

"I've got no other skills," Bernardo lamented.

When he had these crises of confidence Liza would kiss him furiously, stroke his face, squeeze his dreadlocks, and tell him how handsome and talented he was.

He finally agreed, with a depressed exhale, that he "probably wanted
a solo career," one in which he could give vent to his own "stanky,"
sexually explicit R&B tastes, involving adult-advisory lyrics and tracks
of hyperventilating orgasms. Guyzer's bubblegum music, which he
had so convincingly delivered onstage, was repugnant to him now.
Once he had kicked a child's boom box, splintering it all over a parking lot, because it was playing "You're the One," the Guyzer ballad
which had held a #1 *Billboard* slot for several weeks. He gave the upset
kid $200 and an autograph, then smoked a bunch more coke to forget
the incident.

Bernardo's loss of celebrity made the need in Liza only more acute.
Fame smelled *closer*. Bernardo still bore the brand of it; the scent of its
scorch was still on him.

During the last week of the rehab program, the hospital staff began
to pick on Liza and Bernardo, claiming that their relationship was a
sure route to "jails, institutions, and death" (a standard rehab mantra).
During these assaults, they would sit with their arms crossed in the

molded blue plastic chairs, grinding their teeth and staring angrily at the cold floor, or out the window into the hospital parking lot. Both of them had grown to hate every detail of the facility: the 7 a.m. blood-pressure tests and horse vitamins, the formaldehyde death-science smell of the arctic air-conditioning, the shitty food, the pathetic, sobby group-sessions, the smugly righteous ex-junkie counselors.

Liza was not convinced that all of her immediate problems stemmed from an enslavement to drugs and alcohol. She preferred to think of herself as an adventurous "binger," since she never had the kind of "I-must-do-it-all-tonight" fever she'd seen in people who obviously *did* suffer from the disease of addiction.

"Hi, my name is Liza, and I'm a Scorpio," she'd say during visiting AA group meetings, which annoyed everyone but Bernardo, who found it funny.

Liza was persuaded that she loved Bernardo; he was no Roland Spring, but Roland, for all she knew, could be in Tibet, bedding down in a yak yurt with triplet contortionists, and it was nice to have an actual, tangible boyfriend around. Bernardo had real affection for Liza; he'd never seen such crass ballsiness juxtaposed with such goofy insecurity in a girl before; he liked her rude drive and was grateful that he could borrow energy from her at a time when he had none. At the height of their re-hab persecution, Liza and Bernardo resolved to move together to Los Angeles when they got out—a vote of confidence for a love that all the counselors condescendingly informed them was merely a substitute for the drugs they weren't doing.

A call to DelVonn sealed the deal: he was looking for someone to sublet his LA apartment because he was planning on moving in with his boyfriend, a makeup artist named Cupcake who had hit a stretch of unemployment and needed DelVonn to pay his rent. This coincidence seemed to be proof that Liza and Bernardo's plan was blessed by an even Higher Power than the one currently ruling the rehab facility.

Earl, Peppy, and Noreen came to pick up Liza at the end of her month-long stint. Peppy and Noreen looked away in discomfort as Liza said her tearful and tongueful goodbye to Bernardo, who wouldn't be fin-ished for another four days.

"Who's that boy?" asked Peppy, when Liza was finished.

"My rock-star boyfriend," said Liza, proud.

"Why is he here?" asked Peppy.

"Why do you think?" asked Liza.

"Mike is sick," said Peppy, turning around from the front seat of Earl's car and pulling down her large sunglasses.

"What kind of sick?" asked Liza.

"AIDS. He's had it for a long time," said Peppy.

"Bless his heart," muttered Noreen, patting Liza's arm with her pruny, spotted hand.

"Why didn't anyone ever tell me Mike had AIDS?!" Liza was outraged.

"He didn't want you to know. He thought it might scare you."

Liza's brain scattered into all kinds of foolish worries—*Did he cough in this car? Did my mother kiss him and then kiss me? Is Ike dying too?*—then (she couldn't help it) she resented that Mike's illness was upstaging her dramatic release. Everyone was supposed to be in awe of her rehab experience and concerned for her, like she'd just steered her dogsled back from the Yukon, black with frostbite. The Mike announcement was so devastating, it blew away any possible sympathy she might have gotten for her comparatively trivial hardship.

Liza sullenly stared out the car window as the airport flashed by, a mirror reversal of the way she'd passed it a month before. She never got the attention she felt she deserved; there was always something bigger, badder, wilder, prettier, more talented, more tragic, more interesting than she was. A plane was taking off on the runway parallel to the car. Liza wished she could rocket through the car window and land in a first-class seat as its nose tipped upward and the wheels lifted into the sky, going away.

Butch Strange had called daily and hounded Liza with black Centaur postcards the whole time she was in the clinic:

```
Why the hell don't you write more stuff?
Don't you like money?
  Get Well Soon.
  Love, Butch
```

The underground market for Venal de Minus was apparently still expanding. One could now buy the Venal de Minus books through participating comic-book stores, and via mail order from ads in the back of magazines like *High Times* and *Heavy Metal*. Liza's broken finger, which she had been using as an excuse for not writing, had stopped hurting but was now crooked at a permanent teacup-holding angle away from the rest of her hand—an eyesore equal to any bad tattoo, in that it reminded her daily of her Haight Street shame.

She dreaded writing more film-inspired softcore, but at least in the short term, it was her only possible source of income, and she knew she would probably have to support Bernardo in LA for a few months as well, until he got his new career off the ground.

Butch Strange liked vampire fiction, so Liza tried a book wherein Venal de Minus fought vampire Catherine Deneuve for David Bowie's sultry, undead attentions in *The Hunger*.

It was mere minutes until dawn. The limousine had finally pulled to a silent stop in front of the mansion.

"Jo-o-o-ohn," Venal hissed from her perch near the second-story gargoyle. The vampires looked up from their doorstep, John's alarmed green eye glowing under the streetlight as Venal pounced down, knocking him backward onto the limestone stoop with a flying boot tip straight to the jaw. She knew he liked it rough.

Miriam Blaylock watched with mounting fury as Venal took the titanium ice pick she held in her teeth and began ripping John's leather pants to ribbons with a raucous cackle.

"Ya-a-a-ahhh," John moaned, in a blur of interesting and possibly sexy pains.

"Take your hands off my husband," Miriam said with quiet threat, in her clipped French accent.

Venal stared at Miriam. Smiling salaciously, she slid her pointy boot heel into John's mouth, which he began to suck willingly, voraciously, enraging his

wife . . . . Miriam slowly descended the
stairs towards Venal in a lather of
rage . . . .

Patrons and fans of Venal de Minus were delighted by this new install-
ment. "It's bringing you a whole new audience," Butch told her, after
it had been available for a few weeks. "Now you're picking up the
blood-freaks, the necrophiles, and the people who get off on catfights.
You're on a roll."

Liza was less than thrilled with her bizarre gift for entertaining these
strange, if somewhat populous, breeds of perverts.

"Jesus. Who are these people?" Liza wondered.

"Middle-aged women into bondage, mostly," said Butch, "and Dungeons and Dragons-type, fantasy-role-playing feebs. Venal is becoming
a cult character in D and D games around the country. I'm thinking of
having a custom, die-cast lead figurine made of her, for the D&D
geeks . . . whaddaya think?"

"Terrific," said Liza, repulsed.

· · ·

Peppy had her lawyer appeal the civil suit, knowing she would lose, in a
last-ditch attempt to pull whatever last financial tooth out of the theatre that she could. Earl the Mailman helped to convince her that "now
was the time" for her to fall back on and exploit her one inexhaustible
resource—her own talent.

An Evening with Peppy Normal was organized over five nights by Mike's
bedside, with a quart of gin, several chewed pens, and three yellow legal
pads. Peppy would talk and Mike would listen and make comments,
when he wasn't too weak or drugged. Peppy would set her wet, clinking
tumbler of liquor on Mike's bedside table, right on top of his mounds of
wadded Kleenex. Ike was glad Peppy was there to pester Mike and keep
him awake, irritated, and alive. He was so emotionally ravaged by Mike's
advancing illness, he couldn't eat—Ike was thinning at a rate almost as
alarming as Mike, whose body seemed to diminish by handfuls a day. But
Peppy was as self-centered as ever, chattering away. Ike felt that her in-
ability to grasp Mike's impending death preserved a kind of zany levity.

"I'm putting a perfectly ordinary pair of glasses on your face," Peppy told Mike. She had become interested in the art of hypnosis and read a couple of how-to books; she was attracted to the idea of making strangers surrender themselves utterly to her control. She stuck her fingers through the frames for the imaginary audience, to prove there were no lenses.

"With these glasses, when you open your eyes, you'll believe I'm completely naked. Open your eyes at the count of three. One, two, *three.*"

Mike didn't know, while his eyes were shut, that Peppy had stealthily removed her bodysuit. When he opened his eyes, she was completely naked. The shock made him topple over in such a rib-cracking fit of coughing, Ike made her go home for the day.

"Tell her she's improving," Mike whispered to Ike, as Peppy gathered her props.

Ned was a great comfort to Ike, at this hard time; Ike would come and sit quietly in Ned's room among the light-boxes, as a Catholic might sit in Chartres, irradiating and recharging himself to go home and battle the gloom. Ned was inspired by Ike's grieving presence; he wanted his boxes to be worthy of it.

An Evening with Peppy Normal never materialized, since Peppy was unable to rally an adequate support crew. She trudged back up to her bedroom with a tankard of gin to ponder her eviction.

"I dunno, Li," said Peppy, orating from her bed. "Maybe you just ought to go back to school, and learn how to do something."

Liza felt her lungs go brittle with resentment, then crack.

"Oh! Don't get all in a snit," Peppy said, noticing Liza's green face. "I just . . . I've come to the conclusion that this career in the performing arts is impractical. There's too much rejection."

"You don't think your lack of success has anything to do with your lack of talent?"

It was a bad thing to say, but Liza couldn't control herself.

"Hey!" Peppy shouted. "You want to be here? Talk that way to me, you can go sleep somewhere else!"

"What's my father's phone number?"

"Your *father*? Who? You mean *Hal*?"

"I'm sure it's hard for you to remember, but yeah, the man who impregnated you."

"You think Hal's going to help you? Ha. That's a laugh. Good luck."

Liza had an idea of how a conversation with her father should go. He was supposed to weep with joy that she had contacted him. He would drive through the night and they would rendezvous at a lovely restaurant for breakfast. He would be well dressed and driving a white Mercedes. Her hair would be backlit with golden sunshine. They would clasp each other, awash in a rebirth of family sentiment; he would tell her what a beautiful woman she had become, and give her money.

The home number that Peppy had was defunct; the dental office number, however, was still active. Liza left a message. An hour later, Hal Normal called.

"It's him," said Peppy, handing her the receiver over with an expression that suggested sewage was oozing out of the little holes.

"Daddy?" Liza asked, in a too-excited tone.

"Is that Liza?" asked Hal Normal, not quite as excited.

Liza tried to feel a sense of homecoming, a swell of love. She attempted to dazzle her father with a truncated version of how she'd finished high school, moved out, and gotten "a writing job." Hal congratulated her and asked to speak to Ned.

"He won't talk to you," said Liza, "but don't feel bad, he won't talk to anyone except Gramma." Liza told her father a little about her brother, amplifying the fact that he was going to have a gallery show and downplaying his mental illness.

"So, he's talented, huh?"

Liza could sense that Hal was trying to steal pride from the idea that his genes may have made a remarkable contribution to the art world.

"He is, and so am I." Liza spoke passionately of her big plans for "trying out her singing career" in Los Angeles. She could hear Hal anticipating her request for money, and beginning to backpedal, by referencing his seven-year-old daughter Cathy's pricey equestrian summer camp, and his five-year-old son Carter's private swimming lessons.

"That's nice for them. I was wondering if you could help *me*, Dad," Liza said finally.

Hal coughed and blabbered something about "Peppy's decision" and how he had "no legal responsibility." Liza bristled.

"Dad . . . let's put it this way. You cleaned my teeth a few times, but other than that, you were a total zero. If you want me to have any feelings for you besides total disgust, you need to send me, like, fourteen

hundred dollars, right now." (The rent at DelVonn's was $350; Liza fig-
ured she'd need four months' worth of slack.)

Peppy started to cackle.

Hal, doting father that he was, spoke at length about "emotional
blackmail," then succeeded in bargaining Liza down to $700; she set-
tled for half the money, he for half the resentment.

"Ned has some money."

It was late that night; Liza and her mother were drinking beer at the
kitchen table and spearing anemic cocktail onions out of a jar with
crab forks; Liza had just asked Peppy for the other $700.

"Where'd *Ned* get money?" asked Liza.

"That gallery woman Jacqueline helped him get a grant. She wanted
to help him get a bigger work space for the show he has coming up, but
he won't leave that little room. He had Ike go out and get him a bunch
of glue and some plastic, but he doesn't know what to do with that
money. They gave him seventeen thousand dollars."

Liza felt like she'd been struck by lightning—the huge number shot
with blinding voltage through her head, burning a hot black corridor
down to her shoe.

"I've been out there, this whole time, hustling like crazy, and Ned
hides in his room like a retard, and somebody gives him *seventeen thousand dollars*?!"

"Jacqueline thinks his light-boxes are 'important.' She calls him an
'Outsider Artist.' I guess rich people like to look at stuff made by re-
tards, these days."

Liza considered it her solemn professional duty to hit Ned up for the
other $700.

The room that Liza had once shared with Ned was now a fanatically
organized habitat; a concentric expansion of Ned's delicate mind.

The walls were tiled up to the ceilings on all four sides with multicolored lighting-gel sheets. Dishes set on a clean table each contained
different colored mounds of tiny, curving strips of acetate that Ned had
shaved off the gels. The light-boxes were simple: a wooden frame, a
piece of glass, a lightbulb; but the compositions Ned had been gluing together, with limitless care and patience, had become even more rapturous and virtuosic than when Liza had first seen them. Several completed
boxes leaned against the floor, plugged into a power strip. His pointil-

listic, geometrical flowers had evolved into sensuously fluid, curvy patterns in wildly juxtaposed colors—fire-coral women and eggplant wood grain; citrine bones, opal smoke, and black octopi—everything was rooted in nature but longing madly to break into the sublime, like a swimmer with empty lungs, struggling up through an undulating, prismatic corridor to the sun. It hit Liza that Ned, the whole time she had been screwing around with her appalling vanities, had been working like a monk on the tireless creation of pure beauty.

"Ned, can I borrow seven hundred dollars?" Liza asked, suddenly feeling impoverished on multiple levels.

"I gave all the money to Gramma. You'll have to ask her," Ned said, his black wool face barely glancing toward her. Liza saw that she was scaring him—he twitched and fumbled with an X-Acto knife.

"These are so beautiful, it is totally blowing my mind," Liza said, looking with envy at the light-boxes.

"It's easy to spend a million hours doing something stupid like this, when you can't leave your room," Ned said.

"It's *so* not stupid!" admonished Liza. "Don't you feel proud of them?"

Ned thought about it. "Oh, I don't know. It's just so *never-ending*," Ned said, his shoulders dropping in exhaustion. "I always feel like the *next* one is the one that I really want to make, but I have to finish the one I'm doing, first."

"Why don't you just skip one, and work on the one you want to work on?"

"I don't get to skip one," said Ned, very seriously. Liza caught a chilling glimpse of the merciless psychic laws Ned employed to extort these lovely works out of himself.

"Mike is sick," said Ned, with gravity.

"I know. Are you real close to him?"

"I like Mike. But if Mike died and Ike decided to *move away* or something . . ."

Liza could hear, in her brother's voice, his miserably huge attachment to Ike, and how petrified he was of losing him. She knew too well the awfulness of that feeling—that crippled pining for someone you can't have, but who is present enough to keep your soul in a wretched, hopeful limbo with an occasional flash of antler.

"Ike won't go away," said Liza, not knowing anything at all.

"You don't think so?" Ned asked, sadly. "I hope not."

"Ned said I could borrow some of his money," Liza told Noreen, who was ironing sheets with care and patience. *Ironing sheets,* thought Liza. The bleachy clean smell rising off the steaming cotton had an involuntarily poignant effect on Liza, which she repressed. She was not in the mood for an abstractly holy moment. *Who the hell irons sheets?*

"Why do you need Ned's money?" Noreen asked, without suspicion.

Liza explained, with do-or-die urgency, her and Bernardo's risky dive into mainstream Los Angeles. Noreen listened, trying to keep the doubt and worry from her face.

"You be careful. You shouldn't try to be something you're not. You're pretty and sweet and full of life, and spunky and interesting. Don't be jealous of those Hollywood girls who look like they have everything. You scratch the surface, you find out a lot of them are more miserable than you'd ever know. It's a terrible thing to have to be perfect all the time." Noreen parked the hot iron on the board; it hissed in agreement.

Liza had no answer. She wanted beyond all reason to be perfect, if even for just five minutes, as long as there were a few other people watching.

"Look at Ned. Ned's *genuine,*" Noreen said. "That's why he's doing so well. Take this, will you?" Noreen handed her two corners of a warm, fitted sheet.

"Ned hasn't left the house in five years," said Liza, not looking down as she slapped her two corners together.

"He's a worker," Noreen said, her eyebrows lowering.

"I am too. You'll see." Liza tried to sound confident.

"You're balling up the ends, there, dear . . . here, you tuck in the fitted parts into each other first, see? Then you make these corners nice and flat, and you can fold it up nice and square."

Liza wasn't paying attention.

Bernardo Jones was released from rehab and was staying with his mother, Philomena, in Oakland. She bullied him into accompanying her on daily visits to the Baptist church, in order to give him some rudimentary guidance before restarting his life. With the money Liza had scrappily amassed, they bought Philomena's car and sent a month's rent to DelVonn. Status-wise, the hatchback Plymouth Horizon in two shades of metallic brown was an eyesore, but it had been well taken care of. Bernardo helped Liza squeeze her duffle bag and cardboard boxes into it, alongside his own jam-packed clump of meager belongings.

"I'm going to make it this time, or I'll die trying," Liza told Bernardo. "And you're going to have a big, big solo career, and everybody in America will have to kiss your ass. And then, we'll break into movies." Liza's face grew brightest when heaping one fantasy onto another. Bernardo put his arm around her, saying nothing.

"You're going to miss my art show," said Ned when Liza entered his room to say goodbye. Liza hadn't even thought about that, she was in such a rush to get away from Peppy.

"I know. I'm really sorry."

"Hey! Don't worry. I'm going to miss it too."

"I'm stoked for you, though. You're going to be a famous artist."

"God," Ned said in a wavering voice. "I hope not."

Peppy stood outside the theatre door with Noreen.

"When we come back, it'll be in a limo!" Liza shouted.

"Go get 'em, kid." Peppy was distracted—her cigarette had just dropped a clot of red ashes onto her exposed toes.

"Drive careful," said Noreen, pushing a large paper bag full of oatmeal cookies through the window into Liza's lap. Liza hoped her grandmother would live long enough to witness her success.

It was the requirement of all human beings to attempt celebrity. What did you mean in the world, if you lived and died unrecognized? Who cared? Anyone who wasn't famous merely sucked air and died boring, without wealth, pomp, or newsworthy obituary—they might as well have never bothered living.

Liza felt that she was finally doing what she was meant to do, and she pressed her nose into Bernardo's neck, molesting his thigh as he drove down the I-5.

"Don't make me crash!" Bernardo shouted.

"Aren't you happy we're going to Hollywood?" Liza cooed, twirling a finger around a dreadlock.

"I don't know," said Bernardo, who was still haunted by the cruelty of the industry he'd experienced firsthand. Like Humpty-Dumpty, he had a pretty good idea that his former life would be impossible to put back together again.

Liza slugged him in the arm. She wrinkled her nose at the cowshit smell of Coalinga, as they passed. It was the beginning of February; all of the trees they passed looked starving, cold, and arthritic under the cinder block–gray sky. Each town on the drive seemed like nothing but a cluster of gas stations, with an occasional McDonald's or truck stop. Life between big cities seemed useless and unlivable. Liza felt suffocated by the absence of glamour. The car couldn't move fast enough.

Finally, the brown-orange haze of the San Fernando Valley was visible in the sky, and there were signs for Burbank.

What was LA, if not the Emerald City? While it wasn't exactly gorgeous to the eye, with its wavering exhaust fumes, sooty palms, and unkind, black-glass buildings, it held a certain fast promise, like the "Street" films of yore—if one was only slick, sexy, cute, and ambitious enough, anything could happen—a normal girl could ascend to the level of royalty. Liza rolled down her window and felt the warm wind blow down her T-shirt, which bellowed RELAX in an oversize font.

Bernardo and Liza pulled into DelVonn's neighborhood. There were signs in unidentifiable Asian and Spanish; dirty toys hung in storefront windows.

DelVonn, wearing a child's pink plastic raincoat, ran up and slapped the car until Liza opened her door and got out.

"Welcome to Koreatown, bitch!" screamed DelVonn, jumping into Liza's arms. She swung him around like a heavy doll.

"I used to have such a crush on you!" DelVonn shouted, pumping Bernardo's hand. Bernardo showed his trademark chipped tooth in a bashful smile.

DelVonn's basement apartment was a spooky shithole, but Bernardo and Liza acted pleased as DelVonn showed them around. The only real window was halfway beneath the sidewalk and barred on the outside; it was otherwise fully obscured by a taped-up sheet of tinfoil. A weak air conditioner chugged through a cardboard frame in the broken transom above the door. The walls were painted deep purple, emphasizing the dungeonlike feel.

"I only really used this place for sleeping in the daytime," DelVonn confessed.

The acoustical-tiled ceiling, which somebody had half-attempted to spray-paint black, was only six feet high, which was fine for DelVonn, but Bernardo, who was six foot one, had to slouch while indoors. Likewise, the sink and shower nozzle DelVonn had installed were dwarf height; Liza had to bend low to use them; Bernardo had to get on his knees. The apartment was, in short (and shortness), a torture chamber—a feeling underlined by the eyebolts screwed into the walls above the bed area, which Del Vonn had obviously used for torture of a voluntary, sexual nature.

DelVonn treated them to cocktails that night at a Korean strip mall bar named Mr. Bot, where old men with brown teeth slammed dice on the bar out of felt cups all night, getting hot and exuberant on a horrible, milky vodka. DelVonn bought everyone a round; Bernardo, who was white-knuckling his way through a hard-won sobriety, refused his, but Liza didn't blink at the prospect of getting nice and drunk for the first time in nearly two months. She didn't notice the jab of disappointment Bernardo eyed her way as she sucked down her glass in two hard swallows, then reached over to drink his.

Cupcake, DelVonn's boyfriend, showed up at around midnight.

It was immediately clear to Liza that Cupcake was taking rude advantage of DelVonn, who was slobbering over the boy in the full foolishness of Love—paying for his drinks, thrilling over his every smoky exhale. Cupcake was bleach-blond, petulant, bitchy, too young and way too pretty, and doled out his affectionate gestures stingily to DelVonn, like there was a taxi meter on them.

Uh-oh, thought Liza.

Cupcake fawned over Bernardo, gushing about how he used to watch Guyzer videos and imitate the dance moves.

Starfucker, thought Liza, the epithet boomeranging into self-recrimination: *I know I am, but what am I?*

"Liza came here to be a famous, movie-star-celebrity," DelVonn said.

"Yeah, give me some makeover advice," Liza begged, clutching Cupcake's skinny, spike-braceleted-wrist. "What do I need to do?"

"For real? You really wanna know?" asked Cupcake.

"Be blunt. I'm drunk and I can take it," she said.

Cupcake's eyes were sympathetic, but his pink mouth bowed downward. "It's good that you're blonde-ish, but you should dye it, like, way lighter, so it softens your face . . . . I mean, your face is *fine,* but if you want to get into movies or videos or whatever, you might need a nose job and your teeth capped. And you should shave those eyebrows off, like, *tonight*. And if you're not going to get a boob job, at least wear a *hugely* padded bra. And can I say something and you won't get offended?"

"Yeah, what?" asked Liza, her colon tensing.

"You should lose, like, at least fifteen pounds. I mean, you're not fat or anything, but actresses have to be, like, *sick* thin."

"Like *AIDS* thin," DelVonn said nastily.

"And even *then* you have to spend at least four days a week in the gym and three in the tanning booth. And girl, you *can't* wear those boots, they make you look like a dyke."

Liza cast a shameful glance down at her favorite combat boots, the ones Lorna had found in the houseboat Free Box.

"I mean, this place is *brutal* on girls. It's all about sex, and . . . sex." Cupcake giggled nasally.

"Shit, Liza," said Bernardo. "Sounds like you best throw your whole self out and start over again."

Which was what Liza was thinking too.

Late that night, while Liza was shaving off her eyebrows at the miniature sink, she and Bernardo both began feeling flu symptoms. They spent several bad days steeped in fever, sore throats, and malaise. One of those unhappy afternoons, watching DelVonn's portable television while Bernardo was passed out and burbling with congestion, Liza saw a few seconds of an entertainment news show's segment on Madonna. Liza couldn't stand Madonna; Madonna reminded her too much of her own failure to be Madonna. Not wanting to get up from the futon to turn it off, Liza grabbed one of her pumps and threw it across the room in an effort to hit the power knob. The TV flash-cut to a segment from Madonna's European tour, and Liza saw distinctly, unquestionably, for a split second, Roland Spring's holy face on one of Madonna's backup dancers, right as the shoe smacked the TV off, winging the cheap knob across the room.

Liza scrambled to the television to pick it back on with her fingernails only to see a simpering, black-eyed sponge-animal extolling the innocence of fabric softener.

Liza, with bleary eyes and runny nose, crawled over to one of her unpacked boxes and threw objects out of it until she found, inside an old Christmas stocking, the stained hanky that Roland Spring had given her on the final night of *The Sound of Music*. The touch of it clawed at her. She would never catch up to Roland, the Stag was too fast, and too fine.

How do you hold a moon-beam in your ha-a-a-and?

She had most likely already gotten all she was ever going to get from Roland: one stoned romp and a hanky. She needed to blow her nose, but would not use the relic. She folded it, tight-lipped, refusing to cry.

This is what it is to become an adult—accepting the fucked-up truth.

She secreted the hanky away with her socks and underwear.

Financially, Liza was relying heavily on Butch Strange, who was only too glad to pay for all the Venal de Minus material that she could send. Before writing, she first ingested anything in the house that could induce a woozy state of intoxication, no matter how unpleasant—the wormy dregs of a souvenir bottle of DelVonn's mezcal, a handful of Pamprin cramp-tablets, a shot of NyQuil; once she tried to chew the ephedrine-soaked wick of a Vick's inhaler, but the noxious menthol scorched her tongue.

Once sufficiently buzzed, Liza forced herself to spend three hours a day at the Selectric II, brass-knuckling Bruce Willis, reprogramming The Terminator to relentlessly pursue Venal's orgasm by any means necessary, and outratcheting Nurse Ratched in *One Blew into the Cuckoo's Nest* by pioneering new frontiers in electroshock sodomy. It seemed that the more she hated the gig, the crueler her stories became, and the more they sold.

Bernardo was trying, in a snail-like, depressed, and loathing way, to get his life moving again. He still had the numbers of music producers and powerful old friends from his glory days, but most wouldn't return his calls. The stink of having fallen from grace was upon him—to associate with Bernardo one had to feel secure socializing with an acknowledged failure, and nobody in LA was that secure; career death was perceived as contagious.

Wading against the tide of his own purest acrimony, Bernardo was forced to contact the one person from his former life that he knew wouldn't refuse to see him; Douggo, the assistant A&R dude, his ex-Guyzer-mate.

Douggo called back a few hours after Bernardo left a message with his secretary, hailing Bernardo over the phone with a transparent, oversize, professional gladness that made Bernardo wince. He offered to put Bernardo's and Liza's names on the list at the Midnight Earl—an elite hotel bar frequented after hours by denizens and subdenizens of young Hollywood. Bernardo accepted but shuddered as he hung up. He had reveled in some very grimy nights at the Midnight Earl during his coke days and dreaded going back, now that he was feeling all the retrospective shame and disgrace he was too high to feel at the time. Liza was desperate to go.

"You're a new man now! They're your friends! They'll be happy to see you!" she argued.

"Yeah, they'll be happy to see me all broke-ass and unemployed," Bernardo mumbled.

"But *pleeeeeease* can we go? We have to go. It's important to our careers. Please-please-please-please-*pleeeeeeeeeeeeeease*?" Liza mockbegged, dying to get out of the horrible apartment and enter the world of glitz.

"I don't know what you think Douggo's gonna do for us. He's got no soul, no flavor, no dick of his own . . . if he wants to use a dick, he has to send out a memo requesting clearance. And then he probly can't take it out of the office."

"Yeah, but he's got important friends, right?"

Bernardo didn't want to let on how weak he felt.

"I'm scared to be around all them drugs."

Liza covered his face with desperate kisses.

"I'll watch over you. You'll be with me. You won't do anything bad. I won't let you."

Bernardo tried to let Liza untangle him from his creeping dread, but the forced, overoptimistic gleam in her eyes did nothing to assuage his fears.

At 3:30 a.m., Bernardo and Liza parked far away, to avoid pulling up to the front of the hotel in the demoralizing Plymouth Horizon.

As the doorman ran his eyes over the clipboard for their names, Bernardo, who hated being recognized, was suddenly very embarrassed not to be recognized. The doorman asked Bernardo for his ID and scrutinized his face to compare it to the photo. Two girls waiting for a cab who recognized Bernardo noticed and laughed to each other.

"Hang in there," said Liza, squeezing his big hand, once they were inside. "Fuck those peons. Who are *they*?"

Douggo, who was wearing a pristine set of tricolor, padded motocross leathers, ran up and gave Bernardo a complicated Guyzer handshake.

He kissed Liza on the cheek and guided them both through the packed, airless, VIP room to a purple velvet couch that was already occupied by "Hadrian" (not his real name), the especially depraved son of a hugely famous, dead pop star, whose very name still embodies the freewheeling 1960s, psychedelic drug abuse, political dissent, and mass orgies. Hadrian, a small, gawky Brit with a cynical mouth and long bangs hiding his beady eyes, half-stood, and gave Bernardo a half-hug.

"Aaaah, Bernardo," Hadrian drawled, in his British public-school accent. "Back from the dead, are we?"

"Are we?" asked Bernardo.

Hadrian, a bright but ignored child raised by nannies and boarding schools, was a bitter, self-indulgent adult. He had attempted his own recording career and had a hit single once, largely due to his dead father's enduring celebrity, but he was unable to retain the attention of the multitudes and ended up confining his self-declaimed "useless energies" to holding court at the Midnight Earl. Hadrian socialized there nightly, surrounded by women he fondly dubbed his Lesions, "Because, like a herpes outbreak, there's always one on me somewhere. Their name is Lesion."

The Lesions were mostly models from unglamorous backgrounds who hadn't made it into the higher and/or superechelons. Many of the Lesions opted for oversize breast implants and were now "personal assistants" of male celebrities and/or top-shelf call girls. Several got paid huge sums of money to be "guests" of the Sultan of Brunei for a few weeks a year; a few of them had done glossy nude layouts in men's magazines. They clung to Hadrian because he had lots of famous male friends for them to seduce, and he always had cocaine.

Liza looked at Hadrian's harem and realized that most, if not all, would be phenomenal beauties in other contexts—each had surely been queen of some high school, somewhere, but here they were merely hothouse wallflowers. Hadrian treated them all with contempt, calling them "whore" and "trollop." It was supposed to be good-natured, faux-contempt, but it was really *undisguised* contempt. The girls, for their part, acted hard and unflappable, smoked a lot, vanished into the bathroom in groups of two and three, and made a show of brazenness, campily squeezing each other's big breasts and striking joke porn-poses; Liza watched one girl stick her tongue up another's nostril, in an effort to momentarily command any available male attention.

. . .

In the smoky dim, Bernardo introduced Liza to a head that suddenly appeared over the back of the couch: Chip, Hadrian's omnipresent homunculus of a Laotian coke dealer.

"You still owe me four hundred dollars!" Chip yelled at Bernardo, loud enough for Liza and couple of Lesions to hear.

Bernardo looked abashed. "Sorry," he said.

"Just joking. OK? No problem, OK?" said Chip, who suddenly felt comfortable enough to tousle Bernardo's dreads. Bernardo flinched; Chip was Hadrian's servile whipping boy; he would never have dared to touch Bernardo, three years ago—such a trespass might have meant exile from the Midnight Earl forever. Liza watched as Bernardo's self-esteem began to wilt down into itself like cotton candy in fog.

That evening, Hadrian, Douggo, and the Lesions were all kissing Voo Dewey's ass, Voo being the only person on the couch that night whose celebrity was still functional. *"Como Talley VOO,"* Voo's rap single, had been a hit, two years back—Voo's controversial lyrics drew on his "personal experiences," e.g., doing three years' time as a juvenile for participation in a gang rape. There was a much-facilitated rumor that he was a "vanisher" for bodies assassinated by his local branch of Crips. Voo parlayed his reputation into opportunity; white executives loved him, for he was a "thug" from the "Street" and it made them feel manly to be near him ("Street" having a distinctly different Hollywood definition than it did five years previously: now it was "real," a place full of killings and despair, where only da baddest and strongest survived). He was now the impresario behind the wildly successful Strickly LaJit record label, and he surrounded himself with an entourage that seemed imported directly from the county lockup: large, glowering men with guns, do-rags, pit bulls, and presumably ferocious tempers.

Voo appeared to be completely uninterested in Hadrian, Douggo, and all the women vying for his attention, talking instead to a friend with platinum teeth, despite the fact that the entire evening seemed to be arranged for his benefit. Everyone in the group kept turning after they said something clever, to see if Voo had noticed them; he hadn't.

Douggo was enthusiastically chewing on Bernardo about the idea of developing him into a new act.

"You know Justine Bateman? Or that blonde chick from *Facts of*

Life? I want to get you together with one of them, so you guys can write a love duet." Bernardo couldn't tell if Douggo was serious in offering such wretched deals or trying to humiliate him to amuse Hadrian. Drinks kept coming to the table; the waitress neglected to bring Bernardo a 7UP, round after round, instead placing shots of tequila before him, which remained untouched until Liza drank them to fortify herself. Bernardo's face suggested he was enduring a cramp.

Suddenly, Voo's heavy attention turned to the group. Everyone practically jumped in their seats, they were so surprised he was finally interacting with them. He was singing, in a quavering, soft-jam falsetto, lousy with faux-unction:

> *You're the one, girl*
> *And who could ask for more*
> *I opened up the door*
> *And you came in my life . . .*

It took a few seconds for everyone to realize Voo was mocking Bernardo and Douggo by singing Guyzer's #1 soft-jam hit. It had been penned by Pam Derwood, the ubiquitous pop composer, whose simplistic melodies, snivelingly codependent lyrical clichés, and overproduced flights of unsophisticated feeling had been responsible for a staggering number of #1 hits.

Voo continued in his cruel imitation of Bernardo's overwrought style as Hadrian and Co. laughed uproariously. Bernardo smiled, pretending to find it funny.

"Oh, blood, that's cold," laughed Douggo, trying to give Voo a high-five. Voo ignored him, dipping the tip of a marijuana-packed blunt into his cognac.

"I bet Pam Derwood's rhyming dictionary is so small that she can store it in her digital watch," said Liza.

Douggo turned to her humorlessly. "There's only three or four acts in the world that can afford a Pam Derwood song, and Guyzer was one of them. She's the most expensive composer there is."

Liza remained silent.

"Liza sings," said Bernardo, after an uncomfortable second.

"Oh yeah? Is she any good?" Douggo looked right at her.

"Yeah," said Bernardo, looking at the shot glass before him that Liza had just emptied.

Liza's eyes focused on him with a gratitude so intense, he thought she might have tears in them; then he decided she was just drunk.

"Where can we hear you?" Hadrian asked, turning to Liza.

"Well . . . we just got here, I haven't really gotten a regular gig, yet . . . ," she stammered, the glut of tequila in her stomach beginning to churn.

"Liza should sing at your Pimps n' Ho's party, Hadrian!" Douggo yelled.

Bernardo slapped Liza's leg with less enthusiasm than seemed called for. "Here you go. Here's your big break. Let Liza sing at your party, man."

Hadrian reveled in his power for a moment. A few girls had gotten recording deals, singing at Hadrian's parties. They got "exposure" and met the "right people" (usually in the hot tub).

"OK, Bernardo, but you have to do something for *me*," Hadrian sneered.

Douggo grinned. "Oh shit, here it comes!"

Hadrian tossed his bangs, revealing a ratlike eye. He took a dramatic pause. "Liza, you can sing at my party, if Douggo and Bernardo promise to come in their silver jumpsuits and sing 'You're the One' for us."

Voo began laughing crudely. "Oh, shit! Oh! That's fucked up!" he crowed.

Douggo rolled his eyes in appreciation of the merriment at his expense.

"Voo, if you show up, we'll do it! Right, Bernardo?" Douggo jostled Bernardo's tight shoulders.

Bernardo picked Liza's used lime out of the empty shot glass and began sucking it.

Hadrian noticed Bernardo's agony and leapt to feed on it.

"Do it for *Liza*, Bernardo. You want Voo to hear her sing, don't you?" he asked, wickedly. "It could be so *important* to her *career*." Liza felt a tremor of raw opportunism lick up her spine like an ice cube.

"I'll show up if they wear them fuckin' Jiffy Pop suits," Voo giggled. "I gotta see that shit."

"For reals?" Douggo asked gamely, rabbit-punching Bernardo's arm. "Come on, blood, you'll do it, right? You still got the suit, right?"

The waitress came, setting yet another shot of tequila in front of

Bernardo. Liza reached for it, but Bernardo got there first and threw it back, his eyes shutting as the burn slapped the back of his throat.

"Oh yeah, why not." Bernardo looked Voo hazardously in the eye. "What the fuck I got to lose?"

Voo leaned over to give Bernardo a conciliatory finger-shake, still giggling. Bernardo accepted the gesture.

"You'd better be a good singer, Liza, or we're all going to throw hors d'oeuvres at you," said Hadrian, picking his teeth with a miniature cocktail-sword.

"Oh man! Hoo!" Douggo glowed. "It's gonna be so sick, B.! You remember the moves?"

"I remember," said Bernardo, darkly. Liza looked at his defeated face and a lurch in her stomach informed her that she was, in fact, going to be sick. She pushed her way through a slanting and feverish hallway to the ladies' room. The girls Liza wobbled past were towering and bamboo slim; their large, frosted eyes followed Liza's eccentric orbit with expressions of disdain. None of the girls appeared to need a nose job, larger breasts, blonder hair, capped teeth, or a tan, and if any of them lost another fifteen pounds, it seemed to Liza (as she threw up), it would probably kill them.

Liza did not remember leaving the bar. The needle-sharp brightness of morning poked her eyes open through the dirty windshield of the Horizon; her head felt poached in acetone.

"God, Bernardo. Those people are really awful."

"I told you," Bernardo said, glumly navigating his way into the parking area behind their building.

"You actually still have your Guyzer jumpsuit?"

"I was gonna try to sell it to the Hard Rock Cafe," he whispered.

"You drank a shot," Liza said, worried.

"So? You drank twelve. You drank like a damn Romanian," muttered Bernardo, remembering a particularly gruesome night with the band in Eastern Europe. They trudged into the room and fell, demolished, to the futon, grateful, for once, that the apartment was a dark box.

Bernardo was vehemently against going to Hadrian's party, but Liza felt inexorably pulled toward the event, like a masochistic stuntman in a barrel, paddling willfully toward the falls. She purchased, from the drugstore, an ultralight blonde hair dye, which she left to bake on her head until her scalp was scabbed, and the ends of her hair were white and crispy as fiberglass. She vowed to herself to eat nothing but Diet Coke and carrots, at least until the party. The combination of caffeine, starvation, and nerves wound her up into a gear-grinding frenzy.

"Motherfucking Hadrian just wants us to do it so he and Voo can *laugh at me*," Bernardo kept trying to tell her.

"They want to laugh *with* you!" Liza would say with false, manic cheerfulness, aware that she'd say anything to change his mind. "You have to get over yourself! It's your past, you can't escape it, you may as well make fun of it, right?! What better way to put it behind you?"

Bernardo did not see it that way.

"This is the kind of thing you do, here, right?" Liza would ask, with hopeful eyes. "You get offered this kind of opportunity, in LA, and you do it, right? You don't say no to the Opportunity Train, or it skips your stop next time, right?"

She was quoting her former talent agent, Burt Swan.

"But I got *hit* by that train."

"Oh come on, how bad could it be? Everybody else is gonna be dressed like a pimp or a ho. What's one silver jumpsuit, more or less, among pimps?"

On and on it went, with Liza wheedling and rationalizing, and Bernardo growing more sullen, until Liza finally won out by promising to clean the bathroom for a month. Bernardo detested the bathroom, and could only tolerate its punitive confines if it was floor-lickingly spotless.

DelVonn called Liza the night of the party, as she was in a mortal panic, trying to beautify herself in a way that would look more Lesion-y, in the hopes of fitting in with Hadrian's scene. DelVonn was living out his own Grim Fairy Tale; he was the Frog Prince, a lonesome little monster—Cupcake, his spoiled princess bride, was suddenly in a hurry to sever their bond.

"Cupcake's dumping me," DelVonn wept. "I'm totally falling apart. He's out with his new sugar daddy. He's moving out and leaving me in this goddamn apartment all by myself!"

"I knew he was sketchy," said Liza, drawing tiny eyebrows on with a brown pencil and nervously trying to figure out what dress to wear. "He was so shallow and full of shit." She was still smarting from Cupcake's cruel "makeover advice" (which she had nonetheless followed to the best of her ability).

Liza couldn't give her full attention to DelVonn. Though he was shattered and crying, she still felt he was *luckier* than she was: he was supporting himself in the performing arts, he did occasional TV and videos, *what else was truly important*? Of the two ends of the phone line, Liza felt her singing debut was the bigger crisis.

"Can you come over?" DelVonn sniffed.

"No, I totally can't! I'm freaking out! I have to perform at Hadrian's Pimps n' Ho's party!"

"Oh, Lord," DelVonn whimpered. "Can I crash it? Please? I don't want to be alone." This was the night Liza had been pining for: all of her energies were going to fizz and swell; she knew she would be too embarrassed to give birth to her holy Star-Self in front of DelVonn—in his desolate mood, he might throw a wet-dog blanket of self-consciousness over her intended blast of personal power. Worse yet, he might steal her thunder by getting drunk and acting like his usual self. Given his tendency to debauch, he would be a bad influence on her; they would inevitably get fucked up and disgrace themselves, in front of people she was bowel-voidingly nervous about impressing. She couldn't afford any of her usual retardation, on this night of nights, and hence, she couldn't afford DelVonn.

"I wish you could. It's totally invite only. I had trouble getting Bernardo in," she lied, realizing the moment she said it that it would be a difficult lie to substantiate. She squatted and stuffed two ruined black stockings into her bra, trying to make both sides equally round in the dwarf-length mirror.

"So how did *you* get that gig?" DelVonn asked, suspicious.

"It's a long story," Liza bluffed. DelVonn fell silent, then began to sob again.

"Nobody that beautiful will ever hug me and kiss me again, I *know* it."

"Oh, don't be ridiculous," said Liza, opening the closet door and gazing in panic at her mound of stupid shoes. "He was a jerk. He was using you. You'll get over it, I promise." She had no such genuine belief, but she was trying to extricate herself from the call.

"I'm a *freak*," howled DelVonn. "The fact that he wanted me at all was a fucking *miracle*. You don't get that lucky *twice*."

"Oh, don't be such a drama queen! Snap out of it!" Liza knew she was being cold but felt she couldn't afford to stop focusing on herself. She opted for an old outfit from Peppy's Reno past—a fragile silver minidress with a plunging neckline, which shed trails of yellowing sequins like a mangy trout.

"I'm in a fuck-ton of pain. Can you call me later? Please?"

"Yes," Liza lied. "I'll call you later."

"Promise?"

"Yeah."

Liza could not help noting that DelVonn hadn't wished her luck with the gig.

Bernardo and Liza didn't speak in the car. Bernardo wore his black church suit; the silver jumpsuit lay in a garment bag on the backseat. Liza was trying not to sit with her full weight, afraid that all of the sequins over her ass would crack off. They drove among the trees of Laurel Canyon, passing Hadrian's mailbox, hiding the unsightly car up the road. Hiking up Hadrian's curving, private driveway, Liza was momentarily reassured by a sharp, organic whiff of skunk. This was it: the Primordial Forest, the Emerald City, the Yellow Brick Road, oh my.

Unlike the Baumgarten home, which up to this night had been the most lavish house Liza had ever been to, Hadrian's mansion was the result of money without effort, and luxury without mindful choice. It was hugely expensive and modern, but compromised by weak character; the mark of no genius architect was on it—no stunning perversions of space—the house was cold, clunky, and severe, reminding Liza of a ranch-style detentional facility. Glass doors ran the length of the long living room, looking out to a pool that had a Hammond organ marinating disingenuously at the bottom of it. The white concrete patio jutted out over Hollywood, serving the guests to the breezy sky, where the excrescences of LA exhaust and industrial whooping cough made a thick, rusty stripe in the darkness over the hazy, astigmatic lights below.

Liza caught unnerving conversation-bits while she and Bernardo elbowed their way through the party in an effort to find Hadrian.

". . . Anita tried to off herself again last month . . ."

". . . Money is green energy, a tool that is neither good nor evil . . ."

The party was crowded with B- and C-list revelers, wallowing in Hadrian's ersatz Playboy Mansion environment. The Lesions were out in force, clad in costumes fresh from Frederick's and other Hollywood

Boulevard stores that trafficked in absurdly high-heeled, patent-leather dominatrix hip-waders, peek-a-boo rubber nurse ensembles, crotchless jodhpurs, marabou handcuffs, and other fripperies of the fetish world. A goodly number of the "pimps" accompanying the Lesions were enormous, tanned, gay bodybuilders with electric-white teeth, displaying their own cherished steroidal nakedness in spaghetti-string tank tops, pheasant-plumed fedoras, Liberace-pants, and droll platforms from pricey Melrose vintage stores. Liza spotted a white-haired old man in large black glasses, his slack and mossy chest visible under an open silk kimono; he was steering a cushy blonde teenager through the party with clawlike fingers, denting her tube skirt into the cleft of her buttocks.

Liza recognized many people whose names she didn't know—TV bimbos too long-in-the-tooth to be famously fuckable anymore, square-jawed macho guys from forgotten action shows who had lost their hair, or gotten fat. There was a trio of much older women, all victims of plastic-surgery clear-cutting; their skin had the textureless shine of Silly Putty. They flaunted expensive, minuscule dresses far too slutty for their age; their big breasts, barely supported by thin, spangled triangles of sheer fabric, were mottled and raisiny from excess sun; their creased brown necks resembled sheaves of barley bound by garish necklaces. Liza silently thanked whatever God was responsible for making Peppy too poor for surgical enhancements.

Bernardo pointed out a large oil portrait of Hadrian's father looming over the mantel; long hair, embroidered tunic, psychedelic pink glasses. Relics of Hadrian's father were everywhere—numberless gold records, sculptural tributes, photos with Gerald Ford. Liza was struck by how awful it could be to have a parent be so beloved by the world that nobody saw his faults; he had surely been a terrible father, an oblivion-seeker who'd indulged himself to death, and yet Hadrian had nothing but his collateral light with which to redeem himself; his father's presence was still more vivid, some fifteen years after his death, than Hadrian's would ever be while alive.

Liza and Bernardo pressed on, Bernardo looking more and more like a man on a tumbrel cart, creaking toward the guillotine.

. . .

They heard Hadrian shout, "Archbishop! Bring me a goat!" He was poncing about in a lacy Marquis de Sade costume, goosing women and lisping.

"Bernardo! Liza! What a shabby dress. Nice tits, though. Are those real?" he asked, drunkenly, reaching for Liza's chest.

"They're socks," Liza admitted freely, sidestepping his grope. Liza showed Hadrian what she had—her boom box, plug-in microphone, and her tapes of Virgil Ortiz playing synthesized arrangements of Lisa Lisa & The Cult Jam songs.

"Oh, you're *ridiculous!*" Hadrian jeered. "This is *it?* I thought you'd at least bring an *accordion.*"

Liza almost began crying but steeled herself.

"Just let her do her thing, man," Bernardo said in a warning tone that made Hadrian flush pink behind his prosthetic syphilis welts.

Hadrian was dead set against Liza using his main sound system, so he relegated her to a small, empty room in the back of the house, far from the party, where the vibrational whumping of his main music could still be felt through the floor. "I must leave you now, and enjoy the voluptuous sensation of polluting infant schoolchildren, with defilements most foul." Hadrian slithered back out into the hallway, leaving Bernardo and Liza alone.

Liza looked imploringly at her boyfriend.

"You're the one that wanted this, not me," he said.

With that, he abandoned Liza to her little Siberia.

Liza swallowed the sizzling lump of coal in her throat and resolved, with commendable determination, to summon her powers.

Oh mighty Isis, she said to herself, remembering a Saturday-morning TV show; then she got serious. She kneeled, lifting her cheap portable microphone to the heavens in the way she imagined Joan of Arc offering her sword.

By the powers vested in me by my continued pursuit of excellence and magickal star-quality via inner cleanliness and my undying belief in my wishes upon numerous stars, I swear by the precious Golden Stag that this is a night that will CHANGE MY LIFE. Blood and adrenaline roared into her limbs.

In a willful blast of personal might, she envisioned herself as a rock goddess in a wind tunnel, scarves and hair flying, eyes combusting, aura crackling with pink veins of newborn lightning.

She popped the tape in, smiled, shook her newly fried, baby-blonde hair out, adjusted her wadded tits (sprinkling brittle sequins and rotten thread, like dead fairy rot), hyperventilated for a few seconds, and began.

Liza sang her guts out, magnetizing herself, working with all of her powers to draw people into the room. From a distant side of the house, she could hear conversations, uproarious laughter, a separate world of activity, oblivious to her. When her tape was finished, she turned it over, undiscouraged. When side B finished, she turned the tape over again, despite the fact that nobody had heard her yet, and her underused vocal chords were tiring. *They'll come, and they'll fucking LOVE me,* she insisted to herself, taking a quick swig of the small, warm bottle of Jägermeister in her oversize purse, and giving a quick wink to the holy stag of St. Eustace on the label.

On her second trip through side A, two Lesions, one in a pink fishnet bodystocking and the other in a white bridal gown with two ragged scissor holes exposing her breasts, came up and grabbed the microphone and began braying with Liza, rudely, in brash and drunken voices.

"Put on some Journey!" screeched Bodystocking, rifling through Liza's purse. "Don't you have any Journey?"

"You guys, I'm serious, cut it out, I'm doing a gig, here," Liza whined.

"Oh. A *gig*?" the Bride asked, giggling.

"Oh, excuse me, a *gig*," said Bodystocking.

"Have you seen Voo?" asked Liza.

"Why, are you looking to get raped?"

The comment chilled Liza and confirmed something that she had sensed when she walked into the party: there was deep depravity here—even ChoCho's house had a redeeming innocence compared to this scene.

"So . . . lemme get this straight . . . you *only* sing songs by Lisa Lisa and the Cult Jam?!" the Bride squealed, inspecting the tape in Liza's boom box. Bodystocking went over to look for herself. The two girls started laughing so hard they fell down on top of each other.

Watching the tawdry girls roll on the floor, cackling with breathless delight at her stupidity, Liza had a sense of serial déjà-vu: being perpetually dunked back into the Normal Family Theatre dressing room, with naked girls terrorizing her.

What does this mean?

It was then that Liza had the startling realization that she was extremely *lucky* only to have been seen doing her "act" by these nudist barracudas; she had been spared a far more damning humiliation. Liza grabbed her purse, abandoning the boom box and tape to the savage vixens, who were fast-forwarding through the tape at random and screaming improvised, obscene lyrics into her microphone.

A shrill, *phweeking* car-alarm of panic in Liza's solar plexus told her that she must find Bernardo immediately, and they must leave before he'd have to perform the Guyzer song with the repugnant Douggo. She sprinted down the bookcase-lined hallway toward the party noise but was stopped by a familiar, lurid pink on Hadrian's bookshelf. Right next to her knee, between expensive art books of pornography from feudal Japan and the Weimar Republic, stretched the complete, twenty-three-volume collection of Centaur's paperback Venal de Minus series; this discovery was wholly dumbfounding—a karate chop to the larynx.

At this exact moment, Liza heard the horrifying strains of the familiar synth-drum intro of "You're the One" thunking over Hadrian's huge speaker system.

OH NO.

Liza ran down the hall; her vision was blocked by a tight wall of shoulders—everyone was staring at the center of Hadrian's living room. Liza found a place next to a woman who had each of her breasts compressed mammogram-style between six-inch squares of plywood, held flat with C-clamps.

"Ungh! I've always *hated* this song," said the woman, with spiteful relish.

Naturally, Hadrian's entire crowd hated the Guyzer song. Mild hilarity rippled through the guests when they realized what they were about to be subjected to.

Liza saw a dark patch of humanity muscling for sightlines in the back of the room: Voo Dewey and Co. were "in the house," all wearing sunglasses, berets, and black canvas utility jumpsuits. They resembled an elite corps of Black Panther, air force assassins. (Voo, in self-consciously eschewing the "pimp" theme, was inadvertently the pimpingest guest of all.)

At the climactic musical cue, Douggo and Bernardo bounce-walked into the center of the room, wearing radio-microphone headsets, and began their synchronized kicks, turns, and hormonal soul-moaning. The guests burst into high, derisive laughter, drowning out the vocal performance. Women trilled, "Woooo!" with faux-teen hysteria.

Voo and Co. were laughing so hard, they were bent over double and giving each other weak high-fives.

Douggo sang his part with special clownish unction, making sure that everyone knew that he was making fun of himself. *No sincerity here, folks, ha ha ha, I'm one of you.*

Bernardo, however, didn't have Douggo's emotional distance. His voice and dancing were rusty, but painfully earnest. He was actually doing the unthinkable—trying to give a *good performance.*

I'm down on my knees, girl,
Beggin' to please yuh. . . .
Dontcha kno-OOOOO-oOOOOOoow
You're the one, AaaAAAAAwwwwwww

Bernardo did not have the élan to pull off the self-mockery required of the moment, and everyone watching felt it. The laughing became raucous and uncomfortable. Liza pitied Bernardo, but the shameful sting of association with him was even sharper; she wanted to stay as far away from him as possible.

Voo lifted his sunglasses to wipe away a tear of mirth and caught Liza's eye. She began to laugh, as if what Bernardo was doing was actually funny. Voo stared a horrible icicle through Liza's thin dignity, informing her, with his look, that he was laughing precisely because Bernardo was *not* funny. And here Liza made an interesting reflexive decision, without thinking:

So subtle, but such is the banality of evil:

She looked at Voo and rolled her eyes, complicit with him, as if to say: *ha ha ha, yes, poor, dumb Bernardo.*

The song ended, to the relief of everyone, and there was a round of unkind applause.

"I am *discharging!*" Hadrian screamed, rescuing the dying moment with his Marquis persona. The crowd laughed in relief at this.

.   .   .

Days later, Liza would reassemble the small, seemingly meaningless individual moments that contributed to the overall catastrophe.

Twenty minutes after the song fiasco, Bernardo cornered Liza at Hadrian's wall-size wet bar, where she was working on a pint-glass of vodka, trying to recover from his mortification. Liza had hidden from Bernardo after the performance, hoping to reconnect only after he'd taken off the offending jumpsuit, which announced his loserhood like a full-body cold sore. The silver suit, to Liza's stabbing distress, was still on him.

"You famous yet? Voo come hear you sing and give you a great big recording contract?"

Liza flinched at his bitter sarcasm.

"It was total bullshit. Nobody heard me. Let's get out of here as fast as we can."

"Oh no-o-o-o, baby, we're staying for the real party, now. It's so lovely to be back in Hollywood. There are my people. And you're my *girl*." Bernardo seethed with a fury that Liza had never seen in him before. He stalked toward the back of the house. Liza followed, concerned, but ten feet behind.

Bernardo knew his way through the labyrinthine hallway, entering what looked like a thin utility closet; he reached down at the back wall and unlocked a concealed door, leaving it ajar for Liza without looking back at her.

Several steps led down into what was obviously the VIP inner sanctum of Hadrian's compound, or what Hadrian liked to call "The Drug-out." The room was really just a low, round conversation pit, lined on all sides with a red leather couch. It evoked a modern, sinister version of the bottle-house in *I Dream of Jeannie*. A halo of black light on the low ceiling made everyone's skin look purple, their teeth and eyes ghoulish and radioactive. A stereo played murky, beat-heavy music; a black candle the size of a milk carton burned on the onyx table.

"Ohp! Here he is!" giggled a redhead in a rubber corset-dress upon seeing Bernardo. Everyone laughed. Liza recognized the woman as the once-lumpy child star of a family TV show, popular years before—her struggle with eating disorders and breast-augmentation surgery had once made the cover of *People* magazine.

"We knew you'd end up back here, Bernardo, after that performance," said Douggo, looking up with watery eyes and pinching his nose to moisten the burn from all the drugs he'd just snuffed into it.

A flame clicked on atop a shiny lighter, illuminating the otherwise entirely shadowed face of Voo, who took a drag of a glowing and enormous joint, inspecting its construction as he held his breath.

"That a coco puff?" Bernardo asked solemnly. Voo nodded, almost imperceptibly—only one eyebrow actually moved.

"There's coke in that?" Liza asked him, quietly. Bernardo wouldn't look at her.

"Lemme hit that," Bernardo said to Voo. There was a beat while everyone in the room watched.

"Better nail down yo' TV set, Hadrian," Voo joked, passing the cigar-size joint into Bernardo's sweaty hand. Everyone laughed at Voo's cleverness. Liza wanted to scream, but to her great shame, she was still bound to the idea of extracting her last chance for Voo to "discover her"; she found she couldn't say anything that might offend him, she was already at such a painful disadvantage. Liza pinched Bernardo as he took a drag; he slapped her hand away.

"So, how long did that sobriety thing last, Bernardo?" Hadrian sang out, to the delight of Chip, the Laotian, who was graciously accepting wads of cash from people in the circle and handing them phosphorescent Baggies.

"Long enough."

Liza felt her heart trying to crawl out of her mouth and eject itself onto the rug.

I watched Bernardo fall off the wagon and I did nothing, Liza would think, days later. In her mind, The Wagon was a primitive wooden raft with crude wheels twenty feet tall, and Bernardo had been hanging by tender fingertips to its bare and splintered planks, as they crashed down a near-vertical mountain face. Liza had insisted they go this route, despite the fact that she knew Bernardo wasn't up to the ordeal, *I knew it, I knew it . . .*

Bernardo had taken sixty dollars from Liza's purse and given it to Chip and was now snorting a thumb-size line of coke off of the black table. Everyone in the circle became suddenly aware of Voo's intense, predatory focus on Liza.

"Your girl look nice, Bernardo." Voo licked his chops like a lion.

"Yeah?" said Bernardo, subtext: *I know you're fucking with me.*

"I thought she was gonna sing for me. Why she didn't *sang* for me?"

"I did," Liza pouted. "You just never made it into the fuckin' refrigerator Hadrian made me do it in."

"You wear that dress for me, Li-i-iza?" asked Voo, drawing her name out with a lewd grin. His cobra eyes slid down Liza's (now slightly asymmetrical) cleavage with alarming candor.

"You have a bunch of books I wrote on your bookshelf, Hadrian," Liza said, in a dire attempt to change the direction of the conversation.

"You, foul pollution, are an author?"

"I write Venal de Minus," she mumbled. "It's my day gig until the singing thing takes off," she added, painfully. She couldn't believe that in front of Hadrian and his friends, it was the singing that she was ashamed of, and that smut was her only possible hope of impressing them.

"You're Venal de Minus? Get out of town!" said the ex-child-star, suddenly excited. "I love Venal de Minus! It's so hilariously *trashy*. How'd you get that job? I want to talk to you."

"Honey, what are you doing trying to *sing*?" Hadrian derided. "The world has way too many singers and far too few pornographers, if you ask me."

"Music is a filthy profession," said a six-foot, coffee-skinned Amazon with a blonde Afro wearing a sheer, cheetah-print negligee, who Liza recognized—she was a one-hit wonder, an R&B singer who had topped the airwaves with an unavoidable song a few years ago, then abruptly vanished into Never-Again Land. Her low, suede voice was laden with bad experience.

"Believe that," Bernardo said to Cheetah Woman in a near whisper.

"Come here and sit by me, Li-i-iza," Voo said suddenly. "Tell Daddy about cha'self."

Liza shot a look to Bernardo, because although she understood that there was some kind of cruel, group headfuck going on, in which Hadrian, Douggo, and Voo were ganging up on Bernardo, she still didn't know whether to pretend it wasn't happening or not, especially since Bernardo still wouldn't look at her. Liza knew he was blaming her for everything; she felt this unspoken accusation was basically true but resented it anyway.

Liza stood up, with a hard look at Bernardo, edged around the table, and sidled up next to Voo, who cleared a place for her. Everyone watched the move with tremors of apprehension—Little Red Riding

Hood was squeezing in close to the Big Bad Wolf. Liza was aware her gesture looked whorish and decided she didn't care—everyone else was debasing themselves for Voo's entertainment; she was no worse than any of them. Liza reached over to drink Voo's cocktail.

She was reminded of ChoCho's pleasure in subjecting an addict to his stun gun—the primary drug abusing everyone in this hellish little room was Fame. Everyone present, aside from her, had had their hands at some point on some small but active coin of the Fame realm, and instead of enriching and actualizing them, it had sucked them dry. Hadrian and the people around him were malignantly unhappy, vice soaked, and nearly insane. It seemed unthinkable; they had beauty, money, youth, prestige—everything except immediate household name recognition, and the lack of that one thing seemed to be actually killing them all. Worst of all, she knew she was one of them—another lost, self-hating, Stepford-zombie-bloodsucker, wandering Hollywood's purgatorial void. Voo was an atrocious person, a murderer, in all likelihood, and yet he was their king, and here she was, with his larcenous arm heavy on her shoulders, and his lips on her ear, with Bernardo quietly killing himself four feet away.

For the first time in her life, Liza felt actually, truly, deeply sleazy.

Bernardo was, by now, high enough to address the bearbaiting that had been going on at his expense all evening. He went on the attack.

"You didn't really see no gangsta shit, back in the day, did you Voo? You ain't no O.G. Compton Crip. It's all a tall tale, ain't it?" Bernardo asked, boldly. "Where'd you come up, really? Bel Air? La Jolla?"

"What the fuck you talking about, nigga? I was on the front lines of that shit. I got my ass shot off one time."

"You got shot?" asked Bernardo. "When? Your moms stick you in front of the pistol range over at the country club?"

Hadrian cackled loudly.

"I'll show you the bullet hole! Motherfuckin' Blood did a drive-by, took a two-inch bite out my shit with a Glock 9." Voo, whose pants were already low-slung to display the elastic band of his Calvin Klein boxer shorts, turned around and pulled his underwear low enough for Bernardo to see the keloid starburst of scar tissue on Voo's left buttock. Bernardo's heartbeat began fluttering like a rabbit's.

"That shit hurt like a motherfucker. Hadda sleep on my stomach for two weeks."

Bernardo looked at the low ceiling and emitted a funereal chuckle.

"That ain't a bullet hole, Voo," Bernardo said slowly, staring into Voo's right eye.

"Wha'd you say?" Voo asked, turning to Bernardo with a mad-dog, penitentiary stare-down. Stomachs cringed.

"Ho! You *sold your ass!*" cried Bernardo, with terrible conviction. "To that cannibal bitch in Zurich, right?"

The whites of Voo's eyes seemed to vanish as he exhaled smoke through his nose, dragonlike.

"You *high,* crackhead?"

Bernardo had already lost all his pride and felt suicidally bold in the fuck-it-all way that only a coked-up wretch with nothing to lose can be.

"I got that letter too! Euu! She *ate* your *ass,* and *that's* how you got all the money! Hah! I knew it wasn't because you so *talented. 'My hunger is for the flesh of a beautiful star'. . . . ,*" Bernardo quoted, falsetto, from the letter. "And she probly had to put some bacon on your ass to eat it too, it probly stank so bad."

Hadrian's eyes were as huge and petrified as a cat's. A thick cloud of violence had moved over the room, pressurizing everyone's skulls with rage-ozone and coke-paranoia. Douggo became hysterical with frightened laughter.

Voo reached into the front of his pants. Liza yelped in fear and moved to dive under the table. Bernardo didn't even look up at Voo, busy, as he was, chopping himself another fat line.

"Dude! Woahwoahwoah! Don't, like, *shoot* him," babbled Douggo, flapping his hands in terror.

Voo lifted his hand, empty. "I ain't gonna shoot no no-account crackhead. He ain't worf the time it take to pull the trigger."

"Oh *do* shoot him. I want to enjoy the new orifice!" Hadrian squirted, reverting back to his Marquis persona to conceal his fright.

"Shut up! You disgusting, pathetic, dickless has-been!" Liza shrieked.

Hadrian turned to her, suddenly delighted. "Oh, you're *delicious!* Why weren't you ever like this before, Venal?"

"Don't call me Venal." Liza shook with nervous rage.

Hadrian moved to Liza and began stroking her thigh; she slapped his hand away. The psychotic murder-energy between Bernardo and Voo was suddenly *gone,* as if the whole ugly showdown had been a relatively normal social exchange. Bernardo was back at the coke; Voo was rolling another enormous joint.

"Oh, Venal de Minus! Don't be like that! Be *fun*," chided Hadrian.
Fun?

This was supposed to be FUN?

Ordinarily, Liza might have made a spectacle of herself, to at least gain the Pyrrhic victory of a grand, obnoxious exit, but she was no match for the high level of disgrace generated by this crowd. She was seized with an urgency to get out of the tiny, evil, claustrophobic room.

"I'm leaving. Goodnight, everyone," Liza said, standing up. Voo held her wrist in protest, then let his hand drop. "You coming?" she asked Bernardo.

"Nope."

The cocaine animating the muscles of his face made him look like a completely different person.

"I'll be having my cars washed next Saturday, Liza, perhaps you'd like to sing for me then, standing on a little bucket," Hadrian said, with sparkling cruelty. Voo giggled like a child.

"Y'all so mean and nasty," drawled the bored Cheetah, unfolding her own bindle and pouring herself a line.

"Can I call you about that Venal de Minus gig?" the TV child asked Liza, earnestly.

"Why the hell would you *want* to?!" Liza snapped, feeling foul enough to kill them all with one big axe-swipe through all their necks.

"I thought maybe you could give me some tips on how to break in to that kind of job," she said, pitiably. Liza felt sorry for her—she was a victim, a sweet person whose whole life had been marred by the dorkiness of her preteen stint on national television. Liza remembered envying the girl, when she was a kid, and wondering why it couldn't have been her in tight pigtails, saying cute lines on TV that made the whole studio audience say *Awwwww*.

Liza gathered her boom box and tape, which had been pulled apart and strewn in ribbons all over the room, and staggered her way to the car, crying in hard sobs. As she drove down the hill, the oncoming headlights magnified into head-splitting white bowling balls through her tears. Liza thought acidly about Peppy, and how easy it would be to floor the gas pedal, flip into the indifferent canyon and smog-sick trees below, and end herself with a metal and bone–jagging *cr-r-ack,* loud as a mile-wide ice tray.

Ned's gala opening, at the Leighton/Kelles gallery in San Francisco, was a smash success.

. . . boasted the expensive postcards and placards that Jacqueline Kelles had printed for the occasion, with one of Ned's more spectacular light-boxes on the front, resembling a jeweled sea anemone basking in an iridescent oil slick. Peppy and Noreen were intimidated by the affluent, sophisticated crowd—men with large, architectural eyeglasses who spoke in inscrutable nine-dollar words; women with hard, coiffed hair and gumball-size pearls, who spent as much time admiring one another's beaded handbags as they did the art.

The glow from Ned's boxes made everyone in the room look flushed; flirting and exuberant humor radiated from the excited viewers—the group mood was transported by the art, in the stirring way that a crowd will emote together at an exceptional concert or hotblooded wedding.

Since Ned was naturally not in attendance (despite Peppy's attempts to browbeat him into a sudden, miraculous sociability), a blurred photo hung in the alcove at the entrance of the gallery, of Ned cutting acetate in his room with his ski mask on. Peppy had snapped it without his knowing, at Jacqueline's request.

Peppy took a peek at the tags next to a few of the light-boxes, saw they were priced at $14,000 to $22,000, and nearly screamed. She trawled across the room in a panic, to seize the lapels of Jacqueline's creamy silk jacket.

"Jacqueline, honey, you're *insane*. I mean they're pretty and all, but Jesus, they're not made of emeralds! You gotta drop the prices or you won't make a *dime*."

"I was considering raising the prices," Jacqueline said, beaming. "We've already sold four."

The blood leapt out of Peppy's brain so suddenly, she had to concentrate on not toppling into levitation.

"Anybody can get an emerald. Ned's stuff is *truly* rare and exceptional," Jacqueline informed Peppy before turning to a tweedy older man with a heavy gold watch who had tapped her shoulder to gush over her taste.

Peppy stumbled over to find Noreen, who was sitting in a folding chair near the bar table. Peppy grabbed a plastic glass of white wine.

"Four of them have already sold," Peppy told Noreen, in a disembodied voice.

"Oh, how wonderful!" said Noreen. "I think Ned will be so happy, don't you?"

"I don't understand this at all. I don't understand Ned at all."

"Just be proud," said Noreen, patting her daughter's leg.

• • •

Bernardo did not come home the night of the party, nor the day after. The next evening, Liza was still flat on the futon, annihilated under megatons of bitter self-recrimination. All of her previous moral failures were chicken feed compared to how she'd failed sweet, weak Bernardo. Not normally a person prone to flights of guilt, Liza realized that she'd really eaten a plate of dicks this time, and she couldn't pin this fuck-up on the fact that she had been raised by wolves—the credit was all hers.

But Liza didn't learn the full, catastrophic effect of her rottenness until 7 p.m., when she got The Phone Call.

It took Liza a few minutes to realize that the hysterical person on the other end of the line was Cupcake.

The unfortunate boy, freshly beard-rashed from a night of highly narcissistic sex, had expected his return to the apartment to be an uncomfortable event. He didn't, however, expect the morning to shock-blast a black hole into his psyche. When Cupcake walked in, DelVonn was naked, hanging from the bathroom doorknob by a belt around his neck, and unmistakably dead.

Forty-two minutes after Cupcake's hysterical screaming at the 911 operator, a fat, blond detective looked at DelVonn's body and explained to Cupcake that he had died by autoerotic asphyxiation.

"Was there a suicide note?"

"No, I don't think so," Cupcake whimpered, in complete shock from the sight of DelVonn's body and its resemblance to the crispy brown Peking ducks that hung in the window of the Chinese butcher shop.

"Yeah. It's a sex-thing. Most likely, it was accidental—he didn't mean to die, but he cut off all the blood supply to his brain and blacked out before he could unhook himself. It usually goes down in the books as a suicide, but it's not a suicide."

"Why would he want to do that?!" wailed Cupcake.

"Some people are gay, some wear dresses. Some people like kids, others prefer sheep. Some people get off by strangling themselves." The detective shrugged. "Who knows why?"

Cupcake's tear-drenched eyes told of his desire to kill the detective for the good of mankind, since he was obviously the world's most insensitive shithead.

"Poor DelVonn," Cupcake sniffed on the phone. "I can't stand to think of that asshole talking about him that way. It drives me *crazy*."

"But that was the great thing about DelVonn—he always just wanted to be talked about," Liza said, attempting to console both Cupcake and herself. "He didn't care if the talk was good or bad, as long as it was a *lot*."

"He wanted to be famous so bad," Cupcake mewled.

"He wanted you worse," said Liza, plunging the guilt knife into Cupcake to the hilt before she hung up, seething.

Liza knew it wasn't right to deflect blame onto Cupcake, but at the moment it felt better than blaming herself. A few seconds later, she broke down and bawled out her entrails in the full certainty that she was a cruel, bitter, vindictive, despicable, shallow person. DelVonn had called *her,* after all, and she had blown him off to go to Hadrian's accursed party of the Living Dead; she had ignored the S.O.S. of a good friend to swinishly gratify her disgusting ego-greed, her appalling need to be *seen* and *make connections* with *important people . . . .*

Liza tried to call Cupcake back and apologize, but his line was busy.

The weeks that followed were horrendous and frightening; a faceless head staring through a midnight window. Bernardo was completely AWOL on a full-scale freebasing rampage. Liza came home from a grocery run and found that the apartment had been ransacked for anything of value: the cheap mounted mirror had been unscrewed from the wall; pieces of her costume jewelry were missing, all of Bernardo's stereo equipment was gone—he'd even taken their answering machine. He had left, for some reason, DelVonn's little TV, not so much because it was basically worthless, Liza presumed, but out of some last vestige of guilt over leaving Liza alone. Liza found herself taking the phone in her purse when she left the apartment to drive around in the miserable heat, looking for him on crack-infested corners—she would be truly isolated if Bernardo smoked the phone. Liza pined for him and hated him and hated herself so much she could barely eat or get out of bed; her sleep was haunted by the anxiety that wild crackheads could swarm in at any moment, or that DelVonn's unhappy ghost might materialize, chained to the eye hooks above her bed.

Depression festered in Liza's stomach, bound in tight twine like a rotting ham.

When Peppy called, one of those dismal afternoons, with the news that Mike had died, Liza was already so wrung out she couldn't cry. She'd always liked Mike; he'd become part of her family over the years, but it was Ned and Ike she was really worried about. Ned wouldn't come to the phone, and she really didn't feel up to calling Ike.

Yet another example of my totally selfish loserdom.

Death, supposedly—at least in reference to old celebrities—came in threes. In the back of her mind, she was waiting for the third shoe to drop, praying it wasn't going to be Bernardo, or Noreen, or herself.

Three and a half weeks after Hadrian's disastrous fete, Bernardo returned. Though part of her, crazed with loneliness, wanted to cling to him like a child, Liza struggled to control herself and wouldn't open the door all the way (she had gone to the hardware store, after he burgled her, and spent several hours installing a door chain with a hand drill and the wrong type of screwdriver). Bernardo's clothing had the sooty patina of having slept on sidewalks, but he didn't seem high: he was very sincere. As Liza's eye peered at him through the inch-wide gap, Bernardo told her of walking the streets through the lower rings of white-powder madness, his soul devoured by snakes and bugs. Two nights before, at midnight, he had passed by a storefront church called the Iglesia de la Luz de Jesucristo. Although people were singing in Spanish, Bernardo thought he recognized an upbeat hymn, from childhood Sundays in church with his mother. He had stumbled inside, taking a seat in the back row of peeling wooden benches, behind a small crowd of short and squarely built Mestizos—day laborers with Sheetrock frosting their cheap boots, young couples with serious, flat faces and wounded black eyes who huddled together with fingers entwined, and a few old women in housecoats, bobbing like autistics in toothless prayer. All of these intensely poor, exhausted immigrants were offering their heartfelt and humble voices of praise to a God who had beat them up daily for most of their lives.

In this brief silence, Bernardo began to sing (involuntarily, to hear him tell it) a hymn he remembered, and the people turned to hear his voice, because his tone was solid, resonant, and round as a bell.

"It makes me kinda embarrassed to say it, but damn, Jesus Christ walked into my heart right there," he said, now in tears, trying to touch Liza through the chained door-gap. "I knew right then, all the drugs had to be put aside, for reals. And I knew, like *BAM,* it just hit me, that I have to go back to Oakland, and be with my moms, so she can help me look to God for a while . . . . Open the door, Liza, *please?*"

Great, thought Liza, her heart sinking into the wormy earth below the basement. She had known people who had stopped doing drugs, but she had yet to meet anyone who successfully recovered from Born-Again Christianity. The Born Again'ers of her acquaintance, after receiving the Good News that God was an entity to be feared, became allergic to the rowdier aspects of freedom, sex, and human fun. She called them "Bummer-Again Christians," because their main objective, however well intentioned, was usually to annoy and badger their friends into submitting to an airless personal friendship with Christ.

"Come with me back to Oakland," Bernardo implored, gazing into Liza's eyes.

"No. I have to stay here and give it one more chance."

Liza was surprised to hear herself say it. Though she was demoralized, exhausted, and sickened by this prospect, she was even more dismayed by the idea of returning to the Bay Area shrink-wrapped in failure, with a detoxing Jesus-freak. Her ambition was a fever she couldn't shake, reinfected daily by the stories that famous people told, on TV: *Right when I was on the way to buy a bus ticket to move back to my uncle's garage in Trenton . . . Right when I was throwing the master tapes into the Dumpster outside EMI . . . Right when I'd given up and applied for a job as a bar-back at T.G.I. Friday's . . . I got a call from (important person), asking me to (perform somewhere wonderful) and it all went skyrocketing from there . . . .*

Liza promised herself: *My story is going to be one of the happy ones.*

"LA is Babylon, girl. You gotta get out," Bernardo said, wild-eyed with fear of the Devil in that special way that someone who has been Off Coke and On Christ for just under thirty-six hours can be; dead certain of how Good and Evil fall unambiguously away from each other in neat, obvious squares, like a checkerboard.

"If I let you in, how do I know you're not going to just rob me again?" Liza asked, too vulnerable and hug starved to be vigilant anymore.

"I don't have anywhere else I can go," Bernardo said. Liza unchained the door.

They drank some cups of tea, made from dusty old Red Rose bags that had probably been in the kitchen cabinet since 1972, and Liza listened to Bernardo talk about his plummet back into the inferno of addiction, and his frantic new piety. When Liza fell asleep that night, Bernardo was sitting on the floor with his back against the wall, cross-legged with his lips silently moving, in a state of urgent, pleading communion with his newfound Lord.

When Liza awoke in the morning, Bernardo was gone. In reaching for her keys to peek outside for him, she noticed that the car keys had been slid from her key chain. A distraught scramble in her pajamas out to the parking area confirmed that the Plymouth Horizon was, indeed, gone. Bernardo had taped a note to the bathroom mirror with a Band-Aid:

> Liza
>   I M so sorry 4 this but theres nothing left 4 me in LALA and i gotta go home right now and theres just no other way coz I got nothing left and GOD knows I GOT TO CHANGE NOW and i hadda get out B4 i got caugt up innit agian....
>   GOD LOVES YOU i love you 2 + i'm 2 sorry baby but it hadda B like this
>   Peace
>   B.

In swiping the Horizon, Bernardo had sentenced Liza to the worst fate that can befall anyone trying to establish a life in Los Angeles: carlessness. The public transportation system was strictly for the slave-and-criminal classes of non-English-speaking or otherwise disenfranchised human refuse, smashed beneath the poverty line and excluded like lepers from the real economies of the city. Until she got another car, Liza would be in virtual Hades, slow roasting for interminable hours at unsheltered bus stops in a 100+ degree Indian summer, snail-crawling through traffic to stops countless blocks from where she needed to go, walking with damp, blistering feet down miles of empty, cooked sidewalks and across huge asphalt parking lots like bubbling tar pits. He might as well have shot her in the leg.

That evening, Liza took her combat boots and sat them carefully on the sidewalk next to the trashcan at the corner of her building, in case a poor or homeless person might want them. They were the only shoes she owned that she actually loved, and the only ones she could really walk in, but she had to make a substantial sacrifice to some minor god that might assist her in her time of need. Besides, Cupcake had said they made her look like a dyke.

She built a special shrine before the TV set, laying the shredded remains of the infamous silver-sequined dress on top of a cardboard box, and setting a white candle on top, using the nicest teacup she could find as a holder.

Before this humble altar, Liza prayed for a tiny sighting of anything with antlers. *That would be enough,* she told herself; a sign that she should renew her faith, pick herself up, and keep marching down the long, thankless, and masochistic road to mainstream stardom. She would know she possessed the strength to persist in the lightless vacuum of anonymity; to withstand the endless beat-downs of derisive rejection, to hurl herself tirelessly against the brick wall surrounding Hollywood's cream-filled center until finally—no matter how many bones she had to break, teeth she had to sell, pints of blood she had to drink, or pounds of flesh she had to sacrifice—she found a way to break in.

She drank out of a large bottle of single-malt scotch (which she didn't like, but she bought because it had a picture of a stag on it) and she watched TV, and she drank, and she changed the channel, and she watched, for hours. The divine glimpse was not forthcoming.

When half the bottle was gone, her tears began again, unstanchable.

· · ·

She flipped the ON switch of the Selectric II and listened for a moment to its menacing hum. She had planned to write a letter to Noreen, but she was too drunk, too tired, too devastated. A recent pile of Venal de Minus pages sat next to the typewriter, mocking her. She could almost see Venal sitting cross-legged on the card table in a black rubber bra and matching hot pants, picking her nails with a hunting knife, waggling her forked tongue at Liza.

Ha ha ha, said Venal. *I'm famous, and you're not.*

Liza threw all the Venal papers to the floor, stomped on them, and poured a bunch of scotch over them. Liza lifted her bottle, toasting the mess, then took a mouthful of the warm fluid and spat it at Venal's imaginary face.

"See ya," Liza slurred. "Wouldn't wanna be ya."

She got out of her clothes and put on a black slip, her most attractive nightie. From the bathroom cabinet she took five sleeping pills, which she washed down with the remainder of the scotch—more pills, she reasoned, might make her vomit and would therefore defeat the purpose.

Liza turned the gas stove knob to a steady hiss, making sure that the pilot light did not kick on, and that gas was leaking steadily into the apartment.

She got Roland Spring's hanky out of her underwear drawer and clutched it with both hands, crying all the emptiness of a short, unlucky, and disposable life into it. Then she stumbled across the floor, dropped to the futon, and abruptly passed out.

• • •

The projector kicks on, shines its dusty ray at the screen.

A kid, singing Barbra Streisand numbers in full makeup. A terrible but wholly sincere, pathetic performance.

A mermaid wakes up, sliced in two and bald.

Tinkerbell, wired out of her skull, leaps from her branch, suspends for one millisecond in bright ecstasy, then plummets.

A faceless young woman in a fucked-up sequined dress sings songs of love to an empty room.

Venal cracks up, somewhere in the darkness, *Ha ha ha ha.*

The Antlers racing around behind Liza's walls have grown into a forest of towering Mean Trees with big skeleton hands, clenching Liza's head, trying to puncture her skull with their horn-tip fingers; she is a terrified Babe in the Woods and her head is much too soft . . . .

The projector's beam is poisonous: limelight white, quicklime white, boring into Liza's eyes, forcing its deadly white vapors down her throat . . . .

She squints up into the scorching ray, at the fiendish Projectionist . . . .

(And then, the gas from the stove ignited, and Liza's apartment exploded.)

WHOMP

KZZ#%!!TUIZZINGKTK!!CHTKING

(glass blowing out of all the windows)

What had happened was this:

The tiny apartment began to fill with gas, which would have killed Liza, who was completely zonked out on booze and pills, but the gas-cloud finally touched the candle, still lit on Liza's TV shrine to the Golden Stag, and a huge blue fireball rolled out in a bomb-flash, blasting the glass out of the windows and smashing all breakable whatnots in the apartment. It would have blown Liza through the cheap wall had she been sleeping on an actual bed and not a futon, flat on the floor— the safest place she could be. The brain-shattering noise of the explosion shocked Liza upright and deafened her entirely.

The projector has blown itself inside out, she thought, still half-comatose and midnightmare, sitting up on the futon.

The TV was now staring at Liza in static menace.

The liquor-soaked Venal de Minus scripts went up first, then the sequined dress-shrine:

VOOPF.

Venal stepped out of the burning dress, *Ha ha ha.*

SHUFFFF, white-orange antler-flames tongued up, licking the low black ceiling . . . .

Venal kicked over the little TV; its screen cracked open, shorting wires popped open into flames . . . .

The black carcinogenic smoke pouring from the face of the TV snapped Liza's barely functioning mind back on. Struggling to think through her hallucinating half-coma, she made two important discoveries:

1. The apartment actually was on fire, and filling with smoke, and she should probably get out.
2. The front door of the apartment was jammed, having been forcibly bent outward by the explosion, and she couldn't get out that way.

There was only the window, and though it was broken, it still had bars on it, which she couldn't budge. She could hear nothing, not even her own coughing, so she did not respond to loud voices asking if there was anyone still inside. Liza saw that she still had Roland's hanky in her hand, and she ran to the barred window and waved the hanky, screaming, with no noise coming out of her mouth, as far as she knew, and it was this little white flag that was seen by someone—a hand from outside the window grabbed Liza's hand and held it, hanging on as Liza went limp, passing out from shock, pills, smoke inhalation, scotch, life, death, all these things, and what have you.

Time snapped; in what seemed like her very next breath, Liza woke up, and there were a lot of people staring, and a woman in a white coat with thick eyebrows appeared to be screaming at her, but she was also very quiet, and cold air was shooting into her face from a rubbery mask that was squashing her nose, but it was all very peaceful, considering she was lying in the middle of a crowded sidewalk and being screamed at.

Liza sat up, pulling the mask away, and an acrid, dirty whiff of burning wires hit her dry throat. Eyebrow woman was shaking Liza by the shoulder and clapping, inaudibly, in front of her face, and Liza noticed she was sitting on a stretcher, with ambulance doors yawning before her. Liza gently pushed the woman's hands away and swung her legs around to sit on the side of the gurney. It was all very manageable, with the sound off—like lying in a bathtub with the water over your ears, watching the ceiling; you could hear yourself think.

Liza stood, muttering silently to the ambulance woman, *thank you, but no, thanks, I don't want to go to the hospital* . . . she didn't know if the woman heard her, but it didn't seem to matter. The sidewalk was wet and gritty under her bare feet.

Three cops began silently shouting at Liza, pointing at the apartment, wanting to know things.

The lady cop thrust a clipboard at Liza and made her sign her name:

Venal de Minus

This was exhausting; Liza handed the ballpoint pen back to the cop and dizzily sat down hard on the curb. The lady cop gave a "stay right there" signal to Liza, then turned her back and walked closer to the action.

A tall, Hispanic teenaged boy, maybe sixteen, was looking at her, smoking. Liza walked over to him and pointed to his cigarette, and pointed to her mouth. The boy hurriedly reached into his pockets for a menthol Newport, which he lit for her. As an afterthought, he took off his oversize Raiders football jersey and offered it. Liza smiled. She handed him her cigarette and pulled the jersey over her charred slip, smelling his musty boy smell.

The boy had a sweet face; angelic—three stripes had been shaved into his hair over each ear; a Mercedes emblem swung from a thick gold chain around his neck, another necklace suspended *Juan* in thick gold letters over his sternum.

Juan's worried brown eyes communicated an intimate sympathy, and Liza felt a sudden love wash over the space between them; a warm, uncomplicated compassion for a fellow human being, in wartime. She was touched to be wearing his shirt.

Liza sat at Juan's knee; the two of them watched a jet of water pumping from a fire truck through her window, the bars of which were lying on the sidewalk. A piercing, ultrasonic dial tone began to drone in her ears; beyond it, Liza could begin to determine muffled, yelling voices.

It occurred to Liza that she might be in deep legal trouble for having burned down her apartment. She tugged at the hem of Juan's long basketball shorts; he bent down to hear her.

"Could you take me someplace else, before the cops come back?" she yelled.

Juan nodded. He steered her by the shoulders through the fire-transfixed crowd and down the street.

They walked several blocks in silence, slowly, since she was barefoot. Juan guided Liza through the chain-link fence surrounding a basketball court next to the freeway, where she had seen shirtless black and Latin guys playing aggressive street ball. He posited her on a wooden bench next to a heavy Hispanic man with pointy sideburns, who was talking to a kid with cornrows, sitting on a low, customized bicycle.

"Mzzzmmmmpphhsl be back immnmmg," Juan said, looking Liza in the eye, pointing down, *stay here*. He loped off, back toward the fire.

Liza involuntarily slumped against the big Hispanic guy's plaid shoulder. He pulled abruptly away—Liza, spots before her eyes, tilting with vertigo, tried to sit up on her own. The plaid man reached over and tried to pull Roland's hanky out of her death-gripped fist; Liza wouldn't let go; there was a short tug-of-war before he yanked it away.

He looked for a clean spot, then held the hanky in front of her face, indicating, grandma-style, that she should lick it; she licked it. The man then gently rubbed the soot off the side of her face nearest him, then pulled her head back down to his shoulder, with a soft pat. He and the kid on the bike got a good laugh out of that.

Liza dozed off, comforted by the vibrations in the guy's shoulder as he talked.

Liza blinked awake; Juan was shaking her knee. The plaid shirt guy was gone, the sun was high, and the basketball court was now full of young men. Juan had Liza's combat boots in his hand.

"Can you hear me? I found you some shoes," Juan said.

"I can hear now. Hi. Thank you." The sounds were still a little muffled, her treble a little shrill, but it was all returning.

"These are kind of dirty, but they're shoes." Juan shrugged. His voice was just changing; it had that awkward honk to it, but she liked the staccato way he said things.

"Oh, they're fine."

Her boots were covered with a silty black film. Liza sat up and pulled them onto her bare feet, marveling at their return.

"You got someplace to go?" Juan asked. "The cops are still over there, asking for you. I would say come stay at my house but my gramma lives in the building."

"Is her place all right?"

"They contained the fire mostly right away, but your place is *demolished*," he said, enjoying the word.

"I'll be all right," Liza said, though her head felt like a three-hundred-pound cannonball, hurtling through space.

She tried to remove his football shirt, but he insisted she take it. Then Juan saw some friends, and ran off to speak with them, and Liza walked away, out of the basketball cage. *He never asked me my name.*

Loiterers in front of the liquor store stared openly at the blackened girl, her hair in a greasy fright-wig, staggering down the street like she'd just crawled her way out of a coal mine disaster. She lurched several blocks before finding a functioning pay phone, where she made a collect call.

"Liza!" said Butch Strange. "I'm glad you called, there's been some interesting developments."

"I need a favor, Butch."

"You name it, kid."

After the call, Liza sat down on the curb with her elbows on her knees and waited, fading in and out, half-dreaming. An old man in a fly-fishing hat who had been watching her from inside the Off-Track Betting parlor brought her a cup of coffee and a donut, with shaking hands, for which she was very grateful. After an hour and ten minutes, a sleek black car pulled up to the street corner where she sat. Liza raised a finger, and slid elegantly into the back, just as ChoCho had taught her: as if it were the most natural thing in the world.

Six hours later (most of which she slept, a plummeting, feral sleep), Liza returned to the Normal Family Dinner Theatre just as she had promised the day she left.

She had come home in a limousine.

PART VII

Why, It Was Always in My Own Backyard, Or, Just When You Stop Wanting It

HERE WERE NO SEASONS IN LA, particularly, but in Fairfax, leaves were turning crispy, falling off and rotting in the gutters; the winds were wet and cold. It looked beautiful to Liza, because it wasn't LA.

"Oh my, you need a bath," said Noreen as Liza flung her filthy arms around her. "Why do you have black stuff all over you?"

"I just got shot out of a cannon." Liza grinned with relief to see her grandmother's face. Noreen eyed her suspiciously.

"Hello! What happened to you?" asked Peppy, sloshing gin into her Fresca.

"Some Aztecs sacrificed me to a volcano," said Liza.

She walked over to Peppy, grabbed her gin bottle, and took a nice swig, her lips leaving a black ring on the bottle neck.

"Welcome back and everything, but I hope you're not planning to stay too long. We have to move."

"Move where?" asked Liza.

"We don't know yet," said Peppy.

"Oh! Hi," said Ned, nervously looking over his shoulder at Liza as she peeked into his room. She could already feel that he wished she'd shut the door again and leave him alone. "You're back," he said, politely.

"In Black," said Liza, quoting an AC-DC hit of their youth.

"So how was LA?" Ned asked, being wry by ignoring her ghoulish appearance.

"Sort of like high school, to the infinite power," said Liza.

"That bad?" asked Ned.

"You're living an incredibly cool life, Ned."

"I think *you* are. You look like you've had an adventure," said Ned, returning his attention to his glue gun.

"Dude, really, you're not missing anything out there."

"Well, there's probably one or two things," Ned said, finally scrutinizing his sister. There was something new about her, besides the obvious blackface; she seemed kiln-hardened—something in her had galvanized, but he wasn't sure what it was yet.

"You're a real artist, Ned."

"Well, let's not get carried away," Ned muttered, unable to accept the compliment.

"You're going to have to face up to your own greatness at some point. You really are."

Liza didn't want to give up her fire-filth, but Noreen informed her she couldn't keep leaving black smears all over the furniture. The soot felt like a comforting balm—sort of like Pigpen in the old Charlie Brown specials, protected by his self-regenerating dust-cloud.

She looked at herself in the bathroom mirror and started laughing. She was blasted, dark, and greasy; all of her hair was standing straight up; a duck pulled from an oil spill. It was a maquillage that said *I've been through the ringer and deserve respect.*

. . .

Liza sat in the kitchen and tumbled the fire, trying to shake the silt out of her brainpan and mine the weird experience for its subconscious gold.

She also mulled it over on the phone with Lorna, who had taken a job at a Wiccan supply store in the Fillmore district called WANDS OF THULAMIS, selling jars of dried power-herbs, tarot decks, crystal balls, and *I Chings*; Lorna had interesting insights on what she deemed Liza's "shamanistic" experience.

Both Lorna and Liza agreed that the burning TV was obviously symbolic.

Lorna ventured that Liza's fame quest was the disastrous chemical result of mixing unreasonable expectations with years of self-loathing.

"You've always compared your life to *Lifestyles of the Rich and Famous*," said Lorna. It was true, and in doing so, Liza had always found her life tragically lacking in every detail of production: script, genre, casting, wardrobe, makeup, location, mise-en-scène. Movies and TV— especially the harmless PG-rated stuff she'd seen when she was young and impressionable—had been the unlicensed architects of her desires and expectations for everything. Peppy, too, had been raised on fictitious promises of infinitely more and infinitely less than Life actually offered, and had passed these delusions on to her daughter like a hereditary disease.

"You never liked or believed in yourself, unless you were all glamour-pussed out and holding a microphone," said Lorna.

"I *kno-o-o-o-ow*," Liza groaned, balancing the phone on her shoulder while she shined her combat boots; she vowed never to part with them again. She wanted to have them bronzed.

"I told you, the singing-thing was all so *Peppy*," Lorna teased.

"Shut up! I know!" cried Liza.

"Awwww, it's *OK*. *Everybody* wants to be Audrey Hepburn in *My Fair Lady*."

"You never did!"

"That's because I have no talent, thank God."

"What am I supposed to do with my life *now*?" yowled Liza.

"Oh, I'm sure something will turn up, eventually. When you stop obsessing on one thing, sooner or later you find a bunch of other stuff out there you were ignoring."

"Ungh. I'm back to square one. I'm nothing, again."

"No, try to look at it this way: now you really are punk rock. You've *earned* the right to be subversive. It's really *coming* from someplace, now. You're rejecting all of the bad myths you grew up with, just like Hammy Christ did."

"Are you saying I've finally grown into my mohawk?" Liza asked.

Lorna cracked up.

That conversation simmered in Liza over several days, and fermented into the profound realization that she had been needlessly maladjusted, frustrated, and incurably discontent for around ninety-seven percent of her waking life.

It's only a movie, went the childhood chant of horror films, but where else did a young person see life unfold from a safe distance, in endless variations on fixed, repeating patterns? Where else was one trained to be moved by the problems of love, death, and the eternal struggle for individual success, and expect satisfactory outcomes? How was it possible to resist the luxurious hope of happy endings?

The media Liza had consumed in her life were too powerful, too confusing, too ultimately demoralizing: they had corrupted her logic, letting her believe that there was a way that things should be, that had nothing to do with how they actually were. The sanitized, formatted story lines Liza had been raised on were chiseled into her psyche with all of the insidious staying power of myth or organized religion. She had been strung out on fantasies, dazzled and duped by the extraloud, glorious emotional Technicolors that insulted the basic realities of life and nature, at a time when she was too young and trusting to weigh such vapid fairy tales against concrete experience. She had expected her wishes to come true with unrealistic *ease.* Nothing in life was ever clearly drawn, obviously just, or totally emotionally satisfying, but the moment-to-moment stuff of reality featured infinitely more complication, sleaze, struggle, true beauty, unfairness, profundity, passion, and depth of consciousness than she, in her frantic struggle to be somebody other than her unspectacular self, had been previously aware of.

So what does that make me now? A QUITTER?! a resonant, Colleen Dewhurst-ish voice in Liza's mind asked. *Why, YES!* she answered. *Oh yeah. That's EXACTLY what I am: A QUITTER, God love me. I QUIT.*

And for the first time in her entire, misguided life, Liza Normal felt a warm sense of personal integrity.

A month before Liza's return, at the beginning of September 1989, Peppy was finally forced to settle her debt with Pat Morgenstern, who agreed to withdraw all further damage claims in exchange for the deed to the structurally degenerating Normal Family Dinner Theatre; he intended to move in, remodel it, and convert it into a "Writer's Salon" (now that he was no longer critiquing local theatre, he fancied himself a "novelist"). Morgenstern had been good enough to give the family a few months to figure out their next move, mostly out of respect for the well-publicized agoraphobia of "the Outsider Artist, Edward Normal," whose light-boxes had become de rigueur among the wealthy socialites of the area.

At 5:04 p.m., on October 17, 1989, the Loma Prieta Earthquake hit the Bay Area, clocking a 7.1 on the Richter Scale, which made anyone laying on certain shifty areas of bedrock or sandbar feel as if their homes had been built on a dishtowel that Jove had just snapped.

Ike was at the theatre, delivering a box of lightbulbs to Ned, when the jolting started. Peppy and Earl were having their early evening cocktail with Noreen, in the kitchen.

"Oh!" exclaimed Noreen, grabbing the table, which had just bounced her glass onto the floor.

The walls began screaming, and they heard a huge *C-C-C-CRACK* like a ten-gun salute from the basement.

"Everybody run outside!" Earl shouted.

Liza was bracing herself in the swaying front doorway while Peppy, Earl, and Noreen hustled to get out.

"Move!!!" Peppy screamed as the aged wood floor beneath them bucked in a seizure of sickeningly loud, creaking *whaps*.

Liza ran with her family onto the street, where they stared, with the other neighbors, at the telephone poles jumping in their sockets, and the Normal Family Dinner Theatre's window-eyes cracking bloodshot and popping onto the ground with a xylophonic jangle. Right as the ground-spasm began to relax, they heard the moan and fracturing of wall studs, and the people on the block watched in blank astonishment as the whole theatre slumped hazardously toward the back of the lot like a ruined soufflé, releasing the trapped dust of a hundred years in a gritty cloud; the peaked roof at the front splaying downward and outward on whining beams, like it was trying to do the splits.

"Holy shit," said Liza, barely even noticing a small aftershock.

Structurally, the entire theatre had been resting, for the last decade, on a support beam that termites and water damage had whittled down, at the critical back end, from a square eighteen inches to a comparatively splinterlike four inches. This weak, crumbling beam end could not withstand the ground shock, and gave way. And The Normal Family Dinner Theatre met its end.

"Welcome home, Pat Morgenstern!" Peppy shrieked with red-faced joy, after a moment of bewildered silence. "Waltz on in, Patty-Boy! It's all yours! Ha!! I want you to look at me very carefully, Liza. This is the sight of your mother *laughing her ass off*! Wooo! I knew you had it in you, Lord! You old so-and-so!"

Peppy cackled and spat and danced a demonic victory-jig in her terry cloth tennis dress, screaming with blood-drunk glory, until Liza stoically informed her that Ned and Ike were still inside.

Ned refused to leave the theatre, even though his room was a broken trapezoid, the floor was at a thirty-degree angle, all of his supplies had slid and smashed against the back wall, and the building was still hacking out an unfinished death-rattle.

"We have to get out, Ned," Ike said gently as the two of them sat under Ned's worktable. "Come on, let's go."

"I can't," Ned said simply. "You go ahead, though."

"I can't let you stay in here, it's way too dangerous. It's all coming down."

Ike clutched Ned's shoulder protectively as the floor beneath them abruptly jerked down another three inches. Ned seemed unmoved by the situation.

"I'm sorry Ike, but I really can't."

"Ned. Please, knock it off. We have to get out. Let's go."

Ned had never heard Ike speak so sternly; he found it kind of touching, but it had no effect on him.

"Why would it matter, really, if I stayed?" he asked, turning his eyes to meet Ike's. He was composed, dispassionate. "I'm not a part of the world, and I'm not very happy."

Ike, exasperated, looked around the room for something blunt enough to knock out Ned without seriously wounding him, so he could drag him out of the building, but something about the philosophical calm with which Ned was approaching the situation made the latent Franciscan priest-part of Ike's mind kick in, and his panic dissipated into practiced compassion. Ike sighed.

"You're a part of *my* world. I'd miss you terribly," said Ike.

"Well, that's nice of you to say."

"I'm not just being nice, I mean it."

Grrrrrrr-ACK-KACK-KACK-KACK

"We have to leave, Ned."

"Nobody would ever *really miss* me. I mean, I'm sorry to bring it up, but you'd never miss me the way you miss Mike."

"Oh, no? What makes you think so?"

The building cried out and listed abruptly another ten degrees to the left; the plumbing bowed, wailing in outrage. Ike swallowed hard, marveling at how Ned was still unruffled, wondering if it was his medication . . . .

"Cut it out, Ike." Ned smiled. "I appreciate what you're trying to do, but . . . ."

"Ned, I've loved you for years, but it would have been inappropriate in about a million different ways for me to do anything about it."

"You're such a liar!" Ned laughed, slightly hysterical, now. "You're just saying that so I'll come outside . . . ."

Hunks of plaster began to fall in book-size flakes from the ceiling. Ned began to get agitated, shaking his head.

"Aaaauuurrgghhhh . . . . Ike, seriously, please, GO! I don't want to kill *you*."

Ike looked at the one remaining escape route—the fire pole, still steady at one end of Ned's destroyed room—thinking, *how much do you interfere with a person like this?*

"I'm not leaving unless you're leaving," Ike said finally, with unbudgeable resolve.

"NO, Ike! . . . This wouldn't be right for you! . . . It's right for *me*. I'm *really NOT LEAVING*."

"Then I'm not either," said Ike, suffused with peace. "That's all there is to it."

The rusty nails straining in the tilted walls squealed like punctured seals, then collectively broke, and the building violently yanked left-ward another foot. Ike took Ned's hand in his own, and they sat, fingers entwined, listening to gravity chewing away the floor on which they sat.

Fifteen minutes later, two dust-coated apparitions tiptoed out of the tilted front door, with extreme caution, right as a fire truck pulled around the block, responding to Peppy's frantic 911 conniption on a neighbor's phone. Ike's arm was wrapped tightly around Ned's shoul-ders as he walked onto the sidewalk for the first time in years, squinting into the evening light. Peppy stared carplike with glassy eyes and gap-ing mouth as Ike brushed flurries of grit from her sneezing son.

"For the love of Christ, What TOOK YOU SO LONG?" she bel-lowed, furious.

Ned's knees began to tremble. He said something softly, grabbing Ike's elbow; Ike cocked his ear toward the encrusted mouth of Ned's ski mask.

"Ned wants to come to my house," Ike said.

"Uh, OK," Peppy stated flatly, after a beat of silence, unsure of how to respond. She wasn't sure whether the vibes she thought she was picking up were merely due to the shock of watching her house fall down, or if it was Ned and Ike's escape from the jaws of death that made them touch each other in a more familiar way, or if her best friend actually *was* taking this calamitous opportunity to make gay moves on her shut-in son. Whatever it was, Ned and Ike drove away together.

"It's a good thing Ike got him out of there," said Noreen.

It took almost twelve hours for the theatre to totally collapse into a pile of broken beams and powdery wood-rot. Earl the Chinese Mailman realized that this was his moment to stand fully upright in his Red Wing work shoes and display, for Peppy Normal, the full wingspan of his Deus-Ex-Machismo.

"NOW you marry me! HA!" he exalted. "You got nowhere else to go!"

"Oh, you think you've got me cornered, do you?" asked Peppy, an-noyed.

"HA! Unluckiest day in your life, luckiest day in my life!" Earl smiled ear to ear with his big, brown-rimmed teeth. "You wanna be my mother-in-Law, Mama?" he asked Noreen, walking over to squeeze her shoulders and kiss her on the cheek.

"You're a nut, Earl," said Noreen. "I need to lie down."

Earl drove Peppy, Noreen, and Liza to his apartment.

Later that evening, Noreen lay grouchy and exhausted on Earl's overstuffed couch, which appeared to be upholstered in coleslaw. Peppy ate an entire package of Earl's coconut wafers with beer. The women could barely talk. Minute by minute they remembered more possessions they had lost in the collapse.

"My wigs! Jesus!"

Liza took a long bath, in Earl's tiny bathroom. She was homeless and possessionless for the second time in two months, and the freedom was dizzying; it made her completely absorbed in the wonder of the present moment: life had led her HERE, to Earl Tang's orange-and-gold-foil-wallpapered bathroom. She opened and smelled all of the strange grooming products and Chinese herbal pills in Earl's medicine cabinet. Bathing under this new lighting, in a horizontal position for the first time in months, she was surprised to discover she had no arguments with her naked body; it was fine. Slim, proportional—obese, naturally, by LA camera standards, but in the flesh, totally agreeable.

Earl called his entire family in Las Vegas, where he had a number of relatives, to tell them that he was bringing home his fiancée. He was very happy; Peppy was the only blonde woman with big tits he'd ever gone out with, and he was extremely proud of her vivacity, sex drive, and theatrical nature—he even found her tantrums thrillingly cute and artistic. He had long, loud, giggling conversations in Chinese.

"I haven't exactly said YES, yet, Earl," Peppy groused.

"Oh, quit giving the man such a hard time," said Noreen.

"Missus Peppy Tang! How do you like it?" Earl teased Peppy, punching her in the shoulder.

"Peppy Tang. Sounds like I should be on the spice rack somewhere between Mrs. Dash and 'Krazy Mixed-Up Salt'."

Ike dropped by Earl's a little later, with a bag of cheeseburgers.

Peppy was already five Coors into the six-pack, breathing her nicotine.

"Ned wants to live with me," Ike said slowly. "And, I'd like that very much." His normally expressive face was hard to read.

Peppy looked at her friend with a red, hellhoundish eye.

"Oh, so is Ned GAY now? Is THAT what this is?"

Ike traced his rough finger on the edge of Earl's artificial wood coffee table. "Well, maybe you should ask him."

"Well I can't, now can I? He *doesn't talk to me!*" Peppy railed, the accumulative weight of all the day's ordeals rising up in her. Her body shook forward, unleashing a hard sob into her lap. Ike put a hand on her shoulder, but she jerked it away.

Noreen had fallen asleep, with her little nylon-clad feet resting on a stack of Earl's old newspapers.

Liza, fresh out of the bath, latched on to Ike as he stood around miserably.

"Give her some time, she's all fucked up now," Liza whispered. Ike nodded.

Peppy was too emotional to say goodbye to either of them.

"Maybe come back tomorrow," Earl told him quietly, with a wink.

Liza wanted to get away from Earl's and see Lorna, who she knew would let her crash at Elf House. Ike drove her to the bus station hub in San Rafael. He stared straight ahead, his shoulders hunching against a siege of invisible arrows.

"She probably just doesn't like the idea of Ned being gay because she thinks it makes *her* look bad," Liza offered, trying to fix the painful silence. "It probably makes her think she did something wrong as a mom. I'm sure she'll get over it."

"Thanks," said Ike, grateful for Liza's tacit support.

"I mean, really, what *didn't* she do wrong, as a parent, short of molesting us?"

Liza stopped, realizing she might have put her foot in her mouth. She too was uncomfortable with the idea of Ike, an almost-father-figure they'd known since they were kids, suddenly being "involved" with her brother, Ned being as hyperfragile and rare as a zoo panda.

But the idea of Ned being actually intimate with anyone was probably an improvement . . . maybe . . . she didn't know anything anymore.

It was dark outside and had gotten cold; the air was so ice water clear, the arcing streetlights over the bus stop made superbright, pointy shards when Liza squinted at them.

"Have you seen his face yet?" asked Liza.

"No," said Ike, sadly. "What about you, though? Are you OK?" he asked suddenly.

"Yeah! You OK?"

"Yeah. I'm OK. Ned's OK too, you know," he said with a surge of sincerity, trying to really convey this.

"I know."

"You need some money?"

Liza accepted fifty dollars, promising to pay Ike back when she got her bank account straightened out.

He *needed her approval.* This was new for her.

The city bus came after Liza stomped her feet for several minutes in the biting wind, thinking that Ike really should have let her sit in the heated car until her bus came, instead of hurrying back to poor, delicate Ned. Liza was sick of everyone assuming she was indestructible. In the bus, Liza pressed her feet against the seat-back in front of her.

But this is my gift, she thought: *I am the crude boot from the Free Box. I am uncrushable steel toes.*

Liza arrived at Elf House around eleven o'clock.

Greycoat answered the doorbell. Liza had to control herself from gawking, he was so changed. In the months since she'd been gone, he had stopped abusing speed and become pudgy—worse, his beautiful waist-length hair was beginning to thin dramatically—his white scalp was visible, his hair devolving into what would soon be a long, wispy hula-skirt of monk-fringe. What he had lost in hair, however, he had apparently gained in humility.

"Hi, Liza. You look *great,*" he said, in a friendly, almost apologetic tone. The thought flashed through Liza's mind to dismiss Greycoat for having been such a dick to her in the past, but she decided to take the high road.

"Greycoat," Liza said warmly, giving him a hug.

The girls jumped at the sight of each other, hugging and pulling at each other's clothes. Liza felt a flood of homecoming; Lorna, of all the people living, knew her best and still loved her—seeing her face almost made Liza cry.

Elf House had plenty of room, and Liza was free to move in. Slipper, Fawn Bell, Vanessa, Nodnik, and Paisley had all moved out and gone their separate ways; only Greycoat remained to carry the dimming torch of Elfhood through the Haight.

"But I dunno, man, you seem to destroy every house you set foot in these days," Lorna teased, pouring Liza another glass of six-dollar red wine. Liza pulled one of Greycoat's long, shedded hairs off of the couch and marveled at how things can radically change in short periods of time.

For the next few days, Liza spent a lot of time in the shower. She could feel the pressure of a major puzzle piece about to drop into her landscape and resolve a bunch of converging lines—she just wasn't sure what it was. She had money, if she could assemble enough proof of her existence for the bank to give it to her—a queenly sum of something like $4,300. After a few more days of hassling at the DMV to get an ID card, Liza called Butch.

"Gimme whatever you got. I'm totally undistracted, now, I have nothing else going on, and I want cash, cash, cash."

"You wanna try something new?" asked Butch's weird, androgynous voice.

"It depends."

"You've done some acting, right?"

"I'm not taking my clothes off."

"I don't care if you wear a snowsuit, I'm only interested in your voice."

"You want me to sing?" Liza asked. Butch laughed until he coughed.

"I want you to write some 976–phone scripts for Venal. They'll be prerecorded; you'll just have to read them into a microphone."

"You want *my voice* to be Venal de Minus?"

"Well, who else's?"

Good question, thought Liza.

Butch was so enthusiastic about Liza's new venture, he had a courier deliver one of Centaur's computers over to Elf House, so she could start immediately on the first ten, two-page scripts.

Greycoat, who worked as a temporary paralegal assistant by day, spent that evening teaching Liza the basics of word processing. Once she knew, more or less, how to type a document, she spent a week doing nothing but playing computer solitaire, over and over and over.

She was stymied; she couldn't figure out how to be Venal, first-person. Venal hadn't really spoken in any of her books, except when barking an occasional over-the-top S&M command: "Take off your wetsuit!" "Kiss my bludgeon!" etc.—she was more a creature of *action*.

Venal's laugh was the only thing she could really hear in her head—raucous, derisive; *nanny nanny nanny goat.* She didn't know if she'd be able to pull off imitating it and felt paralyzed by the whole project.

Since Liza had escaped the theatre collapse with nothing but her historic boots, some old pants of Noreen's, and an acrylic ski sweater that had sat wadded in the theatre dressing room since the *Sound of Music* days, she had been living out of Lorna's closet; Lorna finally insisted that Liza take a day off from her desultory solitaire marathon to go shopping with her at Thrift Town, a famous, huge old store that had been in the Mission District long enough that nobody in the current generation knew, offhand, why there was an enormous, cryptically life-affirming neon sign on its roof, reading:

17

Reasons
WHY!

The girls picked through old prom dresses and eyeless stuffed toys suffering from open sores and patches of velveteen eczema.

"Look what love will do to you," said Liza, gingerly tweezing the ear of a forgotten elephant, covered with dried fistulas of unidentifiable food matter.

"Why are you having so many problems with that Venal de Minus phone-thing?" Lorna asked, suddenly reminded of Liza's plight as she looked through a yellowing plastic bag, in which the Thrift Town employees had surreally juxtaposed several miniature telephones, plastic doll arms, and yarn God's-eyes.

"She has to actually have a *personality,* now. I have no idea what that personality *is.*"

"I always figured you'd make her talk like those notes you used to pass with Tonto Grosvenor. Those were pretty funny, in a nasty way."

. . .

Liza felt what she had thought were two wholly disconnected parts of her life clicking together, like a snake suddenly biting its own tail and rolling down the street like a hula-hoop. It was so obvious.

What kind of fucked-up evolutionary accident makes Lorna so imperative to my survival? This was transcending mere best-friendship and verging into some fearfully mandatory bee/flower symbiosis. Lorna had reached out, effortlessly, and pulled the near-forgotten ghost of Tonto Grosvenor from the cosmic vapors, ready to pay his karmic debt.

Liza clutched Lorna's arm. "Dude. You're my miracle worker. You are my Angel of the Morning. You are 17 Reasons Why."

"Here, maybe you need these," said Lorna, finding a pair of small leather chaps on the clothing rack—no doubt the pride of some little gay guy, when his wild nights out on Folsom Street were in their fairest blush.

"Yes. Yes. Yes," said Liza, grabbing the chaps and soaring into an imaginary world of black horsehide and steel studs.

After the girls had stripped Thrift Town of all its ersatz bondage-gear, they went to various leather and fetish stores, to load up on some of the real stuff—over-the-elbow black latex gloves, a tall leather police cap—for Liza to get into the mood, as it were.

"I need props to make the proper Foley sounds!" Liza argued with Butch, on a pay phone, trying to get him to underwrite her splurge. She stood back and whacked the receiver several times with her new riding crop, to prove its audio efficacy.

"Oh, *all right,* prima donna." Butch sounded perturbed, but Liza could tell he was pleased that she was finally getting into the spirit of the thing.

Later that night, Liza put on the day's collected garb and stared at herself in the living room mirror. Severely pointy, black-vinyl boots, black chaps, fishnet ass, a buckled leather bustier, the gloves and hat. It was invigorating; she was frightening herself.

"Ooh. You're so *Helga, She-Wolf of the SS,*" Greycoat said, flirtily. "Hit me, baby."

Liza smacked him across the thighs with the crop, harder than she meant to—a little vengefulness from the old days, leaking out.

"Ow!! Shit!" Greycoat yelped, rubbing his pants.

"Jesus!" Lorna giggled, surprised by the severity of the blow.

Liza cackled wildly and was electrified to hear Venal's rude *ha ha ha* coming out of her own mouth.

She sat at the computer, and lines started spooling out like sweet black licorice-whips. It was *fun*; like reaching into her own chest and yanking a hidden rip cord that blew her up into a big, useful, inflatable some-thingorother—she was cohering, all of a sudden. Venal was the com-post heap where all of Liza's old, rotting humiliations could be recycled into creative mulch. She was exacting a satisfying, poetic revenge against a popular media that had always made her feel unpopular. Venal, much to Liza's surprise, had sprouted her own set of antlers.

Later that week, armed with cherry lozenges and a small bottle of root beer schnapps, Liza and Butch took a cab to a small, professional recording studio in Daly City, where she sat in a tiny black sound booth for four hours. Butch and an engineer sat behind a glass window and recorded her, Butch giving occasional snippets of direction over the in-tercom as Liza snarled, chided, coerced, threatened, and lathered in sev-eral different accents into a foam-covered microphone.

The scripts would continue for exactly two minutes and forty-one sec-onds, at which time Venal would come to a screaming, brutish climax, which had to die down to whimpering, purring satisfaction by 2:59 on the digital stopwatch in Liza's right hand. The process involved a lot of "takes," at first, to get the timing down, but by the second hour she pretty much had it down. By the end of the session, the first ten recordings for 976-VENAL were officially laid down on professional reel-to-reel tape.

Butch took Liza to his favorite steak house afterward, ordering her a bloody filet and a bottle of champagne.

"To my sacred golden cash cow," he said sweetly.

"Moo," said Liza, remembering DelVonn with a pang.

Clink.

"And to DelVonn Chaka Khan D'Shawn, wherever he is," Liza added.

"Gone on to that little black dungeon in the sky, God bless him. I miss him all the time. He'd have been so proud of you today."

Tears swam into their vision for a minute, smearing the candlelight; then they changed the subject.

Previous to her LA experience, Liza would have been petrified that her nonexistent "career" would be undermined by this smutty venture, but now she really didn't care, and the money was great. Butch, who always had a keen understanding of the relationship betwixt incentive and employee morale, promised her the usual eight percent for any profit after his expenses were covered. A week after the recording session, Liza saw the ad for 976-VENAL among the other dial-a-porn listings in the alternative weekly paper.

"Hey . . . is this 976 thing *national*?" Liza asked.

"You bet your boots," said Butch.

"Wow," said Liza, astounded by the thought of some masturbating yutz in Omaha shelling out three dollars to listen to her prerecorded joke-porn.

●　●　●

Peppy, Earl, and Noreen were loading their vehicles and "taking their show on the road" to Las Vegas. They would live for a spell with Winnie Tang, Earl's sister, until other arrangements could be made.

"Goodbye, California," Peppy announced, tossing some plastic food-storage tubs and random pieces of mismatched silverware into her trunk. "And good riddance."

Ike stood around, helping wherever he could, looking forlorn.

Ike had been bending over backward for weeks, trying to get back on Peppy's good side. He had snuck back to the theatre, very late the night of the collapse, ducked under the yellow POLICE LINE—DO NOT CROSS tape, and tried, with gloves and flashlight, to find as much of the family's stuff as he could in the treacherous rubble, carefully lifting splintered planks and stepping over yards of broken glass and rusty, upturned nails. He was able to recover a few wigs that had been in their storage boxes, three pairs of shoes, and a few plastic bags of dust-saturated towels and clothing, which he dropped off at Earl's the next day. (In the small "in-law unit," at the back of the building, a few crispy old girly magazines had slid from their hiding places, remnants of Lalo's residency—Ike thoughtfully left them there for some young looter to find.)

Peppy took full advantage of the slave labor Ike kept offering, but she was still fuming and doling out curtness and disgust vibes even as he sweatily loaded Earl's couch into the U-Haul. Peppy could not resist milking every last drop out of her grudge, even though she'd just been

Cintra Wilson

to Ike's house with Noreen to say goodbye to Ned, and Ned was clearly fine. He had been keeping busy, assembling an exact replica of his room at the theatre in what had been Mike's old workroom. Peppy was so obsessed with punishing Ike she barely took in that Ned had actually looked at her eyes, spoken directly to her, and hugged her for the first time in years.

Peppy's cruelty made Liza feel entitled to stealing her white-blonde Elke Sommer wig—a perfect Venal find, which she discovered after opening one of the dirt-encrusted cases. Liza hid it behind a hedge to retrieve as soon as Peppy drove away.

"So you'll come to the wedding?" Peppy asked Liza, hugging her goodbye.

"Yeah. Of course. *Say something nice to Ike,*" Liza hissed.

"Why should I?" asked Peppy, her lips puckering in stubbornness. Peppy's bitter face behind her large, UV-blocking sunglasses looked shrunken and mean.

"Because *he's part of the family.*"

"Yeah, we'll see about that," Peppy clucked, a sarcastic chicken-sound that had always driven Liza nuts. Ike began advancing toward them.

"Goodbye Ike," Peppy said, turning toward him with a hard brightness, extending her hand.

"*Peppyyyy,*" he implored, insisting on hugging her. She endured the squeeze as a teen boy tenses against the overfamiliar kisses of an aunt.

"Ike, you let us know if there's anything we can do for you and Ned," Noreen said, her hand appearing suddenly at Ike's elbow.

"I'm going to miss you all so much," Ike said emotionally, hugging Noreen.

Ike and Liza stood together and watched the little caravan drive away.

"She was such a bitch, Ike, I'm so sorry."

Ike wiped a tear off of his unshaven face. "This is way harder than when I came out to my own parents. I mean, I've basically had to come out *for* him, and be big bad Uncle Pervert at the same time."

There was no resentment in this statement, only weariness.

Liza collected the wig.

"Let's go get a drink," she offered, looping her arm around Ike's. He gratefully accepted. They ended up going to the Lady Tamalpais Café, the bar where Mike and Ike had first met Peppy. They had several drinks, the bar environment adding a new, mature dimension to their relationship; they were both grown-ups now.

• • •

Winnie Tang was divorced and had daughters in college; she was glad to have company in her ranch-style tract house, a few miles off of the Vegas Strip.

"This reminds me of Reno," said Noreen, the hot wind reacquainting itself with her bones, which she hadn't really noticed had been cold most of the time in Fairfax. Peppy was anxious and uncomfortable about being someone's guest, having been the Empress of her own domain for so long, but Winnie was relaxed, amusingly cranky, and hospitable. She poured large drinks the minute the threesome walked in and kindly guided Noreen into a clean bedroom with her own color TV, so that she could rest.

Winnie worked as a bookkeeper at the Whiskey Lane Casino, one of the aged eyesores off the strip that catered to the cheapest cocktail compulsions of the town's cirrhosis-level alcoholics. After hearing of Peppy's theatrical exploits Winnie suggested that Peppy try to bring her talents to the Vegas stage.

"We gotta get rid of the guy doing his act over there, now. He's a disaster," said Winnie, backhanding the invisible act with her gold-ringed hand. "Come see the place, first, and then if you want, maybe we can set you up with an audition."

Later that week, Earl, Peppy, and Winnie went to the Whiskey Lane casino's "Komedy Korral," a small, low-ceilinged room with wood paneling, plastic chairs facing a foot-high stage, and a band of noncirculating cigarette smoke hovering at face level.

The waitress working the Korral was a sixty-year-old woman with a firmly structured silver permanent and a name tag that said PANSY, who had obviously worked as a cocktail waitress since the dawn of table service and had, like an eyeless deep-sea creature, become accustomed to casino life without sunlight or windows, among the truly drunk, where the party never stopped and had never really started.

"Two-drink minimum," Pansy commanded. "What are you having?"

Earl and Peppy consulted a cardboard triangle listing the drink specials:

Dr. Nasty's X-Rated Potion's!
$3 each or 2 for $5
HAND JOB: Peppermint schnapps, Baileys . . . ask for it by name!

NIPPLE-TWIST: Butterscotch schnapps, Baileys . . . think of it as liquid "foreplay"!

FELLATIO: Peppermint schnapps, Baileys, vodka . . . almost as good as sex!

BLUE BALLS: Blue curacao, peach schnapps, vodka . . .
just when you thought you couldn't get any hornier!

BEAVER SHOT: Kahlua, Baileys and vodka. . . . a real eye-opener!

The joke, presumably, was to ask the humorless, elderly "Pansy" for a "Hand Job." Liza watched Pansy drone, "Why, sir, never on a first date," for what must have been the eighty-thousandth time, to a tableful of drunk Texans. *Baw haw haw haw,* they laughed, ignoring the awful thought of Pansy's dry, clawlike hand reaching toward their genitals, her face puckering with vast reluctance.

In a puff of dry ice, twenty-eight minutes after the scheduled show-time, "The Diabolical Dr. Nasty and His XX-Rated Powers of Persuasion" took the stage. He resembled a reanimated Wolfman Jack, if his corpse had been preserved in an urn full of nail polish remover; his skin was red, chafed, and flaky, his thin web of black-tinted hair was spray-mounted into a flimsy and lopsided Elvis-knob, half of his Satanic beard was drawn on in cosmetic crayon. There were only eleven audience members, scattered throughout a room that could hold ninety, the emptiness allowing the *chong-chong-chong-chong-chongs* and jangling nickels of the outside slot machines to drown out the applause for his entrance.

"Where the fuck is my audience?" asked Dr. Nasty, flapping his arms into an outraged shrug. "I need four volunteers. That's half the people in this fucking room. Pansy?"

"Yes?" she asked, in her clipped and nasal voice.

"Could you give me a Beaver Shot, please?"

"What. With all these people watching?" Pansy rasped mechanically, with hatred.

After downing a large glass of thick, black alcohol, Dr. Nasty invited the two drunk Texas couples to participate in an excruciating hour of unfocused, blathering hypno-tainment, during which he pulled scarves out of Pansy's slack, unwilling cleavage, compelled the Texans to do lumbering stripteases for each other's glazy-eyed wives, and invoked the usual itch-in-a-private-place/turd-in-the-martini-glass/uninhibited-love-serenade gambits, culminating at long last in the finale, in which an abused parrot magically clawed its way out of the fly in Dr. Nasty's red tuxedo pants.

"This guy really IS a disaster!" Peppy said, with mounting confidence. Even after all the deathblows Peppy had suffered to her performance ego, she *knew* her act was better than his. "He's Dr. No-Talent and his Potty-Mouthed Powers of Embarrassment!"

"I told you," said Winnie. "He's gotta go."

After the Dr. Nasty debacle, Earl scooted off to play a few rounds of blackjack. Peppy and Winnie barged directly into the back offices of Whiskey Lane to meet the "Entertainment Manager," a man named Van deVille, who kept graveyard-shift hours, since anything interesting that happened in Vegas happened after 2 a.m., when the big shows let out.

"Holy shit," said Peppy, when she went into the office.

"Holy hickory-smoked Moses!" said the Entertainment Manager, whose wood-toned plastic desk-plate said VAN DEVILLE but who was, in fact, an older, less flashy, more haggard, but still unmistakable Neville Vanderlee, Peppy's greatest artistic collaborator.

(Briefly: Neville had left San Francisco in 1987. AIDS had ran-sacked his community and killed most of his friends, and a rather demanding drug problem had caused him to file for bank-ruptcy. So, he escaped to Las Vegas, to live with a kindly aunt. Slowly, he crawled up to his current position, which was lonely and abject but sane compared to the life he had left behind.)

"Honey, I'm going to save your socks," Peppy shouted.

"Crazy Woman, I have a feeling you're telling the truth," said Neville. "Slide your big nylon ass over here and give me some sugar. Winnie! Grab us a bottle of Drambuie and three brandy snifters!"

"Now you're talking my language," Peppy chortled, smashing a waxy magenta impression of her mouth on Neville's concave cheek, squeezing his little balsa-wood bones until he coughed.

"Wow!" Winnie smiled. "You guys know each other from up north?"

"That's putting it mildly. Peppy Normal, I am *so* happy to see you."
And Peppy could tell that Neville was telling the truth.

Neville, after several cocktails, was delighted with Peppy's summary for
An Evening with Peppy Normal; he had a few ideas of his own on how to
"add more snazz." Neville planned to can Dr. Nasty immediately and
begin rehearsals for what he described as "giving the gift of Peppy
Normal to the deserving citizens of Las Vegas."

Peppy was so pleasantly surprised to find herself launching into a solo
project with her favorite director ("The only man who ever really
knew what to do with me," she'd joke), she finally agreed to nail down
an actual wedding date with Earl. She called Liza and Ike (knowing
Ned would never come without him) to invite them to her Vegas stage
debut, and the wedding ceremony, five days later, on Christmas Eve.

"Why don't you come out here and stay awhile?" Peppy asked Liza.
"It's not like you're doing anything important, over there. If you do
something cute with your hair, you can be my stage assistant!"

Liza clamped down on the rude comment that sprang reflexively to
her lips.

As much as she itched to put Peppy in her place, she didn't want to
tell her about 976-VENAL, which was an instant hit, exponentially
more successful than even the books had been. It took off for a reason
that nobody could have predicted: ironic Generation X-ers. Lonely
S&M fantasy geeks weren't the only ones into Venal anymore—now
she had reached the smart-ass college crowd, who found Venal's hi-
camp domination hilarious. Bootleg snippets of 976-VENAL had been
heard on college radio stations in Texas, Wisconsin, Illinois, Michigan,
Iowa, and Vancouver. The Internet was just beginning to seep into
homes, and there were already several Web rings devoted to the discussion of Venal, from different fan perspectives: feminist, slash-fic-crit,
grad-school-postmodern-cineaste, Dungeons and Dragons, and, naturally, the usual alt.sex aficionados, who mostly complained that Venal
"wasn't hardcore enough" and "needed more foot-play."

"I dunno," Liza told Peppy. "I'm not that jacked up about living in
Nevada. I mean, isn't it just kind of smarmy and grotesque?"

"I thought you liked that kind of thing," said Peppy.

Liza had to wonder if this wasn't true, given that her life experience
hardly suggested otherwise.

Butch invited Liza to meet him at Cape Horn for their notorious, annual "Pre-Holiday Karaoke Turkey Truss." Liza had been dressing as Venal to go out to nightclubs with Lorna, enjoying the power-high of visual intimidation more than she had since high school. Butch enjoyed squiring Liza around town. He felt she was his creature, and he was very proud of her growing underground celebrity (besides, having an excitingly perverse Liza on his arm aided him in cruising the she-male escorts he consorted with).

Lorna sifted through the karaoke songbook binder and started laughing when she saw "Superstar," the Carpenters' song that she knew Liza had embarrassing childhood fantasies about.

"No way!" Liza protested, cringing at how dumb she'd been, as a child.

"Do it *as Venal*!" Lorna said, jumping up and down on her bar stool. This was a fun idea, so Liza mounted the stage in her dominatrix regalia and talk-screamed the song in a gutteral Nico-of-Velvet-Underground-cum-Cloris-Leachman-in-*Young Frankenstein* voice:

> DOHN'T YOU VEMEMBAH YOU TOLT ME
> YOU LAHVED ME BABEH.
> YOU SETT YOU VOULD SOMEDAY COME BECK ZIS
> VAY AGAYNE, BEYBEH. . . .

The bar boys went wild, and Liza walked offstage a sensation, showered with hoots and whistles.

Butch was rapt, chewing his cocktail straw like mad.

"*Ka-ching, ka-ching,*" he said in Liza's ear, when she came back to her seat.

"What?"

"Live Venal show. Onstage. *Ka-ching*. Dollar signs."

"Forget it. No. No no no no no no no."

By the end of the night, she'd sung four more songs in Venal style—by the last chorus of Manilow's "Could It Be Magic?" both she and the audience were pretty sick of it.

"See?" she told Butch. "It gets old fast."

Butch shrugged.

. . .

Ned and Ike rented a minivan and planned to drive straight through to Vegas, apart from a few planned veers down side roads, so Ned could relieve himself in foliage and avoid being subjected to gas stations. Liza was flying in a few days later, but she came to see Ned and Ike off that frosty morning, since Ned was traveling for the first time in his adult life, and everyone was nervous about it.

A realtor's FOR SALE sign was mounted on a post in Ike's yard.

"Are you guys moving?" Liza asked Ike.

"Yeah, there's too much old mojo, here . . . this was Mike's house. We want to start somewhere else. Besides, I want Ned to have a real space to do his work, for once."

"I miss Gramma," added Ned. "I want to live closer to her."

This comment, for some reason, reminded Liza that behind this acrylic-knit mask was the only coparticipant of her childhood. Ned's mental illness had seemed such an obvious, intelligent response to their shared experience, she had always kept a nervous distance from him, afraid that his shunning of society and her reckless belly flop into it were two sides of the same chewed-up coin.

"I don't want you to live far away from *me*," Liza told Ned, some hidden hook from her chest suddenly casting out and fishing for him, with a starved urgency.

"Really? That's sweet of you to say."

They hugged awkwardly. Liza felt a visceral need to de-estrange herself from her strange brother. He had been invisible to her for so long, then all of a sudden he was a firebird, an untouchable phenomenon; now, for the first time, he looked like a three-dimensional human brother.

．　．　．

"I just had the yarrow stalks thrown for me, and they totally confirmed that we've made the right decision: Jimbo and I are moving out next month, and we're buying a huge old truck from a moving company, and we're converting it into a totally self-sufficient land-yacht, and we're going to live in it."

"Wow. How come?" Liza asked, having no idea what yarrow stalks were or how they could yield advice about trucks. She and Lorna were in the Elf House kitchen, pitting beer against Liza's general malaise.

"Because. We want to be able to move around whenever we feel like it, and we're never going to pay taxes, ever again."

"Excellent," Liza said. "If you can avoid taxes, maybe you can avoid death too."

"Exactly," said Lorna, with a wink.

"I totally don't know what to do with myself," Liza said, in despair. "And now *you're* leaving."

"You need an oracle," Lorna sympathized. "Here."

Lorna reached behind her head and pulled a Magic 8 Ball off of the microwave. Liza was nonplussed.

"Dude. You're trying to make me entrust my entire future to a plastic triangle floating around inside a fake pool ball."

"What makes the gestalt experience of this oracle any less valid than any other oracle?" said Lorna, mildly affronted. "You're the one who makes an oracle real. If you grant this plastic ball the ability to reveal the will of whatever divine entity you want advice from—then it can give you solid information. Frankly, I think the Eight Ball gives solid information whether you grant it special powers or not. It's always worked for me."

"OK, gimme," said Liza, reaching for it.

Oh Magic 8 Ball. Oh Spirit of the Guiding Light of Direction in the Universe, hear my plea. Should I stay here, in San Francisco?

(shake shake shake shake)

Should I move to Las Vegas?

(shake shake shake shake)

"Try it again," said Lorna, looking over her shoulder.

(shake shake shake shake)

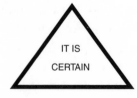

"It thinks I should move to Vegas," said Liza.

"I think that's a really good idea," Lorna concurred. "Go to the desert. The mountains and hills are really beautiful. All the nastiness is concentrated into that one urban area."

There was no reason not to go to Vegas. Everything she owned could fit into a duffle bag. She could write filth for Butch anywhere with e-mail or a fax machine, and if there wasn't a recording studio in Vegas, she could always fly back to do more phone tapes. Greycoat sighed when Liza told him the news. It was the final nail in the coffin for Elf House; he had to face up to the painful truth that his Haight Street glory days were unresurrectable. He would give up the lease, move back to the Peninsula, and find a computer job. He began calling himself "Greg" again; a bittersweet farewell—he was mortal again; his Elfishness, henceforth, would live only in cyberspace.

The plane to Vegas was smallish, loud, and empty save for a beer-swilling pack of purple-faced corporate louts in large nylon shorts. Liza felt like she could cry, undetected, and she did. Her Future Life seemed way too large, vacant, and hazy, like she might step off the plane and just blow away—so little held her to the world, it all fit in an overhead compartment.

. . .

The street posters in front of the Whiskey Lane Theatre read:

NOW APPEARING
IN THE
KOMEDY KORRAL:

EMPRESS PEPPY TANG:
RISQUÉ COMIC HYPNOTIST

Empress Peppy emerged onstage to a smashing gong, unfurling dry ice, and "Oriental" background music—synthesized wood flute, ploinks of meditative Koto. Wearing a tall, black beehive geisha-wig bristling with ornate chopsticks and tiny lanterns and a long, imperial Chinese bathrobe that emphasized her ample cleavage, Peppy bowed to the audience respectfully, thanking them for being there, and asked for "most honorable volunteers."

Liza and Ike gave each other glances of nervous horror, but Winnie and Earl were grinning ecstatically; they had filled the room with black and red helium balloons for Peppy's Vegas debut. There were a lot of Tang-connected Chinese people in the more-than-half-filled audience—amazingly enough, they didn't seem offended.

The gimmick was that Peppy would begin the show feigning elegance and royalty—then, over the course of her standard group-hypnosis act (wherein she essentially did the same tricks Dr. Nasty had done, but with a bad Chinese accent), she would gradually become more and more raunchy.

"Ah, so. Since I am a hypnotist, I would please like you to view my most honorable hypno-tits," Peppy would say, toward the end of the show, shimmying her shoulders to foist her beaded glands into the face of a giggling, grimacing VCR repairman from Modesto, to shrieks of laughter from the audience. Neville fidgeted with pride.

Peppy was clearly having a blast.

"She really fits in here," Liza told Winnie.

"It's eerily perfect," Ike agreed.

. . .

Earl and Peppy were married at the chapel of the Gold Nugget casino, where Earl's brother Frank was a Pai Gow dealer. It was a short, pleasant ceremony, followed by a simple reception in one of the corporate meeting rooms—there were some folding chairs, a table, some chrome platters of cold cuts and crudités, a wedding cake with a Chinese bride and groom on top, and an aluminum Christmas tree.

Sixteen Tangs showed up at the wedding, all teasing and pinching Earl, in his rented burnt orange tuxedo. Peppy, wearing a daffodil yellow sundress and a ginger-colored wig in a respectable, Barbara Walters shape, was blushing so hard the burst veins in her nostrils turned purple. Frank Tang's contribution to the wedding was the Entertainment: a karaoke machine, operated in DJ/Emcee manner by a heart-throbby young Chinese guy in a collarless white dress shirt and eyeliner, who announced the various tracks in enthusiastic English and Cantonese. Liza stared at the emcee's glossy, 8 × 10 head-shot, taped to the front of a speaker—hair moussed into a savage wedge-shape and wrapped in a checkerboard headband, eyebrows plucked and angry.

RICK LIN—ENTERTAINER

Oh, poor Rick Lin, Entertainer, thought Liza, who knew she was about three millimeters away from being Rick Lin, Entertainer, herself (and not even as together—at least he had a karaoke machine).

The Tangs got up and sang unabashedly gooey pop songs in Chinese, as well as traditional American radio favorites. When there were no karaoke volunteers, Rick Lin sang ultrasincere pop ballads, with a quavering vibrato and Chinese accent, including, to Liza's wincing horror, the Guyzer song "You're the One."

Liza surprised herself by actually having a good time. The Tangs were the first functional family Liza had ever been around, and Liza was a huge hit when she finally got drunk enough to sing "Little Red Corvette."

Peppy toasted Winnie and Earl with a plastic champagne glass, and drained it. "You got a bride!" Winnie shouted, poking Earl in the arm. "How'd you do that? You tell her you were rich?" Earl buried his smiling red face into Peppy's neck.

Ike suddenly appeared in a rented tux with red cummerbund and tie. He made a beeline for Peppy and Earl and congratulated Earl earnestly, kissing him on the cheek as he shook his hand. Brimming with champagne, the milk of forgiveness, Peppy turned an unguarded face toward Ike for the first time since the earthquake.

"Can you come out to the car, for a second?" Ike asked her carefully. "Ned's here, he wants to congratulate you."

"Oh!" said Peppy, for once not making an annoyed sigh at the extra demands of Ned's condition. "He wants to talk to me? Really?" Ike nodded.

"Don't go anywhere, I'll be right back," Peppy told the table, linking her arm to Ike's.

Peppy clambered into the backseat of the minivan to sit with Ned in the casino parking lot. He was wearing a new red, Mexican wrestler's mask that Ike had bought him. It was made of light nylon and had fetching yellow vinyl flames.

"Hey! Congratulations!" he said, leaning to give his mother a sideways, seated hug.

"You dressed up," said Peppy, suddenly overcome.

Ned took her hand. They sat in the dry chill of the desert night, letting silence soak up the unmanageable emotion for a minute.

"I think Ike and I might move near here. I forgot how much I liked the desert."

"You remember living in Reno?" sniffed Peppy.

"Yeah. I love how it looks like you can see the roundness of the sky."

"I figured you'd want to get as far away from me as possible." It was a self-effacing joke, but she knew it was true when it came out of her mouth.

Bridal tears that had been damming up all day behind her lashes began to sluice down Peppy's cheeks. Ned tucked his hand inside his sleeve and carefully blotted her tears with his shirt cuff.

(He would cut this shirt cuff off, later, to preserve the peach, pink, coral, and black smears, flecked with tiny sparks of glitter. "That is my mom," he told Ike as he hung it on a nail.)

After drunkenly flirting and singing Christmas duets with Rick Lin for a while, Liza snuck out of the Normal/Tang wedding to roam amongst the midnight lights and twinkling rivers of runaway coinage. The evening had a magic to it, and she wanted to hunt for her Path, some auspice that would reveal itself and connect her dots. She walked the strip, absorbing the whiplash attention-grabbing of it all, searching.

It was Christmas Eve, wrought in trashy, rococo Vegas dementia: American "fun" as an all-night orgasm of lights and sinful temptations: a color-saturated imagination turned toward glitzy salacity, designed to help good people forget themselves and ride the Devil's tail in the eternal twilight. Ancient waitresses of Ancient Rome served antifreeze margaritas to robot-gods; topless mermaids swam in walls of angelfish and eels. Vast fortunes in sapphire pinky rings and executive biofeedback accessories lay wet and ripe in the open lips of spinning velvet pirate chests, for your Bacardi-blackout, impulse-shopping pleasure.

"Ho Ho Ho," said a black Santa, handing Liza a postcard advertising a show: "Santa's Helpers," bending over in flocked red minitunics to reveal their bethonged ass-cheeks, pressed together side to side like a row of dinner rolls.

"Hey, I got a present for you!" Santa shouted as Liza started to walk away, folding the card to drop in the nearest trashcan. Liza turned.

"You been a good little girl?"

Black Santa reached out and handed Liza a pair of green foam-rubber, novelty reindeer antlers. There was a whole cardboard box of them sitting behind Santa Claus—he was handing them out indiscriminately—but she couldn't help clutching them to her chest like they were a material kiss from the Great Beyond.

Christmas Day was spent hungover at Peppy and Earl's suite in the Whiskey Lane Casino hotel.

For the sake of Ned's comfort, the guest list was confined to Ike and Neville, who Ned remembered from the theatre days. The "Yule log" burned strangely on the mute TV; the day was one of relaxed drinking and the massacring of walnuts. Earl was wearing Liza's foam antlers, smiling in a boozy honeymoon delirium; Peppy was cozied next to him, wearing his gift to her: a ruffley, transparent Xmas housecoat.

Ned sidled up to Liza and handed her something book-shaped, mummified in toilet paper. "Merry Christmas," he said. "This is also from Ike. Actually, he picked it out."

"You did the wrap-job?" Liza teased.

"Yes, I'm a wrap-artist. They call me Special N'Ed." He pronounced this Nuh-ED. It was an old history book, entitled *Erotic Literature Through the Ages,* replete with naughty, nineteenth-century illustrations.

"Let's see . . . Oh!" said Noreen, peeking over Liza's shoulder.

"We thought it might help you with ideas for your phone dominatrix thing," Ned said, thoughtfully.

"Thanks *loads,* Ike," Liza said, wide-eyed with outrage.

"Oh, come off it. Everybody knows," he said, simply. "You should be proud of Venal de Minus! It's a cool thing!"

She had told *Ike* about her job, in confidence, but she had taken great pains to keep it a secret from the rest of her family; she had always used the euphemism "vocal gigs" when they asked where her sudden rolls of money came from. Liza was pissed that Ike had suddenly cast himself as the Normal family minesweeper, publicly detonating all the buried secrets. Ever since Mike died, Ike had very definite ideas about how Life should be Lived, in a full-disclosure, maximum intimacy kind of way . . . .

"This is *us*. You don't have anything to be ashamed of," Ike said, putting an arm around her shoulder. She wanted to elbow him in the stomach for this well-intentioned gesture. Instead, she topped off her supermarket eggnog with a large dose of rum. She had to admit, she felt a tiny inkling of relief that she could relax her personal and professional boundaries.

* * *

In the first two weeks of her stint, Empress Peppy Tang could safely be considered a minor hit. Attendance picked up for the 9 p.m. show at the Komedy Korrall. Neville quickly placed more ads in all the local magazines, replete with new critical recommendations:

"We all laughed till our bellys hurt!"—Jimmi S., Iowa City.

"Did you make that up?" Liza asked, knowing it was just Neville's arch sense of humor to type up such an unsophisticated review, to better attract dull-witted hickweeds.

"I took out the apostrophe *'s* he had written on *belly's,* but other than that, it's a genuine quote from a satisfied audience member."

Peppy's sudden success as Empress Tang made her walk a bit taller through the world. "It's like that line in *My Fair Lady*: 'The difference between a lady and a flower girl is not 'ow she behaves, but 'ow she's treated,' " Peppy announced, sashaying to the front of the breakfast line at the Original Pancake House. The hostess had recognized her black wig from one of the local newspapers and importantly whisked her past other patrons.

Scanning tourist brochure write-ups of the local floor shows, Liza figured out that it was possible to have face-recognition-level celebrity in the isolated oasis of Las Vegas and nowhere else. Vegas was a parallel entertainment world to Hollywood or Broadway, but wholly disconnected, tackier, and more meaningless. The relative anonymity was alluring in that there were no stakes: Vegas fame didn't particularly *count,* as far as the rest of the nation was concerned—therefore, success or failure in Vegas was inconsequential; there really was nothing to lose, not even face. Liza decided to investigate the town's various stage acts, to see if there was any slot where she might fit in.

After several weird nights sitting alone in tourist-filled audiences drinking weak Greyhounds, she noted that a few distinct schools of entertainment thrived in Vegas:

1. **Spectacle:** topless six-foot showgirls in chandelier hats doing ostrich prances up and down flights of stairs; the featured performers were really their huge, motionless breasts, tinted and professional as sports equipment.

2. **Spectacle Plus Sentiment:** Older, conservative country acts that were once truly famous, but could now only be found in Vegas or Branson, Missouri.

    Elvis was once The Lord of these; crooners in rhinestoned jumpsuits singing massively overproduced versions of "God Bless America." Through a miraculous combination of large music, trembling unction, raw patriotism, and the love of Christ, they would launch their audience—mustachioed, drunk, older, white Republicans, and their second or third wives—into tearful, fist-biting, baptismal meta-catharses.

3. **Comedy:** Unthreatening prop-gaggers and guys who did impressions of celebrities born before 1941: James Cagney, Johnny Carson, adenoidal Woody Allen.

    The more successful ones spliced in cloying, Heartfelt Moments: "You're always young, especially when you're young at heart," they'd croak in their best Jimmy Stewart, and the white-haired audience, conscious of the encroaching presence of death, would clap wildly with lumps in their throats.

4. **Magic:** There were the top-hat-and-cape variety guys, who forced disposable white doves out of hidden pockets, and their more expensive counterparts, "Illusionists," who traded in the raw sex appeal of billowing white pirate shirts open to shaved chests. Rare lions would explode out of hydraulic trapdoors, armored showgirls would goose-step to the fascist majesty of the *Carmina Burana* soundtrack.

5. **The Death-Defiers:** Evel Knievel and trapeze artists without nets, or Liza's favorite act: four guys in leather jumpsuits and

pancake makeup who rode minibikes into a stationary, mesh metal ball, chasing one another around upside down and sideways and giving the audience the sensation that they were about to see a horrible accident, live.

6. **Superstar Imitators:** A Michael Jackson, talc-covered and contour-pencilled to look as Kabuki as the real thing; an oversexed Madonna in ice-blue Cleopatra eye makeup who threw her skirt over her head to reveal her black thong, and a Cher warbling in feathered Cherokee-restraint-straps.

Some could sing the part, some could dance it, some looked startlingly like the people they imitated, but all three criteria were never pulled off simultaneously. There was, Liza noted, no Lisa Lisa & The Cult Jam imitator, and this was probably no accident.

When the seventh show she'd seen in eight days let out, Liza abandoned hope and wandered out to the endless parking lot to find Earl's car. She looked up at the enormous SIEGFRIED AND ROY AT THE MIRAGE marquee towering above her; fifty square feet of backlit twin Magnus Apollos: heliocentric hair, iconic bronze jawlines, photovoltaic eyes, and saintly, manicured hands at rest on groomed albino predators.

There is no place for me on the Vegas stage.

Then she looked down.

She'd half noticed, outside of every theatre she'd been to, that the parking lots were littered with flyers for escort services and erotic massage, but it was not until she dropped her keys that she really noticed the omnipresent Day-Glo pink one, the one she'd stepped over blizzards of, the one that littered every hotel garage like Mardi Gras confetti.

They were ads for 976-VENAL.

There she was, thousands of her, being walked on by lucky Americans, many of whom were apparently wishing to get walked on by *her*.

• • •

After consulting with several real estate agents, Ike found a ranch in Overton, NV, about an hour's drive from the strip. Its asking price had been thrice reduced, after festering on the market for several months. "It's a real horse property," said the agent. It had once been a cattle ranch—720 acres of overgrown sagebrush, datura, and mistletoe, with a natural spring well and three ponds. On all sides, the property was surrounded by brick-red sandstone striped with eggnog-colored silica. Wild mule deer, sage hen, quail, and jackrabbits skittered around like they owned the place.

The ranch house was a fixer-upper that hadn't been remodeled since the mid-1970s, but it was large, and had four big bedrooms. Ike and Ned were mostly interested in the old barn, which was huge. As soon as all the papers were signed and the deal was closed, Ned and Ike were moving to the ranch.

* * *

Liza's hand was sweating as she held the phone.

"Butch, I'm thinking about doing that live Venal de Minus gig . . ."

"Am I dreaming?"

"No. Could I do it in Vegas?"

Butch paused, thinking about it.

"That's probably exactly where it should be."

"OK. I have one condition."

"What. Spit it out. What do you want? Dancing eunuchs? Hydraulic torture-racks?"

The words stung Liza's throat. She strangled them out. It was traumatic, like birth. ". . . Venal could sing, right?"

Butch couldn't stop laughing.

At the end of January 1990, right around the time when Lorna and Jimbo moved into their truck, Butch Strange boarded a plane bound for the great Southwest, to begin the development of Liza's show with Neville, who Butch had vaguely known for years, from the periphery of the Cape Horn scene.

"Smut is like hard liquor," Butch told Liza as they sat in a floating hotel bar designed to be artificially rained on every forty minutes. "It's hard to swallow at first, but after a while, you don't really notice the harshness anymore," said Butch, his smooth cheeks flushing after his second Jack Daniel's. "Besides, this is for Vegas, so it'll be more like *family* smut."

"OK," said Liza, psyching herself up for the role like a proper actress.

Liza hurled herself into the role of Venal de Minus, Queen of leg cuffs, ball gags, bamboo canes, flamethrowers, and spark-cascading chainsaws. The show, planned over a week of loud brainstorming in a Whiskey Lane corporate boardroom, involved a little bit of dance, a little bit of singing, and a lot of stage combat, but was mostly wink-wink, sadomasochistic-double-entendre-laced insult-comedy, adapted from the 976-scripts.

By putting ads in the local trade papers, Neville easily found unemployed celebrity look-alikes and impressionists who could play Venal's leading-man-victims.

"You're scary," Neville proudly told Liza, with a shivering grin, during rehearsals. "I like to think I was influential during your inappropriate childhood. I'd like to feel that in some way, I created this monster."

"In some ways, you did," said Liza as she practiced stomping out the breakaway sugar-windshield in an engineless stage Cadillac. *So did Tonto. And so did DelVonn. And Lorna, and ChoCho, and Butch, and Mom . . .*

Four months later, Liza had her first genuine marquee, at a small club a few miles off the strip that Butch leased for the "workshop production":

VAN deVILLE PRESENTS:

<u>NATIONAL CULT SENSATION</u>

VENAL De MINUS

LIVE!!!

AT THE PANTENA GENTLEMAN'S CLUB
IN
VENAL DOES HOLLYWOOD . . . DIRTY!
A CENTAUR PUBLICATIONS PRODUCTION

Liza's two-month run in the midnight slot at the 120-seat Pantena Gentleman's Club caught on quickly by word of mouth and sold out within two weeks; it unexpectedly became a kind of ersatz *Rocky Horror Picture Show* for frat boys at UNLV.

"Oh, this is *ideal*," Neville gushed when he saw fans in the audience decked out in bondage-wear. Butch was feeling like Flo Ziegfeld, wearing tailored suits and flying back and forth between Vegas and San Francisco with his new lover, a tiny Filipino transsexual named Tonya.

Liza was enjoying herself. Her childhood dream of being an irony-free, singing princess had been shot down in flames, but rising from the ashes was a hardy acceptance of her role as an icon of camp depravity. Her fans were people she didn't relate to at all: hooting, drunk, collegiate boors and trembling old deviants, and Liza made it a point never to meet them; she slipped through the back exit in disguise, into a waiting taxicab. She had learned how to build mystique, interestingly enough, from Ned: the art world was obsessed with seeing him, mainly because he wouldn't let them. Ike had fielded phone calls from *The New Yorker, Vanity Fair, Artforum, Vogue*—all begging Ned to sit for a formal portrait for articles they wanted to do on Jacqueline Kelles and her "discovery." Ned always had Ike graciously refuse; hence, a photo of Edward Normal was a Jackie O.–like prize that hungry young paparazzi yearned for.

Liza's run at the Pantena was extended for a third time, and a fourth. Venal de Minus was becoming a reliable, medium-size piece of Las Vegas entertainment, with ads in all the tourist magazines, pamphlets, and novelty maps.

Neville had the brilliant idea of printing up Venal de Minus signature souvenirs, which he sold on a folding table next to the Pantena snack bar—black T-shirts, coffee mugs, baseball hats, sun visors, and key chains, all emblazoned with *Venal de Minus Does Hollywood Dirty*™ in slashing red. The T-shirts were a big hit; college kids bought them by the stack. Neville sold out of the first run in less than a week.

When the show was six months old and still going strong, The Phone Call They Had All Been Waiting For came: The Nexus, one of the older hotels just off the main strip, was interested in having Venal de Minus replace a show the following year, since their star, a vivacious forty-five-year-old singer best known for her infomercials, was going on "maternity leave."

This was a big, big deal. Butch and Neville flipped out.

"Oh, shit! Now we're really at the Copacabana!" enthused Neville.

"Bigger ticket prices too," said Butch, aglow with naked greed.

The Venal schtick was so brainless and trashy, Liza almost felt guilty it was becoming so legitimate.

Lawyers were hired; contracts were signed. Liza was given a fairly impressive "Welcome to the Nexus Family" bonus.

The show would be expanded for the larger stage: more dancers, more explosions, bigger and better props. They would develop the production with a seasoned choreographer for the next nine months, and then unleash it on the Vegas public.

"You need to do something with your money," Winnie told Liza, after accidentally glancing at one of her bank statements. "You should buy a condo or something. You shouldn't leave so much cash sitting in your checking account."

Ike suggested that Liza buy the adjoining lot to his and Ned's, which was owned by the same previous owners and had also been foundering in the disinterested market. This idea was appealing in that Liza would have to build a house from scratch. Most Vegas stars built secluded, ranch-style Xanadus out in the desert, where they decompressed from the demanding life of the stage by wildly overindulging their every self-coddling whim—giraffe pools, ice-climbing walls, ostrich polo, Brazilian rosewood bowling alleys. Liza wanted her own cool, customized destination—a place she could drive home to every night and think, as she pulled into the driveway: I'm home.

Ned and Ike had done great things to their barn; it had tinted skylights and a poured concrete floor, covered with ratty old Persian rugs from Ike's old house. Ned was given a large bare wall to begin construction on new light-boxes. Ike gave the ranch house a scouring face-lift so that Noreen could live there.

Liza purchased the adjoining lot, with Winnie's help.

"I want to build a totally whacked-out, architectural folly," Liza told Ike and Ned.

"Excellent," said Ned.

Liza rejected several drawings by young and eager architects: a Hobbit Hole, dug into the hillside; a Parthenon; a windowless tower, ten stories high; a round, igloo-type dome structure that would be built entirely out of white PVC. Finally, Liza, Ned, and Ike did the rudimentary sketches themselves, then hired engineers to figure out how to achieve it: Liza's home was to be tall, churchlike, and made of concrete; the roof would be a cluster of turrets, which Ned drew to resemble streamlined, art deco arrowheads and bullet-trains, pointing upward . . . embedded in the concrete exterior would be millions of pieces of broken green bottle glass, which Ike figured out how to buy from a Mexican recycling plant. The glittering final product was intended to resemble the skyline of the Emerald City of Oz, as seen from the enchanted poppy field, where Dorothy and Co. had all succumbed to the witch's spell, and fallen asleep.

"If Hollywood is the Emerald City, then what is Vegas, if not the enchanted Poppy Field?" Liza cackled. She sounded a little bitter, but Liza had a droll sense that Vegas quasinotoriety was actually where she had been heading all along. It was only by pursuing Hollywood immortality so doggedly and failing that she'd arrived, by default, at the interesting place she was—like Peppy, her flawed nature had sunk to its true audience, and it was surprisingly OK.

Liza wanted to lavish gifts on her grandmother, now that Noreen was living at Ned and Ike's ranch house.

"If you wanted anything, what would you want?"

"I don't want anything. This is already too much for me."

"No! Think about it. If you could have *anything*."

"Well. I have to say, I have been missing my little cactus garden, I used to have," said Noreen, reminiscing about her little slice of Mars, back in Reno.

Liza had a truckful of assorted cacti, several dozen plaster gnomes, and four birdbaths delivered later that week. She hired two workers to plant them and pour pink gravel.

"Who do you think you are? William Randolph Hearst?" Noreen teased.

Liza was indulging decadent tastes, and spending all the cash she brought in. She'd never had money before; the novelty of its buying power was intoxicating. She bought herself a strange, savage, tusk-and-antler throne from the 1930s, upholstered in leopard skin.

"Idi Amin would have *loved* this," Liza gushed to the curio dealer as she shelled out the goodly wad of cash.

As an act of unregenerate extravagance, Liza experimentally purchased two albino peacocks to wander the grounds and be decorative. She made an enormous wall-collage, a primordial, enchanted forest on her largest wall: odd and mismatched flora cut out from dozens of expensive, illustrated coffee-table books on botany. When it was finished, Liza sat in her tusk chair and stared at the wall and the mutilated book-husks with a twinge of guilt.

I spend money like an idiot because I'm lonely as hell.

While there was always some ardent, goofball fan-boy dying to take her out on dates, there was only one person Liza was interested in, and she had no idea where he was. *Even NED found love, for crying out loud.*

With a big, safe, isolated living space, Ike by his side, and his family within arm's reach, Ned's love for his life expanded suddenly and wildly, and for the first time, he felt the melancholic sting of knowing he was unbelievably *lucky*. There was an initial anxiety to feeling plunged into an almost unbearable happiness, but by baby steps and degrees, he began to relax into something like stunned gratitude. His work became broader and less self-torturing—he used bigger pieces of acetate, making simpler, larger, more abstract designs.

Critics would later argue that happiness made Ned's work suffer, but his light-boxes were still beautiful, if less neurotically obsessive, and Jacqueline Kelles was still enthusiastically "repping" him through her gallery. "Don't fall into the trap of doing the same thing over and over again, just because everyone liked that first batch. Artists have to *evolve*. I think this is your best stuff yet," said Ike, and that was good enough for Ned.

●　●　●

Since the Venal de Minus show was physically demanding, what with all the nightly beatings she had to perform, Liza accepted a free membership at a fitness studio owned by the Nexus and began taking yoga classes to increase strength, maintain flexibility, and to try to achieve some kind of athletic connection to the divine that was both mindful and cardiovascular. It was the urban compromise between ascetic Godliness and Buns of Steel—an act of worship occurring somewhere in the pantheon between step-aerobics and crucifixion.

The fitness studio, whimsically named "Ohm on the Range," was little more than a dressing room, a large wooden floor, and central air-conditioning. Hanging alone in the center of the main wall, behind where the instructor sat, was a large, batik wall hanging of a Swastika, with a sign posted next to it:

Wait!!
. . . *OPEN YOUR MIND.*

Before you start freaking out, read on!

"Swastika" is a Sanskrit word that translates to "well-being." A clockwise Swastika is an esoteric Buddhist symbol for the positive life force in motion, a symbol of evolution. The counterclockwise Swastika is a symbol of natural dissolution. The positive vs. negative, "churning" movements of the clockwise and counterclockwise Swastikas represent the dance of the natural paradigms: creation/destruction, evolution/decay, positive/negative, inhale/exhale. The "rolling wheel" at rest represents equilibrium: Nirvana, balance, and harmony between body, mind, and spirit.

Don't let the bad hype of the Third Reich destroy the rich history of this powerful symbol! We hope you will let our Swastika be a "bell of mindfulness" reminding you to "look beyond appearances."

~ Namaste ~

It's still a fucking SWASTIKA, thought Liza, perturbed. *"Hey There, Georgie Girl" is the Barbie doll theme song, now. "Anticipation" is the ketchup song. It doesn't matter what it was before. The Nazis had a bigger ad campaign.*

Liza decided to try to ignore the wall hanging, since it was the best yoga school in Las Vegas; so, thrice weekly, she set up her mat in the back corner of the room, as far from the swastika as possible, closed her eyes, and attempted to Breathe.

"Um, I have an announcement? I've changed my name to Shiva-Sunyari?" announced the tattooed instructor, a former showgirl who had a bleached mohawk and large breast implants. Liza recalled that only last week, she had been named Linda, and noticed that in addition to the new name, she had also recently adopted an Indian-Holy-Person accent, which made all of her statements curl up at the ends, like a question: "So, when you see that name on the Tuesday class schedule, you will know that it is still I?"

Shiva-Sunyari hauled out the melodeon, a little red squeeze-box, with a little keyboard, and made it whine out a minor chord to kick off the chanting.

She sang with Carlos Santana–like pain, moaning Ohm (in her native Californian: *Eeeeeeeuuuuuuuuuuuooooohm*) full-throatedly with her eyes shut, grimacing with emotion. Shiva-Sunyari looked an *awful* lot like an Aryan skinhead . . . but Liza tried her hardest to ignore the fascist signifiers and "let them go" by chanting along with Shiva-Sunyari's questionably subjective English interpretations of Sanskrit texts.

The workout often made Liza intensely competitive toward the women around her, trying to stretch farther and in more noticeably beautiful ways. Shiva-Sunyari would roam through the class, pontificating on the nature of consciousness:

"If you are comparing yourself with other people . . . that is not yoga? If you look at your neighbor, and think, I am doing this pose better than my neighbor, then that is not yoga? That is your ego? Perhaps, instead of concentrating on gratifying your ego, you can channel your energy toward someone who makes you angry, and send them love?"

I am sending you love, "Shiva-Sunyari," thought Liza, but she had to be nice, because Shiva-Sunyari was about to start teaching a Thursday night class entitled "Fit to Be Tied! Venal de Minus™ Tortureobics," a ballistic workout involving bullwhip cracking and modern jazz dance in high heels, for the local trophy-housewife-cum-wannabe-dominatrixes. (The Nexus was test-driving this exercise conceit as a potential franchise opportunity, marketable to gyms nationwide.)

The choreographer hired by the Nexus to work alongside Neville was a Ben Vereen type named Halston T. Quarters III, a real Vegas warhorse of solid reputation, who had worked steadily on different shows in town over the last eight years.

"We're gonna whip you up some new slave boys, Liza," he joked.

Venal was now quote-unquote-respectable enough to merit auditions by veterans of other shows—"real" dancers who were between productions for various reasons—age, drugs, injury.

"We are low budget no longer," Neville was proud of saying. "We're midbudget. Now we get dancers who are almost *talented*."

It was curious for Liza to be on the other side of the table, remembering the spate of miserable commercial auditions she'd survived as an adolescent. Headshots stacked up as she, Neville, and Halston surveyed the auditionees with poker-faces and clipboards.

"I know this next guy, a little," Halston said, after the threesome dismissed yet another tall, oversexed-looking blonde in her late thirties with more body parts than talent.

"Is he any good?"

"He's OK. He did Michael Jackson over at Superstars for a while. I heard he got sacked for attitude."

Liza was tired and didn't want to be doing this anymore. She wanted to drive home, take a bath, and read the hilariously filthy autobiography of Klaus Kinski.

When he walked in, the atoms of Liza's heart smashed. *Roland?!*

And then she squinted, looking at him closely . . . . . *No.*

She relaxed into her usual state of disappointment.

Wait.

This couldn't be Roland. She grabbed the clipboard from Halston to read the auditioner's name.

Oh my God, it IS.

He looked *smaller*. His posture had changed; his face was downcast; his expression was so uncharacteristically hangdog as to make his features unrecognizable. His poverty, which had always looked nobly ascetic before, now looked feral and a little desperate. Older white women probably clutched their handbags a little tighter when he walked by.

"Hey, Liza, you remember me?" he asked, with awful supplication.

"Of *course* I do, Roland. God."

The greenish eyes behind his glasses had lost their incandescence; the sparkling nimbus of thrill he had always projected was gone. He squeezed her hand shyly, clearly ashamed to be so visibly defeated; Liza's mind was bleeding out of her ears. She was embarrassed to be in such a stupidly glorified position.

". . . I heard you were holding auditions, so I just thought I'd come by and say Hey, do my thing, drop off my headshot." So bitterly humble. It was horrendous to see him this low; reason enough to kill the world.

He could barely dance anymore; even his wonderful body was shot through with the poisons of his evident depression. He was listless, uninspired. *Unbelievable.* Liza couldn't stand watching him move, so she read his résumé and discovered that according to the dates, she'd actually *seen* him doing Michael Jackson in the Superstar show, and *not recognized him.* White pancake makeup notwithstanding, this was *Roland Fucking Spring,* for God's sake, whose *back* she had recognized in pitch darkness, whose *presence* once gave her chills from twenty feet away, before she even realized it was him; whose impossibly bright, peerless, exultant energy had been the lighthouse of her soul, the lamp by which she had read the mystery of her own heart. . . .

What could have been an effortless triple pirouette was a wobbly double. It was clear to Liza that he was so unhappy he was sabotaging the audition, to spite himself.

"Roland."

"Yeah."

"You're the most talented guy in the entire world. What are you doing?"

Neville and Halston looked at Liza, trying to conceal their surprise.

"I'm sucking ass, I know." Roland stared at his feet and twisted in agony. "I don't mean to waste your time."

"I'm going to talk to him," Liza whispered to Neville. "Roland, can you come with me a sec?"

Roland shrugged, looking busted. Liza pulled Roland out of the room by his elbow.

"Thank you," Halston T. Quarters III yelled at Roland, in a professionally dismissive tone. Liza gave him a nasty look.

They walked out onto the bright sidewalk. Roland immediately lit a cigarette and assumed a dejected slouch against the building. Liza walked in front of him, bending her knees to look up into his downcast eyes, which kept darting away when hers made contact.

"Hi. Hi. Roland? Hey. Hi."

He couldn't say anything; he was beating himself up too hard. ". . . I'm sorry . . ."

"No! Stop it! Why are you apologizing?"

"Well . . . shit, Liza, you're all *famous* now, and I dunno . . ."

Liza's head was hearing what it had always wanted to hear, but in the worst way imaginable; this wish fulfillment was blown violently inside out like a cheap wind sock; only the seamy underside was visible.

"Can I take you to dinner, after the show tonight?" Liza suggested. "Let's catch up."

He accepted with discomfiting eagerness.

After he left, Liza abandoned the audition process to leave a crying message on Lorna's voice mail to call her as soon as possible.

"I injured my knee," Roland told Liza with a shrug as they sat at the strip's best sushi bar, watching a smack of miniature jellyfish wafting in a backlit tank.

It was a predictable story, and Liza should have guessed it: "The Business" had used him badly and discarded him.

He'd been on the Madonna tour in Istanbul when, during a particularly aeronautic piece of choreography, he'd caught a girl badly and damaged a tendon.

He was summarily replaced and sent back to LA, where he lived off of workman's comp and endured several months of physical therapy. Once recovered, he'd decided to try New York, where he quickly figured out that his color was a problem when it came to traditional Broadway leading roles. He went out for exactly two carefully selected auditions and landed both parts. Forced to choose one over the other, he chose *Orange Flag,* an intensely popular, long-running Off-Broadway show with a small cast. He had reasoned that since the performers were all painted bright orange, his success would be unimpeded by his skin tone and based on the merits of his talent.

He was fired after three weeks of performances: he was so much more talented than the other performers that he ended up receiving a disproportional amount of applause, during the curtain calls. He was "becoming a star in what was supposed to be an ensemble," and this was counteractive to *Orange Flag*'s "egalitarian social message"—at least this was what they said when they fired him.

He performed in subways for a while, playing washtub-drums and singing. Music industry professionals gave him their cards daily; he ended up performing at nine or ten private parties for rich people, but "The Industry" had no use for his originality, music-wise. There was really no such thing as the kind of musician he was—free-jazzish percussion, with smatterings of old-school bebop, scat, and a capella gospel, evocative of old Smithsonian recordings from the Deep South.

A&R people, while they slobbered about his talent, were only signing gangsta rappers or R&B balladeers; a few tried to get Roland to sing what he called "Down on my knees, beggin' ya please," songs, which he found too hokey and bathetic to sing with any conviction.

"It comes down to this: if I want money, I'm not allowed to express myself, and if I want to express myself—and I *do*—I starve."

To top off this string of bad experiences, Roland's mother was diagnosed with diabetes. The Michael Jackson gig had, at least, made it possible to send money to his mother and keep dancing—"Michael may be freaky, but he can still can dance like a motherfucker." But eventually Roland's creativity got the best of him, and he got in trouble with the show's choreographer for embellishing the moves.

"And now I have a bad reputation," he added, painfully.

Liza was dying.

Roland had gotten the shit kicked out of him by pop culture's brutally infantile, polar simplicity: In or Out, Hot or Not—absolutes arbitrarily decided by the momentary cash-cults that formed whenever the mass attention-span swung unpredictably onto something and stuck for more than three seconds. The man she worshipped had been creamed by the unfair rules of success—*Roland,* of all people.

Since he was looking at her with eyes of appalling deference, Liza found herself talking about parts of her life that had pained and embarrassed her the most, knocking herself down in an effort to raise him up again. It all came off like a comedy routine, to her chagrin.

"It's really good to see you." Roland smiled, taking her hand and kissing it. "You are really very funny, Miss Liza."

Liza wanted to slap him for not knowing who he was.

Liza dropped Roland off at his apartment. He made a play for her mouth, but she kissed him goodbye chastely and platonically on the cheek. They made a date to go hiking the following afternoon, since Liza wasn't performing, but she planned to break it.

"There is nothing so fatal to an ideal as its realization," Lorna told Liza as she freaked out on the phone, late that night. (Jimbo had been reading Schopenhauer).

The un-Rolandness of Roland felt like a deathblow. He was her last Pure Fantasy, her most sacred inspiration, and the world wouldn't allow her even *this*.

"No . . . *all* my dreams have to get fucking shot down. Everything."

"Wait and see . . . life is long and full of surprises," said Lorna.

"You and your Zen-hippie wise-woman crap," Liza lashed out.

Lorna laughed, unruffled. "Why else do you call me?"

Liza almost didn't answer her phone the next morning when Roland was supposed to call her, but the horror of his change was so magnetic that she found herself picking up on the first ring.

A few hours later, Liza and Roland drove out to the Valley of Fire, past the Red Rock mountains.

The sky was enormous, high, blue, and endless, making Liza feel that she was reflected in the half-dome of a 1970s fish-eye mirror. At visitors' posts they read wooden planks, learning the names of the spiny plants in the area: catclaw, screwbean, ocotillo. They walked up red hills and looked at crude, prehistoric petroglyphs—stick-animals, snakes, and suns that the Native Americans had carved through the black desert varnish and into the sandstone . . . some jackass had carved KAYLA '85 and yet another criminal had spent hours chiseling SHOW ME BOOBS into the ancient landmark, but the overall effect was still more or less interesting.

They weren't really talking. There wasn't enough to say.

The rocks at the Valley of Fire were a surrealistic joke: huge, bulbous red boulders, twenty feet high or more, filled with portholes and little round caves and smooth, intestinal corridors, that looked like tactile wood-art or enormous dinosaur skulls arranged in a geomantic, Stonehenge-y way; the wind blew through the rock cavities in soft hoots, like late-night lips on a beer bottle.

They climbed to the top of a particularly inviting, double-dipped boulder. The sky formed a black curtain at the far right of the horizon, which began muscling forward, bruising the air beneath into papaya orange-pink and viscous brown. A gray wall of rain let loose, less than a mile away. Liza and Roland stood breathing in the mineral hit of ozone, watching the storm sweep toward them. It was so mesmerizing they forgot their melancholia and stood in rapt awe of the hugeness before them.

Warm rain began sploshing down in drops the size of peach pits, and lightning marbleized the charcoal sky with spleen-shaking cannonball BOOMs; slashes of light lingered on their retinas.

Liza and Roland clambered inside a crawl space in one of the rocks. They could still watch the storm, through portholes in the red boulder. It was an ion-charged moment; nature had overwhelmed the day in its infinite majesty, and there could be no secrets in this ancient red skull, only truthful confessions, like the one that had been combusting in Liza for nearly a decade:

"Roland, I've always thought you were the most magic person alive," she told him, studying his sad face.

"So I'm a pretty big disappointment now, huh?" Roland asked, messing with the sand beneath his elbow. "Life's a bitch, right?"

Liza marked an internal gear-change. She knew she had to either sub-mit to the random, blind will of the world, all its sadness, and the weight of all of the children who fell through its cracks, or decide, with alarming hubris, that she would right the wrongs in This Rock, Right Now, by the divine power vested in her by *Herself*.

"You're the kid who came into my theatre with a plastic bucket when I was fourteen and made me cry. You didn't lose your magic, *I have it,* I've been carrying it around for *years,* I am the Bank of Roland. I know who you are. You're my Golden Stag. I *found* you that night in Golden Gate Park . . . ."

" . . . . ."

Liza stopped, suddenly gagged by tears of frustration because she re-alized she was starting to sound insane, like an acid casualty, trying to explain with druggy-sounding, fucked-up metaphors how his incredi-ble specialness was *intact* in her, as if she had been waiting for him to need it again—how could she convey her huge belief in his *essential Rolandness?* . . . She was sounding like a burnt-out stalker . . . .

Maybe I did give myself brain damage, because now when it's the most im-portant time to speak and really say something for a change, I have no . . . . .

"I sound crazy, don't I?" Liza strangled out. "Do you think I'm crazy?"

It was then that Roland Spring flashed Liza his *old* smile, the good old, wide, gap-toothed one, the magic rocket ride. And he kissed her.

The silica sand under them was soft as pollen, and there was gorgeous, luxurious kissing, agonizing, wonderful.

Liza's teeth clenched as she squeezed him from her poignant sense that such seconds of ridiculous, high-octane bliss are not built to stay—such is their golden and fleeting nature—but her all instinctive subatomic parts prayed for everything to stop forever, right here, so that she could have enough time to properly thank the empyreal waltz of space explosions that had somehow, over trackless millennia, managed to assemble *This Perfect Roland* . . . .

The back of Liza's fluttering eyelids burst into ornate patterns, delicate bats and vines and urns and bees, jellyfish, koi, and hibiscus as she and Roland gift-wrapped themselves in each other, and gave each other back to each other as gifts exponentially more precious for having been so wrapped. *I love you, love you, love you, Roland Spring, with the most serious, mysterious, eternal and dizzying love, forever and ever, amen.*

* * *

Lorna and Jimbo came to visit Liza in their nearly completed land yacht, a month before Liza's Nexus premiere (which had kept being pushed back due to various budget cuts but would surely open eventually, once "the usual union shit" was sorted out). Ike invited Peppy and Earl over, since it was a good excuse for a barbecue. Neville was bringing Ned a batch of fireworks purchased from the nearby Moapa Indian reservation.

Ned took to Jimbo right away. After a long conversation, Ned announced that he wanted to get his entire face and head tattooed with glow-in-the-dark tattoo ink. It would be invisible in the daytime, but in the dark, if he turned on a black light, he would be covered with glowing, greenish swirls.

"It will be perfect. It will be like I have a built-in mask on, all the time," said Ned.

Nobody really identified with this logic, but everyone wanted to see Ned's face again.

"Well, I did it," Peppy said to Liza and Ned as everyone sat around the barbecue pit on plastic chaise lounges, that pink evening. "You kids are both successful artists. I've done my job in this life. I've done damn well."

Liza nearly leapt over and strangled Peppy, but Roland's hand on her thigh gently, reassuringly, squeezed.

Happily Ever After.

THE ROLAND STONE
OF MRS. SPRING

OR

YOU CAN'T ALWAYS
GET WHAT YOU WANT

ERE IS WHERE OUR PATHS DIVERGE. I, your Author, betray my function and deliberately annoy you by telling you what happens after the final shot where everyone was captured in freeze-frame, laughing and jumping in midair.

Liza once saw a game show where a man stood in a Plexiglas box, and dollar bills swirled around him in a miniature tornado, and thought, *Life is Like That*: you can keep whatever you can catch, but it's all whipping sideways past your head so fucking fast, and how were you supposed to tell which were the big bills and which were the small? How could one train for such an infuriatingly stupid challenge? How could anybody catch *all* the beauty in the Present Moment, when, after years of misery, there was suddenly a day when all the wonderfulness of life unexpectedly blew down from all directions all at once? And how were you supposed to store *joy*, for the ugly days when the bleakness returned?

Human beings can't stand for too much happiness in their lives; it's not as interesting or educational as the Obstacles.

While Peppy and Earl became remarkably chummy over the years, they drank too much, and this led to health problems as they got older.

Noreen, being an old person, died a few years after the move back to Nevada, and everyone missed her terribly.

Ned and Ike's relationship, while very stable and loving, was eventually sexless.

And Liza and Roland, after a few years (like all relationships, after a few years), needed Work.

Liza had been in love with her projection of love, which she had shone on the silver screen of Roland with the glamorizing light of her heart's desire. When she had been in love with him from afar, she hadn't known him well enough for his normal faults to hamper her ability to conceive of him as the one who would rescue her from the terrible woods, and carry her away, steedlike, on his mighty golden legs, as she swung safely in the cradle built for her between his splendid antlers.

It was sort of like that for a little while, and then, naturally, Life set in.

Ned tried to summarize an article he'd read on string theory one morning at breakfast. "I'm sure I'm screwing this up, but . . . the essential nature of matter is interconnections, because photons and electrons connect everything on a physical level, and light is both particles and waves, but you can't get a Unified Field Theory that works on a microscopic and a macroscopic level unless you account for multiple dimensions and mathematically describe that everything is made up of invisible wiggling loops of string that just happen to be attracted, for some reason, to other invisible loops of string. So, supposedly, the force of attraction rules everything."

.   .   .

Nobody at the table understood anything but the last sentence, and they all silently provided variations of the same addendum in their own heads: *and attraction fades.*

When dissolution sets in, new connective glue must be mixed, if one is to resist the natural drift of the invisible stuff that moves us, even when we want, badly, to stay put.

Roland was, after all, just a guy—enormously special and talented, but flawed like all men, and though reasonably happy in his recent gig as a drumming acrobat in a large French circus at the Mirage, he and Liza got in terrible fights about stupid things, sometimes.

"You can't tame the Golden Stag," said Liza's psychotherapist. "If you catch it, and tame it, it can't be the Stag anymore, because the Stag is wild. It is passion. You can't keep it in a cage."

Shit, thought Liza.

The Passion, said the paid professional, would come back. Then go away again. Then come back. Antlers, of course, are deciduous—they fall off, they grow back, they fall off again.

Such is the unsexy math of life, but Liza had learned to accept it on its own terms, without looking at it through the Vaseline-smudged and filtered lenses of false hopes or false eyelashes.

Liza found other, more elusive Stags, to stimulate her romantic imagination—characters in old foreign movies or books. A glimpse of the divine ideal would reveal itself to Liza, periodically, and show her where, when lost in her forest, to run.

The sum of love increased between Liza and Roland when there was an excess of kindness (a hard-to-find gift on a birthday; a sudden, passionate bite on the neck), love decreased where there was selfishness and bad communication, and in the end, their relationship evened out, like all of life on a karmically lawful planet, to a bland zero, a perfect zero, a divine, Arabic zero.

. . .

Why? Because.

(An unforgivable way to end, but anything else would be too sentimental or pedantic or religious or pessimistic or tidy, and wouldn't properly
encompass how unanswerable that "Why" really is.

And I wouldn't want to shortchange you, Kind Reader, not when
you've been so hospitable.)

Fin

In the end, what we need is some hygiene, some cleanliness, disinfection. We're smothered by images, words and sounds that have no right to exist, coming from, and bound for, nothingness. Of any artist truly worth the name, we should ask nothing except this act of faith: to learn silence. . . . Such a monstrous presumption, to think that others could benefit from the squalid catalogue of your mistakes!

—*The Critic, from Fellini's* 8½

But where are the clowns
Quick send in the clowns
                    —*Stephen Sondheim*

ACKNOWLEDGMENTS

My magical agent, Bill Clegg, and my gorgeous and brilliant editor, Courtney Hodell, were vital to every aspect of this book. Their friendship, guidance, and overwhelming support were my primary fuel. I couldn't be luckier. I love them like crazy.

I have huge gratitude for the beautiful works and/or intellectual contributions of these beloved Golden Stags and Stag-ettes: Austin Young; Necia Dallas; Dave Cook; Rebecca Wolff and Ira Sher; Jon Rubin; Nick Carlin; Bill and Valeria Walker; Becky Smith of Bellwether Gallery; Wayne White; the Fourth Estate crew: Rachel Safko, Carrie Kania, Amy Baker, and Michael McKenzie; Jessica Craig and Arlo Crawford at Burnes & Clegg; the Dutch guys at Prometheus: Job Lisman and Peter Abelsen; Daniel Reitz; and Naked Angels' *Tuesdays at Nine* series.

I tip my hat to Adam Parfrey's *Apocalypse Culture II* for providing key research material on slash fiction and cannibalism.

For being generally inspiring, I thank the following muses: Jules Beckman (a brief sighting of whom triggered the whole idea), Steven Felty, Matt Prager, Mark Johnson and Mark Stanger, Mitzy McFate, Muire Dougherty, Michael Kudler, Ilya Brodsky, Robbie Caponetto, Eugene Robinson, John Bowe, Joanne Carthey, Heidi Pullen, the Wilson family (inc. my mother, who is *not* Peppy), the Bernards, and Sasha and Badr Karram.

And, of course, the late great Kevin Gilbert.

Alafia